MOTHERLESS CHILD

Kathleen S. Cunningham

PublishAmerica

Baltimore

First printing

ISBN: 1-4137-3008-6
PUBLISHED BY PUBLISHAMERICA, LLLP
www.publishamerica.com
Baltimore

Printed in the United States of America

Sometimes I feel like a motherless child
Sometimes I feel like a motherless child
Sometimes I feel like a motherless child
A long, long way from home.

Old Negro Spiritual

Thank you... Bill Shorrock... for taking the time to edit and advise. To my husband Dale for making the coffee at 3 AM and patiently listening to every word. And special thank you's to Gretch, Donna, Elaine, and Jeannie.

Lovingly Dedicated to LIZ
Now will you stop bugging me and Rest in Peace?

TABLE OF CONTENTS

PART 4

PART 1

Chapter 1

1915

She was not a pretty child, nor was she destined to become a beautiful woman.

Anna MacGregor was born on September 7, 1897, in the steerage section of a ship bound for America. Her frail mother, Nellie Lee, struggled to nurse the infant girl while she fought for her own life, but died soon after the ship docked. Malcomb MacGregor buried his young wife in New York, and made his way west to Richmond, Indiana, enlisting the assistance of any and every available female along the journey who would take pity on the motherless child.

Upon arrival in Richmond, Malcomb called upon a fellow Scotsman who had urged him to settle there with promise of work. Malcomb was neither ambitious nor skilled, and jobs were not readily available to him, so he sent at once for his widowed mother. Mrs. MacGregor was a stern and humorless woman who seldom spoke, and then did so primarily in parables and cliches. She brought her life's savings, certainly not a fortune, but enough to make a down payment on a modest house and provide for the three of them until they somehow prospered. Her quality of mercy was not without strain, however, and she never missed the opportunity to remind her son and granddaughter that the roof over their heads, the food they ate, and the very clothes they wore were the result of her considerable generosity.

"Pretty is as pretty does," the old woman would chant as she rocked rapidly and regarded Anna with a scowl. "You are like your mother in that regard... about as pretty as a Irish pig, and you have no pleasing talents. You'd best be working your brain, girl, and try to be smart, for you'll get no help from your worthless father, taken as he is with the drink."

Anna's first eighteen years were as unworthy of notice and void of color as was her physical appearance and sober countenance. Tall and big-boned like her father, Anna was hefty and clumsy. She played very little, and always alone, preferring instead to sit quietly and read. Whether drunk or sober,

Malcomb was never abusive, but neither was he caring or nurturing. Father and daughter saw little of each other, while Malcomb floated from one odd job to another. Anna, meanwhile, managed to mature in much the same way that a large ugly weed flourishes among roses, somehow always overlooked and desperately grabbing that which it needs to survive.

Anna went looking for her father one cold morning in 1913. She searched three pubs before she spied him, dozing on the bar, an empty bottle of Scotch in his hand. She returned the crude stares of the men who moved aside and shook Malcomb's shoulder roughly. "Wake up and come home," she ordered him. "Mrs. MacGregor is dead."

Anna offered scant explanation of the "accident," stating only that the old woman had "tripped on a piece of loose carpet and tumbled down the stairs." The funeral was thrifty and swift, producing little sorrow or sense of loss. Relieved to be free of her grandmother's rules and constant whining, Anna eagerly took control of the house, and Malcomb.

"If you expect to eat, you will work," she told him. "You will bathe once a week and come to the table sober." Malcomb shivered under his daughter's gaze, for she was as tall as he and heavier. Her cold gray eyes bored into his soul with fierce determination not unlike his newly dead mother. Within two days, Malcomb had secured a full time position as a janitor at Richmond's Savings and Loan.

Anna rocked and fanned herself one hot August morning in 1915. It was already ninety-three degrees at 10 AM, and Anna was suffering the humid air in her long cotton dress and petticoats, although she was barefoot and without bloomers. Her mood was dark as she reflected on her boring life, oppressing poverty, and lack of social grace or stature. A knock on the MacGregor screen door broke her reverie. She sighed, pulled her bulk from the chair and walked slowly down the darkened hallway, where she confronted the broad grin of a handsome young man.

"Just passin' through, Miss," his voice purred with a smooth Irish brogue. "Wouldja be havin' a cold drink for a thirsty salesman?" His black eyes twinkled as they took in every inch of her five foot eleven inches, broad hips and ample breasts. She was alone and ripe for the taking.

"What are you selling?" she inquired; although, it did not matter, for she had no money. Mrs. MacGregor had not permitted strangers into her home, but then it was no longer the old girl's home because she was finally dead. Anna could do as she damn well pleased. So Anna was damn well pleased to swing open the screen door and smile at the beautiful creature on her porch.

There were very few preliminaries other than small talk and a shared pitcher of lemonade. Anna delighted in his rapt attention, for she honestly believed that he stayed for the pleasure of her nervous conversation.

There was no struggle, no request for consent; none was given. The ease of her seduction was pathetic in its execution.

He drank one last glass before he departed that morning with a wink and a wave. He briskly trotted down the hot street, leaving her disheveled, bewildered, and pregnant.

Chapter 2

John Templeton Sterling, "Jack" to his friends (if indeed he had any friends), liked to refer to himself as a "self-made man." He had forgotten, evidently, that he had inherited a large fortune from his father. To his credit, he continued to expand nicely on his financial good luck for the rest of his long life. At thirty, he was short, fat, and almost totally bald. While his personality did not lack humor, albeit primarily directed at some unfortunate other, he was often self-absorbed, sometimes mean-spirited, and usually uninteresting. His mother admonished him often that he was destined to live out his life as a bachelor, given his undesirability as a husband. Jack pretended that he had no wish to become a social animal, to learn the lessons of etiquette that might earn him an appropriate wife.

Like his father had been, Jack was ambitious and industrious. Already a vice-president of Richmond Savings and Loan, he had an uncanny ability to make money when everyone else was losing theirs. His firm was more "loan" than "savings." He called himself as a banker, while he was actually a loan shark of textbook definition. His office charged interest rates that left his borrowers weeping, while he took particular satisfaction in the "repossession" phase of his duties. Jack had little tolerance for anyone, but none for those who defaulted on a debt. His private finances were, after all, in perfect order, for he owned free and clear the largest and finest home in Richmond, Indiana. "I own most of this town, and sooner or later I will own the rest," he liked to boast, "and nothing happens here that I don't already know or won't find out."

There were, of course, Jack's incredible blue eyes. So intense was the color that it overflowed to the whites, commanding immediate attention. His gaze locked on contact and held until Jack "dismissed" the looker, for there was no pulling away once he had you. But they told you nothing about the man, for there were not mirrors to his soul.

Jack had few passions, other than money and his own personal comfort. Children interested him… he liked to watch them in the park near his office while he ate his lunch. They were beautiful creatures, laughing and playing, and he envied them their joy. He liked good music, classical usually. He dressed well, drank expensive liqueur, and smoked fine cigars. He always knew where everything was, arrived exactly five minutes early for every appointment, and never missed a day's entry to his personal journal, where every encounter, every detail of his uneventful life was recorded for posterity.

He was heterosexual by nature, but not actively. Women were a mystery, too complicated, too moody, and too much trouble. He visited the local brothel on a regular basis and equated the experience with a good bowel movement. His only other characteristic of note was his intense bigotry. He disliked most people while he tolerated those that he must, for business reasons or to avoid confrontation. His accountant's mind categorized them on a descending scale... Jews, Chinamen, Mexicans, Irish Catholics... and finally, at the very bottom of the list, "niggers."

Sterling had positioned himself at the bar next to Malcomb MacGregor one cool October evening of 1915, and persisted in leading Malcomb into conversation. The pub was crowded, for prohibition was still five years away. A newspaper on the bar announced an average income of $1800.00 per year, a gallon of gasoline sold for 10 cents and the war in Europe raged on. The small article that caught his eye, however, was the life-expectancy prediction of 52.1 years. That fact alone reinforced for Sterling the urgency to alter his life.

"It only makes good business sense," Sterling was saying to MacGregor, "it is the only solution." When Sterling took a long draw on his beer mug and slammed it down loudly, Malcom jumped and stared stupidly at the foamy moustache on Jack's upper lip. "Mr. High and Mightly" sure looked silly, Malcomb thought, but then he was more than a little drunk himself.

"I am responsible for the care of my invalid mother," Jack was saying now. "She needs a companion, a young lady who reads well. I am also compelled to fulfill certain social obligations that are difficult without a woman's touch. Your daughter Anna will be a welcome addition to my household, and I am in a position to offer you five thousand dollars in cash. In addition, I will dispose of the mortgage I hold against your late mother's property. Do we have an agreement?"

Malcomb's head was buzzing, but he forced his attention back to Sterling. He was nervous while his eyes swept the room for familiar faces. He did not like sitting next to this man... what the hell was this meeting all about? Did he just say five thousand dollars? The best Malcomb had hoped for was five hundred to get the girl back to Scotland, to rid himself of her shame once and forever.

"I don't think too fast, Mr. Sterling, but I am not stupid. If you want to pay my daughter to work in your house, what does that have to do with me? She's a bit old to adopt, doncha know, and slavery's illegal. What the hell are we talking about here?" Malcomb's tone was slurred and impatient, barely concealing his contempt for the conversation. What will happen when Sterling discovers (and soon!) that Anna's gone and gotten herself "that way," without benefit of clergy, husband, or means of support? Will the pompous ass next to him then cry "Foul!" and demand his money back, money paid for "spoiled goods"?

It was Jack's turn to look startled. "Good God, man, I intend to marry her!"

Chapter 3

Their nuptials were perfunctory and without adornment, like their introduction and short engagement. She, a non-practicing Presbyterian, and he, an excommunicated Catholic, had no need of clergy and were met at the Union County courthouse by Judge George Steinburger. Anna and her father were out of breath from the long, hurried walk, and she was tense because Malcomb kept reminding her that if they were late, Jack might change his mind and leave. This was only the second meeting of the couple, and Anna was very confused regarding Jack's marriage proposal.

Malcomb stifled a laugh when he observed them standing side by side in front of the judge. Jack barely reached Anna's shoulder and a comic vision crossed Malcomb's mind of the two in the marriage bed, lips to lips, toe to toe. Malcomb indulged this fantasy so long that he missed the pronouncement, recovering just in time to see the two of them turn to each other in confusion. There was no kiss. Jack took Anna's elbow and guided her firmly to the door. This time, Malcomb had to hurry to keep up with her.

"You forgot this," he called out, and extended the battered valise. The trio stood silently uncomfortable until Jack finally offered his hand to Malcomb. "Well, good luck to ye," Malcomb mumbled as he weakly returned Jack's firmer grip. He tipped his hat in Anna's direction but carefully avoided her gray eyes. His long legs carried him swiftly past them and he trotted down the busy street in the rain, patting the bulging envelope in his coat pocket.

They drove in silence. "I need to throw up," Anna said finally, and Jack obligingly stopped the car and stood with her at the side of the road, holding his umbrella. He offered his handkerchief, but she shook her head and produced her own from her sleeve.

"My mother is a grand lady," he told her when they resumed the drive. "She is very particular about her house and her precious collections. Be good to her and she will repay you in kind."

Anna nodded. "Will she be angry?" she asked.

"About what?"

"Us."

"I don't expect that she will," he answered. "But her condition is delicate and she cannot tolerate any kind of conflict or shock. There is no need to tell her of your condition just yet. It can wait." It was the first and last time Jack ever referred to Anna's pregnancy. He asked for no explanation and none was offered him.

It was late October, and the cold rain turned to sleet, threatening snow. Anna wanted to ask for heat, but they were already approaching a massive house at the end of a long driveway, and she sensed that she would soon be very warm. She caught her breath, for the sight of it was impressive indeed. The circular driveway wrapped around perfect gardens. They passed the front door, a huge oak structure flanked by large imposing columns and stone lions. Jack's car finally came to a halt at the rear of the house, near a door that held the sign "Deliveries."

He offered to carry the valise, but she shook her head, hanging on with white knuckles in a death-like grip.

"Good evening, Mrs. Kennedy," Jack greeted the small woman seated at the large kitchen table. "And to you, Helga. Is my mother in her room? Has she eaten?"

"Good evening, sir." Maureen Kennedy spoke to Jack, but her eyes never left Anna. "Helga prepared a light tray and took it to her several hours ago. Her appetite is very lacking tonight, I'm afraid. Shall I have Helga fix you something?"

"No, thank you. Maybe later." Jack turned to Anna, now clutching her valise in front of her slightly protruding belly with both hands. "Mrs. Kennedy, our housekeeper," he announced, "and Helga, our cook. You will meet the others tomorrow." His deep blue eyes locked onto Maureen Kennedy's. "This is Mrs. Sterling. Tomorrow you may show her the house and see to her needs."

Mrs. Kennedy held his gaze and nodded curtly. If she was stunned, she took great pains to conceal it. "Of course," she said, and took a step toward Anna, hand outstretched. "May I take your bag?"

Anna, startled, stepped back so swiftly that her heel struck the edge of a braided rug and she stumbled. Jack's steadying hand was once again at her elbow while she regained her balance. Anna shook her head and moved the little suitcase up her long body until it fully covered the lump of a tummy that she imagined was huge and shouting "and I am her bastard brat... how do ye do?"

Jack watched the three women with amused interest as the little drama played out. Females had dominated his entire life; as the only child he became the only resident male after his father's death, excluding the staff, of course.

He liked to watch the women as they interacted, always hoping to observe a good "cat fight" firsthand.

He smiled at Mrs. Kennedy and said, "Mrs. Sterling is very tired. We will go up now." He gently removed the valise from Anna's rigid fingers, took her arm and led her up the back staircase.

Anna ran her hand lovingly along the polished surface of the ornate railing as she climbed. "So lovely", she whispered, but her interest in the beauty of the house did not completely take her attention from Maureen Kennedy. The two women continued to make eye contact until they lost sight of each other.

Jack settled her into a guest bedroom, inquired about her comfort and said goodnight. "I'll ask Helga to bring you a pot of hot tea and something to eat," he said in a tone that was soft and concerned. "Breakfast is at seven; I'll call for you then." Again, there was no kiss, and he closed the door quietly behind him.

Anna sat down on the massive bed and looked at the huge oaken headboard that nearly touched the ceiling. A crystal chandelier gleamed in the gaslight. The room was warm and beautiful, and she felt safe for the first time in her life. So this was to be her wedding night... spent alone in a stranger's house, where she would lie awake for hours and contemplate the incredible past few weeks and the unknown future. She was not afraid.

Jack was also alone downstairs in his cozy study, a double scotch in one hand and an expensive Cuban cigar in the other. He stretched his short fat legs as far as they would extend and sighed with satisfaction. Today he had become a husband. In seven months he would become a father! His mother was wrong... he could be like other men. His father had been right... there is nothing that money cannot buy.

Chapter 4

The eggs were cold and tasteless, but it did not really matter. Had they been hot and delicious, Anna could not have choked them down. She may, in fact, never eat again if she had to eat at this table. She looked to her left and studied her bridegroom of less than twenty-four hours. What did she know about him, other than the fact that he was rich and lived in a big house with his mother and his mother's servants? There had been no time to learn anything else. Jack, she concluded, had arranged everything, and Malcomb had simply done as he was told.

"You will do this thing," her father had said to her just yesterday morning, "or you will go back to Scotland to live in shame with your Aunt Mary, and everyone will know what you are." What was that exactly? Was that thing that she had done with the handsome stranger so very terrible? The lump in her belly began to object to her attempt to eat, so she concentrated on stacking the sausages into a neat "log" pile between furtive glances at the man to her left and the old woman to her right.

"Mother Sterling," as Anna had been instructed to call her, sat very erect and silently stared at the intruder seated at her table. Anna wanted to scream at Jack, "your mother is rude... make her stop!" Instead, she filled in the log pile with scrambled eggs. *Maybe the old girl is dead*, thought Anna; *she sure looks dead!* The possibility suddenly delighted Anna, and she unsuccessfully tried to stifle a giggle. The effort did not go unnoticed, but brought the old woman's eyebrows to a stiff arch and caused Jack's newspaper to inch down, exposing black rimmed half-glasses and tight, thin lips. He lowered the paper to his lap and cleared his throat.

"Mother," he began, "this is Anna. We were married yesterday."

There. It was said. He waited. Hearing no response, he continued, "Anna will be a companion to you. She is very well- read and I am sure that having another woman in the house, I mean someone who is family... will be of some comfort."

Cold silence prevailed. Jack slowly folded his paper, laid his napkin on the table and rose. He walked to his mother's chair and kissed her temple. "I must go to work now," he announced. "Enjoy your day, ladies."

Jack's departure seemed to go unnoticed by both women, as they continued to lock stares. Finally, Anna broke the trance and rose to her feet.

"Thank you, Mother Sterling," Anna said quietly. "I am indeed as pleased to be here as you obviously are to have me!" She held her napkin high and then dropped the costly piece of linen to the floor. Anna kept her back very stiff as she left the room and took long strides through the house that made the wood floors groan in protest. When she reached the kitchen, she found Mrs. Kennedy seated at the long table blowing into a cup of hot tea. Helga hummed at the stove as she stirred a large pot of soup. *Like a witch and a caldron*, thought Anna, and she addressed the cook first.

"I will take my meals in my room until further notice," Anna said loudly. Helga jumped and turned. When she saw Anna's face, Helga could only nod, her mouth comically gaping. Anna continued, "I will prepare a list for you." The new Mrs. Sterling then turned to a startled Mrs. Kennedy. She was next.

"After lunch we will tour the house, and I will give you your instructions. And by the way... I think it would be appropriate if you would rise to your feet when I enter the room." In spite of her bulk and the horrible taste of rising bile in her throat, Anna managed to spin on both heels and exit the kitchen with the dignity of a queen, leaving two very stunned women staring at her back.

Lillian Sterling sat in a wheelchair at her bedroom window. In the garden below, she watched her daughter-in-law stroll leisurely, inspecting first this plant, then that shrub. Growing tired of this distraction and the pain involved in holding back the Irish lace curtain, she turned away... then turned back just in time to witness Anna on her knees, hanging on to a stone bench while she forfeited her scanty breakfast.

So... there was to be progeny, was there? Jack would pay dearly for this folly!

Chapter 5

1916

Anna stared at the face in the mirror, her hand suspended in midair and gripping the silver hairbrush that Jack had given her in honor of their first anniversary. What was the thought that just now whispered past her mind? Oh yes, that day over a year ago, when she had rolled on the sofa with the father of her baby. Strange that she would think about him now... now that she had so much to content her.

It had been eight months since the funeral of her mother-in-law, that miserable hag who had snubbed her. "Well, guess what?" Anna said aloud, "I win." The event had been well attended by their new found friends, would-be friends, and Jack's business associates, a fitting send-off to honor not only the deceased, but also Jack and Anna, who now enjoyed a prominent place in Richmond's social register. There were flowers everywhere, and catered refreshments; important people patted Anna's shoulder while she sniffled into a linen handkerchief, and they repeated again and again how wonderful she had been throughout the whole ordeal, caring for Jack's mother the way she had.

Anna thought that the family doctor acted somewhat strange when he was asked about the cause of death. "She was old and infirm," Leonard Bennett said. "What more do you need?" But then he had looked directly at Anna, and she thought she saw something in his eyes. Well, she certainly couldn't explain why the old woman refused to eat, practically starved herself as some sort of protest, she supposed. What did it matter? She was dead and now this house was Anna's, just as Mrs. MacGregor's house had been Anna's; only this time she would see that no one took it from her.

As for Jack's mother, she never spoke another word to Anna until the morning she died, two months after the baby was born. "You did well for yourself, girlie," she gasped between labored breaths, "see to it that you take care." Anna was never quite sure what that admonition was supposed to mean, but she knew well that the old lady had not been as easily fooled as Jack. And where was Jack when his mother was dying, leaving Anna to keep the bedside vigil?

The cradle's occupant made a sleepy sound, and Anna smiled. He was almost one year old, her beautiful MacGregor. At the first twinge of hard labor, Anna remembered, she had ceased her chores and sent for Mrs. Kennedy. The housekeeper scurried across the large hallway to find Anna on her knees, casually waxing the staircase spindles. Something very exciting was about to happen, Maureen suspected, and she very much wanted to be a part of it. Quite to her chagrin, Anna instructed her to take the rest of the day off, go out shopping, or visit someone.

"But I had plans... spring cleaning... the guest room rugs are filthy."

"Too bad," Anna snapped, "I have plans of my own." Anna maintained remarkable composure during the exchange, her pains now minutes apart and very intense. She slowly pulled herself up to her full height, stiffened her spine and held her breath while Mrs. Kennedy continued to protest. Anna stood silent, her gray eyes boring holes in the housekeeper's forehead while white-red waves of pain racked her body. Mrs. Kennedy was still speaking, but Anna could not hear. Finally, agitated beyond further debate, Mrs. Kennedy swiftly turned and left the hallway, heels clicking and keys rattling loosely from her leather belt.

The journey up the long oaken staircase was agony that seemed to take hours, causing her to pause and bend as each new pain demanded. Anna locked the door and pulled the shades against the warm May sun. She continued to labor and prepare, stripping the large bed of its fine Irish linen, replacing it with heavy padding that she had stored in the closet. She then removed the large sharp kitchen knife from beneath the mattress and placed it on the bedside table, along with a full bottle of Jack's scotch.

"There is one advantage to sleeping alone," she mumbled to herself. "No one is inconvenienced when you mess up the bed!" It was true; nothing had changed since her wedding night in regard to cohabitation. No time to think about that now, there was important work to be done.

Anna conceded to herself that naked would, no doubt, have been preferable, but she was never at ease with nudity, not even her own. She was nineteen years old and had no one in which to confide her fear, her ignorance of the birthing process. She was healthy, however, and strong, and determined to prove that she needed no one. She lay down and waited in her flannel nightgown, for although the room was very warm, her skin felt cold and clammy. The ascending pain that approached caused her to brace, and she bit her lip until she tasted blood. The next was even worse. Anna feared that she would die in this bloody bed. The third contraction was unbearable, bringing with it the compulsion to bear down, and while it required all of her remaining strength, bear down she did to push this strange object from her belly once and for all, dying be damned! The result was a large red male child shot out between sweaty thighs, squalling loudly and throwing his limbs in protest. Anna stared at him in wonder for long moments, catching her breath. Then calmly and with expertise that surprised even her, she cut the cord and wrapped the baby in a clean towel. She held him very tightly, rocking and smiling. So this was new life... her reward at last for being poor, and homely, and lonely, and motherless.

Her next reward was a warm and numbing swig of the best scotch money could buy. She'd have one more, she told herself, before she rang for Emily.

Chapter 6

So absorbed was he in thought about the day's Wall Street closing, the Dow Jones average at 90, gold at almost $18.00 an ounce, that Jack approached his front door without thought about a key. The door was locked as he had expected, but he decided not to ring the bell. Shifting from side to side, transferring briefcase in the process, he dug the elusive key out of a pocket and slipped it into the lock. Jack preferred the kitchen door, the one that opened to the warm and comforting haven of Helga's kitchen.

The late afternoon shadows danced with intermittent rays of sunshine across the expensive tiles of the foyer. Too warm for May, he thought. The house was very quiet, as usual, and just as he liked it. It did seem odd, however, that no one bothered to greet him, not even the young maid, Emily, whose toothy grin and exuberant bounce gave him a chuckle. "Where is everyone?" he asked the silence. He shrugged and carried his briefcase into the study, tossed it to a leather couch and headed for the bar. Suddenly he stopped and listened. Something was... not wrong exactly, but different. He forgot about the drink, turning instead to the rear of the house, to the kitchen where he found Helga mutilating a large bunch of carrots with a cleaver.

"Hello, Helga," he said. "Where is Mrs. Sterling?"

"In her room, I'd be guessin', been there since right after breakfast." Helga's mumble was barely audible above the slaughter of the carrots. She continued to pound without looking at him. Jack decided that Helga was not referring to Anna, who would not spend an entire day in her room.

"I was asking about my wife," he clarified, "not my mother."

"And so was I. Too many Mrs. around here these days, if you ask me, which, of course, no one did! How's a body supposed to keep track? Not my job anyways, beings I'm just the cook!" SMASH! Another pureed carrot.

Jack had just experienced one of the best days of his year. War bonds were soaring and blue-chip stock was high. His mood mellow, he tried again. "And Mrs. Kennedy?"

"Banished by the young Mrs. mid-morning. Probably hiding out in her room since she was told, and not too nicely, that she was not permitted on the second floor. Treated like a naughty child she was, and for no good reason I could see. I'd be out early, too, except then you'd all starve to death. Mighty strange goings-on around here these days, if you ask me!"

Jack decided to leave the room quietly, before he was forced to endure another "if you ask me." He made a swift exit up the back stairs, shaking his head at the many moods of the female. His knock at Anna's door was answered immediately by an obviously euphoric Emily.

"Good afternoon to you, Mr. Sterling," Emily effused. "How wonderful to see you at last!"

Good God, was she drunk? He pushed past Emily to Anna's bedside, while Emily bowed and swept an arm in that general direction. Anna herself had the look of someone he had never seen before. She was propped on a bevy of satin pillows, smiling sweetly. Long chestnut hair flowed to her shoulders. He had never seen her hair down, and now a pretty blue ribbon held it away from her face, a face radiant with a dewy flush.

"Are you ill?" His tone sounded concerned, but Anna couldn't be sure. Perhaps he was merely curious. Stepping closer, his leg brushed the small cradle, and it moved. Looking down at the sleeping, naked infant, Jack's heart pounded. He was on the brink of an overpowering emotion, a new experience and not totally welcome. This child... his son was beautiful. Yes, his son. It had never mattered to Jack who fathered this child... it was his, by legal right.

"It's a boy," Anna whispered. "MacGregor Sterling, if that's all right with you."

"That's just fine with me." She now had his full attention. How brave she had been, how efficient. Now smelling of fresh lavender sachet and Palmolive soap, perhaps they could, after all, be the couple of the year. She was almost lovely! With Anna's assistance, he held the baby, stroked his hair, and counted his fingers. She had earned his gratitude forever. From this moment and for the rest of their lives, he would deny her nothing.

"Since you managed this without messing up your hair, let's have one every year!" he teased her.

She forced a thin smile. When he rose to put the baby down she mumbled, "Over my dead body!" but he missed it.

Chapter 7

1918

"I have developed an intense dislike for that woman."

Anna was almost as startled to hear herself speak the words as Jack was to hear them. She was staring at the back of Maureen Kennedy's head as the housekeeper exited the room, and somehow the thought just blurted out.

Jack slowly lowered his newspaper and gave his wife a puzzled look. *Here we go*, he thought. *Everything is going well, we have harmony and peace, and life is as good as it gets… so naturally you must find something, anything, to remedy that situation!* He allowed this thought to settle back into the dark recesses of his brain before he spoke, "And why is that, dear? Has Mrs. Kennedy done something to offend you?"

Anna's snappy comeback was on the tip of her tongue, and she wanted to say, *Do you mean the way she treats me like poor white trash?* But this time she was in control, so it came out, "Mrs. Kennedy doesn't know her place. I am the mistress of this house, not she, but I am continually made to feel like an unwelcome guest in my own home."

Jack sighed and folded his newspaper, a sign of surrender that signified that the reading was over, pre-empted by a serious matter indeed. Anna avoided his stare, kept her head down, as she suddenly became intensely interested in the needlework in her lap. Now that she had his undivided attention and was armed for battle, she considered for a moment that she might lose. He waited. Carefully choosing her words, she began again.

"I'm sure that Mrs. Kennedy has given you and your family many years of loyal service." So, it would be the concerned, tactful approach. "But she is certainly of retirement age, and her services here are no longer required." That was as gracious as she could be… it would have to do, because she could think of nothing else to say.

Jack allowed his mind to wander for a moment, considering how he might best avoid the landmine clearly buried in this conversation. What he lacked in sincerity, he compensated for in careful double talk, often disguised as tact. He smiled to himself, pleased about his correct prediction that there would sooner or later be some trouble among the ladies of the house. Maureen

Kennedy had been in residence since before his birth; she was actually the first to hold him, taking him gently from the arms of the mid-wife.

It was Maureen to whom he ran when he fell, and it was she who carefully washed his dirty knee and applied the stinging salve that somehow didn't sting quite so much, because she urged him to watch for the "little people" who might any moment dash under a chair. It was Maureen who smuggled in hot bread and milk when he had been banished to his room by his irate father. It was Maureen who, God forgive him, had unknowingly become the object of his pubescent fantasies; a secret that whispered to him of incest since he often silently wished that Maureen had been his mother. Jack had never known life without her, nor did he desire to. "Your personal audience," he had once read, "is comprised of those few people in your life whose opinions of you truly matter." If that were true, Maureen Kennedy was front row center. It was her approval that he sought, her disappointment that he tried to avoid.

She had returned as a personal companion with his mother, whose European tour had extended to Ireland in 1884, a year before his birth. *Must have been some homecoming*, Jack chuckled to himself. Mrs. Sterling struck up an unlikely friendship with Maureen's family, and their request that Maureen Flinn be permitted to immigrate was granted, due to intense and increased fighting in revolutionary Ireland. Maureen lived her life believing that Mrs. Sterling had probably saved it. An arranged marriage to Paddy Kennedy, complete with the finest wedding ever bestowed upon an "Irish domestic" further endeared "Mother Sterling" to Maureen, and she remained fiercely devoted to the old woman—of whom she spoke with whispered reverence. Oh, yes. This was going to be very difficult indeed. Better to proceed slowly, feeling his way out of this dilemma.

Anna waited for an answer, worried by the silence. Had she pushed too far? Was he thinking that his life had been far less complicated before this marriage? Did he know how significant the issue; would he honor his pledge to grant her every wish?

"I sincerely doubt that Mrs. Kennedy has 'forgotten her place,'"Jack finally spoke. "I'm confused about the phrase, by the way. Just where is 'her place'?" He gave Anna several moments to reply. When she did not, he continued, "Mother's death has been very difficult for her. They were mutually devoted."

Devoted enough to inherit a handsome pile of money, Anna thought. *Why is she still hanging around when she has more than she needs to retire? Is she to be my bequest, left here to drive me crazy after months of catering to that old woman?* Out loud she said, "My point exactly. Mrs. Kennedy was devoted to another mistress of this house. That one is gone forever. Her loyalty was to your mother, not to me, and never will be. We need to make a change."

"All this gibberish and you still haven't told me what terrible thing she has done." Jack's tone was considerably louder and strained. He rose and crossed the room quickly, as if the bar had suddenly become a finish line to be reached at any cost. He poured a large scotch, added ice, and half-turned to his wife, remembering his manners. "Drink?"

"I am nursing," she said in an undertone that implied, *and if you were paying attention to me, you would know that.*

"Just as a matter of curiosity," Jack retorted, "why is that? The little bugger can walk and talk... can't you teach him to drink from a cup?"

Anna started to say something, but changed her mind and clamped her lips tightly shut while she considered her husband's belligerent tone. This discussion was getting out of hand, not going at all her way. She must be careful here or there could be no escape, unless, of course, she acquiesced and left the room.

"It keeps him close to me," she lied. Doris Steinburger had told her that nursing would prevent pregnancy, although God only knows that her chances of getting pregnant again were extremely slim, given the lack of sexual interest by her husband, her infrequent lover. "If that answer is satisfactory, may we resume our original discussion?"

Jack forced a smile. This repartee was taking a nasty turn. "Certainly, dear. What exactly has Mrs. Kennedy done?"

Anna sighed loudly. "I have already told you. She has no respect. None of my requests have been honored. It's as if your mother were still here these past two years. My decorating suggestions fall on deaf ears. I offer ideas for the menu, but these dishes are never served because the cook would not dare offend 'her.'" Anna had once again worked herself into frenzy; her voice grew louder, her speech faster. She took a long, deep breath and blurted it out at last, before she lost all courage... "Offer her a generous severance and let us be done with her once and for all. I want that woman out of my house!"

Standing at the bar, his back to her, Jack literally saw red. A vivid band of crimson flashed behind his eyes, blinding him. He was trembling, his face was on fire, mandibular muscles contracted and released. *Her house?* Who the hell was she, this come lately to his quiet life to dictate her wishes? Hadn't he given her everything, taken her in, she and her child? Hadn't he saved her from shame, provided a home, allowed her charge accounts, secured for her a prominent place in society? *His name!* His name, for Christ's sake, his most precious possession! How could she be so ungrateful, this petty female who now decides who may or may not live here? A chorus of demons exploded in his brain, shouting obscenities he dare not repeat, mixed with less offensive verbiage like "divorce" and "murder."

Silence roared. His volley. Keeping his voice level and controlled, he spun to face her, splashing ten-dollar scotch on his sixty-dollar lapel. "Why in the name of heaven do you persist in this folly? Are you so insecure that you must control every aspect of this house, depriving yourself of luncheons, tennis, bridge, and, of course, the continued indulgence of your precious son? Why, when you have a perfectly competent housekeeper to do it for you?"

She stood, returning his icy glare. "Why," she retorted, "do you persist in visiting your whores when you have a perfectly competent wife?"

He looked at her for a long moment but did not blink. He crossed the room and opened the French doors. "Please ask Mrs. Kennedy to join me in the study."

Anna slowly sank into the nearest chair. For the first time in her life, she wished that she could cry, but years of suppression had dried the source, she suspected, because despite the sting in her eyes, the tears would not come. Crying was a sign of weakness, she reminded herself. Only babies and silly schoolgirls could afford the luxury of tears.

Right at this moment she must force herself under control and assess the damage. To the casual observer it may appear that she had won... but she knew better.

Chapter 8

1919

Mary George was so excited she could hardly contain herself. The Wednesday afternoon bridge game at the club was about to begin and the ladies were wasting precious time discussing Lady Aster's appointment to the British Parliament. Who the hell cared? Mary finally had a juicy tidbit to share, a rare commodity for her, as she was, alas, always on the receiving end of information.

"Listen!" Mary interrupted with such enthusiasm that Doris Steinburger, Anna Sterling, and Sophie Hughes at once ceased their chatter and stared wide-eyed at the speaker.

"I simply must tell you this before I burst! Shirley Layton caught her husband John with a prostitute last night, down on Canal Street. Seems she had hired a detective to follow him, and there he was, in all his naked glory... 'red-handed,' so to speak. I told Fred that if he ever humiliated me in such a manner, he'd better leave the county fast because I'd kill him!"

The news was titillating indeed. Everyone started talking at once, seeking more detail, speculating about divorce settlement, and probing deeply into the philosophy of sex and marriage. Everyone except Anna, that is. She flushed a deep crimson and caught her breath. Canal Street. She knew the area. She had walked that way once or twice on her way home from school, and she had wondered about the painted ladies that stood in dark doorways and taunted her when she passed. She also knew that Jack went there. Not often... but he went there. Lost in thought, Anna almost missed Sophie's shocking theory about the "why."

"They do things that no lady would ever do," Sophie announced. "Horrible, unspeakable things!"

"What things?" Anna wanted to know more.

"You tell her, Doris. But tell her later... I don't want to hear about it; I don't even want to think about it. It just makes me sick to my stomach!"

Anna looked around the table at each pinked face. She was twenty-two, the youngest of the group, and the most recently wed. No one had ever spoken of these matters in her presence. Only once, when she had been twelve or so and had begun to menstruate, had her Grandmother MacGregor, in a rare mood brought on by a third glass of wine, ventured daringly into the subject. "There are certain things that men expect," the old woman had said. "You must put up with them from time to time in order to keep a happy home." Anna's gaze now fell upon the knowledgeable Mrs. Steinburger, who was having some difficulty disguising her amusement.

"Later, dear. We'll have a little chat."

"Good!" said Sophie. "Now can we play bridge?"

"What things?" Anna persisted.

"Damnit, Anna, are you writing a book?" Sophie snapped.

"No, but I would certainly like to read one," Anna retorted. Almost everything she had thus far learned about life, she had learned from her books. How could she have missed this subject? She was a grown-up, a married woman who had given birth. Her sole experience had been a tryst on her grandmother's sofa, a bittersweet moment of newly awakened passion. That was true, of course, unless one counted the few (very few) clumsy attempts by her husband since.

Doris gave Anna a look that signaled that this particular discussion was over.

"Later," Doris announced.

****

"Two hearts."

The bid had been declared, but the game was stalled. The three other women at the table looked at Anna and waited. She seemed to be entranced, lost in her own world.

"Anna?"

"Oh, … sorry! Pass." Anna recovered in time to realize that her bridge partner was looking at her very strangely, and her face flushed. "I guess I am a little preoccupied," she explained, and then fell silent, not wishing to share her thoughts.

"Happens to all of us from time to time," Doris said. "But it seems to be happening to you quite often these days, dear. Is everything all right at home?"

Anna smiled. *Nice try, Doris. But I won't bite.* Aloud she answered, "Of course."

Things were actually fairly lousy at home these days following the sudden departure of Maureen Kennedy from the "Great House," Anna's pet name for the Sterling mansion. While she had expected that Jack would sulk for a day or two, she was totally unprepared for his continuing display of intense displeasure. Communication between the two of them had ceased on every level. Jack stayed overnight at his private club for several nights a week. When he infrequently visited his home, he arrived long after Anna had retired and left again before dawn. Anna tried to conceal her hurt and confusion. Her "victory" seemed indeed hollow. Above all, she told herself, she must maintain appearances, so she made half-hearted excuses to the staff, a necessity that provoked her already bad humor. After two evenings of dining alone at the huge mahogany table, she requested a light dinner tray be sent to her room. Cook Helga, still seething over the discharge of her very dear friend Maureen Kennedy, delighted in the opportunity which now presented itself: she served Anna's least-favorite menus. Anna hated fish, so fish became overabundant in the Sterling household. Bread was stale, fruit overripe, and everything else burned almost to a crisp. *You may also be replaced, Helga. Watch your step.*

"George said that he runs into Jack almost every evening." Doris continued to push the issue. "Are you redecorating again, Anna?"

Anna wanted to ask Doris why George was spending so much time at the club but thought better of it and replied quietly, "Jack has been working later and later." It was a lie and they all knew it. "Could we just play bridge?" Anna asked, her free hand rubbing at her forehead.

Doris smiled, satisfied. She had accomplished her goal, struck a raw nerve. Anna should know better than to spar with an expert. She could now swing wide into another direction and score point "two." "Have you hired a replacement for Mrs. Kennedy?"

Sophie and Mary exchanged knowing glances. This game was over except for going through the motions. When Doris wanted information, wild horses couldn't hold her until she got it, and none of Anna's vague and evasive answers would put her off track. The two ladies silently agreed to just sit back and enjoy the exchange, occasionally tossing a card on the table, as tribute.

"No need," Anna mumbled. She had the beginnings of a terrible headache and was suddenly very weary of this game. Why wouldn't Doris just shut up? Anna stared at the cards in her hand until she could no longer stand the silence. Her head jerked up so suddenly that a searing pain assaulted her, accompanied by a loud snap. "What?" she demanded.

All three were staring at her as if she had just proclaimed Wilson a Republican who supported the Suffragettes. "Surely you are not suggesting," Doris spoke very slowly, "that you intend to manage your own house! I am appalled and distressed that I need to remind you that it just isn't done!"

Anna glared at her, damn the social graces; she was ready to fight. *Drop dead, Doris. I am sick of your stupid, snobbish rules. I have been keeping my own house since I was twelve, and I don't need you or anyone else to tell me that I must hand it over!* Good sense gained control and she asked, "Why? I have plenty of help, you know. Emily is there and Helga, and…"

"Not another word!" Doris slammed the cards down hard and everyone jumped. "As usual, I have the solution that will prevent disaster! Mary, who was that wonderful woman who worked for your sister before she moved to Atlanta?"

"Millie Anderson," Mary replied. "She was the absolute best domestic my sister ever had and she begged Millie to go with her, but she had family here and…."

"There, you see, all settled. Mary, can you arrange for Millie to visit Anna tomorrow?"

Anna's outburst was so sudden, Mary didn't have time to answer. "But… she's a Negro!" Anna almost whined.

Again the table vibrated in shocked silence. How would she ever explain her reasons while her friends looked at her as if she were an ignorant ass? None of them knew anything about Anna MacGregor Sterling, about her humble beginnings, her background; none of them had ever visited, she was sure, the seedy part of town where she grew up. She remembered Millie Anderson very well, for they were classmates at the old, dumpy public school a world away from the New England private institutions that her bridge partners attended. She remembered most how kind Millie had been to her that day when they were about ten, how Millie had helped her pick up the books and papers scattered by cruel boys who tortured them on the walk home from school. How ironic that dear Millie, who had become her only friend, was the one person in this entire city that Anna would be happy to see again! But there was also Jack, and there was no way in hell or heaven that he would allow a Negro in their home. How could she make them understand? What could she say that would explain that her situation was very precarious? Her fragile marriage, on the verge of destruction, was the only asset she possessed. She dared not risk his wrath any further, or she and her son could very well find themselves on the street.

"I…" Anna was at a loss for words. Perhaps she could tell them how Jack, not merely intolerant, was enraged about the Negro race; how he would rant and rave for hours about the liberals and their efforts to offer social programs and encourage integration. Perhaps she could add that he detested Negroes only a little more than he hated women who want to vote!

Doris needed to take control of the moment. Although she had exhausted her short supply of patience with Anna's whiney excuses, she recognized that further debate would only make matters worse. "Let's move on," Doris ordered. Doris tried to choose her battles carefully, and then only those she was certain to win. She would discuss Anna's social faux pas with her privately, some other time.

"Perhaps you would have no objection to another suggestion," Doris continued. "Rachel Spencer Unger is available, I happen to know. She is from a very good family, even if they are poor." Doris shot Anna a long condescending look, but Anna's head was down, and she thankfully missed it. "Poor Rachel married none too wisely... handsome devil, but determined to haul her off to Kentucky or some God-forsaken place where he got himself killed in a mine explosion. She has returned to Richmond with her small son, about MacGregor's age, I think, and she badly needs a job."

Silence. Anna was thinking about Rachel, another schoolmate from PS 23. *'Saint Rachel,' we called her, the pretty, petite blond admired by the girls, adored by the boys. Just what you need, Anna, some other reason to feel inadequate!*

Sustained silence was consent, Doris reasoned. "It's settled then. I will have Rachel call on you tomorrow."

Anna was neatly trapped. Doris had won; after all, the discussion was over. The constant nagging pain in her head had finally evolved into a full-blown migraine. Anna needed to get out of here soon or she would lose her lunch, faint, or worse. She needed to go home immediately, to the sanctuary of her darkened room, to the blessed relief of her pills and the warm comfort of hot towels on her throbbing head.

Chapter 9

Jack Sterling also had a headache. While Anna and Doris played bridge and danced around the discussion of oral sex, Jack and George tried to enjoy a late lunch at the club. Both men picked at various objects on their plates as they read newspapers, a habit certainly frowned upon by Emily Post as a major violation of good manners. There was no need of active conversation, for they were both comfortable in their mutual silence. An odd friendship, this one... they had little in common other than their fascination with money and their endeavors to acquire and keep it.

George was gregarious and outgoing, an excellent candidate for politics had he not pursued law instead. A well-known and highly respected senior attorney for a prestigious firm, he had achieved his judge's chair just in time to officiate at the Sterling wedding. Jack was an admitted introvert who had little time or tolerance for anyone. They seldom agreed on any level, except finance and, on occasion, world affairs and the importance of putting a Republican into the White House.

"Goddamn Krauts!" Jack exclaimed. He angrily mashed the paper into a large ball and tossed it under the table.

"Careful there, my friend, you are talking about my noble ancestors."

"Your noble ancestors refused to sit down at Versailles unless the Allies promised military honors! Why didn't they just ask us to bend over and kiss their German asses?"

"They signed the treaty, didn't they? What more do you want?"

"Nothing less than total monetary recovery for the war, and a personal apology to each and every American."

"Only Americans?" George chuckled. "Well, if we Germans don't need to include the French and the rest of the Allies, I suppose we could consider it."

Jack wasn't amused. He looked at his friend for a long moment. "I may have made a terrible mistake," he said, very serious.

George was about to quip that no, the Germans had definitely lost the war, but something in those intensely blue eyes stopped him. This was a new twist, a different side of Jack, and something was very wrong.

"How so, Jack?"

"I suppose you would be elated to hear me say that I have become a cliche," Jack answered slowly. "I have perhaps, as they say, 'married in haste,' which, of course, leads to repentance at leisure. Who said that?"

"I think you just did."

"This is no joking matter, George. It hasn't been easy, you know. My quiet, orderly little life is falling apart since I took that woman into my house. Now that fool in Washington wants to let her vote! What do women know about politics, George? Why do they want to vote?" Jack's tone was excited and above the level of casual conversation. Club members were looking in the direction of their table.

"Take it easy, Jack, calm down. Is all this really about the suffragettes?" It occurred to George that Jack was babbling, jumping from one thought to another, and not making much sense.

"I had to fire Mrs. Kennedy because Anna didn't want her in 'her house.' Do you have any idea how long that wonderful woman has been employed by my family? What right has she to just toss her out like so much baggage?"

"I had no idea you were so devoted to your housekeeper." George was straining to maintain a straight face. This was all so strange... what the hell were they talking about?

Jack launched into a long tirade about Anna, the pregnancy, the only reason he married her actually was the pregnancy, his one chance for a son to carry on his honorable name. Why didn't he just give her money and adopt the boy? Now he was stuck with this controlling female who wanted to manipulate him into submission. "I need legal advice, George. Will you help me?"

"Jack, if it will make you feel better, I will hold your hand while you talk to your lawyer. I'm a judge now, remember? Since I am no longer a practicing attorney, I cannot represent you. Sorry."

"I already have an attorney... I need a friend. Walter will see to the particulars when the time comes. Meanwhile, just tell me, what's the worst that can happen if I file for divorce?"

"Well," George replied carefully, "off the record, of course. First, what are the grounds, other than the chance that she may vote for a Democrat? It will be costly, certainly; the courts protect abandoned wives. What about the child? Your seed or no, he is yours by law, owing to the fact that you were her husband at the time of his birth and hung your honorable name on him without protest. The French have a saying, actually... 'may all your wife's children be yours.' C'est la vie!"

Jack was silent. He had hoped that George would assure him that the dissolution of his marriage would present no real problem, that he could somehow undo what seemed so easily done. What about the boy? He didn't think he could bear to be without him. He tried to think of some terrible thing that Anna had done, but he was coming up blank. The Kennedy matter was really more a matter of the challenge to his authority since she was nearly at retirement age anyway. Now that he had vented, it all seemed rather silly.

As George waited, he could almost read Jack's thoughts. Carefully, so carefully, he ventured some sound advice. "All marriages have an adjustment period, Jack. Some last for years. Your life is enriched by your little family, no matter how you managed to arrange it. Anna is devoted to you in her own way, and perhaps if you would consider a change in your approach, you might get things back on track."

"What changes?"

George was pleasantly surprised that his friend was actually open to suggestion. He was feeling very wise as he continued, "Soften a little, cajole a little, speak quietly and keep the big stick behind your back. Give her whatever it is that she wants and she will do anything to avoid rocking the boat. And while you're at it, whisper in her ear on the eve of the election and you will have doubled your vote! You must learn how to play the game, Jack, or the women will drive you crazy."

Jack felt much better. This little problem wasn't going to cost him a fortune or interfere with his preferred lifestyle as long as he could hold his temper in check. He could do this. He had been lonely too long to go back to that life. Everything would be all right if he only maintained control. He began again to replay the words that George had just spoken, weighing and analyzing each item. Suddenly he blanched and blurted protest. "Subtle and tender manipulation, George? Are you suggesting that I seduce my bride?"

"Can't hurt. It's been done before, actually. Married people have been doing it for centuries and it may even grow on you." *Besides, my friend, the sweet inexperienced Anna has little to compare you with... she may begin to believe that she has a tiger in her bed!*

****

Anna opened her eyes and attempted to focus. She wanted to recall the dream, the long sensuous dream that had pleasured her with an unfamiliar excitement, a vague memory of another time when she had experienced that strange, wonderful feeling. She could not recall the face of the man who had made love to her in her dream, but she knew that it was not her husband. She smiled and stretched just as Emily drew back the long heavy drapes and flooded the room with warm summer sunshine.

"Good morning, Madam. I have your tray ready, and a surprise!"

"What time is it?"

"Almost noon, Madam. When you're ready to receive her, Mrs. Unger is in the drawing room. Presented Mrs. Steinburger's card, she did, and insisted that you were expecting her. No hurry, though. She's quite settled in, beings she's been here since mid-morning."

Good Lord, she had slept for eighteen hours! The headache was blessedly absent at last... a killer this one, but thank God for the pills. How many had she taken? Didn't matter, she supposed, they had stopped the terrible pain and she was still alive.

Emily approached the large bed , her silly grin hidden behind a crystal vase of long-stemmed roses. "Your surprise, Madam."

Anna read the card three times before her foggy mind recognized Jack's script. "To my lovely Anna. A new beginning. With apologies, Jack."

Yesterday's bridge game, the worst headache of her life, the pills, the roses, the card, ... it was all too much to absorb when she had so little time. Always organized, Anna realized immediately that she could ill afford to offend Doris by keeping her guest waiting any longer. "Please serve coffee in the drawing room," she instructed Emily as she hurriedly dressed. "And have Helga prepare a light lunch. Mrs. Unger will be joining me... in the garden."

As Anna swept down the massive oaken staircase, she thought again about her grandmother. The number "three" was divine, she told Anna, because it was the number of the trinity. If you heard something three times, it was undoubtedly true. Three on a match was unlucky... why was that? Oh, yes. Three cigarettes lit in a foxhole, because it took exactly that long for a sniper to take aim. Why was she thinking about 'three'?

Because she had decided before she reached the bottom riser that Rachael Spencer Unger's "interview" would be a formality. She would offer her the job, bring "saint" Rachael into her home because: 1) it would get Doris off her back and repair any damage done at yesterday's fiasco and 2) it was poetic justice, this opportunity to be Rachael's superior after years of envy and feelings of inferiority. She looked over her shoulder at the rainbow of beautiful colors that radiated from the Tiffany window on the landing. It was indeed a glorious day!

But what was the third reason?

Chapter 10

"Boys! Stop now!"

Anna rounded the corner just in time to observe a breathless Helga reaching for two small male children who were jumping from leather chair to sofa in a fit of obvious glee. The scene was chaotic, and Anna laughed heartily for the first time in weeks. The boys squealed and giggled as Helga attempted to position them, one on each hip and under her fleshy arms, while flour dust from her apron rubbed all over them.

"Mama!" Mac shouted when he spied his mother, and in a second he had wriggled free to run into her arms. Helga slowly lowered the kicking playmate to his feet, where he stood watching the mother and son, thumb securely locked in his little mouth. A small blond woman suddenly appeared and the three women stood silently and helplessly by when the boys made another dive for the furniture, piercing the air with a loud war hoop.

"I am so sorry, Mrs. Sterling!" the pretty lady stammered. "I have no one to watch him."

"Please, Mrs. Unger, don't give it a thought. What a joy it is to hear children's laughter in this house! I'll ring for Emily to watch over them while we chat." Anna's sweet answer prompted Helga to stare at her mistress with wide-eyed wonder, and she shook her head and stomped off to the kitchen, mumbling Swedish obscenities.

The ladies seated themselves on the large leather sofa and smiled at each other.

"I understand you are seeking employment," Anna began. "Can you be ready to begin Monday next? The salary is $90.00 a month and, of course, includes the small apartment adjacent to the main pantry."

Rachael Unger smiled thinly and nodded her understanding, concealing the fact that she did not at all understand. Her small delicate hands held the letters of reference that she had so carefully collected, and she wondered if she should now present them. She had expected that there would be a getting-acquainted period, a formal interview and a "I'll let you know" dismissal. Mrs. Sterling was behaving as if she had already been hired and the details were now open to discussion. Where was her little boy, her Paul? Rachael felt a slight chill as her imagination whispered that the child was somewhere in this massive house, crying for his mama.

"I am so sorry," Rachael interrupted suddenly. "I'm afraid I've misunderstood. What apartment?"

Anna continued to smile. She was feeling very tolerant today and everything was, of course, going to go her way. "It is I who should apologize. I assumed that you knew… this position is a 'live-in,' full time. The quarters are really quite nice. I can show you now if you prefer, or we could have our lunch first."

"Mrs. Sterling," Rachael began…

"Please call me Anna."

No more surprises, please! Rachael jumped to her feet, tipping the cup on her lap and sending it crashing to the Oriental rug. She starred at the stain, fighting back tears.

Anna looked up into Rachael's face. She stood slowly, towering above her visitor, and gently slipped her long arm around a trembling shoulder. "Don't bother about it," Anna said softly. "It is only a cup. Come with me and we will take the tour."

They walked through the big house very slowly, almost strolling. Rachael had never seen such a magnificent house, a cleaning challenge, she imagined. Anna explained that there was adequate help, "more than adequate, actually. I'm afraid we are overstaffed."

Rachael shot her a look that said, *Then why do you need me?* Anna hurriedly covered her blunder when she added that while the maids were competent, they needed "direction."

Besides, dear Rachael, I have other plans for you.

As the afternoon progressed, Rachael saw as much of the house as time would allow. They approached Jack's study where Anna was surprised and embarrassed to discover that she could not enter. "Stuck," Anna offered as explanation. "Emily, come here please." The maid arrived, breathless as usual. The boys were down for a nap, she reported, assuming that the ladies were concerned about the children.

"Why is this door locked?" Anna's tone was suddenly and harshly accusatory.

Emily was nervous when she answered her mistress, "It's always locked, Madam."

"How do you clean in there?"

"Late at night, Madam, when Mr. Sterling is in there. He allows me to come in and dust and such, but no one gets in excepting he's there."

Odd, Anna thought. She would speak to Jack about it later, demand to know why there was an area in this house that did not welcome her. Or perhaps not.

The housekeeper's apartment was very nice, far more than Rachael would have expected had she thought about it at all. A large, nicely furnished parlor, small dining room which seated six, a master bedroom with its own fireplace, a cheerful room for Paul, their own private bathroom, and a nicely outfitted kitchen and back porch overlooking a fenced play area. A private entrance and personal mailbox near the gate lent an aria of privacy, a sense of "this is your own space."

"You may always use the main kitchen, or have Helga prepare something for you," Anna explained. "Or you may prefer your own kitchen, especially on Sunday."

"Sunday?" Rachael was still staring at all the lovely things.

"Your day off," said Anna. "I thought you would want to spend the day with your child, after Mass, of course."

"Mrs. Sterling," Rachael began again… what was it that she was about to say? She had known no real comfort since leaving her mother's home with John, setting out for a life of love and adventure, he had said. They had so little time together, and most of that time was taken up with the struggle of the long journey to Harlan County, Kentucky. The wagon was up to its hub in mud every day, and the poor old horse finally plopped down and died on the last day, leaving the newlyweds to find their way in underbrush. The "company cabin" assigned to them upon their arrival in the camp was no more than a shanty, sparsely furnished and very dirty. The older women in the mining camp gathered around her like a herd of old elephants, protecting the young. They helped her clean the dingy shack, tore pieces of muslin for hand-sewn curtains and saw to it that the "youngsters" never went hungry. "Take care," they told her, "or you will owe your husband's wages to the company store!" The warning came too late; she was soon over her head on the account books.

Anna had read about the Harlan County riots. Children of miners begged in the streets for food. It was certainly a rough existence, paying only about nine dollars a week.

"They posted a notice," Rachael was now telling Anna as they sipped after-lunch coffee. "John signed up for special duty. He never told me about it, that it was very dangerous. The explosion happened so fast, was so intense that it rattled the windows in the cabins. I ran as fast as I could, but I never saw him. I begged them to let me bring him home, for a decent burial, you know, but the camp boss said that there wasn't enough left of John to bury."

Anna noticed a small tear beginning to bother the corner of Rachael's right eye. *Of course it was dangerous, you silly goose, how could you be so naïve? So... your husband blew into a thousand pieces because you couldn't pay your grocery bill?* "It must have been terrible for you," Anna said aloud.

"I was seven months along with Paul, so I had to stay there until I delivered. I was afraid the management wouldn't let us leave after John died, because they said I still owed them money. One of the women managed to get out long enough to telegraph my brother in Richmond, and he came to get us. At gunpoint. It was the most frightening day of my life." Rachael dabbed at her tear with a small handkerchief. "You have been most kind, Mrs. Sterling... Anna. It is far more than I had hoped for. I accept your terms."

Anna smiled. *Naturally you do. You may be a ninny, but you are no fool, Rachael Spencer. I have just offered you more money than you could ever hope to earn, and you will keep my house and do my bidding, and I will never have to feel that you are the better ever again.*

Mac and Paul ran into the room, followed by a tired, happy Emily. "They have eaten every cookie in the kitchen!" Emily exclaimed. "And Cook is taking a nip of the brandy in the pantry." Anna watched Paul with great interest as he climbed into his mother's waiting arms. A beautiful child, and a playmate for Mac. *Reason number three,* she realized. Another wonderful child in this house, and she didn't have to put forth any effort, no morning sickness, no horrible labor. Jack will be pleased.

"We will send one of the gardeners to your address tomorrow to help you fetch your belongings," Anna offered. "One more thing... Mr. Sterling requires complete quiet when he is at home. Housekeeping activity must cease, the Victrola kept to a low volume, and above all, peace and a calm atmosphere. He works very hard and this house is his haven. Do you understand?"

"Yes," replied Rachael. "I completely understand. But little boys do make some racket, although I'll do my utmost to keep Paul quiet."

"A major part of your duties will be the care and handling of Mac," Anna informed her. "I trust you see that they both behave as little gentlemen. As for noise, some is indeed expected, but I am sure that you will see to it that all is serene when Mr. Sterling is at home. Don't be overly concerned. My husband adores children."

Part 2

Chapter 1

1920

For six months following the birth of his baby sister, the Sterling boy-child continually asked, "Why?" He chanted the word night and day, even in his sleep. It became his standard reply to every question put to him and every instruction given him. The constant "why" was a source of irritation to Jack and cook Helga, an amusement to the ever-patient Rachael and a prophetic echo of her own thoughts to his mother. "Why indeed?" she began to answer the toddler, for she considered the birth of Lillian Gretchen Sterling an unnecessary inconvenience.

Almost a year before the baby's arrival and very soon after Mrs. Unger and Paul moved into the small apartment adjacent to the kitchen, the household settled into a cheerful, well-organized period of contentment. Rachael was, to Anna's complete surprise, worth her weight in gold, guiding effortlessly every housekeeping detail. Every member of the staff adored Rachael, whose quiet, subtle suggestions were immediately implemented. She seemed to accomplish the impossible with such ease and grace that even Anna grew to depend upon Rachael to keep her life running smoothly.

"You have made an excellent choice," Jack told Anna. "I am duly impressed." Anna was pleasantly surprised at Jack's expression of approval, and she accepted it proudly without concern that it was also a compliment to Rachael. Rachael, in turn, deferred to Anna in a manner that was never obvious.

"Where did you find these wonderful cigars?" Jack asked Rachael one evening.

"Mrs. Sterling suggested I look for them," she answered, unaware that Anna was within hearing distance. "She was sure you would like them." It was a fib, harmless, but a fib nonetheless. Anna smiled her approval.

Rachael was beginning to be more than merely pleased with her new position. As she reported to Father Mackey during their weekly chats that passed for confession, for Rachael had little to confess, "I am truly blessed." Her generous salary was far more than she would ever need to support herself and Paul, so she was able to save with new regularity. St. Rose's Parish became a beneficiary when Rachael more than doubled her tithe to a full twenty-five percent, dropping it every Sunday morning into the collection basket. She was delighted to discover that she could attend daily Mass as well, since no one in the Sterling household seemed to care that she left her sleeping son under the care of Emily and walked to church in the pre-dawn chill.

Anna and Jack ended the decade on a definite note of harmony. Everything that had divided them suddenly disappeared with Rachael's arrival and Jack's change of attitude. They threw themselves into an entertaining frenzy, gave lavish cocktail and dinner parties, after-the-theater parties, bridge parties and sometimes, "just because it is Friday" parties. Their social stock rose to new heights. Anna took a sudden interest in her looks, experimented with new make-up and hairstyles. She was now a fashionable lady who kept her dressmaker in a hurry to keep up.

As 1920 dawned, the country was in a hopeful mood. The war over, life could return to normal. Women would finally vote by August, a new president was on the horizon and "jazz" would become the newest craze, along with shorter and shorter skirts and longer and longer cigarette holders. New Year's Eve approached in an aura of excitement, due to the anticipated ban of alcohol that would impose itself on society on the twentieth of January. Each party planner feverishly worked to outdo the next, for this would surely be a party to remember!

"I leave the matter entirely to my social secretary," Jack told George. "If Anna wants a party, then so be it. I have suggested to her, however, that she might better show off her new dress if we make the rounds."

George nodded in agreement. "Besides," he ventured, "it will be far less costly, and there will be no morning-after mess."

Jack sold the idea to Anna over dinner that evening. "We will have our favorite dinner at the club and go from party to party. I'll even buy a new tuxedo for the special evening."

When the couple arrived home in the wee hours of January 1, 1920, they were warm and giddy. The evening had been perfect, from the roses on the dinner table to the nightcap that Jack prepared before they climbed arm in arm up the beautiful staircase still draped in Christmas holly and bright red bows. They shared the same bedroom that cold January morning, indeed the same bed, the same passion.

It was a new beginning.

****

Dr. Leonard Bennett rubbed his tired, reddened eyes and sighed deeply. A family-practice physician for thirty-two years, he had become accustomed to eighteen-hour days and nights without sleep. The clock jarred him with a loud chime, an announcement of the midnight hour, and a mocking reminder that he had been at Saint Rita's Hospital since early afternoon. He had delivered two healthy babies, and the sour taste in his mouth brought back the memory of cigars shared with happy fathers. He had dutifully done his rounds, and looked forward to a routine, quiet afternoon of seeing patients in his office, actually ahead of schedule for once. Around one o'clock his nurse interrupted his examination of a large boil on the hairy buttock of a grouchy milkman.

"Better get over to Saint Rita's," the white-capped head instructed him."Fast."

The doctor smeared drawing salve on the large, red lump and stepped into the hall.

Miss Johnson was waiting for his questions. "It's Anna Sterling," she said, her eyes rolling to the right. She considered adding"trading one pain in the butt for another," but passed on the remark.

Bennett ignored the implied message and did a quick mental calculation. It was early September. "Baby's early." He frowned as he shed his white jacket and reached around the corner for his suit coat. During the drive to the hospital, Leonard recalled the past six months of Anna's pregnancy. It had been rough on patient and doctor, from the first moment he had diagnosed her condition.

"That's not possible!" Anna exclaimed. "I won't have it."

He understood that this particular news was not always well received. He smiled a warm concern for his patient and sat down behind his desk, lab report in hand. He waited. Usually, after a few moments, a few tears, some token protest, the mother-to-be settled down into quiet, if somewhat reluctant, acceptance. Anna looked genuinely ill, her color very pale and pasty. He watched her carefully, feeling for the spirits of ammonia capsule in his pocket. Looking back, he should have referred her at that very moment to a specialist, perhaps even a psychiatrist, someone else to see her through what became a tense and tiresome ordeal.

Before the clock in the doctor's lounge had finished striking twelve chimes, the door opened and Dr. Thomas Anderson, a specialist in Obstetrics and Gynecology at Fort Wayne's largest hospital, joined Leonard. The newcomer extended his hand.

"You must be Bennett. Sorry it took so long to get here. I was held up at the hospital and got a late start. Are we going to deliver tonight, or can we sleep?"

Sleep? Leonard wished he could grant them both the luxury, but things were not well in room 104, as evidenced by the hair-raising screams that erupted every seven minutes.

He returned Anderson's handshake and opened his mouth to speak when the quiet was once again shattered by loud wailing, a full two floors away.

"What the hell is that?" Anderson jumped.

"Your patient, Doctor. Anna Sterling. I checked her twenty minutes ago, and she is less than three centimeters. Contractions every seven. We have a long way to go."

Anderson groaned and crossed the room cluttered with white bed screens and gurneys. He reflected for a moment about the stark difference between this, "the doctor's lounge," and the well-equipped concession at Western. *Back to my roots, I guess.* He found the enamel coffeepot and grabbed it greedily. Empty.

Shit!

Bennett felt a pang of guilt. He was not a good host, he decided. "I'll go get some," he offered, and started for the door.

"Just tell me where," Anderson replied. "You need some rest, and I need to take a walk."

After twenty minutes, Leonard started to wonder if the visiting doctor might be lost somewhere in a dimly lit corridor. He rose to seek him out just as Anderson reappeared, carrying a tray of coffee and sandwiches. "Had to bribe the kitchen people," he grinned.

Leonard could have kissed him! He suppressed his guilt and poured a cup of steaming liquid. "I was beginning to worry about you." Leonard was eyeing the food as he blew on the coffee.

"I stopped off to examine Mrs. Sterling," Anderson reported. "Nothing much happening except for the noise. 'Primips'! God, you gotta love 'em."

Leonard's sandwich halted halfway to his mouth while he gave Anderson a puzzled look. "She's no first-timer," he said. "Gave birth to a boy about four years ago, in her own bed and entirely alone. Even cut the cord, sterilized the knife with some very good scotch, I'm told."

Anderson stared in surprise. "Amazing! So why the fuss with this one? Everything seems rather routine. I guess we'd better get to the official 'consult.'"

Leonard tossed his half-eaten sandwich into the wastebasket and dropped his weary head into his large hands. He was very tired and no longer hungry. Anderson had every right to expect a full and completely candid briefing about the impending delivery of Anna Sterling's baby. Leonard began to remember just how and why he had become involved in the process. Had she been given a choice, he was certain that she would not have chosen him to attend this birth. A case of default, he supposed, since he had been summoned to the Sterling household on the afternoon of Mac's birth to examine mother and child. There he was surprised to find a glowing young women in excellent health and a robust baby boy nursing greedily at her breast. Dr. Bennett had only one patient in this family, the elder Mrs. Sterling, who required regular visits, considerable medication, and for whom he held a sincere concern.

"I don't know very much about her, actually," Leonard sighed, at last lifting his head to address Anderson. "She was almost in her second trimester when she first visited my office, and so shaken by the diagnosis that she didn't return again until well into her third."

He wanted to blurt it all out, the tantrums, the verbal abuse she had heaped upon him, the obstinate insistence that he continue to prescribe her headache medication, which he did against his better judgement. He wanted to "confess," to purge the memory of the past six months that produced a lump in the pit of his stomach every time he had to see her. He must proceed carefully. Tell Anderson what he needed to know… no more, no less.

Anderson listened and nodded. "Did she request that you abort her?"

Leonard was stunned! How did he know that? She had pushed the issue so persistently that he had, in desperation, threatened to inform Jack of her intentions. That exchange had put a stop to the request, but had gained him a formidable enemy, he was certain.

Anderson studied his colleague. "Rather simple procedure, technically speaking. I gather you wanted no part of it. Why didn't you just refer her to another doctor?"

"I… we… this is a Catholic hospital, Dr. Anderson. I am a simple GP, a family physician."

"And a devout Catholic," Anderson stated, matter-of-factly.

"Yes."

Anderson rose and stretched. "Well, Dr. Bennett, shall we go take one last look at our patient? At this rate, I doubt that we will deliver before morning."

Chapter 2

Doctor Thomas Anderson was visibly worried. Anna was unconscious, her blood pressure alarmingly low, and her pulse weak. Her contractions were suspended due to an almost complete system shutdown. When he looked down at her, Leonard 's immediate reaction was that she was dead. Anderson moved rapidly from one side of the bed to the other, pushing nurses out of his way and sweating profusely. Leonard stood back, in semi-shock, feeling stupidly like a first-year intern. Whatever it was that was going wrong would be his fault, he was sure. He should say something, do something. No point in speaking to Anderson, whose stethoscope was pressed firmly against Anna's contracting belly.

"That's it, just as I suspected! Full-blown fetal distress here. We need to get this baby out quick, or we'll lose them both. Don't just stand there, Doctor. Get me an OR, stat!"

Sister Mary Gabriel appeared almost out of nowhere, her small feet moving silently and rapidly across the tiled floor to Anderson's side. Only the whisper of rosary beads that suspended from her belt could be heard. Her Dominican headdress that extended a full six inches above her forehead gave the impression of equal height with the doctor. "The room is ready," she offered. "I will assist, of course. Dr. Bennett, will you be attending?"

Leonard searched Anderson's face for approval. There was no indication that he had even heard the question, so deeply involved was he in his attention to Anna. He pulled off the stethoscope and laid his ear directly to the underside of her abdomen. His face darkened and he turned suddenly, oblivious to the nun beside him. His right leg struck out savagely at a bedside cart, sending it crashing across the room. Anderson moved quickly to the bed's headboard, maneuvered his small frame behind it and began to push the bed across the room.

"You people better move your asses!" he bellowed. Two startled nurses jumped back and braced against the wall as the bed rolled past them, barely missing a foot.

"What the..." A protest began, but a warning glance from the diminutive nun silenced the effort. Mary Gabriel put her shoulder to the headboard and pushed, nodding toward the surgery's double doors as the bed entered the corridor. Leonard followed closely behind, clutching at the patient's chart, which he had hurriedly grabbed from the bed's footboard in an effort to appear useful and occupied.

"Caesarian section, Sister," Anderson said to her questioning look. "Ever assisted on one of those?"

"Yes, doctor."

"Good, because I don't have time to train you. Bennett, get up here and monitor her pulse. Vital signs aren't good. Where's the husband?"

They were running now, two doctors, two nurses and the nun, who was also moving her lips almost as fast as her feet. "Hail Mary, full of grace," she whispered over and over, as the foot of the bed hit hard against the double doors. After the transfer to the table, Sister Mary Gabriel finally looked into the faces of her teammates, noting that a question seemed to be hanging unanswered. What did he ask? Oh, yes… the husband. Mr. Sterling. Where was he?

Anderson rolled his eyes. "Never mind. Get someone in the waiting room that will approve the surgery. No telling at this point what we'll find when we get in there."

Bennett snapped out of his confusion and gratefully pounced upon the opportunity to do something useful, and get out of the room. "I'll take care of it," he announced with willingness that, even to his ears, sounded too enthusiastic. His long legs moved out the door and down the hall before anyone could protest.

****

"I simply cannot believe that you could do such a thing! How could you be so stupid? Ignorance is no excuse, George. How could you just give Jack the keys to the cabin and send him off on a fishing trip, for Christ's sake, when his wife is about to have a baby?" Doris Steinburger lit another cigarette and blew smoke across the front seat of the large Buick in the direction of her sleepy husband. It was 2:25 AM.

"You haven't shut up since the phone rang, Doris. I told you, I'm sorry. I make mistakes on occasion. Now will you please be quiet and help me look for this address?"

Doris leaned forward, narrowed her eyes and peered out into the darkness. This was a very bad neighborhood and one flophouse looked like every other. They had to find Anna's father, the doctor had said. With Jack out of reach, a blood relative needed to give permission for the surgery that was necessary to save her life. Doris shivered, despite the warmth of the evening. It was difficult to believe that Anna might actually die. "Damn you, George," Doris continued. "I begged you to put in a phone! You and your fishing buddies, silly overgrown boys, off on a lark and can't be disturbed! If that poor woman dies, it will be on your head."

George groaned. He knew better than to argue with Doris, it only made matters worse. Better to just let her rant and rave until she got it all out of her system. He supposed he deserved it, but damn, was she going to go on all night? He hit the brake hard and sent them both dashboard bound. Doris drew a deep breath for a new attack when George announced, "This is it."

Doris recovered in time to grab at his jacket when he started to exit the car. "Don't you think for a moment that you are going to leave me sitting in this car alone in this neighborhood, mister. I'm coming with you."

It took considerable time to locate the drunken, incoherent Malcomb and get him into the back seat of the Buick. George badly wanted a drink himself, and Doris held her hanky to her nose, fighting the waves of nausea brought on by the smell of dirt and drunks. She insisted that all the windows be wide open on the wild ride across town to St. Rita's, George's large foot pressing the gas pedal to the floor and running every traffic light, green or red.

When the trio entered the front door of the hospital, the night receptionist almost laughed out loud at the sight of the Steinburgers and their "guest." Malcolm MacGregor hung suspended between the couple, an arm over each shoulder. His eyes were red, he mumbled incoherently, and his potent aroma extended beyond a twelve-foot radius. His feet glided along the floor, although not of his own power, for he was more than merely supported, he was drug along like a rag doll. George looked confused and disheveled, his dark suit wrinkled, his trousers only partially closed. Doris reminded the nurse at the desk of Medusa, the Greek goddess of snake-hair fame.

"We are the Steinburgers," George announced. "This is Mrs. Sterling's father, Malcomb MacGregor. We were told to get here as soon as poss...."

Doris interrupted, "There is Anna's doctor."

Leonard was hurrying toward them, paper in hand. There was no time for the usual courtesies, he decided, for he recognized the Steinburgers and deduced that the other member of the group must be Malcomb MacGregor. "We must have this authorization signed immediately," he said. "Please bring Mr. MacGregor over to the desk."

George was fully recovered now, ready to assume his pompous demeanor. "Hold on," he said, "I am Judge Steinburger and I am obligated to inform you that this man is obviously unable to understand anything well enough to sign, and…"

"I know who you are, and quite frankly, I really don't care" Leonard's face reddened. "There is no time to play legal games; he must sign, and I must get upstairs immediately."

George bristled, "I will repeat for your understanding, doctor…"

"Shut up, George!" Doris hissed.

Malcomb moaned louder, this time his complaint could be heard. "I gotta piss," he insisted. Doris looked around the lobby frantically.

"The men's room is over there." Leonard motioned with a nod of his head. "Take him, George."

George started to protest but caught his wife's icy glare. God, when will this nightmare end? He pulled Malcomb toward the door marked "Gentlemen," contemplating how he, a prominent judge, a church elder, and pillar of the community whose noble name graced the very foyer of this hospital, found himself in the humble position of assisting a drunk in the act of relieving himself!

As soon as the door had closed, Leonard turned to Doris. "Mrs. Steinburger, I know you to be a sensible and compassionate lady. Your friend will die if we don't operate very soon. The fetus is in distress also. Can you help us?"

"He'll sign," she answered quietly.

The surgical consent signed, albeit illegibly, Leonard hurried off to join the drama currently playing in OR 2. He congratulated himself on a job well done. He was no sissy when it counted, he told himself. He scrubbed quickly and put on a white gown and cap.

When he at last presented himself across the table from Thomas Anderson, he was more than a little surprised to discover that the incision had already been made, exposing the internal organs of Anna Sterling.

Chapter 3

"Mr. Sterling is here to see you, Doctor," Miss Johnson announced, "with another gentleman." Her knowing look said, "Who is probably his attorney," but she decided to edit the comment and let the good doctor draw his own conclusions. Bennett looked up from the pile of charts in front of him and forced a smile. He was dog-tired, couldn't remember when he had last slept. What was he supposed to do now? Anderson had left town, returned to Fort Wayne after the successful Caesarian delivery of Anna's baby girl, six pounds even. Anna was in recovery and stabilized. The infant was incubated as a precaution, for although her weight was within normal limits, she had undoubtedly suffered some pre-natal stress. Was he now supposed to notify his attorney that a lawsuit was probably pending? Too late. *Anderson gets all the glory and I get to dance with the tough guys. Shit.*

Johnson's head reappeared. "They're still waiting."

Bennett closed his eyes and silently called upon God. Hearing no reply, he rose, put on his jacket and surprised his nurse when he said, "I'm coming out there."

Attorney-at-law, Walter Bernstein, was seated in a large armchair in Bennett's waiting room, thumbing through a magazine and chain-smoking. Jack stood at the large window, his hands in his pockets, foot tapping impatiently. Leonard ignored the lawyer, forced a smile and crossed the room, right hand extended. "Hello, Jack. Good to see you again. How was the fishing?"

Jack whirled. His large blue eyes sought out the doctor's, but his hands remained hidden. "Fine," he said flatly. "How was your most recent delivery?"

Holding his stare, Bennett took a deep breath and took his best shot. "Are you willing to sit down with me, alone," he gestured toward Walter, "and discuss the condition of your wife and daughter in full and in private? I give you my word as your mother's physician and friend that I will be as candid as possible."

Jack continued to hold the doctor's eyes. Only the sound of the waiting-room clock broke the silence. Finally Jack nodded curtly, and only then did he look in Walter's direction. Walter was shaking his head slowly. Leonard turned to lead Jack to his office, almost tripping over Walter's long, sprawling legs. "I will call you if I need you," Jack said in passing. When the door closed, Walter threw the magazine across the room and lit another cigarette.

Somehow, after the two men had seated themselves, they were both more relaxed. Jack sheepishly offered Leonard a cigar and they lit up. "What happened?" Jack began.

"I'm not entirely sure," Leonard replied. Jack didn't like the answer, but the doctor's sincerity calmed him and perhaps at least he wasn't going to hear medical gibberish and excuses. "I got to St. Rita's a little after one o'clock. She had been admitted, prepped, and medicated. Her contractions were mild and spaced at about seven to ten minutes. She was very comfortable, a little giddy from the medicine. Everything was normal, just taking longer than expected. When her labor did not progress, I sent for Thomas Anderson, a specialist, because I knew you would want the very best for her."

"She was alone?" Jack interrupted. "Why? Wasn't Emily or Rachel with her?"

"The admitting clerk said she was dropped off by your driver, Jack. I don't have any more information, but I can try if it's that important."

"Never mind," Jack mumbled. "I'll find out from my staff."

"Anna likes to do things on her own." Bennett made a feeble attempt at humor. "I'm impressed that she even came to the hospital."

"Anna doesn't like you or trust you." Jack's demeanor took on a dark look. "Why is that, Doctor?"

Leonard looked away, studying the glass front of the bookcase to his right. Not yet. He knew the answer, but he may not have to tell Jack. Not yet. "There was no fondness between us, true, but I always treated her with care and concern, just as I did your mother, Jack. Perhaps it was a personality clash, just one of those things. What else would you like me to tell you?"

Jack was staring again. Bennett was lying, but Jack couldn't be sure what information was being withheld. "How do things stand now?" he asked quietly. He needed to stay calm, extract more information before he acted.

"If the baby continues to improve, and I expect that she will, you can take her home in a week or so. Anna's recovery will be slower. A normal delivery with no complications requires seven to ten days. I would expect that Anna will be with us for perhaps a month."

Jack's facial muscles visibly relaxed, and he seemed satisfied with the prognosis. Now it was time to give him the bad news. "Jack, there's something else."

Here it comes. Excuses, not his fault... someone else to blame.

"The surgery was... well, difficult. There was the excessive bleeding, we had to transfuse her twice... and then the scar tissue, so when she finally heals..."

"What caused the scar tissue?" Jack interrupted briskly.

Perhaps Jack would take the news better than Leonard had anticipated. He was giving the doctor a chance to explain. He was calm. He was listening carefully. Bennett traveled on safer ground now. "Scar tissue is the natural result of any intrusive procedure, Jack." Leonard's tone was soft and even. He was calmly explaining the technical aspects of Anna's surgery and even he was impressed with his own presentation. Perhaps he should seek a teaching position. If he could so completely hold the attention of Jack Sterling, imagine how well a class of would-be doctors would receive him.

"When tissue is cut or torn," Bennett continued, "the site will eventually close, but there is always a hardened healing edge." The doctor rose, picked up a sheet of paper, and walked around the old desk, a chipped leftover from the last doctor who had occupied his office. Perched casually on the edge, foot swinging, he tore the paper very close to Jack's face, a face that simply stared blankly back at him.

"Watch the frayed edges," Leonard told Jack. "They fit back together and will reattach, but they will never be the same, not like they were before."

Jack continued to stare while the doctor watched his face for a sign of acceptance. He looked at the paper, trying to imagine that it was a piece of Anna's body. *How did this little demonstration explain why they cut her open?* he wondered. Aloud he asked, "Whose permission did you obtain before you did this... this surgery? Did you or Anderson discuss it with Anna?"

Bennett's face flushed, and he rose quickly and returned to the other side of the desk. He needed a moment to construct a carefully worded answer, for the conversation was again taking a dangerous turn. Again, he decided to turn the topic back to the technical dissertation where he had appeared to be making progress. "Dr. Anderson was very careful, of course," Leonard said quietly, pretending that he had not heard the question. "There was so much blood... so hard to see, and he was forced to hurry."

"Why?"

Another *"Why."* Jack was playing with him, he realized. Letting him stumble around, pretending to accept the answers while his mind had already convicted. His only hope was to get it all out and hope for the best. "Anna's vital signs indicated that she might lapse into a permanent coma at any time," Leonard sighed. "It was an emergency situation, life threatening. We had no choice. I am obligated to inform you that the result is permanent sterilization. Anna will have no more babies, Jack. I am truly sorry."

There. It was said. Bennett closed his eyes for a moment and rubbed his throbbing forehead. He waited, but there was only silence. What did he expect to hear? Loud protests of disbelief? Ranting of an irate husband? Gunshots? When he opened his eyes, Jack was still staring at him, dispassionately, patiently waiting for him to continue, waiting for an answer to his last question. What was it?

Jack held a small notebook in his left hand, a pen in the other. His countenance betrayed no sign of emotion, any sorrow or anger. He had the look of an interviewer, a detached seeker of fact. "What hospital is Dr. Anderson affiliated with? And the permission for the surgery?" he repeated softly.

This was a goddamn cross-examination, Bennett concluded. He was on trial for his professional life. Christ, he should have taken his chances with the attorney! He had one shot left, one chance at a closing statement that could turn it around. "Dr. Anderson did an admirable job, Jack, considering the circumstances." If he could keep the focus on Anderson, perhaps Jack would be reasonable, see the whole picture."You should consider yourself a very fortunate man. After all, he saved them both, you see, Anna and... what will you name her?"

"Lillian Gretchen."

"For your mother, of course." Bennett rose, a gesture intended to signify that the session was about to end, and one he hoped would not appear too obvious. "A fine name, Jack, a fine name indeed." When Jack didn't move, didn't return the notebook to his lapel pocket, didn't blink, Leonard felt a little stupid. If he sat down again, the grilling would certainly continue. Should he walk to the door? What the hell was Jack waiting for? What more was there to say? God, those eyes were downright spooky. When would he let go?

"The authorization for surgery, doctor?" Jack continued to push the point.

Once again, that question. *What does it matter, Jack? What's done is done. It can't be undone. No turning back.* Bennett was still standing. He picked up a chart and pretended to read it. After a long moment, he lowered the chart and sought out those piercing blue eyes. "When baby Lillian goes home, it is imperative that she is breast fed, and will require constant monitoring. I have taken the liberty of securing a wet nurse for her, an excellent woman, one of my patients. Millie Anderson."

Jack looked confused but only momentarily. His reaction registered almost immediate understanding, and he delayed his protest long enough to indulge in a little dark humor. "Is she, by chance, related to the good doctor?"

Leonard was once again thrown off guard, but he used the opportunity to diffuse the tension with a hearty laugh. Too hearty, when he realized that he was laughing alone.

"Hardly." He quickly composed himself. "She is a black woman."

The corners of Jack's lips curled up, suggesting a slight smile, followed by what may have passed for a grin except that the rare exposure of his short yellow teeth clearly defined the expression as a diabolical snarl. He stood, finally, propelling his five and one-half foot body out of the chair in one smooth movement, leaning over the expanse of desk with little effort. As if by silent command, Bennett slowly lowered himself to his seat, until two pairs of eyes were locked in parallel embrace, inches apart.

"Listen to me, you lying son-of-a-bitch! I never considered you much of a physician. I put up with your fumbling incompetence because my mother thought you were some reincarnation of St. Luke! You've gone too far this time, Bennett! Just how stupid do you think I am? Do you believe that George Steinburger drove seven hours to the Michigan Upper Peninsula to bring me home so that we could chat about the weather? He told me how you strong-armed my father-in-law into signing that worthless piece of paper. Malcomb McGregor is a homeless drunk. Did you honestly think that little trick would get you off the hook? You allowed my wife to be butchered! Now you want me to congratulate you and be grateful that you have 'arranged' for my only daughter to suckle a black tit! Oh, yes, I am fortunate indeed. I'll get most of the money from Anderson, but I'll get satisfaction from you. When I'm finished, you won't be able to treat sick cats!"

Leonard wished desperately to lift his right hand, which felt strangely fused, palm down, to the desk surface. He needed to wipe the spittle from his face, a most unpleasant sensation. He was surprisingly calm, however, for he could finally be certain that he was beyond Jack's vengeance. The words flung across the barrier desk did not offend him, for they were the raving of a madman, a blur of verbs, pronouns, and obscenities. He did not feel particularly threatened since he knew Jack to be a non-physical type who stomped, bellowed, and rattled his saber, but would not strike. Only the dampness on his face troubled Leonard… that, and just the close, overwhelming presence of this little man. It felt almost like a perverted intimacy, and Leonard was repulsed.

Jack's eyes bulged, his face, a dangerous shade of scarlet. Bennett considered for a moment that his adversary might have a stroke. But Jack was now on his way down, taking in deep breaths of air while his chest heaved. He brought up his right arm, and Bennett flinched slightly, a reflex, he supposed. Jack crudely wiped the sleeve of his jacket across his mouth, pivoted swiftly on his heels, tucked his notebook away, and was at the door when Bennett spoke.

"Do you know a man named Fred Veh?"

Jack stopped, stood very still, but did not reply.

"He is an old classmate of mine," Leonard went on. "I wanted General Practice, but he became the Union County Coroner." The sound heard next was that of a drawer opening, a creaking protest from the old desk. "Here is the latest correspondence from Fred." Leonard had to force himself to speak slowly in his new excitement. His heart pounded, and he knew that his pulse was racing. This was his *swan song*; it had better be good! "Would you like to read it?" The doctor spoke now to the back of Jack's baldhead. "Perhaps you would like me to read it to you. This paragraph is interesting, I think.

"'So, dear Leonard, given the strange condition under which Mrs. Lillian Sterling breathed her last breath, i.e. near starvation and definitely dehydrated, and the observation that the deceased, despite her advanced age and medical problems, evidently enjoyed relatively good health until the marriage of her son, and the sudden and unexplained demise of Anna Sterling's own grandmother some seven years ago, one might reasonably conclude that relationship to Anna Sterling is indeed unhealthy. As for Anna's immediate concerns, you might consider referring her to a good psychiatrist, whose advanced training could provide an intervention of her apparent addiction to codeine and her continued insistence of the abortion of her child.'"

There was no response from the man at the door. "You may have this letter if you want it, Jack. A keepsake, perhaps. Don't be concerned for me, I have other copies. One is on file with my attorney, the other in a safe deposit box." Leonard smiled, wondering if he should perhaps pay a visit to his priest this very afternoon, to confess what must surely be a mortal sin, for it was giving him so much pleasure.

Jack turned the doorknob and entered the waiting room, where he found a distressed Walter. "What the hell... I couldn't even go to the men's room, waiting for you to call me in there. I read one magazine six times and smoked two packs of cigarettes."

Jack gave Walter a long, cold look. "I said I would call you if I needed you," Jack snapped. "Obviously, I didn't need you." Jack's short legs were moving down the corridor so rapidly that Walter had to hurry to catch up.

The attorney looked at his watch. "I'm not so sure about that, Jack. But you're going to pay me anyway."

Chapter 4

Open your eyes, Anna. You must wake up and get out of this bed! Open your eyes, now. Anna made the attempt, but her eyelids felt as if the heavy copper pennies she had seen in books on the bodies of outlaws blanketed them, and so like a lazy schoolgirl, she silently begged to be allowed to sleep. *Now, Anna. Open!*

The voice was louder this time, and it startled her. Her eyes popped open as if pulled by a string, and she struggled to focus. Where was she? Slowly scanning the large room, she recognized the fireplace mantel just as the clock on its center chimed the half-hour. More familiar objects came into view, the large oil portrait above the fireplace stared back at her, and her mind acknowledged that the woman in the beautiful mink-trimmed robe with the large, sad gray eyes was herself.

"Well, so we are finally awake, are we?" a different voice said, a voice equally foreign to her ears, but from a source outside her mind. "We thought you would sleep all day, Mrs. Sterling." A large white blur floated over her.

"Who...?" Anna tried to ask, but found that the words wouldn't utter. She choked, sending her body into a coughing convulsion that produced stabbing pain somewhere in her body.

Strong arms were suddenly around her and the blur said, "Easy now, let me help you sit up a bit."

The horrible pain somewhat subsided, Anna's conscious mind began to clear. She now saw the blur clearly, a strange woman in a white nurse's uniform bent over her. "Water," Anna gasped.

A cup touched her lower lip almost immediately, along with the admonition, "Just a sip, and slowly."

The water soothed like liquid gold on her parched lips and dry throat, but when she swallowed, the demon below protested violently, returning the unwelcome water to her mouth along with bitter bile. The stranger deftly caught the return in a soft towel and then released Anna's head to the coolness of the pillow behind her. After a moment, the woman in white spoke again. "Do you know where you are?"

"In my room," Anna answered clearly. She was sufficiently awake now, awake enough to register the pain that radiated from her abdomen. "Where are my pills?" she asked. "Who are you?"

"So many questions!" the woman chuckled. "I am your private nurse, Jessica Rawlings, Mrs. Sterling. Are you in pain?"

Anna nodded emphatically.

"I will find out what Dr. Powell has prescribed for you. Do you remember coming home yesterday?"

Anna shook her head. *Just get the damn pills, and stop asking me silly questions.*

Rawlings left the room, and Anna took a deep breath and tried to think. Who the hell was Dr. Powell? Where was Jack? What had happened to her? She probed at her mind; she must remember! Slowly, a vision floated up to her, as if through a long tunnel. There had been pain, labor pain. Someone put her into a car and took her... where? To a place where the hurt continued, she recalled. Men in white coats put their hands on her and the pain had stopped. Eyes so heavy, so tired. Closed. Halfway closed, her eyes sprung open again. Her baby! Where was her baby?

The nurse returned, carrying a bottle of pills. "Dr. Powell will be here shortly," she explained. "Meanwhile, he said to give you one of these, to relieve your discomfort. They will make you very sleepy. Do you want the medication now, or would you prefer to stay awake awhile?"

Anna extended her arm and held her hand open to receive the solitary tablet offered to her. She shook her head at the water, suspecting that it would only force the pill into another towel. Rawlings looked surprised when Anna swallowed it dry, but she put the cap back on the bottle and set it on the bedside table. "How are you feeling now?" Rawlings asked as she moved around the large bed, smoothing covers, tucking corners.

"Fine," Anna answered flatly. "Where is my baby? My husband?" Her belly felt like fire. She wanted to reposition her aching legs, but the slightest movement sent rails of agony across her body.

Rawlings continued to tidy up the room, fluffing here, spot-dusting there with her hanky, adjusting wall hangings. Anna found the activity annoying, but listened carefully to her chatter. "Mr. Sterling is on his way home to see you. Your darling little daughter is asleep in the nursery and your little boy... Mac, I think... is playing with his friend. I am new in the house, so I'm afraid that is all the information I have. You will see them all very soon. May I get you anything?"

Anna shook her head and closed her eyes. Her bottom was sore from sitting up and she could, she supposed, ask to lie down, for it seemed that the medication was taking effect. She remained still and silent, however, until Miss Rawlings said, "What a lovely name you and your husband chose for your little girl… 'Lillian Gretchen Sterling'… an old family name, I gather."

Anna's eyes again sprung open and she wildly looked around the room until she saw the nurse. *Good God in heaven, was she joking? Jack wouldn't do that to her… he would know how furious she would be. 'Lillian Gretchen Sterling'? Would that mean old woman never leave her?*

She finally focused on Rawlings, across the room, her back to the bed. Anna reached to the bedside table and wrapped her hand around the pill bottle. She unscrewed the top and quickly swallowed two pills before redepositing the bottle to its former position. She would deal with it later. Right now, she needed to sleep.

Chapter 5

In addition to his regular duties at the Savings and Loan, Jack made his "rounds" two afternoons a week. He would leave his office at noon sharp, after eating the light lunch that Helga had prepared for him, and knock on the doors of humble homes in the ethnic sections of the city, collecting payments due on risky loans. It was a simple system. He never offered a receipt, but if one was requested of him, he scribbled the amount paid on the record pad that he carried and handed a copy to the debtor. Few of his customers could read, so when the balances didn't seem quite right, it was easy to explain. Some of the cash collected did indeed apply to their debt; the rest was applied to Jack's pocket.

It was late October, and the snow clouds threatened the horizon, prompting Jack to hurry through the afternoon's business and go home early. He didn't want to wait any longer for the warmth of his study, and his scotch. Since Anna's return from the hospital, Jack had avoided the great house, and he missed his "nest," that special room that was only his. It gave him particular comfort today, as he worked on his accounts. The late afternoon sun added to the quiet atmosphere of fireplace and Chopin. There was a light knock on the door.

"Who is it?"

"Me, Mr. Sterling… Emily. May I come in and dust?"

Jack rose and opened the door. With the exception of Rachael, Emily was the only woman in his house who didn't frighten him, and he was always happy to see her. The Sterling household seemed overrun with women these days, he thought, and the image of the ever-efficient Maureen Kennedy played in his mind.

He moved to the large leather chair and watched Emily. Her feather duster flew across the first editions, the massive oak desk, and the mantel. She hummed and chattered. "… So I told Miss Rachael that, to my mind, the nurses were not guests, they were help, just like me, so if they think I'm going to pick up after them, they surely have another think coming!"

Nurses? How many "nurses" did he employ? Oh, yes, the Anderson woman. Well, she wasn't really a nurse, Jack thought. She was a feeding system, a necessity forced upon him by that idiot doctor and not here for the long term.

"What about the other one, Rawlings?" Jack inquired of Emily. "Does she do her duty well?" If you wanted to know what really goes on in the house, his mother had once told him, ask the servants.

"She's an odd one, she is." Emily stopped dusting and looked at him. "Mrs. Sterling doesn't like her, I think. Yesterday, when I told the Missus that Millie Anderson was in the house, why, Missus perked right up, she did, and then she sent for her. That Negro woman was in her room a long time, sitting next to the Missus, holding her hand and whispering."

Jack frowned and retreated deeper into his thoughts. Long after Emily had left the room, he sat very still, contemplating the recent events of his life. Primarily, of course, was the recent birth of his very own child, Lillian. She enchanted him the very first moment he laid eyes on her, so small and fragile, so in need of his protection. Her existence gave him another opportunity to take control of life, to guide the present gently (or forcefully) into his fantasy future. She was truly his, and he would always be able to influence her. It did trouble Jack, however, that the one exception to his total dominance was the regrettable fact that all his money could not nourish her. He must tolerate the infant's wet-nurse for now.

As for the mother of his child, he had begun to recognize that unlike traditional couples, he and Anna had no romantic history. Strangers when they wed, they were little more than strangers still, for he knew very little about her past or her preferences. If he was questioned about his wife's favorites, for instance, he could not name her preference for color, or book, or piece of music. Her womanly cycles were a complete mystery to him, so how could he be blamed for his lack of participation in her childbearing duties? She had been aloof, cold even, during his rare and infrequent visits to her sickbed. When he had attempted to be warm and solicitous, she had rebuked him, pleading pain or fatigue. Just yesterday, when he had entered her room unannounced, he had been unnerved by the sight of Anna's exposed belly, for nurse Rawlings was changing her dressings. It had been the most that Jack had ever seen of Anna's body, and it was not a pretty sight. He hadn't visited since.

His mind moved on, to the matter of Veh's letter. Item by item, he reviewed the charges against her. *So she is addicted to codeine. So what? He had arranged to obtain all the drugs she needed, if it kept her quiet and happy. So she may well have "helped" her grandmother down the staircase. What has that to do with him?*

73

There remained two additional concerns that warranted more thought. He rose from the chair and returned to his desk, where he unlocked the drawer that held his journal.

He wrote, "I am unable to accept the possibility that Anna was in any way responsible for my mother's death. Even if I could entertain the thought, what recourse do I have?"

Pen suspended, Jack dallied into a daydream scene. George Steinburger's gavel banging for order in the court, Anna led away in shackles, the shame and humiliation of it all, and Jack left alone with two small children. The entire suspicion was too horrible to consider, and so he dismissed it. He continued to write.

"I have no reason to believe Bennett's accusation regarding abortion. All women, I am told, are extremely emotional during pregnancy, and Anna is certainly more high-strung than most. In any case, it didn't happen. The matter is closed."

Jack returned the journal to the drawer and congratulated himself on the efficient discharge of his doubts. If the rest of humanity could only imitate his swift rationalism, he thought, the world would be far less troublesome. He turned his attention to his accounts. Another large ledger came out of the drawer, and Jack made meticulous entries of balance, payments, his "take" and his immediate investment plan. Each and every Monday, he put to good use his obsessive study of the Wall Street Market reports and made his choices accordingly. Most of his "pocket money" went to his bookie. Both ventures were highly successful, and this very rich man was becoming richer.

Another tap on the door, followed by a soft voice, brought Rachael into the room.

"I hope I haven't disturbed you, sir," Rachael began.

Jack smiled at the sight of her and rose to his feet. Something about Rachael brought out the gentleman in him. He was genuinely glad to see her. During the past weeks Rachael had once again proven her value, as it was she who kept everything running smoothly.

"Come in, Rachael," Jack greeted her. "Sit down, please. I have missed our little chats."

"Things have been very... well, excited around here," Rachael sighed as she took her seat. "I need to ask you about the incident in the nursery."

Jack looked worried. "What happened?"

"Mac got away from Emily and somehow found his way to the baby's room. He opened the double doors all by himself, and tossed one of his toy trucks into the bassinet."

"Was the baby injured?" Jack held his breath.

"Not really, thank God." Then Rachael added, "And Millie. She was there in a wink, and intercepted. Took a nasty scrape on her hand. Lillian was startled, but no real harm done, except for a small bruise."

Jack was thoughtfully silent, and Rachael continued, "If Mac is to be punished, it must be done quickly, as four-year olds have short memories."

How had he become so detached, he pondered, from the activities of this household? Perhaps he had left too much to Anna. He would need to take charge now, with Anna lying upstairs in her medicated oblivion. Finding another doctor to attend to her had been easy. Jack had handed Powell a blank check with instructions to defer to her wishes at all times. He wished that he could so easily solve the problem with Mac.

"Mac needs a sound spanking," Jack proclaimed.

"That is, of course, your prerogative," Rachael sighed, her subtle indication that she did not approve of corporal punishment. "Shall I send him to you?"

"To me?" Jack's eyes widened at the suggestion. He had never struck a child, never struck anyone really. There had been that awful time in eighth grade when the confrontation with the nun had gotten out of control, and she lunged at him. His natural defense, he had rationalized, was the cause of his expulsion from the school. His right arm swung out in protest, his hand grabbing at any object that might prevent his fall. The ensuing sound of ripping material and a loud scream frightened young Jack. He recovered his balance in time to get a good, up-close look at Sister Marie Stephen's frontal exposure, which extended from her neck to her navel.

It was a painful memory, but not as painful as the look in his mother's eyes, and not as painful as the beating administered by his father. No one believed his version of the incident. He never returned to that school, or any other; nor did he ever set foot inside a church again.

So then, it followed; physical punishment was a father's duty. "Send him to me," Jack said.

Chapter 6

"The president is dead."

Jack looked at George Steinburger in disbelief. "What did you just say?"

"I said that Harding is dead. It just came across the teletype. He was out West somewhere, California, I think, and he just dropped over. Heart attack. I wonder if this Teapot Dome business had anything to do with it?"

"I can't believe it!" Jack stammered. "Are they sure?"

"Reasonably, I suppose, since they seem determined to bury him." George poured them both another shot of scotch from his "private stock," the topshelf brand that he kept in a desk drawer, an expensive indulgence that had become even more so on the black market. "Drink slowly, Jack, I may soon have to mortgage the house. Thank you, Carrie Nation."

Jack raised his glass. "Meddling bitch!" he toasted. He made himself comfortable on the leather couch, lost in the latest headline. "How do you suppose this will affect the market?"

"Difficult to say, but my educated guess is that it probably won't," George said between sips.

"At the risk of sounding cold, it is probably just as well," Jack ventured. "By the time Cooledge runs for re-election, the county will have forgotten about the scandal. Harding would have never earned the nomination again, and then we'd have another damn Democrat!"

"Now why would I interpret that remark as 'cold,' Jack?"

They were both silent for several minutes. George had learned not to hurry Jack. He never "just dropped in," never wasted time on a social call, so sooner or later Jack would get to the purpose of this meeting.

"Anna is gradually becoming a woman of means," Jack said finally. "I thought her business venture would bore her eventually, but I seem to have miscalculated. The dress shop is quite busy, and now she wants to open another."

"Why did you think it would fail, Jack?" George questioned. "Anna is resourceful, hardworking, and smart."

"Did I say 'fail'?"

"No, but that's what you meant. In order to fully control Anna, you must keep her dependent upon your good will and your money. So, what happens now?"

"Lillian will be three years old next month. Anna has delegated her maternal duties to Rachael and that black woman, who absurdly continues to arrive at my back door every morning and draw a salary regardless of the fact that there is no longer a baby to nurse."

"Simple enough, dismiss her," George advised. His casual tone belied the fact that he had already heard the entire story from Doris. Anna blocked the discharge of Millie Anderson, and she had something on Jack, or by now it would have been fait accompli.

"Not that simple," Jack groaned. As usual, he told George far more than he would tell anyone but stopped short of complete disclosure. George was his friend, or the closest substitute that he had, but Jack worried about confiding secrets that could be used against him. "Besides, the Anderson woman is now working at the dress shop. Anna insists that she is vital to the business."

"Once again, Jack, I fail to understand your problem. If Anna were making money, it would seem that you could give her less. The children, I take it, are well attended, so what exactly is your objection?"

Jack sighed, reached into his coat pocket and handed George a piece of paper. It read:

> Dear Mr. Sterling,
>
> I regret to inform you that since our last discussion regarding MacGregor's inappropriate behavior, his demeanor has become increasingly worse, rather than improved, as we had hoped. It is not a matter of mere inattention in class. MacGregor is disruptive, disrespectful, and refuses any and all attempts at guidance.
>
> You and I have talked at great length about MacGregor's problems, and I'm afraid that our staff has exhausted all avenues of reason and discipline. It pains me, therefore, to request that you make arrangements for MacGregor's education elsewhere.
>
> Very truly yours,
> Thomas McKay, SJ
> Thomas McKay
> Headmaster

George returned the letter to Jack and waited for his friend to let him know what he wanted to hear.

"I swore I would never support another Catholic school," Jack announced. "Public school was good enough, I thought, but his mother insisted. I have been very generous. I suppose that Mac must have given them considerable trouble or they would have put up with it."

George smiled and pondered how Jack had changed. Never one to give the benefit of the doubt, Jack was uncharacteristically understanding of Father McKay's position. He seemed to George somehow mellower, more tolerant. Perhaps fatherhood had been good for Jack, exposing a kinder aspect of his usually dark persona.

"For once, I am at a loss to advise you, my friend," George said quietly. "Much as I like giving advice, Doris and I are childless, so parenting is a little over my head. May I presume, however, to ask a very personal question?"

Jack nodded slightly, suddenly cautious.

"Has Lillian's birth brought out the loving father in you because she is truly yours?"

Jack reddened; his immediate reaction was regret that he had allowed the question. The uneasiness passed after a moment, however, and he gave the query serious thought before he answered. "I think so, yes. I felt some of the same emotions with Mac, at least in the beginning because he was so small and helpless. The sensation is far more intense this time. I will do anything to keep her safe and happy."

From your lips to God's ear, Jack. Here's to a lifetime of control!

George raised his glass to Jack and smiled. "My brother enrolled his son in an excellent military school last year. Robert Jr. is about the same age as Mac, seven, I think. Robert Sr. is quite pleased with the result. The fall term begins in September, which is next month. As a matter of fact, my brother and his wife are packing the footlocker as we speak. Usually these elitist schools require a pound of flesh, but I am sure that your tenacity, combined with that ultimate persuader that you call your checkbook, will have the boy enrolled before the end of the week."

"That all depends," Jack mused, "on the women."

Chapter 7

Anna shrieked and threw her silver hairbrush across the room in the general direction of her husband's head. The "weapon" flew evenly between Jack's ear and her prized globe lamp, and she was more relieved that she had missed the latter.

"Christ, Anna!"

"You... you bastard! How could you?" She stood and crossed the room until she towered over him, breathing heavily in an obvious state of intense anger. Her eyes scanned the room for something else to throw... something, perhaps that would impress upon her intended victim the exact quality of her rage. Lips curled into a grotesque smile, she hissed at Jack, "You will never take my son away from me. I will kill you first!"

Jack was not afraid. He thought he vaguely recognized the scene as one from a movie recently viewed at the Quillna on Market Street, and he almost chuckled at the thought that Anna played it more convincingly than Bernhardt did. He was becoming all too accustomed to Anna's theatrics. He took the chair next to the prized lamp. No point in taking any chances, he might be safer there. He forced himself to relax, look casual. He crossed his legs and waited while Anna paced rapidly around the room.

"All you ever wanted from me," she ranted, "was only what I could give you from my belly! I almost died giving birth to Lillian, but I suppose that would have been preferable to you! Now you want to take my son away, send him off like a naughty little boy to some toy soldier school. Why, Jack, why? Have I been such a terrible mother?"

Jack was very still, lost in thought, carefully choosing his next words. Anna was openly sobbing now, and while he didn't doubt the sincerity of her tears, he remained passive. What was her question? If he spoke frankly, he would tell her that her sin had been one of omission, not commission. She had freely delegated her children to the care of Rachael, whose purpose had been that of housekeeper, and to Millie Anderson, whose purpose had long since ceased to be anything at all. She had simply resigned her position of motherhood, evidently in favor of that of shopkeeper. He could see no advantage in sharing this thought with her, so he maintained his silence and watched her cry.

"You have managed to take them both from me," Anna wailed. "It was insidious with Mac, I didn't see it coming. But you were bolder with the baby, snatching her away while I lay in that dreadful hospital and naming her after your mother!"

"What would you have called her?" Jack asked. He already knew the answer. While the couple had not discussed a name, Jack knew that Anna's preference was "Nellie Lee," named for the mother she had never known. It was a part of her past best forgotten, he reasoned, and he had indeed moved quickly to honor his own mother at the birth of the granddaughter she would never hold. It was his right as a father, he told himself.

Anna held Jack's stare, opened her mouth to speak, and then closed it again. She was beaten, it became suddenly clear. There was no point in this conversation for he was merely allowing her to spend her fury, and in the end he would have his way, as always.

At the same moment, each replayed a scene of past dispute, the dismissal of Maureen Kennedy. Never again, he had vowed, would he allow her to incriminate or manipulate him. It had been her one and only victory, for he no longer feared offending her. If she chose to leave him, she would do so alone, for he would not forfeit the children. He held the winning hand, and no amount of tears, or threats, or pleas for mercy would alter the inevitable fact that he was in control of their lives, now and forever.

He supposed he could afford to play out the scene as a loving husband and father who, after all, wanted only what was best for all concerned. He went to her side and offered his handkerchief. "It will be good for Mac, for all of us," Jack assured her. "He is registered for the fall term, next month, in fact. We can discuss his progress during the holidays." He patted her shoulder lightly and quickly left the room, leaving her to regard her red, puffy eyes in the dressing table mirror and contemplate her sorrow.

****

Jack was pouring his third scotch when Rachael's tentative tap jolted him. Some of the precious liquid splashed and he wondered if he had downed the first two drinks a little too quickly, or had the recent domestic standoff shaken him more than he had realized?

"I am sorry that I kept you waiting, sir." Rachael's lyric voice turned his attention to the doorway of the study. "There is a small problem with the boys. Again."

How fortuitous! With such a lead, they could get right into the matter, for Jack was feeling rather drained and a little drunk. He was certainly in no condition for another confrontation with a female-in-residence.

"What is it this time?" Jack asked Rachael, attempting to keep his tone level.

She eyed him questionably, sensing that she had intruded upon one of his dark moods. She smiled and tried to minimize the remark. "Oh, nothing really. Boys... well, you know."

Jack decided immediately that he didn't care to dance around the subject. "Has Mac hit Paul again?" he asked.

Rachael looked surprised. "So, you know about Mac's problem?"

"I have seen Paul's bruises, if that is what you mean. Perhaps you had better tell me about them."

"It's just... children play roughly sometimes, especially boys. I'm sure that Mac means no harm. It's just that Paul doesn't seem to want to defend himself. I am really more concerned when Paul is bitten, nasty infections and all."

Jack dropped into the nearest chair and sighed. "Rachael," he began slowly, "I have found it necessary to enroll Mac in the Vermont Military Academy for the fall term at least. I apologize for the attacks on your son. I'm afraid Mac is out of control, and I must do something about it, and soon."

It took several moments for the information to sort itself out in Rachael's mind. Poor Anna! Rachael imagined she must be very upset by the news. She wished she hadn't mentioned the "roughhousing" between the boys, particularly the biting thing. Had she made too much of it? Was she responsible for Mac's banishment?

"I am surprised." Rachael found her voice. "I can't imagine that Anna could bear to be separated from Mac, that she would want this..."

"What Anna wants is not the issue," Jack retorted and rose, avoiding Rachael's eyes. He poured another drink. He hesitated, had a thought it seemed, and poured another, offering it to Rachael. She shook her head.

"Your choice." He shrugged. "You may need it." He knew he was being cryptic and even rude, for he hadn't even invited her to sit down. But he was on the defensive and pulling his courage from the bottle.

"Why would I need it?"

He walked past Rachael, and the confusion in her eyes followed him to his chair. He needed to say it quickly, he decided, get it over with. "I have enrolled Paul also. He will be taking the train with Mac. The application is filed, tuition is paid. I have taken care of everything."

She stared at him, stunned and speechless. This was madness! Did he expect her to thank him? Her ears began to buzz; she felt faint, her legs suddenly unable to sustain her. She groped her way to the bar, her right arm reaching out for chairs and tables to steady herself. Once there she moved a shaky hand through the bottles until she finally gripped the elusive glass of scotch that kept inching away from her.

Jack was at her side before she had taken the last swallow, the one that sent her stomach into spasms and closed her throat. "Easy, Rachael, easy," Jack whispered, helping her to the nearest stool.

"Please hear me out," Jack pleaded. He handed her a napkin and held her shoulders tightly while her choking subsided. "I understand that you are upset, that I have taken too much on myself, but you will come to realize that I had no choice. Mac's future is at stake here. He is badly undisciplined, a dangerous child."

He was so close, she thought. She hadn't been so close to another human being since John's death, and somehow the sensation was of some strange comfort, like a warm blanket on a cold night. She searched his face, trying to understand. "Am I to blame?" she asked him. "Am I the reason he misbehaves? Is that why you are punishing me?"

He tightened his hold, but only for a second. Then he moved away and began to pace. "I am not punishing anyone!" he shouted, and the anger startled her. "I am trying my damnedest to do the right thing. No one is being punished, because no one is to blame, or we are all to blame. What difference does it make? The women in this house coddle him, you and his mother more than the rest, I suppose. I am still learning how to be a father and it is difficult. Too harsh, too soft... what is the answer? I only know that he is not going in the right direction, not the son I want him to be, and if I don't intervene, he won't be the man he can be."

Rachael had recovered, was thinking clearly again. Her insides felt very warm, the scotch, she supposed. Dreadful stuff, but she felt stronger, and she was ready to fight for her son. "It is out of the question," she told him boldly. "Paul is happy at St. Rose's, an excellent student. There is no good reason to disrupt his life. Send Mac if you must, but Paul belongs with me."

When Jack did not reply, she forged ahead, suddenly aware of the opportunity to vent her frustration. "Coming here was a mistake," she said, not caring if he heard or did not hear. "I see that now. From the very first week, you and Anna have tried to control every aspect of our lives. Whatever was determined for Mac applied to Paul.

"He had to wear Mac's discarded clothes, play only with toys that Mac no longer wanted. They are not twins, Jack, not even brothers. I feel I have sold my soul for thirty pieces of silver, God forgive me! Now you want to send my baby to some terrible barracks, to march and salute and... for what possible reason?"

Jack brought his fist down hard on the desk. "Because Mac won't go without him, that's why! In God's name, Rachael, I'm not sending him off to war! It is an excellent school, with a fine reputation. The waiting list is three years, and I pulled a lot of strings just to get them in. What do you see in your son's future? Do you foresee a good education on your salary? What will happen to him if you have no salary, Rachael? Would it make a difference to you if I were to secure Paul's schooling, if I were to put enough money in a trust that will guarantee his tuition to Harvard, or Yale, or any college of his choice?" Jack tried to read the reaction to his proposal, and he thought he saw a glimmer of interest. He pressed on, driving home his point with a desperate hammer. "Perhaps I have misjudged your aspirations for Paul," he said so quietly that Rachael had to strain to hear his words. Yes, he had her full attention now! "Perhaps you would prefer to keep him safely nestled to your breast, shackled to your apron. I suppose you could then, when he becomes a man, send him off to the coal mines."

Seconds ticked by. The silence hung between them like a heavy fog moving stealthily in and out of the channels of their minds. Finally, the pale, shaken Rachael said, "Put it in writing, sign it and have Walter sign it. Six months, half the term. Then we will rethink and renegotiate."

"Thank you, Rachael. I owe you more than money."

She was at the door when she said, "Not only are you not a gentleman, Mr. Sterling, you are not a nice man."

After the door had closed behind her, Jack raised his glass in tribute. "So I've been told," he said aloud.

Chapter 8

1925

"I'm happy for you, Jack. Have you considered, however, that you may have just paid a fortune for a worthless piece of property?" George asked. He puffed rapidly on his pipe, a habit that signaled that he was somewhat apprehensive about the conversation.

Jack smiled patiently, not discouraged by George's apparent lack of enthusiasm. "That is one possibility, of course," he conceded, "but wait until you see this place, George! You'll regret that you didn't find it first."

"Hardly. Somehow I can't imagine us with a 1200-acre horse farm, especially one that is perched atop a West Virginia mountain. My guess is that Anna will be equally unimpressed. Whatever prompted you to buy that place, Jack?"

"I got a tip two months ago, and the price was right. When I drove to Vermont in October to visit the boys, I took a side trip coming home, just to check it out. The house is huge, has so much potential. I can turn it into a showplace."

"You already live in a showplace, Jack." George tapped his pipe on the edge of a large ashtray. "Your house is the talk of the town, you know."

"Truthfully, it is only a valuable asset." Jack frowned. "It has never really been 'my' house... it was my father's house, then mother's, now Anna's. I have never been consulted about anything having to do with the place, not even so much as changed a lightbulb. This new property is a chance to build, or rebuild, something of my own. Maybe I'll go broke doing it, but what the hell, I can afford it!

"By the way," Jack went on, "thank you for sending Billy over to see me. He is very good with the cars. I have put him on full time."

"You surprise me, Jack. Billy is a Negro, you know."

"So what? He doesn't look like one. Besides, I will need help with the ranch."

As usual, George was only receiving part of the information needed from his impulsive friend. Jack could not confide that very soon after learning of the horse farm in West Virginia, Lillian had snuggled into his lap one evening and requested a pony. A less complicated, and less costly approach would naturally have simply involved converting one of several buildings into a small barn, fencing in a large grazing area, and buying a pony. Too easy! If his little girl wanted to ride, she will ride only the very best. He closed his eyes now and imagined it. Lillian, decked out in all that fancy horse-riding gear, leather boots and crop, jumping hurdles on a big, beautiful thoroughbred.

"Of course she's just a baby," Jack was talking out loud, to himself. "But with the proper trainer and animal, she'll take the Grand Championship before she's ten!"

"Who?"

Jack did not answer. He was lost in his own happy daydreams.

****

"You did what? Have you gone completely mad?"

Both women were staring at him in stunned disbelief, but it was Anna who found her voice first. "You can't be serious, Jack! Where the hell is West Virginia, anyway?"

"West of Virginia, I think," Rachael quipped, somewhat recovered.

Anna glared at her. "Thank you, Mrs. Unger, for the geography lesson."

Rachael ignored Anna, a recent habit that had become her own unique defense mechanism, and directed her concern at Jack. "You can't possibly mean that we'll spend the holidays there! What about the boys?"

"The boys will come home on the train, as planned," Jack answered quietly. "Or, even better, we can arrange for them to meet us there. Think of all the beautiful snow! The children will love an old-fashioned Christmas... so much to do. I can rent a sleigh, maybe even teach the boys to hunt!"

"With guns?" Anna gasped.

"No, dear, with slingshots." Jack chuckled at his little joke, but no one else was laughing.

"I think we should discuss this matter in private," Anna huffed. "First of all, I cannot believe that you would make this decision without consulting me."

"I assume you are referring to your own good example," Jack retorted. "You mean, no doubt, like the manner in which you consulted me when you decided to open a dress shop?"

Anna blushed. "May we discuss this in your study?"

"Since it concerns Rachael and Paul, it is only polite to include her." Jack delighted in pointing out Anna's lack of consideration. "I think I can save us the time and effort, however. Every summer we spend weeks at the house on the Upper Peninsula, a property that you purchased without my knowledge. It is a matter of 'goose and gander,' my dear. I have decided that where we spend the winter holiday is, therefore, my choice. We will take Emily and Helga with us, if you prefer. In any case, start packing. We are going. Pack warmly; it's cold up there."

"What about the house?" Rachael looked as if she may cry. "Who's going to look after this house?"

"We'll close the damn house, if we have to... that's why they make sheets!"

****

Anna packed, continued to protest, citing her business obligations, the need to shop for Christmas, and complained daily that her migraine headaches had returned with a vengeance. Rachael put in longer than usual hours, organizing and overseeing the closure of the "Great House" with the same attention to detail that Meade must have implemented at Gettysburg. Jack contacted the school, made the necessary arrangements and sent written authorization for Mac and Paul to board the train to Clarksburg, or Pittsburgh, in the event that heavy snow closed the former, three days before Christmas. Jack told Anna that she could safely leave the shop in the care of her beloved Millie, one-time wet nurse become seamstress, now full partner. Anna recognized the comment as a trap, a direct challenge to her to deny that Millie was capable, so she deferred quietly, albeit still seething. He instructed Rachael to calm down; Billy would remain to insure that the house was safe. Jack himself was euphoric. Never in his life had he taken time away from the office, except for the few days spent each summer at the family's summerhouse and, of course, his infamous fishing excursions. Lists were written and rewritten. The house became a beehive of excited activity, even though the reason for the excitement varied with each occupant.

Five days before Christmas, the family departed Indiana for the snowcapped mountains, three vehicles loaded with more supplies and luggage than one might expect to transport to Europe for a full year of sightseeing.

Jack drove the lead car in the caravan, a large black Buick. Lillian sat on a pillow beside her "papa" in the front seat. Anna and Rachael shared the back seat, silent and moody. Helga's burly brother John followed in the second car, with Helga and Emily.

James Ashley, the family's long-time chauffeur, and the gardener manned the third, carrying most of the luggage, Christmas presents, and supplies.

The journey took two full days, but the roads were blessedly clear of snow and the temperature warmer than normal for late December. They cut across southeastern Ohio into West Virginia, stopping overnight to eat and rest. After a few hours in the car, Anna and Rachael loosened up and began to chat, rather formally at first, then more merrily and eventually nonstop. They discussed fashion, made decoration plans for the "holiday house," and planned menus. Jack relaxed and began to enjoy the company of "his women," especially Lillian, who delighted her father with hours of childish prattle. Jack even arranged to stay overnight in Clarksburg, preferring that the group arrive at their destination late the next morning, after a good night's rest.

After a hearty breakfast at Clarksburg's finest hotel, Jack left his "troop" sipping coffee while he walked down the street to the offices of Burton Luddock, Attorney at Law, who held the keys and the deed to the property. In his lapel pocket was the check that represented final payment.

"Good morning, Mr. Sterling," Luddock greeted him warmly. "I trust your trip was pleasant."

"Very." Jack returned his handshake. "I am a little nervous about the mountain, however, since I haven't navigated it since fall. How much snow do we have to contend with?"

"Considerable, I'm afraid. Not to worry, however. I have taken the liberty of arranging experienced drivers to take you up there. It will be necessary that you take everything with you, however. God only knows when you'll be able to get down."

"Perhaps the ladies should do a little more shopping," Jack laughed. "I'm sure they won't mind."

Luddock pulled a file from the steel cabinet and very soon they concluded their business. Jack thanked the attorney for the drivers, and agreed on a meeting place, departure scheduled in two hours.

"Oh, I almost forgot! This wire arrived for you this morning." Luddock handed over a telegram stamped "Urgent." Jack's smile faded very quickly as he recognized George's return address. It read:

> December 22, 1925
> Mac en route by train to Pittsburgh PA alone, estimated
> time of arrival 4:35 PM today stop Paul taken suddenly very
> ill and is confined to school infirmary stop Academy

physician requests Rachael's arrival as soon as possible and that Mac be quarantined upon arrival home stop Merry Christmas stop George

Jack's face suddenly paled and he sank into the nearest chair. Luddock watched him carefully. Obviously the news was not good, the attorney deduced, so he waited until Jack had composed himself, and then cautiously asked the vital question. "Will you be required to change your plans? Forgive my asking, but I will need to let the drivers know soon."

"No!" Jack exclaimed, a little too loudly. "We will proceed as planned." He rose again, shook hands, verified the meeting place and time, and hurried down the street. There was a cold, brutal wind that forced the collar of his overcoat to flap sharply against his face, and it was snowing very hard.

Chapter 9

1926

"Lordy, but that chile sho do love dat man!"

Millie was gazing absently across the expanse of lawn, that portion of the Sterling estate that flowed into the circular driveway. Jack had just exited his black Buick, an action that sent the soon-to-be six-year-old Lillian into a joyful frenzy. She raced to the car and jumped into his arms, wrapping her long legs around his rather rotund frame as far as they would reach.

Next to Millie, in a matching wicker rocker, Rachael laughed heartily. They shared a pitcher of iced tea, laced with bourbon and a sprig of mint.

"Better go easy on that stuff," Millie teased. "What's so friggin' funny?"

"You are. You go to such pains to conceal the fact that you are a 'cum laude' graduate of Ohio State University, with a masters in English. How I envy you! Why do you talk like a ...?"

"Ignorant black woman?" Mille smiled.

"Please don't say things like that to me, Millie. I don't deserve it."

"Sorry. You are absolutely right. You don't deserve it. Just call it a natural defense, a reflex reaction. Most people expect me to talk that way, and the sight of Jack Sterling never fails to remind me of that fact."

"I know. He treats you shamefully. Aren't you ever tempted to remind him that you are a member of Mensa, and he didn't finish the eighth grade?"

"Tempted, yes. Compelled, no. It would only make things worse. Hush, now... here they come."

At Millie's signal, the conversation was suspended. Jack climbed the steps with Lillian in his arms, looking rather dapper in his white linen suit and Panama hat. *Amazing what expensive clothes could do for a toad,* Rachael thought.

"Good afternoon, Rachael," Jack greeted her. He threw a curt nod in Millie's general direction, obviously unhappy about being somehow obligated to do so. Rachael acknowledged him with a nominal nod of her own, then proceeded to freshen drinks. She did not offer one to Jack. He smiled thinly, nodded again, and carried Lillian into the house.

Silence prevailed as the two rocked, sipping their tea. The late afternoon sun burned hot, but there was a cooling breeze on the shaded veranda, and the ladies had their fans. Millie drained her glass, stood and stretched. "I guess I am no longer needed here. Lillian has her 'papa' now. I'll go and check the roses. Would you care to join me in the garden?"

It was an unusual request. During the years that they had known each other, the pair had shared very few private conversations, as Rachael's duties centered on the management of the house while Millie's role was first wet-nurse to Lillian, and then that of constant companion to Anna. Rachael caught Millie's look, almost pleading. She had something to say to Rachael. "I need to look in on Paul," Rachael told her quietly. "I'll be out shortly."

Passing the closed door of Jack's office, where she imagined Lillian perched cross-legged on his massive desk, Rachael peeked into the kitchen on her way to her private apartment. Helga was banging pots and pans while she sang loudly. Rachael was mildly surprised to find Paul still sleeping soundly, but then he slept several hours each afternoon, and twelve hours at night. Dr. Powell assured her that his recovery would be complete, given enough time and loving care. She sat beside his bed, just as she had for so long during those horrible days in Vermont when he had hovered between life and death. Too many bad memories, she thought, and she shook them off.

She reached out to push back the blond curls from his damp forehead. There was still the occasional low-grade fever; he could not tolerate the slightest chill. It was eighty-five degrees this summer day, but two heavy quilts were drawn to his small chin. He was thinner than a ten-year-old should be, and pale. But he was alive! Even now, breathing in his sleep, he grew stronger with every breath, and would again run and play. "Spinal meningitis," the academy doctor had announced when he escorted her to his room. "Spotted fever. Nasty stuff." Rachael shivered, again pushing away the memory, and rose to seek out Millie in the garden.

"How is he today?" Millie asked when Rachael had closed the gate.

She wanted so badly to say "better," but if he truly was, the remark may jinx it. "I really don't know, Millie. Some days I think he is almost like he used to be. Other days…"

"You are a strong woman, Rachael. I wonder if I could bear up as well, given all that you have been through. First your poor husband, you were widowed so young. Then to have your only child so afflicted… well, I just admire your courage."

"Thank you. It has little to do with courage, however. It's really more a matter of total faith in God."

Millie looked away, thinking. She pulled a pair of snips out of her pocket,

90

put on a glove, and attacked a rose bush. "Do you think that God wills us to be born poor, and that we only serve His purpose if we remain poor? Is it wrong to want more?"

"I don't understand the question," Rachael answered quietly. Millie's chatter was going in a strange direction, and Rachael's innate caution warned her to proceed carefully. "God is a loving, generous Father to us all," she told Millie. "He wants us to have what we need, to be happy. It is only when we become more concerned with the material things of this world than with our spiritual well-being that we offend Him. Are you fearful of becoming too rich, Millie?" Rachael's question was partly good-natured teasing and partly a lead into a deep conversation, for she was now more than a little curious.

Millie continued to prune the roses, obviously troubled in her thoughts. She decided to be blunt. "Why do you stay here?" she asked quickly, whirling around to face Rachael.

"I... I work here," Rachael replied. Caught off-guard, she thought the answer sounded silly. "I came here to do a job, fill a position. The salary is very good, so I hope to save enough to take care of Paul and myself for as long as I need to. Why do you ask?"

"Because you have compromised yourself, Rachael, just as I have. You put up with Jack's controlling attitude, his moods, his incessant demands about how the napkins are ironed, how his French cuffs must extend three inches below his sleeve. Anna is not particularly kind to you, I know. She is so wrapped up in her business that she doesn't even notice the children, let alone concern herself about you. What did she do to you last winter, when Paul was so sick?"

Rachael moved to the stone bench and sat down slowly. "I don't know what you are talking about," she said.

"How did it happen that Paul was enrolled in that school to begin with? Was it your decision, or did Jack pressure you to send him there? Tell me about it, Rachael. Please."

Almost without conscious consent, Rachael began to talk about what she had suppressed for months, the 'West Virginia affair.' "It is true," she heard herself saying. "Mac was displaying some serious behavioral problems, even before Lillian was born. He was so small when I came here to take the position of housekeeper. I hadn't planned to be his nanny, but Anna more or less delegated that duty to me. When Jack decided that Mac must be sent away to school, he persuaded me to allow Paul to go with him. It was a terrible mistake, a regret that I will carry for the rest of my life." Rachael began to cry softly, and Millie ceased her labor of the roses and sat beside her. It seemed that her questions had opened old wounds, and Millie wished that she had not pressed the issue.

"I'm sure that you acted in Paul's best interest, Rachael. You are a good mother. But surely your decision was not made for Mac's sake, to keep him from being lonely?"

Rachael was crying harder now, relieved somehow to purge the guilt that she had felt for so long. "No, Millie. I made a 'contract' with Jack. He promised to pay for Paul's education, the kind of schooling I could never afford on my salary. I suppose I 'sold out.'"

Millie was silent for several moments, allowing Rachael to compose herself. Was that what she was about to do, 'sell out,' to Anna's promise of a full partnership in her business? Would she ultimately regret that decision? "What about now?" she asked Rachael. "Will he honor his pledge to you now that Paul is no longer at the academy?"

"I don't know. It doesn't matter to me anymore. Paul is here with me where he belongs and I will kill before I will ever allow any more harm to come to him."

Mighty fierce words for a devout Catholic lady, Millie thought. She had one more question. "What happened in West Virginia, Rachael? Why did you go alone to Vermont?"

"Anna and I were at the hotel, waiting for Jack to conclude his business with the attorney. She didn't want to be there, but neither did I for that matter, so we were actually trying to make the best of it. When Jack arrived, he ordered coffee for himself and left to make a phone call. Mr. Luddock came rushing into the dining room, asking for Jack. Anna invited him to sit, but he was excited about 'another' telegram, he said, concerned that Jack would be waiting for its arrival. That's how I learned about Paul. The wire was from George Steinburger."

"Didn't you wonder why Jack hadn't told you about the 'first' telegram?"

"I didn't think about it at the time. Anna handed me the wire and I was so upset, I just left for the station at once."

"Alone?" Millie asked her. "With no traveling money?"

"I had enough put back to pay for my fare to Vermont. Not much left over, however. When I arrived at the station, a very kind man and his wife took me to the school. I just needed to get to my son. You can understand that, can't you?"

"Of course. I just don't understand how Jack and Anna could let you go alone, as distraught as you were, with no better provisions for the trip. You had to stay for several weeks. Where did you sleep? How did you eat? Did you hear from the Sterlings?"

"They had Mac coming in on the train, and Lillian to think about. Helga and Emily and the men needed to get back to Indiana. Things were very confused. Emily offered to come with me, but Anna wouldn't hear of it. When I arrived at the academy, the doctor said that Paul had spinal meningitis, spotted fever. He told me to prepare for the possibility that Paul might die. After a few weeks of treatment and constant nursing, he recovered enough to bring him home. That's the story." Rachael looked away. She didn't want to talk about it anymore. But there was more, a bitter confrontation with Anna that had left her so angry, so shaken that she stopped praying, stopped going to Mass.

Millie waited. Finally, Rachael said, "When I telephoned Anna to make arrangements to bring Paul home, she told me to go somewhere else. She said that she didn't want the other children to be exposed, but Dr. Powell said Paul was no longer contagious. I was devastated, frightened. Where was I to go, with a sick child and little money?"

"Good God! What did you do then?"

"I called a local attorney. It cost me my last cent, but I was not going to be put out of the only home I had left. My lawyer contacted Jack, and left it to him to deal with Anna. Things have been somewhat strained between us since. But, as you see, I am still here. Why does all of this matter to you, Millie? Why do you need to know?"

"I have some serious decisions to make. I am trying to understand what I am dealing with, that's all. I have tried to be a friend to Anna and she, in turn, has been very generous with me. She has offered me a full partnership in the business, the opportunity to make more money than I have seen in my entire life. But when I think about those children, Rachael, I have to wonder how a loving little boy evolves into a tin soldier, and that baby girl... she has no mother!"

"I know," Rachael said sadly. "I know. I worry about Lillian, too. She is too quiet, keeps to herself. She only comes to life, it seems, when Jack comes home. Otherwise, I don't think I have ever seen her laugh... come to think of it, I have never seen her cry! Can that be natural?"

"I don't know, Rachael." Millie stood to resume her rosebush inspection and slowly shook her head. "I can't get close to that child, I doubt that anyone can, except her father. Natural or no, it's the way she is, the way they made her, and it will be Jack and Anna who will reap what they have sown."

Chapter 10

1928

Millie looked at the piece of paper in her hand, certain that the figures must be wrong. Anna sat across the large cutting table and watched her friend's face as one watches the expressions of delight and surprise upon opening a Christmas present. "How does it feel," Anna asked, "to be independently wealthy?"

"This can't be true!"

"Why are you so surprised? We have worked very hard, struggled and stitched until our fingers bled, worked all night to finish a special order. You have been right here with me since the very first day, and now it's payoff time. We are a success!"

"I have no idea what to do with all this money," Millie protested. "Will you help me?"

Anna laughed and reached out to pat Millie's trembling hand. "I can help you spend it, or invest it, or burn it... whatever you'd prefer."

"For the time being, I just want to think about it, Miss Anna. I have been poor all my life, and I wonder if I could ever be anything else. Just think about all the babies I can take care of now! So much to think about and... bless me, Miss Anna, I haven't even said 'thank you'!"

"No need, you earned it. But we've had enough excitement for one day, so I will ask Billy to take you home. We are still in business and tomorrow is another day."

After Millie had hugged her and said her goodnights, Anna locked the shop door and returned to the back room where she and Millie and the finest seamstresses in the city toiled for hours over exclusive fashions. She opened the oaken cupboard and greeted the bottle of scotch that nestled neatly behind stacks of thread. "Good evening, old friend," she whispered."Thank you for being so dependable."

Anna often spent the late hours of her long day in this room, sipping scotch and chain-smoking and reflecting on the preceding twelve hours. Her work had become her obsession, she knew, but she felt no guilt.

She mentally checked off the list. Wife? Not really. Jack didn't want a wife, didn't need a wife. They continued to play out the happy couple role, still dressed to the teeth and partied at the club every weekend. They still entertained with more style and extravagance than any of their social rivals, still slept in separate beds, separate rooms, at opposite ends of the wing. There were no arguments anymore, because Anna and Jack limited their conversations to pleasant small talk or stock market analysis. No, Jack wouldn't wonder why she hadn't come home yet, if indeed he was at home himself.

Homemaker? She was no longer needed. The "Great House" had been carefully and extensively renovated down to the last detail, so much so that it now resembled a residence worthy of royalty. Anna had poured over books and swatches for hours, planning and plotting color and design, and from the Ming vases in the foyer to the gold candlesticks on the huge dining room table, every adornment was in place. To Rachael's credit, Anna conceded, all that remained was the maintenance, and that was better left to the housekeeper, who carried it off with utmost efficiency.

Mother? To whom? Her beloved Mac was a stranger in a cadet's uniform, polite and reserved, with barely a trace of the spirited hell-raiser left in him. He was twelve years old, on the verge of manhood she suspected, but already old at heart. When Jack drove her to the Vermont Military School, Mac liked to salute his mother, draped in her mink stole and white gloves that matched his own from the parade ground. Once he had even teased her about her overpowering hat…"Do you keep birds in there?" and she thought for just a moment that she saw the old twinkle in his eye, but one stern look from Jack dampened the boy's fun, and the moment passed.

Lillian had distanced herself from Anna, it seemed, at the exact instant of birth. The child had been brutally yanked from her womb, Anna reasoned, and given over to more competent caregivers. Anna battled for weeks following the delivery of her daughter with a severe sadness, and would have lost not only her sanity, but also her will to live, had Millie not been constantly at her side. Weak and medicated, Anna watched Millie nurse the infant, each time terrified that Millie would insist that Anna hold her after the feeding.

"I can't!" Anna would wail. Millie ignored the protest, laid the sleepy, contented baby next to Anna, and each time Anna held her breath and waited. Lillian soon screamed so violently that Millie was forced to retrieve her within seconds.

"Next time," Millie would assure Anna, but it was always the same.

"Isn't it ironic," Anna asked Millie, "that I seemed to have finally failed at the one thing that I thought I could do well?"

"Hush now," Millie had whispered, "you are not a failure. Mothering doesn't always come easy." Eight years had passed since Millie had assured her that it would somehow resolve itself, and nothing had changed. Lillian greeted her mother politely when she was prompted; reluctantly "kissed" her mother when strongly instructed to do so, but otherwise stayed out of Anna's line of vision. The brutal truth, Anna concluded, was simply that they did not like each other.

"Why are you so filthy?" Anna asked Lillian when she came into the house by way of the back door as required. The question was so abrupt that even Helga looked up from her cookbook to give Anna a disapproving look. Little girls who played with little boys, who were, in fact, in the "tomboy" stage, were more often dirty than clean. Everyone who had any contact with children knew that! Helga was childless, her only knowledge about children was through her sister's two girls, but even she knew that it was pointless to ask a child "why" they behaved in a particular manner.

"I guess I got dirty playing with the boys," Lillian answered quietly. Her lower lip quivered a little, but Helga was certain that the child would not cry, no matter how hard Anna tried to intimidate her.

"I have told you over and over that nice little girls don't play with boys! Why do you persist in disobeying me? Look at your dress! It's ruined. Why can't you just behave like other young ladies?"

Helga rolled her eyes. Again with the "why's"! She wondered how intense this confrontation was to become. Should she leave the room? Damn, this was her kitchen! Let the Misses leave if she wanted privacy.

"Why can't you just leave me alone?" Lillian shouted. She spun around and ran up the backstairs, her ugly brown oxfords pounding hard on the oaken risers. Anna looked at Helga, but there was no clear message in the seconds that their eyes met. Did she want confirmation that she was right? Sympathy for her beleaguered patience? Helga shrugged and looked down at the book. Anna abruptly left the kitchen.

The scene was an old one, replayed over and over again as the years rolled away. Anna would make a point to speak to Jack as soon as he came home. She would complain about *his* daughter, and he would be angry and defensive. But he defended only himself, never Lillian. Anna would hurry upstairs, slam the door to her room and take her beloved medication for the headache that by this time was blinding. Jack would drink scotch until Emily brought his dinner tray, and then he would continue his love affair with the bottle until he either fell asleep on the leather couch or climbed the stairs to his own room.

And the child Lillian would crawl through the small attic space behind her dresser, pull at her hair and cry for hours in this special crying place where no one could see her cry, for no one would come to look for her.

Chapter 11

1929

Lillian Gretchen Sterling stared down at her horrible brown shoes and wondered what life would be like if her mother were dead.

Contemplating a favorite poem, she lapsed into a silent, dark parody of Elizabeth Barrett Browning's "How Do I Love Thee?" and the revised version was "How Do I Hate Thee? Let Me Count the Ways." Anna was again the target of Lillian's wrath, as she was somehow always at the core of any emotion that visited the child.

"None of my schoolmates have to wear shoes like this," Lillian announced to her father. "We have money to buy anything; why can't I have something decent to wear to school? The other girls make fun of me."

They were sitting on two large boulders that hugged the lake's shoreline, a strange choice of location considering that it was uncomfortably cool, and a misty spring rain dampened father and daughter. The ducks seemed content to be there, diving for the stale bread Jack tossed into the water.

It was almost time to leave the beautiful lake. Jack had driven here on Friday, his "fishing buddy" Lillian chattering merrily beside him all the way from Richmond. He now reflected on the strange fact that she had not mentioned her mother all weekend. Only the depressive "going home" mood, it seemed, had solicited this most recent complaint about Anna.

"You must make an effort to get along with your mother," Jack stated. He liked the way it sounded... profound, fatherly.

"Why?"

The question startled him, and he laughed. He knew he shouldn't have, this was one of the moments when such an important statement lost its value when contaminated with humor, but he honestly had no reply. He turned to look sternly at her, but she was laughing too, and soon they were both chuckling while they tossed bread on the water.

Having lost the opportunity to resolve his daughter's problem, not that there was any real resolution, he changed the subject. "You are becoming quite an accomplished fisherman, Dizzy Lizzy, you almost caught more bass than I did. Won't Helga be surprised?"

"Do we really have to leave?" she asked. "I love it here."

"We can't hide out up here forever. We'd starve!" He reached over to poke his finger into a small rib, and the laughter began again. "Anyway, they'd find us sooner or later."

He sighed, stood up to brush the wet grass from his trousers, and offered his hand to Lillian. "Best get going, girl. We need to get these fish home."

Lillian curled up in the back seat of the Buick with a book, her constant companion. Soon she was sound asleep and Jack was grateful that there would be no more debates that he would surely lose, no more questions that he could not answer. The two-hour drive gave him some time to contemplate Anna's latest demand that he involve himself in the investment of Millie Anderson's newfound wealth.

"Use your own broker," Jack had replied. "The ladies man with the phony French accent."

"That would be my preference," Anna said, her tone spoiling for a fight. "He is out of the country, I believe. I haven't been able to reach him."

"Oh, well, he'll be back. He'll need to fleece some silly woman when he runs out of pocket money." *Some 'other' silly woman!*

Anna gritted her teeth. She hated having to ask Jack for a favor, especially one that was such a long shot. He was not likely inclined to do anything for Millie, and she regretted that she had asked. Did he have to add insult to injury? His mean remark about her friend, Clayton DeBoe was a direct hit, designed to goad her into defense. What Jack didn't know, she decided, was that her interest in Clayton went beyond her investments in the stock market. Lately, the attention heaped upon her by her broker had spawned the type of fantasies she had not experienced before, and the little voice in her mind suggested that one rich husband was as good as another.

"He's so perfect!" Doris Schoonover had gushed. "What a huge, handsome hunk of man! Not my type, though. Clayton's not the marrying kind. It would take a woman with the Queen's money to put a ring on that man's finger."

"You made investments for Rachael," Anna retorted. Her tone was still hostile and peppered with the flavor of accusation. She lapsed into silence, leaving the last remark to linger for his reply.

Jack smiled. If he didn't know better he might think that Anna was implying some sort of sexual involvement with Rachael. Her mind did not function that way, however, and even if it did, jealousy of Rachael in connection with Jack would be a long stretch. It was momentarily flattering;

he might just let it ride. Or perhaps he should come clean, confide in Anna that his contacts had recently warned him about the market, in spite of the "bull." To hell with it! He would simply react in type, for he was tired of this game.

"As usual, madam, you are badly misinformed. I personally made no investments for Mrs. Unger; I simply referred her to someone who can be trusted to protect her small savings. Stop acting like a cat, Anna. It doesn't become you."

"Well then, can't you do the same for Millie?"

"I suppose I could. I don't choose to. Is there anything else?"

He was angry, therefore beyond reason, Anna decided. She hesitated. She wanted to talk to him about Mac, to ask if he could come home. The timing was not good, she recognized, so she had silently left the room.

Jack drove on, lost in thought about Anna and Clayton DeBoe. He wanted to believe that her libido was so underdeveloped that no man would tempt her, let alone an obvious gigolo like DeBoe. The nagging notion that kept pecking at the corners of his mind, however, was that there might be nothing wrong with Anna's sexual inclinations after all.

"Papa?"

"Yes, Diz?"

"I don't have any friends."

"I don't really have any friends either, dear. We don't mix well. We are shy, I suppose, more withdrawn than most people. Don't worry about it, you will always have me, and your mother, and your brothers."

"But Paul isn't really my brother. Besides, he is so sick all the time and Mrs. Unger closes the door to keep me out. I sneak in sometimes though, and read to him when he's asleep."

"Don't let her catch you, Diz."

"Papa?"

"Yes?"

"When can Mac come home? I'm so lonely without him. He used to play with me, and I miss him."

"I'm not sure, honey. I will talk to your mother about it, and we'll let you know."

Jack was surprised to find Anna in the kitchen when they arrived home with the big, smelly fish. She was so rarely home, almost never in the kitchen, and never wearing an apron like the one she was wiping her hands on. The smell of gingerbread filled the large, warm room, and even more surprising,

Anna seemed happy to see them.

"How many?" she asked.

"Six big ones!"

"I hate fish."

"We know," Lillian answered, "so we didn't catch you one."

Jack braced himself for the lecture that Lillian would surely receive from Anna, and when it didn't happen, he settled into his office for a drink. There was to be peace in the house tonight, he thought. Enjoy it while it lasts. He looked at his calendar. It was late April 1929. Next month Mac would be thirteen, ready for high school next fall. It was time to bring him home. He would surprise Anna and Lillian, he decided, make arrangements for Mac to be dismissed early and drive to Vermont alone to get him.

He took a long swig of scotch and breathed deeply. The smell of the gingerbread filled his nostrils with pleasant memories, and he found himself thinking of Maureen Kennedy, and happier days.

Chapter 12

1929

Colonel Paul Tornow quickly removed the soggy cigar stub from his mouth when his aide entered the office. Professional military decorum dictated "moderate" use of tobacco in the presence of students and subordinates according to the Vermont Military Academy Cannon of Regulations, and Tornow was a stickler for the rulebook.

"General Hodges to see you sir," the aide announced.

Since rank prevailed, the arrival of the General explained why there had been no warning knock. Tornow leaped to his feet, at attention and snapping the traditional salute.

His right hand was still gripping the cigar butt, and he silently prayed that the General wouldn't notice.

"At ease, Colonel. You may sit."

Tornow sat, privately amused. The General was a pompous ass who refused to sit on the other side of anyone's desk. He preferred to tower over his host or pace the office with his hands clasped tightly behind his back. Tornow gave the General his full attention and waited.

"The purpose of this visit is twofold," Hodges began. "I am instructed to advise you that the fall term applications for admission are lower than usual, resulting in some understandable concern. You are to immediately review all rejected applications and consider them again with a more liberal attitude."

"Yes, sir." Tornow had no questions. The order was clear.

"Secondly, it has come to my attention that the Sterling boy is being excused early at his father's request and will not be returning to the Academy in the fall. For what reason?"

Colonel Tornow was momentarily lost for words. It had not occurred to him to inquire about the reason for Mac Sterling's departure, and the boy's father had offered none.

"I don't know, " he replied.

"You 'don't know'? That is not an acceptable answer, Colonel. Show me the written request from Mr. Sterling."

"There is no written request. Mr. Sterling called. He said that he would be here to pick up Cadet Sterling during the week of his birthday. It is to be a surprise for the Cadet and his family. I assured Mr. Sterling that we would have him ready to go."

"You took much upon yourself, Colonel. No formal request in writing, no notification of your superior officers. Am I to also assume that no dismissal conference has been scheduled?"

"Under the circumstances, it didn't seem advisable."

"What 'circumstances'?"

Tornow reddened. This was a "chew-ass" mission, and for some reason that he could not immediately comprehend, he was in trouble with the brass. What was the big issue, anyway? The father calls and says he wants the kid to come home. The kid goes home. Why is this simple procedure giving him grief, stirring up his stomach acids?

He proceeded carefully, spoke slowly and deliberately. "As I reported, the homecoming is to be a surprise. I could hardly conference with the Cadet if he was not to know that he was dismissed."

"I see. Well, we can certainly clarify that oversight." Hodges opened the door to summon the aide, almost colliding with the young man who hovered outside the door, listening surreptitiously. "Find Cadet Sterling and order him to report to this office immediately," Hodges barked. The aide saluted and scurried away, relieved to be free of the area and thus far unchastised for his eavesdropping.

Hodges returned to the office and sat down on the leather couch. He had made his point, he could now relax a bit... besides, his feet hurt and he was tired. Uncomfortable with silence, and feeling obligated to continue the inquisition, he turned his attention again to Tornow.

"Perhaps we might find some possible answers while we wait. Has the Sterling boy been a disciplinary problem?"

"No, sir... not for some time. He was a tough nut to crack for the first few years, but he has worked through all that and has behaved exemplary for the past three years."

"That's what they pay us for, Colonel. The brass is very worried that if the stock market continues to fluctuate wildly, fewer and fewer fathers will require our services. How are his grades?"

"Average, but within the range of acceptability. The boy is no genius, sir."

Hodges considered the information for a moment. Not a behavioral issue, grades good enough to allow a proud papa to brag. "What about that business four years ago, the brother got very sick and was sent home. Does that have any bearing?"

"I doubt it. Cadet Unger is not related to Cadet Sterling. Paul is the housekeeper's son. At any rate, why would that prompt Mac's withdrawal after all this time?"

Hodges almost said "I don't know", but he suppressed the comment. It wouldn't do to repeat the phrase after taking Tornow to task for the same. "Is he himself ill? Homesick?"

Tornow sighed and lifted himself from his chair. Damn, let's get this over with and get this pain-in-the-ass out of his office. He pulled a file folder from the cabinet and fanned papers until he found what he was looking for. "This is his latest physical report," he offered. "Everything is in order, no indication of physical problem." He wet a finger and went a page further. "Physiological examination was done the next day, dated 14 April, 1929. 'Cadet Sterling is well adjusted and suitable for duty,'" he quoted. "Nothing here to get excited about."

"Very well. We wait."

A light rap on the door directed both men's attention to the entry of Cadet Sterling, accompanied by his senior advisor, Cadet Babcock. The young men stood at attention and saluted their officers. "At ease, gentlemen," Hodges ordered.

Tornow was trapped at the filing cabinet, trying to decide if he could resume his seat, or if he should remain standing, in deference to the senior officer. Was he supposed to interview the Cadet, or just stand there looking stupid? Hodges was in his element, so he would control the meeting. "Everyone may sit," he announced. "This encounter is informal and off the record."

Tornow sat immediately, relieved. Babcock made a beeline for the couch. Hedges walked to the door and opened it far enough to look down both directions of the corridor. Seeing no one there, he returned to where Mac continued to stand, next to the desk.

"Don't you want to sit, soldier?"

"No, sir. Thank you, sir, but I prefer to stand."

General Hodges moved his large frame between the boy and the desk. Mac stood stiffly, staring straight ahead, and he did not move to accommodate the officer. Hodges chose to perch on the corner of Tornow's desk because he could strike a casual posture that put him at eye-level with Cadet Sterling.

Tornow observed the maneuver and was duly, if reluctantly, impressed.

Clever. Must be why they pay him the big bucks.

Hodges took his time. He smiled benevolently at Mac, who continued to stare past him. After a long moment, Mac's eyes moved quickly to the left, where the General caught them like fish in a net. Once contact had been established, Mac dared not look away.

Hodges grinned at the boy, as if the two of them now shared a private joke. "Are you happy here, son?"

Tornow and Babcock exchanged meaningful looks. *This guy was smooth.*

"Happy, sir?"

"Is there somewhere else you would rather be?"

"Like where, sir?"

"Home, perhaps?"

Mac had begun to relax slightly, but he stiffened again at the inquiry. Hodges thought he detected a flicker of... something in the boy's eyes, but he could not be sure, for it was vague and fleeting. He pressed harder. "Would you like to go home, son?"

Mac pretended to consider the question, but his answer indicated that he had really no desire to choose. "I have no preference, sir."

This conference was not going well. Hodges needed to probe deeper, but carefully. "I well remember my first few years away from home," he said absently. "Most of the time I was so busy with the drills and the lessons that time passed quickly. But when I missed my family, got homesick, it was bad. I would become very melancholy, depressed even. I missed my parents, my brothers, my dog." The General studied Cadet Sterling's face like a map, searching for that path that might lead to a reaction, any reaction. There was none. General Hodge's purpose for coming to the school had been to impress upon the Colonel that the unnecessary loss of tuition revenue was a critical problem. He hadn't planned to become personally involved in the particulars of the Sterling matter. But something about this student's obvious lack of concern intrigued him. The face that looked back at him was without expression, the eyes without life.

Mac said absently, "I don't have a dog, sir."

"I believe that you miss your family, Cadet Sterling. I'm sure that they miss you."

Mac swallowed hard. "I don't think so, sir. No."

"Then it matters not whether you remain here or return to Richmond?"

"No, sir."

"Very well, Cadet, you are dismissed. You may return to quarters."

Mac snapped to attention, saluted. He pivoted on his heel and rapidly left the room, looking at no one.

The men exchanged confused glances. "Babcock," Hodges said, "do you have any insight into this matter?"

Babcock rose to his feet, required protocol when addressed by a senior officer. "Cadet Sterling has been somewhat withdrawn, sir. He doesn't talk much about his parents, but he does correspond regularly with his sister, I believe."

Tornow sprung to life. "The sister, yes. I remember now that Mr. Sterling told me that the boy's sister wanted him home!"

Hodges looked surprised. "And how old is this sister?"

"I believe she is about nine, sir," Babcock reported.

Hodges slowly shook his head. This institution had succeeded in transforming a seven-year old hellion into a miniature military prototype, a perfect little soldier. After a six-year investment, the army would lose him now to a willful little girl who evidently had considerable influence with her father. Hodges picked up Mac's file from the desk and began to read the drill reports.

"Tornow, either your clerk is very sloppy or this boy is an extraordinary marksman. These scores are the best I've ever read."

"Sterling is very accomplished, General. Unger was even better... broke all academy records, I understand."

"Pity. Gentlemen, we have somehow managed to lose the two best cadets we've had in many years. For all our sakes, let's hope that the trend doesn't continue."

Chapter 13

"I know a secret."

Paul looked at Lillian and waited. They were seated on the edge of the garage roof, dangling bare feet in the warm spring sun. The building, which had once served as a carriage house, now held Jack's fleet of automobiles, six in all. The small basket between them that had been filled with contraband cookies from Helga's kitchen was almost empty, and Paul wanted to snatch the last one quickly.

"Aren't you going to ask me what the secret is?" Lillian asked him.

"You'll tell me when you get around to it," Paul laughed. "Otherwise you wouldn't have mentioned it."

"Paul Unger, sometimes you can be so aggravating!" she snapped.

"Well, I'm not going to beg you, if that's what you're waiting for," he teased. He flipped open the basket lid and grabbed the cookie, holding it behind his back when she reached for it. "Be careful, you'll fall," he warned her, "and you'll get all smooched on the ground, and I'll be in trouble because I stole the cookies."

Lillian giggled. It was so wonderful to have him back, just like he used to be. Dr. Powell had told Rachael that Paul was completely cured now, and could resume "normal activities." It had been a long, lonely convalescence for both of them.

"Mac is coming home," she said.

"When?"

"In a few days, I think. Maybe tomorrow."

"How do you know?"

"I listened while Papa was on the phone to the military school. No one else knows, just us."

"Why is he coming home? Did something happen at school?"

"I don't think so. I asked Papa to bring him home because I really miss him."

It must be wonderful, Paul reflected, to have a father who granted every wish. He was silent, thinking about his own father. All the boy knew about John Unger was what his mother had told him, how he had been such a good, brave man. Paul visited the "shrine" every day, the picture of John on his mother's dresser next to the burning candle and the lock of blond hair. His thoughts turned to Mac. It would seem strange to see him again, after all this time.

"I have another secret."

"Wow, Gretch. You are just full of surprises today. What else?"

Lillian smiled at the sound of "Gretch." She collected nicknames in the same manner that some people collected stamps or coins. Each one was exclusive to one individual, for she really didn't care what anyone called her, as long as it wasn't "Lillian." Papa called her "Dizzy Lizzy," or just "Diz." Mac called her "Sis." Rachael referred to her as "Liz," while Helga usually addressed her as "Missy." Her mother, of course, refused to call her anything but "Lillian," but since Anna seldom spoke to her, it didn't matter.

"Well? What's the other secret?"

"Papa says we can have a dog."

"No kidding? A dog? That's great!" Paul was very excited, he loved animals and had always wanted a puppy, but Rachael made excuses, finally reminding Paul that they didn't live in the right home to accommodate a dog. He began to think about what the dog would look like, what they would name him. He was so wrapped up in "puppy dreaming" that he almost didn't see Billy coming out of one of the outbuildings.

"Get down, quick!" he whispered to Lillian. "Keep low and move back, or we're in trouble."

She saw him, too, and started to "scoot" backwards, kicking the cookie basket over the edge. "What the hell?" Billy cried as it bounced off his head. One quick glance in the children's direction told Billy all he needed to know. He made almost instant eye contact with Paul, and gestured for the boy to come down immediately.

"Stay here for now," Paul whispered to Gretch, who was belly down somewhere near the center of the roof. "I don't think he saw you. I'll go down and take the heat."

"You sound like one of Capone's goons," she giggled. Paul pressed his finger to his lips and exited the roof though the door that led to the staircase. The rule of the house, he knew, was that any adult could intervene with any child in routine matters. More serious infractions were referred to the parent of the offender. If Lillian were caught on the roof, she would be disciplined by Anna, in Jack's absence. Paul's experience with Anna's brand of punishment prompted him to take all the blame, for he would fare far better with Rachael.

"You know better, Paul," Billy scolded him when Paul stood before him, a few moments later. "That is a dangerous thing to do, and you have been told about it before. Go and find your mother and tell her why I sent you inside."

"Yes, Billy. I'm sorry." Paul turned toward the kitchen door.

"Oh, and Paul?"

"Yes, Billy?"

"Better tell your friend that she can come down now. Wouldn't want her up there all night, eh?"

Paul grinned and caught the basket that Billy tossed to him. "You can come on down, Gretch," he called out." Billy doesn't see you!"

Chapter 14

Jack was disappointed when he rolled the Buick up the drive. Paul and Diz were nowhere in sight, as he had expected they would be on such a warm, sunny day. He loved surprises, as long as they were for someone else, and today he had, in fact, outdone himself. A puppy for the kids, and very soon he would bring Mac home, securing his title of "Hero" once and for all. He might even get to like this damn dog, if it didn't make a habit of peeing all over his linen suit, as it was doing now.

He should have driven around the back, he decided, but he had already cut the engine and had an armful of canine. He walked around the house to the kitchen entrance, where he unexpectedly ran into Anna just inside the door. She took a long look at the furry creature in his arms and said, "I hope it is not your intention to bring that filthy beast into my house."

The gauntlet was down. Jack was really not an admirer of dogs, never had been. It had been an impulse, really, like so many other things he did for his family without considering how it might be received. Lillian had joined her parents in the kitchen, as had Paul, who begged his mother to let him go to the kitchen and atone later for his afternoon indiscretion. If Jack had even considered yielding to Anna's wishes, the faces of the children emboldened his resolve to win this new war.

Jack handed the pup to Lillian, a Boston Terrier, properly pedigreed and expensive enough to impress even Anna, if she would allow herself to be impressed. He pulled his watch chain out of the small pocket in his trousers and removed a silver key from the fob.

"This is the key to my office, Paul," he said quietly. "Take Diz and the puppy in there for now, since it is a part of Mrs. Sterling's house that belongs to me."

The children looked at him just long enough to relay pure adoration, then hurried away before Anna could protest, for they had no desire to stay for round two.

Anna was less unhappy about the pup than the challenge to her authority. They looked at each other for a long moment and Anna decided to test a new technique.

"So," she said lightly, "it seems we have a dog. Does our dog have a

110

name?"

Caught off guard, Jack mumbled, "The children can name him. I call him 'Buddy.'"

"Well, if 'Buddy' spends the night in that room, it will smell like a barn by morning, I can assure you. Wouldn't a bed on the back porch make more sense? I can have Emily come and help Paul and Lillian tuck him in."

Jack nodded, stunned.

"Good, that's settled. We have our Monday night dinner reservations for eight, don't forget." With that she climbed the staircase and disappeared.

The new persona felt so comfortable and intriguing that Anna continued it upstairs, as she dressed. She would be pleasant and charming through dinner, she decided, and she hummed a few bars of the newest show tune, "You're the cream in my coffee." She re-read Jack's note to her, left on her dressing table this morning. "I will leave early in the morning for a business trip," it said, "and will return by Sunday evening."

Six glorious days to do completely as she wished. The stores could be left to Millie, and Anna would board the train to New York to shop, have her hair done in the best salon. She would stay at the Plaza and order room service. She would call Clayton DeBoe and arrange to meet with him. She smiled at the reflection in the mirror. Yes, she would tolerate the puppy; she would play the contented wife and mother. And then she would be free to go off for a few days and enjoy whatever happened her way.

The image in the full-length mirror confirmed what she already knew. She was no beauty, true, but she was chic, fashionable, and women gave her admiring looks and told her that she "carried herself well." The new dinner dress, long and black, was a Paris original, for shop-made frocks, even those from her own boutique, were for the working class, not Anna Sterling. Hours of practice at her dressing table had provided an expertise with make-up, and the short, expensive hair cut flattered her large, long face. As she fastened the clasp on the beautiful pearl necklace, a thirty-first birthday gift from Jack, she silently declared the result almost lovely, certainly adequate.

Anna's jubilant mood endured throughout the evening. Dinner was pleasant, for only trivial small talk passed between the Sterlings. There was no reason to remark upon Jack's upcoming departure, so they chatted about the Lindbergh wedding and the recent arrest of Al Capone. Friends stopped at their table, men chomping on cigars and speculating about the end of prohibition, their wives fawning over Anna's newest Paris creation. It was a tiny utopia in a sea of trouble, a few hours free from the worries of galloping inflation, European conflict, a difficult daughter and an absent son. More satisfying, however, was the reprieve that the social occasions provided them, allowing Jack and Anna to forget that they were held captive in a passionless marriage, bound by an unspoken mutual contract.

By the time they arrived home from the club, Jack had re-thought his travel plans. The prospect of driving for days with a sullen, silent Mac unnerved him. He would take the train, he decided, where he could at the very least escape to the club car. They would more likely arrive home sooner by train, given the traffic and the need to stop to eat and sleep. Yes, this was a better idea. Jack was so preoccupied with pleasure in his new plan that he forgot entirely the note he had left for Anna on her dressing table.

After Anna had retired to her room, alone as usual, Jack tiptoed into Lillian's room. As he bent to kiss her warm cheek, a wet tongue assaulted him. He pulled back the covers to expose the welcoming "Buddy," nestled lovingly in his daughter's arms. She stirred and smiled at him.

"Hi, Papa."

"Hi, Diz. I'm going to take your friend downstairs now. I'll come up and get you very early tomorrow morning, if you'd like, and you and I will take the train to Vermont."

"Oh, Papa! Are we going to visit Mac?"

"Not exactly, dear. We are going to bring him home. But it's a secret, a big surprise."

He pressed an index finger to his lips and backed out of the room. At the door he thought he heard her say sleepily, "I love you, Papa."

Chapter 15

1930

It was a very bad year. The nation was still reeling from October's devastating crash, unemployment spiraled out of control, and the lines of the hungry grew longer and longer. Pittsburgh football fans mourned the loss of the Rose Bowl to Southern California, and on the anniversary of its tenth year, prohibition was hardly the cure-all that it was intended to be, as alcoholism soared and Americans died drinking contaminated bootleg whiskey. Gangsters freely opened fire on the streets of Chicago, and Swedish actress Garbo finally spoke in a film, requesting coincidentally, a shot of booze.

Although never a haven of peace and tranquility, the Sterling household reflected the general mood of the country, and tensions were stretched beyond compromise. Anna suffered tremendous financial loss, and she was able to salvage only one boutique, the original store that she had created ten years before. Unable to support a payroll, all of her seamstresses were laid off, including her partner Millie, who accepted unemployment in lieu of any financial responsibility in the bankruptcy. "Don't you give it another thought, Miss Anna," Millie said. "I still have most of the money I squirreled away when times were good. I'll be just fine." Jack's refusal to invest Millie's funds had been, ironically, a blessing after all, Anna conceded, and the fact that she had almost invested with DeBoe on Millie's behalf gave her a cold chill.

"Why couldn't you have come to me?" Jack asked her over and over again. Anna wondered what angered him more: the lack of confidence in him or the loss of the money. Her would-be lover, DeBoe, it seemed, had robbed her blind, throwing her funds into risky Florida real estate schemes with a keen eye to skimming off the top until it all came tumbling down. Anna fleetingly considered the purchase of a small handgun, the kind that fitted neatly into a ladies purse, when DeBoe gallantly saved her the trouble and threw himself off the roof of a twenty-story building.

Jack's portfolio, however, was quite safe. Anna couldn't understand how Jack had managed to not merely maintain, but gain and prosper. Jack's nonchalant "I told you so" attitude poured like salt into a wound, compounding their already-strained relationship.

Rachael was not a heavy investor, and what funds she did venture were protected by Jack's watchful eye, so her losses were minimal. It became a telling moment for Rachael, however, for she began to weigh her options about the future. She wanted to put some distance between Paul and Mac, who was now home to stay and more troublesome than ever. If she worked just a little while longer, saved her money seriously, she could afford to sever all ties to the Sterlings.

"Why is Paul being so hateful to Mac?" Liz asked Rachael. "He needs a friend, and Paul makes excuses to avoid him."

"I don't know, Liz. Have you asked Paul?"

"He says that Mac is different now. I know that he is, but he's still Mac. He and Buddy follow Paul around with the same look... 'please be my friend'!"

Rachael studied Liz and tried to remind herself that this child was only ten years old. *She has wisdom beyond her years*, Rachael thought. It must be all the books she so constantly reads. Rachael had her own concerns about Mac, but she could hardy discuss them with Liz. "I'll speak to Paul," she promised.

The discussion with Paul was unproductive, and Paul seemed uncharacteristically sullen and reluctant to share any information regarding Mac with his mother. "It's just not the same," he kept saying, "Mac is not the same." Rachael gave Paul her canned speech about God and love, and let it go at that. Rachael was not the same. Although still devote and almost saintly by any standard, Rachael was no longer the naïve pushover she had been when she presented herself to Anna for employment. "Tough times make tough people," she told herself when her all-loving conscience began to nag at her. "I must look to my own first" became her new mantra. At fourteen, Paul was on the verge of manhood, she knew, and soon there would be an entire new set of concerns.

As 1930 moved into spring, there was little to indicate that better days were ahead. America was officially "Depressed" and The Great Depression would hang on for nine long years. "So what?" Jack quipped, his cryptic humor amusing no one except himself. "It has been depressing around here for a lot longer than that!"

"The paper says that Babe Ruth's yearly salary is $80,000. That's more than Hoover makes," George advised Jack at their weekly luncheon.

"That makes sense. Ruth does more than Hoover."

George chuckled, and Jack thought that his friend was, at last, appreciative of his wit.

Actually George's funny bone was tickled by Jack's jibe at a Republican, a rarity that George never expected to live long enough to hear. The men's "arrangement" that had been instituted many years before continued to prove profitable for their "partnership."

Jack continued to bilk the poor, unsuspecting clients of the Savings and Loan, and George continued to use his judicial powers to legitimize the process.

"I have to agree with you this time, Jack. Those fools in Congress have sealed the fate of American industry with that damn Tariff Act. It certainly doesn't seem prudent to increase duties on imports when twenty-five percent of the country is out of work. By the way, how is Anna's shop doing these days?"

"She is covering her overhead, but doing it alone. That little dalliance in the market set her back ten years. She was mad enough to kill that bastard DeBoe! I love it when I'm right."

"Doris called her last week to ask her to play bridge. She is worried about Anna. Says she is very withdrawn, depressed."

"She'll snap out of it when she finds another project. At the moment she is obsessed with Mac. He's been back for almost a year now, and it has finally dawned on her that he is not her baby any longer. That fancy military school shook all the piss and vinegar out of that boy, and when his mamma wasn't home to hug him... well, let's just say that Diz and I are about the only members of the family who aren't depressed."

To the uninformed observer, Jack's remarks might have seemed cold and cynical. George sensed a deeper tone, one of sadness that Jack had never revealed before."I'm sorry, Jack," he told his old friend.

Embarrassed, Jack quickly changed the subject. "Bet big on Gallant Fox, George. My contact assures me that he will take the Triple Crown at Belmont."

Chapter 16

1931

"What is that you are reading?"

Lillian looked up from the book in the general direction of the voice. A boy stood on the wooden bridge that spanned the creek; at least she thought it was a boy, for the late afternoon sun blinded her view of the bridge. She was enjoying her solitude, the soft ripple of the water, the feel of the velvet grass under her bare toes. Maybe if she just ignored him, he would go away.

"Are you hard of hearing, little girl, or just rude? I asked you a question."

"Fitzgerald," she said, without looking up this time. "*The Great Gatsby*."

"His best," the voice said. "I read it last year. Liked it better than *The Beautiful and the Damned*. Kind of racy though, how old are you?"

Lillian's head came up and she glared at the intense burst of September sun on the bridge, the one that seemed to radiate from the form of the intrusive young man. "Old enough to read what I please! If you insist upon annoying me with stupid questions, please have the courtesy to step out of the sun. I'm getting a headache."

The figure on the bridge laughed and swung his body over the railing, dropping into the shallow creek with the ease of a dancer, in one quick, smooth movement. "I can do better than that, little lady." He landed easily on both feet, and slowly waded toward her, careful not to splash. He was quite tall, about six feet, she guessed. His skin was the color of chocolate, and he grinned down at her with what appeared to be an endless supply of dazzling white teeth. A few feet away, the intruder removed his cap and bowed deeply, sweeping his arm in comic exaggeration. Lillian giggled a rare expression of amusement that prompted her to press two fingers to her lips.

"Isaac Thomas Anderson, at your majesty's service," he grinned, "'I.T.' to my friends. And who might you be?"

"I 'might' be Alice in Wonderland," Lillian joked, tilting her head in a subtle, but openly flirtatious manner. "But, unfortunately, I am, in fact, Lillian Sterling. Since I have no friends, you may call me 'your majesty,' and I will call you 'It.'"

Isaac gestured that he sought permission to sit, and Lillian nodded, moving slightly to the left in invitation to sit beside her. He propped an elbow on his knee and regarded her for a long moment. "So," he said, "you are the princess, daughter of the lord of the manor, Mr. Sterling. I find it hard to believe that such a lovely young lady has no friends, but I am nevertheless delighted to make your acquaintance on such an auspicious afternoon!" He crossed his eyes and wiggled his ears, again invoking her laughter.

"Auspicious word, 'auspicious.'" Lillian was still smiling. "You are quite well spoken for a..." she trailed off, suddenly conscious that she was about to offend him.

"Negro?" Isaac asked. "Some of us actually read, you know."

"I'm sorry." She blushed. "I don't know what I meant to say."

If he was suspicious of her quick apology, he didn't let it show. She was obviously uncomfortable, and he had no wish to embarrass her further. His warm smile prevailed, and he jumped to his feet and grabbed a low-hanging tree branch.

"How do you know my papa?" Lillian asked. She wanted to change the subject, put Isaac at ease. She was surprised to find that she liked him, found the conversation easy.

"I will call you my friend, 'Princess Liz,'" he said. He began to lift himself to the branch, displaying strength in his upper torso. Lillian continued to look at him questioningly. "I work for the man," Isaac said suddenly. "I am what you might call 'one of the domestics.' Millie Anderson is my aunt; her husband and my father are brothers."

"Why have I never seen you before?" she asked.

"I work late at night, cleaning the kitchen, washing the cars. I can't miss school, but my family needs the money. We still have babies at home, and times are tough. I am not sure that your father knows that I even exist, and perhaps it is better that way."

"Why?"

Isaac was thoughtful. Should he tell her that her "papa" was a racist? Would she know the meaning of the word?

"Tell me about you." He hedged the question, better left unanswered. "Is this your 'special place'?"

How did he know that? "Yes."

"You come here to read, to be alone, to think. If something goes very wrong in your life, if you are hurt or sad, anyone looking for you would find you here, right?"

She looked at him suspiciously. "How do you know so much about me?"

He released the branch, dropped to her side again. "I am a student of life, Princess Liz. You are a very unhappy little girl."

"I will be eleven next week," she snapped. "Hardy a child!"

"I stand corrected. Please forgive me for overlooking your gray hairs, dear lady!" He took her hand and pulled her to her feet. "Walk with me awhile?"

They walked slowly, kicking at the crunching leaves along the bank of the creek. Isaac pulled some bread from his pocket and they fed the ducks. They talked about their favorite books, analyzing plots and characters like seasoned critics. They sang "The Wippenpoof Song," and Isaac taught her how to "bah, bah, bah." They shared dreams, and secrets, and fears. By the time the long shadows had moved into twilight, then darkness, they knew that they would be the best of friends, that they had somehow known each other forever.

"You had better go now," he said with concern. "Your brothers will be looking for you soon, and if they find us both, there will be trouble."

"'Brothers'?" Lillian laughed. "I only have one brother. His name is MacGregor."

"But I thought…" he stammered, "Who is the other boy that lives in your house?"

"Oh, you mean Paul." She smiled. "He is the housekeeper's son. Almost like a brother I guess, but not really. He's been there forever.

"Will you teach me to hang from trees?" she asked him.

"Of course, your majesty! Will you teach me to properly pronounce the King's English?"

He watched her cross the bridge and run across the massive front lawn of the estate. When she turned and waved, he walked away, satisfied that she was safely at home. It was a rare, unlikely friendship; this bond between the sad, lonely rich girl and the grandson of a slave.

Chapter 17

Winter 1931

Mother and son ate their dinner in silence. It was not an uneasy silence, more a testament to the degree of comfort each found in the other's presence. Both Paul and Rachael were lost in thought. Paul wished he could tell her about some of the feelings that were somehow taking over his life, had been plaguing him for almost two years. His health teacher had spoken privately to the sophomore boys about puberty, had shown the group illustrations that explained in clinical detail the male and female reproductive system. Satisfied that they now understood all that they would ever need to know, he moved on to the subject of circulation, skipping over the final two pages of the chapter that encouraged questions and discussion. And there were certainly no instructions about what one should do when one awakens in the middle of the night with one's penis in one's hand.

Rachael's mind was on the meager balance in her savings account. Her market losses could have been much worse, she knew, had she not been so conservative. She closed her eyes and whispered a grateful prayer, thanks be to God that while so many were so wanting, she and Paul at least had a warm home and a regular income. She watched him eat with his usual enthusiasm, sopping up chicken gravy with bread. At fifteen, he was almost six feet tall and blond like John. He was, in fact, so much the image of his father that it was as if John had never left her at all, for Paul was so near the age that John was when she had first known him. So beautiful, her beloved son. It made her smile to see him eat, although he was never full, and he remained so thin. But unlike so many other Americans, Rachael didn't fear that they would starve. As long as she could remain in Anna's good graces, there was always Helga's kitchen to fall back on.

"After dinner, you have homework to do," she reminded Paul as she cleared away the plates, and she then went to the main kitchen on another mission.

"There is some leftover roast beef," Helga told her. " I can slice some for you."

"Thank you, but I roasted a chicken. I will need a tray for Lillian, however.

She went to her room without dinner, and that girl is skin and bones. If I take something up to her, she just might eat."

The room was almost dark when Lillian answered Rachael's knock, shades and heavy drapes pulled against the cold November wind. Rachael had expected to find her reading. The food was quickly refused.

Finally Lillian asked, "Do people know when they are going to die?"

This incredible girl loved to catch her off-guard, Rachael decided, and delighted in asking outrageous questions. Rachael had learned how to play Liz's game, go along until meaning suddenly became clear.

"I suppose that some do," Rachael replied. "Do you know someone who is going to die?"

"I think so. Me."

Rachael repressed a smile. "Why do you think so?"

"My mother." As usual, Lillian's comment was direct, crisp, all-telling. Strange, Rachael thought, how Liz always refers to Anna as "my mother." It was a title, not a name, certainly not a term of endearment.

"She keeps taking me to see Dr. Powell, but he never says that there is anything wrong with me. I never know why I am there. And she is always checking my... my..." Lillian flushed.

"Your what?"

"My panties!" Liz 's face burned like fire, so humiliated was she to reveal this latest indignity even to Rachael. "What is she looking for in my panties, for Christ sake?"

"Take care with your language, young lady!"

"Sorry."

Rachael busied herself about the room, lit a fire in the massive fireplace. She cleared off a round piecrust table and set out the contents of the dinner tray. She was stalling, thinking about what she could tell the child that would explain Anna's behavior. This newest psychosis, Rachael suspected, was the result of the deep depression that Anna carried after the near-loss of her business empire and most of her financial holdings. Clayton DeBoe's suicide had taken a toll on Anna, as he had been one of her few friends. Rachael's mind began to creep toward the old suspicion that Clayton and Anna had perhaps been lovers, but she quickly pushed the thought away and turned to speak to Lillian.

"I don't really know, dear. Your mother has been under considerable strain of late, and sometime grownups act strangely. If I were you, I would just try to overlook some of the strange things that she says and does. It will pass."

Rachael picked up a novel from the nightstand. "Fitzgerald? I thought that British royal history was your latest phase. Is this appropriate for your age?"

Lillian laughed, a rare but pleasant sound, and Rachael smiled in response. They were seated at the table now, Lillian actually putting food into her mouth and chatting happily about her boredom, for the present, with the Tudors and Plantagenet Kings of England.

She talked on and on about Henry VIII, listing each and every one of his wives in remarkable detail. Rachael listened intently, chin cupped in her tiny hand, as if she were truly interested in the lesson. When the last of Liz's milk left a comical moustache on her lips, she confided, "I have a new friend. His name is 'IT.'"

Rachael laughed this time. "Does Buddy know about your new pet?"

"He is not a pet. He is a very grown-up boy, and he likes me. We walk in the woods and read poetry, and I may marry him someday."

"Oh, pardon me, miss! I obviously misunderstood. Do I know this wonderful young man... does he perhaps have another name?"

"Isaac Thomas Anderson. He is Millie's nephew. I call him 'IT' because those are his initials, get it?"

Rachael's heart skipped a beat and she took in a shallow breath. Where in the name of God were the parents of these children? Mac, she was relatively certain, was sexually active to the extreme, buzzing about town like a pollinating bee, building a shady reputation as "the stud." Paul was evidently trying out for "second runner up," hiding his girlie magazines under his mattress, as if Rachael would never think to look there. Now Lillian, barely eleven and as pure and innocent as the driven snow, was proclaiming her undying love for a black boy old enough to be dangerous. She was only the housekeeper, she reasoned. Why was it that she was apparently the only adult in the house that recognized the prevailing wind of pubescent disaster?

Too much to think about. "Good night, dear," she said as she hurriedly gathered up the dishes and left the room. She dropped the dinner tray off in the darkened kitchen and was almost out the door when she impulsively returned to grab Helga's bottle of brandy from the cupboard over the sink. Yes, she would most assuredly pray tonight, she decided. Then she would have a nip or two, just to take the edge off the day.

Chapter 18

Dr. Bennett walked through the hotel lobby with considerable apprehension.

He regretted that he had given in to Powell's insistence that they meet and discuss the Sterling family. He had ignored the warning signals that were exploding in his mind while he listened to the voice on the phone, Bennett had agreed to have lunch with his colleague here in the Richmond Hotel dining room.

"I have some questions about the girl Lillian," Powell had said. "I got your name from the birth record. You are listed as the physician in attendance."

Why was that, Bennett wondered, *when Anderson was the surgeon who delivered Lillian?*

Leonard recognized him immediately, a smallish, black-haired man who had more the look of an undertaker than physician. Powell stood at the table when Bennett approached, rubbing his hands together in obvious nervousness.

"So good of you to see me, doctor, I know how busy you are. We all are."

Leonard nodded, grunted, and shook hands. They ordered coffee and Powell got right to the point.

"I apologize for this imposition, Doctor. I understand your reluctance, but I am not able to treat the patient until I fully understand the problem."

Leonard was defensive. "Did I indicate that I was reluctant?"

Powell smiled. "I made that assumption, perhaps, because I suppose I would be."

"Why?"

Powell sighed and blew into his steaming cup. Bennett was not going to make this easy, that was obvious. Neither of them had the time to pussyfoot around this subject, so he would need to be more aggressive.

"Look, Leonard... may I call you Leonard?"

Bennett nodded.

"I'll take the plunge here and you can decide at that point. Jack Sterling requested my services when Lillian was two days old. Since you had been the former family physician, it didn't require much information to deduce that something had gone sour. I treat Anna and the children. Anna is a healthy woman, as far as I have been able to determine, for I seldom see her, except when she brings Lillian in, and there's the rub. She has that girl in my office every three or four weeks, demanding that I examine her genitals. Can you help me figure out why, because, to be perfectly frank, I am beginning to feel like a pervert."

Leonard narrowed his eyes and glared at Powell. What did this man want from him? If his professional conscience was so compromised, why did he allow a neurotic drug addict to dictate to him? Leonard didn't want to revisit his association with the Sterling family, and he had no particular interest in assisting Adam Powell. To what end? What difference could it possibly make?

"I'm afraid you have wasted your time, Dr. Powell. I have no information that could possibly shed any light on the problems of your patients." They were, after all, his patients, not Leonard's... any longer. He had escaped a major lawsuit by the skin of his teeth; he was not about to go down that road again!

"I understand," Powell said quietly. It was not acquiescence. However, it was not closure. It was a meaningful statement. He understood that Bennett's refusal to discuss Lillian and her mother was more than professional discretion. It was raw fear.

They lapsed into tense silence. Powell busied himself with his salad; Leonard picked at a roll and finished his coffee. He wanted to leave, just get up and say some sort of half-hearted, semi-cordial "goodbye" and get the hell out of there. Why then was he still sitting there, groping for something to say that might make him feel less like a jerk?

"What is it that you understand?" Bennett ventured.

Powell lay down his fork and looked him squarely in the eye. "I understand," he answered, "that you do not trust me and therefore you will not confer with me. There is really no reason why you should, certainly no obligation. Your reasons are your own, and I will not press. I am sincerely concerned about the girl. That's really all there is to it."

"What is she like... Lillian? Is she like her mother?"

Powell sighed again and rubbed at his eyes. "That's the point, Dr. Bennett. If Anna has her way, Lillian will be a duplicate copy, neurosis and all."

On guard again, Leonard made the accusation that had been nagging at him. "If Anna is still taking the codeine, which I assume that she is, you have to be the source. Why would you continue to prescribe medication that she doesn't need? Does Sterling pay you?"

For a split second, Powell's look was white hot angry. He wondered if his right hand would reach across the table far enough to sink Leonard's smug expression into his soup. A cooler mood prevailed, however. At least the good doctor was conversing with him at some level, and something productive may come of this meeting, if Powell could tolerate Bennett's condescending attitude.

"Of course he pays me! That's not the point. I have a lucrative practice… don't need his money. Anna Sterling has an unusually low tolerance for pain, and she suffers with migraine headaches. What was your treatment, doctor?"

Bennett flushed. "Codeine."

The tension passed, Powell continued. "I attempted several times to get her in for tests, perhaps a chronic sinus infection, I thought. I even considered the new wonder drug, penicillin. But she refuses to be concerned about her own health, or Mac's either for that matter. She is obsessed about Lillian, is a follower of that old quack, Pierce."

"The one who wrote 'the book'?"

"The very same. Some kind of nut case, that guy. He even built a 'menstruation museum,' of all things. She can recite every word of that old book, circa 1883, I think."

"I remember that we studied him in med school, sort of a 'how not to.' His views are considered radical and dangerous."

"So you now understand my problem."

"Yes. Tell me more about the girl. Does she resemble her mother?"

"Somewhat, but has the potential to be pretty, even striking. She is very thin, and all legs at this stage. I expect that puberty will bring out the best in her, physically speaking. Emotionally…"

"What is your greatest fear, Dr. Powell? What haven't you told me?"

Adam took a deep breath, and hesitated. "Confidentially?"

"Of course."

"Anna has hinted at various 'treatments,' ranging from female circumcision to complete hysterectomy. I feel like I'm dancing on hot coals. Can you help me, Leonard? Can you give me any reason for this woman to want to do this to her own daughter?"

Bennett sat back in his chair and regarded Powell for a long moment. No longer suspicious of Powell's agenda or motive, he wished he could help him. Something was very wrong with this case. How in God's name would such extreme measures serve as a 'treatment'? Treatment for what? Growing pains? He was stunned, speechless. He might venture a guess, but it would be only that, speculation.

"I suppose I owe you an apology, doctor. I recognize now that you are truly worried about the girl, and you seem to find yourself between the proverbial rock and hard place. I'm afraid I can't offer anything that might help, except perhaps, have you considered consulting with Mr. Sterling?"

"He won't return my calls. I went to his office once, but he was too busy to see me. I think he himself has an unnatural aversion to discussion of these topics. I have considered professional 'abandonment,' take my chances with the courts, but I have been unable to find another doctor to take the case. What will happen to Lillian then?"

"Unfortunately, my new friend, that is not within your control."

Chapter 19

It was almost dark when Mac and Paul came out of the woods. The setting sun cast long orange shadows on the driven snow, and the expanse of field in front of them looked endless. Mac carried both shotguns, while the pack on Paul's back held the day's kill, two large rabbits.

"Why don't you run up to the barn," Mac suggested, "and hitch the hay wagon to the tractor? Then you can come back for me."

"Why don't you kiss my ass?" Paul laughed.

"Such a bad mouth on such a good Catholic boy," Mac chided. "Does your mama know you talk that way?"

Paul ignored the question. He was beat. Up at 5 AM, they had hunted all day, trudging through knee-high snow up and down the mountain. Too tired for the usual friendly banter that was the hallmark of their relationship, he walked in silence, listening to the crunch of snow beneath his boots.

"Are you up to going into town tonight?" Mac prompted. "Maybe we can find those cute little gals who were so friendly the last time we visited Clarksburg."

"Don't you ever run down?" Paul laughed. "I'm so tired I can hardly walk, and you want to go get some action! I'm betting five dollars you won't be able to get it up."

"You lose, Buddy, cuz it's never down. See?" Paul glanced at the prominent bulge Mac pointed to and flushed. "Pay up." Mac extended his left hand, palm up and wriggled his fingers in Paul's grinning face.

Paul put a gloved finger into his mouth, bit down on the tip and pulled off the glove, freeing his hand to dig into his pocket until he had produced the bill. "That's my last five, asshole!"

"For a good cause, little brother, good cause. This sawbuck is our ticket to paradise. Tonight we can indulge our fancies in 'carnal knowledge,' just like the good book says."

"I keep reminding you that I am not your brother," Paul sighed. "And I'll thank you not to trouble the Bible."

"You sure are in a pissy mood today. We'd better stop at Shorty's and procure a pint of his homebrew, or you won't be any fun at all. Then we'll go looking for the girls. Can't bring them up the mountain this time, though,

Dad's due here early tomorrow."

Paul was thoughtful and somber. He wished he could, just once, say "no" to Mac. He sincerely doubted that his problem stomach could tolerate any more of that rot-gut whiskey that the locals called "moonshine," and he had no desire to roll around with another one of West Virginia's homespun hussies. But the shame and discomfort of a night on the town with Mac wasn't nearly as bad as the argument that was sure to follow his refusal. Mac would berate him, call him a sissy, pout, and turn mean. It was just easier to give in, go along. He supposed he was a coward.

"It's probably just as well that way." Mac was still making plans. "A little hooch, a little 'slap and tickle,' then home early. Dad will be pushing his big Buick up the driveway at dawn, and I'm not packed. How 'bout you?"

"Didn't bring much," Paul answered. "Might as well leave the skis and the hunting gear here, since there's not much snow in Richmond."

The two-week holiday break had passed quickly for the boys, alone at the farm for the first time, with only Billy to cook and "chaperone." They had successfully squelched their laughter at that parental announcement, for they knew that all Billy would require was a non-ending supply of good bourbon and they'd hardly know he was there. Two glorious weeks away from school and mothers. Two weeks to ski Canaan Valley, hunt the copious woods and "taste the local flavors," as Mac had so eloquently put it.

The barn was fifty feet ahead now, and Paul wanted to get out of the wind. "Hurry up," he told his companion, "I'm freezing."

Mac bathed and changed into fresh clothes while Paul cleaned both rabbits. Mac cleaned off the Chevy truck, the only vehicle that would insure their return if there was a fresh snowfall, and warmed up the engine while Paul dressed. They stopped at Billy's door and listened, smiling at each other when they heard loud snorts and snores on the other side.

"Hungry?" Mac inquired as they descended the mountain.

"Starved!"

"We'll stop at the diner, maybe can get our pint there too."

"Why isn't Prohibition in effect in this state?" Paul asked.

"It is, silly. It's just that nobody pays any attention. Just like home... you don't see Jack going without his scotch, do 'ya?"

Paul passed on that question. He had another matter on his mind. "Are you going after that girl again...? You know, the one you did last fall?"

"Sure, why not?"

"No reason, it's just that she might think you are going to marry her or something."

Mac hit the brakes and doubled over, laughing. "Marry her? You've got to be kidding. She's a good time, that's all. Convenient. What's wrong with you?"

"Nothing. I just wondered." Paul slipped into silence and the truck resumed its rather rapid descent. He wanted to tell Mac to slow down, for he could feel the tires as they gripped for traction, then slid again on ice. But he was lost in thought, gone back to that night last October when they had picked up those two girls and parked Mac's car on a lonely logging road. Paul's face had burned when he sobered enough to realize what was happening in the front seat, and then "his girl," what's her name, was all over him, pulling and tugging at his shirt and pants and then... and then he had forfeited his virginity to someone whose name he couldn't remember.

The experience had been less than euphoric, but Mac was so damn happy about it that Paul pretended enthusiasm. Both young men were shaken, however, when they arrived at the farm late the next day, home from a day of horseback riding, and found Marilee and Shirley sitting with Billy on the front porch, sipping beer and laughing like welcome old friends. Mac's eyes wandered off, looking for the Buick, and he was relieved when he did not see his father's car. Jack and George Steinburger had evidently gone off on an adventure of their own, probably golf.

"Well it's 'bout time," Marilee had purred at Mac, rising from the wicker rocker to wrap her arms around him. "We just didn't want to wait any longer for your call, handsome boy, so we came on up here to get us some more of that 'Yankee lovin.'"

"Swell," Mac said dryly. He looked at Paul, a look that said, 'What do you want me to do?' then at Billy, who was grinning. The party of four bedded down in the barn that warm October night, while the men slept and snored soundly in the house. The girls were abruptly hustled off in the pre-dawn gray morning.

"Y'all come back now," Paul joked as the battered old pickup sped away, billowing clouds of gray smoke that almost entirely covered the waving occupants.

****

The boys exited the diner by the back door, having parked the pickup in the alley, rather than on the street. Paul didn't know why, but he never questioned Mac's decisions. Perhaps his friend had seen too many westerns, where the hero left in a great hurry, leaping to his horse from a second-story window. As they stepped into the truck, both boys were grabbed from behind, Mac thrown up against a brick wall and Paul sent sprawling, face down, on the gravel surface of the alley.

First to his feet, Paul came up blindly swinging his arms at the unseen attacker. Mac sat, stunned, peering into the cold darkness at the huge outline of a man standing over him. "What the hell is your problem?" Mac demanded, wiping a trickle of blood from his lip. Paul was lifted off his feet by his collar, carried swiftly by two assailants to Mac's side of the truck, and deposited next to his friend.

"You rich northern boys think you can have anything you want," a voice growled. "We're here to teach you otherwise. You been messin' with my sister, fancy man, and Ma says she's probably pregnant. That means you pay. Plenty!"

Mac shook his head, trying to grasp what was happening here. For a fleeting moment he regretted his soft life, for even his six years at the military academy, with all that talk of warfare and such, had not prepared him for this. Perhaps he came home too soon, should have finished the program, learned how to fight. Maybe the soldier boys could have taught him how to get up and beat the shit out of this goon.

Both boys were pulled to their feet at once, like puppets. They suddenly found themselves inside the truck, where they listened carefully to the specifics of the "plan." "We're gonna play, rich boys," said the head goon.

"Ten minutes head start, just to be sportin,' then we're comin' after y'all, pound your playboy asses into the ground, and maybe, just maybe, we'll decide you can live. Gentlemen, start your engine." The truck doors slammed in unison, and as quickly as they had appeared, the night visitors disappeared.

Paul was trembling. His head hurt badly, and he wanted to throw up. He wondered if he might have a concussion, given the symptoms. Mac sat very still behind the wheel of the truck, staring into the blackness, a stream a red liquid dripping off his chin.

"Move this thing, man!" Paul shouted at him. "Let's get the hell out of here!"

Mac jumped and leaned forward, obedient to the command, started the ignition and pulled the gearshift into reverse as he stomped down hard on the gas pedal. The truck lurched backward, and Mac was forced to brake. "Get out," Paul said. "I'll drive."

Mac didn't move, so Paul opened his door, moved quickly to the driver's side and pushed him across the leather seat. The truck was stalled now, so

Paul let it set while seconds ticked by. He reached across to lock Mac's door, then his own, while watching the mirrors for another assault. He had never known this kind of fear, bone-chilling terror. These guys weren't kidding; they wanted to hurt the boys from Indiana. What little Paul knew of the area confirmed in his mind that there was no recourse to the "law," due to vast rural expanse and the probability that "boys will be boys" mentality ruled here. Where would they go to find "the law," anyway? With or without help, where would they go?

The engine responded to Paul's silent pleading, and he drove the Chevy to the end of the alley, stopped and looked both ways. Right? Or left?

Chapter 20

"Go on," George prompted. "What happened next?"

Jack took a deep breath. He had never been a good storyteller, had never before captivated an audience, even an audience of one. He wouldn't hurry, he would draw it out, make it last.

George looked pained at the pause. Jack continued, slowly. "Well, neither one of the boys knew the area very well. This was only their second time at the farm, and when they were there in late October, you and I were with them, remember?"

"Do you mean to tell me," George was incredulous, "that those two played in the barn with local girls while we were in the house?"

"Apparently. I guess we missed all the fun. But if you will recall, I offered recreation. You begged off and went to bed."

"Bullshit! 'Gin rummy,' you said. I heard nothing about an orgy."

Jack was teasing his friend and enjoying the result. "The business with the girls was not planned, and I certainly would have put a quick stop to it, had I known." Jack was dead serious now, and continued to relate the boy's story.

"Paul drove around for awhile, but he wasn't sure where he was or where he was going. Mac had done most of the driving, but he was no help... in shock, I guess. The Walker boys were right on their tail, and gas was running low. Paul tried to remember if he had enough cash to buy fuel, but he knew that the pickup behind him would follow him wherever he went, and he didn't like the idea of getting out of his truck and going around with them again. The snowfall heavier, the roads icier, Paul headed up the mountain as a last resort. He gunned the engine up the drive, grabbed Mac and ran like hell for the house."

"Did he make it?"

"Yes, but barely. One of the Walkers wedged his foot in the back door and came in, big as you please, right behind Paul, who by this time had remembered the loaded 12 gauge he had left in the pantry. Walker slowed down considerably when he looked down that barrel."

"Great God Almighty! Paul didn't shoot him, did he?"

"No, of course not! I imagine the kid was peeing his pants at that point, but it was gutsy, nonetheless."

"Gutsy enough to get him arrested for attempted murder, anyway," said the judge."But I suppose West Virginia takes a lighter view than us 'Yankees.'"

"Nobody got hurt. Billy came in and talked Paul down, not that the boy needed much persuasion. I got the impression from Billy that the Walkers were bluffing, just playing with the boys, and the gun business brought everyone to their senses."

"So that's it? The bullies went home and Paul and Mac had a good laugh, I imagine."

"Not exactly. The whole experience had a sobering effect on the boys, I am pleased to report. Billy, it turned out, was the hero of the day."

"Billy?"

"When he came downstairs, the scene was pretty tense. Paul was wild-eyed and waving the shotgun around, Mac was scared shitless, and the Walker boys were worried. One of them asked Billy if he was Jack Sterling, and he answered that he was indeed!"

George hooted loudly, laughed harder than he had ever laughed in his life. Jack smiled and waited patiently while George enjoyed the moment, until George had composed himself and wiped tears from his eyes.

"I suppose I don't need to ask why you find that so amusing!"

"Continue," George said between chuckles. He tried to force a serious look, then began again to indulge in gales of uncontrolled laughter.

'One of your boys has gone and gotten my sister in the family way,' Walker told Billy. 'This mess is gonna cost some money, so I guess you pay.' Billy took the gun from Paul and sent the boys upstairs. Then he wrote the Walker brothers a sizeable check."

"What?" George exclaimed. "He actually paid blackmail to those thieves?"

"'Your sister,' Billy told them, 'if she is indeed your sister, is hardly a spoiled maiden. She is rather easy with her favors. She and her companion spent a few hours here with me, in fact, last fall. I'm sure that if I made some local inquiries, I could confirm that the miss in question is widely known for her friendly nature.' Having made his point, Billy wrote the check and they left in a hurry."

"Incredible!" George said quietly, shaking his head. "So how much did this little drama cost you, Jack? And how in the world did they ever mistake Billy for you?"

"He is very light-skinned, 'passes' all the time. As for the cost, not one red cent! Billy had the forethought to write the check on the old household account... been closed for two years!"

"Clever man, Billy. I hope you had the decency to give him a raise?"

Jack puffed on his cigar and smiled. "I 'took care' of him," he answered. "Even offered an additional incentive if he would court that Anderson woman and get her out of my life."

"Just brothers under the skin, eh, Jack?"

Jack's smile faded quickly. "Don't push it, George!"

Chapter 21

1932

Rachael was listening very intently to Paul's explanation of his science project. These were the moments she cherished, the times alone in their cozy kitchen, sipping hot chocolate and talking, sometimes long into the night. She allowed her mind to wander from his "rods and wires," just to look at him and reflect upon her joy. So handsome he was! So like his father, taller maybe, over six feet, but his heavy blond hair and fine facial features were John's.

"I know I can win, Mom," he was saying. "If I can just get the transmitter right. But I need a few more things from the hardware store."

"My purse is on the sideboard." She smiled. "Take what you need."

It was still early, not yet seven on this Friday morning, May 13,1932. As usual, Rachael had attended Mass at dawn, accompanied this time by her son, in remembrance of his father's birthday. An announcement from the pulpit had saddened the small group and Rachael and Paul had stayed to say the rosary. "The body of the Lindbergh baby was found yesterday," the priest said. "We must all pray for God's strength, for the family, for all of us."

Rachael put down her knitting and closed her eyes, silently praying for Anne Lindbergh. A knock on the back door interrupted her thought, and she rose to find an excited Emily peering though the window.

"Have you heard?" Emily gasped. "They found that poor child. Oh, imagine the horror of it!"

"Yes, Father McKay announced it at church," Rachael answered. "Sit down, dear. Would you like chocolate or tea?"

"Nothing, thanks. Good morning, Paul, how's the project coming along?"

"Almost finished." The boy grinned.

Emily turned to Rachael. "There's something else," she whispered. "I went upstairs just now to waken Miss Lillian, and..." Emily glanced in Paul's direction. He was watching her, evidently interested in the conversation. Emily seemed reluctant to continue, and Rachael was confused.

"What is it, Emily?" Rachael prompted. It was too early for mysteries, and Emily was often overly dramatic. "Is she sick?"

"Not sick, exactly," Emily continued. "Her bed is soaked in blood. Her 'time of the month' is upon her and it's a mess, I can tell you!"

Rachael shot a quick look at Paul. He had smiled slightly and discreetly moved away to the desk in the dining room, finding sudden interest in a textbook. What a gentleman he was, Rachael thought. "Did you get her what she'll need?" Rachael asked Emily. "Belt and pads?"

"I tried, but couldn't find anything." Emily was near tears. "She is very upset, yelled at me to get out! I took the linen and left her with a towel."

"I'll go. Paul, I need you to go to the drugstore as soon as it opens."

"Give me a list," he called back. "I can go early and bring it back before school."

The relieved Emily gone, Rachael left the apartment and hurried up the back staircase to Lillian's room. Hearing no reply to her knock, she tried the door. Locked.

"It's Rachael, dear. Let me in."

"Go away!" The child was crying, a frightened, pitiful cry.

"Everything will be all right, honey, just let me in so I can help you."

"No one can help me," Lillian wailed. "I'm dying."

Rachael stifled a laugh. She tried to remember how it had felt to be twelve and bleeding from strange places. Where was Anna? A girl needed her mother at a time like this! Oh, yes, Anna was in New York, on a buying trip. Jack? No matter. Men were no help. She would have to do this alone.

It required a full half-hour of quiet pleading, but the door finally swung open and Lillian collapsed into Rachael's arms, sobbing.

"Now, now," Rachael cooed. "First, a hot bath. Then we'll pad you and get you dressed for school."

Lillian had stopped crying, but she still sniffled, wiping her nose on the back of her trembling hand. "I can't go to school!" she protested. "Everyone will know."

Rachael handed her a hankie from her sleeve. "No one will know," she said quietly. "Even if they did, so what? It's just a natural part of life; girls and women do it every month, for years and years. Better get used to it."

"I'll never get used to it! I don't want to be a woman if that means I have to do this! Besides, Mother said I should stay in bed and take the pills she gave me."

"What pills?"

Lillian moved away from her and walked across the large room to the dresser. Large droplets of blood trailed behind her, staining the Oriental rug. Opening the top drawer, she produced a bottle and handed it to

Rachael."Anna Sterling" the label said, "take one every eight hours for pain, not to exceed three in 24 hours." In large letters was inscribed the word: "WARNING."

Rachael quickly dropped the bottle into the pocket of her skirt. She put both hands on Lillian's thin shoulders and turned her to the bathroom. The girl resisted, attempted to hold her place, but Rachael pushed forward in desperate insistence. "I'm not supposed to bathe, either," said Lillian, "or wash my hair or get my feet wet. Give me back my pills!"

Rachael was angry now, almost as angry as she had been on the day John died. How dare that woman give Lillian narcotics? Rachael had long known of Anna's drug dependency, but to drag the girl down the same path! Rachael had been silent too long, she decided; she would not stand by while more lives were ruined. Anna's coolness toward Rachael was one thing, her disregard for her own destitute father was another. But this!

Lillian made a frantic lunge at Rachael's skirt pocket and when Rachael moved quickly away, the material tore. Rachael restrained the girl's arms, and was maneuvering into a more controlled position when Lillian's right foot caught Rachael mid-thigh, sending her sprawling. While Rachael struggled to her feet, Lillian headed for the bathroom where she could lock the door.

Rachael led with her shoulder against the closing door, wedging her already-bruised right thigh between door and jam. Outweighed by thirty-five pounds, Lillian finally lost the standoff, reeling across the bathroom and sliding down the far wall like a rag doll. Before she could scramble to her feet, Rachael was on her, pinning her slim arms against the wall while she straddled the girl's legs.

For a moment, they simply panted. "You have two choices," Rachael breathed. "You may continue this loathsome conduct, in which case I will call upon the men of the house to assist you with your bath, or you may stop immediately and put your ass in that tub. Either way, you are going to have a bath, because, quite frankly, you smell like a goat!"

After another moment, Lillian nodded slightly, her tear-streaked face screwed into another onset of serious crying. Rachael released the arms, one at a time, and rose slowly, watching as Lillian's head fell to her chest in uncontrolled sobs. She began to fill the tub, moving cautiously around the room to gather soap, face cloth, and towel, never taking her eyes from the pathetic child on the floor. When the bath was ready, Rachael extended her hand to Lillian, who accepted it almost gratefully, allowing herself to be lifted to her feet.

"You are a young woman now," Rachael said softly. "You can undress and take your own bath." When the door closed behind her, Rachael leaned heavily against it, held her breath for a few seconds, then inhaled deeply.

"Rachael?"

"Yes?"

"I'm sorry."

"I know you are, dear. I will be out here when you are finished."

Chapter 22

1933

It was beyond belief. Paul stared at the letter, afraid to read it again for fear that this time the final line would read "April Fool!" It certainly looked official, however, on Harvard letterhead and signed by the president of the university. But how could it be true?

He was little more than an average student, and he had not participated in sports because of his lingering health problems. Even the award he had won last year in the science fair would not qualify him for admission to Harvard. It was a cruel mistake, he decided, and he returned the letter to his pocket and went to look for Mac.

"Hey, Paul!" Mac called to him from the steps of the library, where he was, as usual, surrounded by admirers, primarily female. "Great news, huh?"

Paul approached slowly, confused. "What is?" he asked Mac.

"Aren't you the cool one? Are you trying to pretend that you didn't receive a letter from Mr. Preston about your admission to college?"

"How did you know that?"

"Because I got the same letter, you silly boy. Looks like we'll be roommates."

Paul felt his face flush and his pulse quicken. He didn't understand why he felt as if he would choke if he didn't flee immediately. "I need to go, right now." Paul hurried away from the coed "court" and hopped on the nearest cross-town bus. It was all so overwhelming. He needed desperately to talk with his mother.

"Must have been something I said," Mac laughed. He nuzzled the girl next to him while another pressed up against his broad back. He was truly the reigning king of the Richmond Central set, he told himself and no doubt his good looks and charisma would serve him just as well on the college scene.

At almost the same moment, Jack sat with Rachael and Anna in his office, reading to them the contents of his letter from Harvard University. Never had he been more proud of himself. Against the odds, Jack had called in almost every favor due him, and spent hours, days and weeks on the acceptance of "his boys" to the hallowed halls of Harvard. Then there had been the contributions. "Who says that money can't buy happiness?" he joked as he held the letter over his head and sent it fluttering down slowly to the desktop.

"I don't understand," Rachael protested. "Why did Paul's acceptance letter come in your name? I am his legal guardian, his parent."

Both Sterlings stared at her, surprised at her bold statement. This was the new Rachael, and Anna, at least, liked her even less than the old one. Jack's mental antennae went up, something was going on here, and Rachael was not reacting as he had expected. He answered softly, but with a condescending tone. "Because, my dear, I paid Paul's tuition, that's why."

Anna's eyes widened and she struggled for control. "And why is that?" she asked.

Rachael and Jack exchanged glances. Without warning, they realized, they were now in the position of explaining their long-ago agreement, one that Rachael had written off. Well, she would not be the one to bring it all up, Rachael decided, and she rose and quickly left the room without another word. They could discuss this later, after the fallout.

Anna stared at him silently, without blinking. He considered his options, and then spoke, "I made a promise to Rachael when the boys went to school in Vermont, years ago. I promised to secure Paul's education. I always keep my promises."

"Oh, how well I remember! Like the one you made to keep yourself 'only unto me'?"

"Don't start with that crap again, Anna. Stop pretending that you have a care where I sleep or with who."

"With 'whom,' dear." She was spoiling for a fight and he knew it. It seemed such a waste of time and energy, so he would silence her, bully her, shout if he had to, but he would have the last word.

"I would think that you would be more appreciative, considering that I passed on the opportunity to embarrass you during your little fling with DeBoe."

"What are you suggesting?"

"I suggest nothing. The facts speak for themselves. You left town very suddenly, missing the homecoming of your precious son, and spent several days in a New York hotel with your broker, the one that 'broke' you." Jack had to chuckle at his little joke; Anna was not amused.

It was not a pleasant memory, that week almost four years before, but Jack had now forced her to replay it all in her mind. Business matters had delayed her departure for New York, so she was unable to return by Saturday as she had planned. It was Jack's fault that she had missed Mac's arrival; if he had simply told her about it, she would never have gone to New York in the first place.

She had taken a taxi from Grand Central, and checked into her suite at the Plaza. Clayton DeBoe had not been difficult to find, and yes, he was free for dinner. Her hair freshly coifed, she had looked rather stunning that night as they drank expensive wine and talked about Anna's extensive investments.

"You are, no doubt, a very wealthy man, Clayton. How fortunate that you have all this money to play with," Anna had subtly teased him. She was fishing for information... just how rich was he?

Clayton smiled and offered her the dinner check for her signature. "I do all right," he answered evasively. What was the lady up to now?

Anna pulled a cigarette from a silver case and held it for Clayton's lighter. She cupped his hand with hers in a suggestive manner, and Clayton smiled knowingly, for there was no breeze in the room. It was quite obvious to him that she was flirting... clumsily, of course, but flirting nonetheless. "You do much better than 'all right,'" she said. "The word about town is that you could have just about anything you want. Or anyone."

Great God in heaven, she was making a pass! He hadn't been sure at first, but by now there was no mistaking the "come on" look, the casual touching, oh, this was a woman on the prowl, all right, and he was in her sights. He must handle this one very carefully, or he could lose a great deal of money. Months, years in fact, of flattery, manipulation, playing the fool for this dreadful creature was almost over. Anna's signature on the Florida land-purchase contracts were the last phase in DeBoe's master plan. He would then have all or almost all of her funds, and he would be on his way to South America.

"You seem preoccupied, dear Clayton. Shall we order another bottle of wine and continue this discussion in my room?"

There it was. The final challenge. He had to think quickly, get out of this mess before all was lost. His mind fanned though some of the excuses he had used in the past, for he had found himself the object of unwelcome desire more than once. While he was not normally averse to playing the love game, there was no way on God's green earth that he was going to jump under the sheets with Anna Sterling. He smiled sweetly, preparing himself for the best performance of his life.

"My darling, wonderful Anna." He cupped her hand in both of his and pressed his warm lips to her sweaty palm. "I have loved you for so long, dreamed about the day when we might be together like we are now. How would I ever be able to tell you…?" Tears welled at the corners of his large brown eyes and he looked like a man in agony.

"Tell me what, dear?"

"Terrible, unspeakable war! I often wish I had died in France, along with the rest of me… my manhood, Anna. I can never be a husband to you, and the reality of that fact breaks my heart."

He continued to cry as she sat riveted to her chair, staring at him in disbelief. She wanted to comfort him, tell him that it didn't matter. Oh well, what the hell? When she had her own money she wouldn't need him anyway, anymore than she would need Jack.

Vindicated and off the hook, DeBoe was grateful that Anna was not a particular fan of the cinema, lest she recognize the scene.

****

"Are you listening to me, Anna? You seem miles away." Jack's abrupt question brought her back to the discussion of the boys, and Harvard.

"I'm sorry. What did you say?"

"I said that we will take the boys to the club for dinner tonight to celebrate. Tomorrow you can call the caterer and make your usual arrangements for the party of the century. Rumor has it that prohibition will end soon, perhaps even before the summer is over. Everyone will want to attend. You'll probably get your picture in the paper, on the society page. You can be proud and happy, Anna. I have arranged for your son to go to Harvard."

"Yes," she said absently. "Yes, proud and happy."

Chapter 23

1933

"Dinner at the club," a regular ritual for the Sterlings, was agony for Rachael and Paul. Jack would accept no excuse, everyone was expected to attend the celebration, and Rachael was in tears as she sorted through her limited choice of appropriate dresses. At the last moment, Anna reluctantly offered something from her collection of expensive frocks and Jack's remark about the difference in their sizes only managed to aggravate Anna's sour mood.

Lillian flatly refused to go, pleading a headache. "Besides," she told her father, "this night is for the boys."

Jack was in his glory as his party made their entrance, and as they were ushered to their usual table, club members greeted them with enthusiasm. The announcement of the boys' admittance to Harvard spread like wildfire in the Sterling's social circles and Jack was "the man of the hour." Anna, of course, was impeccably dressed and bejeweled, so all that was left for her to do was to play the admiring wife and get quietly drunk. Rachael was completely out of her element, knew no one at the exclusive club, and picked at her food, anticipating a sleepless night of indigestion. Paul kept tugging at the knot in his tie, wishing he were somewhere else... anywhere else.

The ordeal finally over, Mac came to Paul's rescue. He requested taxi fare, and the boys left the adults sipping brandy and went home early. Mac had plans, big plans.

"I need money, darling baby sister," he whispered to Lillian when she opened her bedroom door. "I know you have a banker's stash." Mac's allowance was often spent before he received it. Lillian carefully saved hers in a cigar box under her bed, and the box was stuffed with twenties. It was one of the little jokes she shared with her father, as Jack always handed her a crisp, new twenty dollar bill each time she approached him with a complaint regarding Anna.

"You still owe me for my bike," she scolded him as she handed him a twenty. "I can't believe you actually sold it to buy booze."

"Hey, times are tough. The old man will buy you another one. Thanks, doll." He brushed her cheek with warm lips and rushed out to join Paul in the new yellow convertible, an early graduation gift to Mac from Jack.

"When did he give you the keys?" Paul asked.

"He didn't. But he left them on the hall table for me," Mac laughed.

They had changed from suits and ties to corduroy slacks and light jackets. Armed with twenty dollars, a full tank of gas, and hormones in overdrive, Mac and Paul set out on yet another night on the town.

****

The telephone rang at 1:56 AM, but Jack didn't hear it. He was snoring loudly on the leather couch in the library, dead to the world. Anna had turned off her phone and taken two pain pills, followed by two sleeping tablets for good measure.

The telephone rang again at 2:16 AM. No answer.

At 3:05 AM, after an additional three-phone attempt, two uniformed police officers pounded insistently on the service entrance door of the Sterling mansion, having received no response at the front door. Helga stumbled out of her room, her robe open to expose a filmy nightie. She stared at the men through bleary eyes, slow to comprehend the message.

"I just told you what the problem is," one officer growled. "There has been some sort of accident. The hospital has been trying to call, but there is no answer. I don't have any other details."

Helga let them into the kitchen, and hurried off in search of Rachael.

Very soon the household came starkly alive, a beehive of confused activity. Rachael hurried in circles, clutching her rosary with one hand while she dressed with the other. Emily ran upstairs to arouse Anna, while Helga pushed at the lump called Jack on the couch like she was kneading a pile of bread dough. Richmond's men in blue remained just inside the kitchen door, standing by, to assist however they might.

Jack entered the kitchen, his friar's cap of thin hair standing comically on end. He was semi-dressed, in trousers and sleeveless undershirt, barefoot. "What happened?" he addressed the policemen.

"We don't know for sure, Mr. Sterling. Your son," the officer consulted the report he was holding,"your son, Mac, and his companion were involved in a traffic accident. They have been transported to St. Rita's hospital. Would you like us to drive you?"

"No." Then he added, "Thank you, no. I'll drive myself. Where is Anna?" He scanned the room with a wild look. There was no one there to answer him. "Where the hell is everyone?" he bellowed. Rachael came running down the back hallway, Lillian just behind her.

"Go back to bed," Jack ordered the girl. "Rachael can ride with me. Where is your mother?"

"Out cold. Helga and Emily are up there making enough noise to wake the dead. I'm coming with you."

"You two ride with them." Jack pointed to the cops. "Then they can bring you back home. Let's go!"

"Papa, put your shoes on," Lillian said as she and Rachael exited the door with the policemen.

Jack was there first, running every red light in the city. He didn't bother to turn off the ignition, leaving the car to idle at the Emergency Room door as he dashed into the building. Personnel attempted to stop him, but he ran to every cubicle, pulling curtains aside to stare at every occupant. Rachael and Lillian found him turning around and around in the center of the corridor. "I can't find them, " he exclaimed, as near tears as he had ever been in his entire life.

"Mac is in the waiting room," Rachael said quietly. Jack and Lillian turned to go in the direction of Rachael's nod, but she didn't move. "Where is Paul?" she whimpered.

Lillian left her father's side and went to Rachael. "Come with us," she said gently, slipping an arm around Rachael's shoulder. "Mac will know where Paul is."

Mac sat with elbows on his knees, head in hands. He was visibly shaken, but otherwise unharmed.

"What the hell happened?" Jack shouted at the boy.

Mac pulled his hands away and looked at the trio standing a few feet in front of him. He was pale, his cheeks tear-streaked; he seemed confused, unaware of the identity of these people. "Mama?" he said, and he began to sob.

Anxiety, frustration and despair were painfully evident on the faces of Rachael and Lillian. They wanted Mac to tell them what they so desperately needed to hear, that Paul was all right. Jack's face ran the extreme from ashen to scarlet. "Your mother is not here, mama's boy! She's at home, sleeping off a drunk, and she won't be here to coddle you this time. This time you'll have to act like a man! Now you tell me... where is Paul?"

Mac couldn't hear Jack, because he was chanting louder, "Mama, Mama, Mama." Jack's short arm swung in a backhanded reach and caught the boy at his temple, sending him sprawling across the leather sofa. He landed on his knees where he remained, blood and spittle mixing with the thick mucus that streamed from his nostrils. Jack looked down at his clenched fist. Should have hit the boy opened-handed, he thought, for the side of Mac's face was already a strange color.

"Papa!" Lillian exclaimed as she grabbed for her father's arm. Once again, he underestimated his own strength. Because he was short and stocky, he gave the impression of softness, while he was actually quite well built and muscular. He tried to intercept Lillian's contact, but his body betrayed his intent, and she too was sent reeling across the room.

"Diz..." he began, but Rachael was screaming and several large uniformed men were upon him, pinning him against the wall. Suddenly the small waiting room was overrun with large, excited men, shouting instructions. The white-coated male nurses and interns focused on Mac, pulling him to his feet and rushing him through the doorway to the Emergency Room across the hall. He signaled that he could walk, but fainted before they had reached the corridor and had to be carried. A young man gently assisted Lillian to a chair on the far side of the room. "Are you alright, Miss?" he inquired. She nodded, crying quietly.

A large, horse-faced nurse pulled Rachael backward and away from the area where Jack was forcibly seated. "Come with me, please, Mrs. Unger," she said. "I will take you upstairs and you can be with Paul."

Rachel stopped breathing when she looked down at him, for she was sure that he was dead. When her lungs demanded that she take in air, she gasped, and grabbed the side of the bed for support. Rachael would never forget the date. It was April 19, 1933... the day that he was accepted at Harvard.

Chapter 24

Margaret Powell put the telephone back in the cradle and frowned. She detested lying. Only Adam could induce her to do this thing, and she promised herself this would be the last time, even for him. She walked into the living room, where she found her physician husband stretched out on the sofa with his favorite cat, the Persian Shasta.

"Don't ask me to get any further information," she warned him. "Even your nurse friend at the hospital is getting suspicious. She just asked me where in Alaska you went on your fishing trip."

Adam ignored the confrontational tone. "Who is the surgeon?" he asked. "Drake. Is he good?"

"Very competent. The best St. Rita's has, actually. Paul will be fine."

"First of all, you can't know that for sure. Secondly, Adam, why are you doing this? Hiding from your patients? It just isn't like you. Just go down there, you know you want to. Go down there and be a doctor."

"I know that I have disappointed you. I'm so sorry, honey, truly I am. I can't do it anymore, not even for Paul and Rachael. He's in good hands, my being there would make no difference. It's not something I can fix. The boy didn't skin his knee or even break his leg. His head went through a windshield, for Christ's sake. It's beyond me. Besides, I just can't deal with that family anymore."

"And you won't tell me why."

"Can't."

Mrs. Powell threw her hands up in exasperation and stomped out of the room. Nothing could be that bad, she thought. Adam was a good doctor, a caring man who worked long hours and stayed awake nights worrying about his patients who were sleeping. The telephone rang again. Probably the hospital again, or the office. What was she supposed to tell them? "The doctor is having a breakdown," she mumbled to herself as she reached for the phone. "He's playing with the cat and can't be disturbed."

Seconds later Margaret reappeared at the archway. "Adam, there's a Leonard Bennett on the phone. He wants to speak with you."

At first he thought she must have been joking. Behind her slim hips he could see the receiver lying on the hall table. "Tell him I went fishing."

146

"Tell him yourself, asshole! I am not your secretary; I am your wife. For now, anyway. It is only seven o'clock in the morning, so if you will kindly arrange for someone else to take your phone calls, I'll go back to bed!" This time she stomped up the staircase and slammed the bedroom door.

Never in twenty years of marriage had Margaret uttered an obscenity, he mused. "Sure has gotten herself a burr under her saddle this time."

When Dr. Powell picked up the receiver, Bennett was ranting. "Where the hell are you, Powell? You have a patient on the critical list and my information is that you have not been here all day."

"What are you, my mother?" Adam retorted. "I thought we discussed this family. I told you I was giving up, phasing out. You, yourself, as much as admitted that the Sterlings are psycho!"

"Forget what I told you, or what you think you heard. This isn't about Anna or Jack, or even the girl. This is about Paul."

"The surgery went well?"

"There are complications," according to Drake. "Paul needs his own doctor. You treated him for the meningitis, every childhood ailment since he was four. That poor woman is up there all alone, and she needs you, too. If I don't see your ugly face in this hospital within the hour, I'm coming over there. Get it? 'Fishing' my ass!"

After Adam heard the click, he stood at the bottom of the stairs. "Margaret? Honey?"

After a moment, the bedroom door opened and she answered, "What now?"

"Don't wait supper for me. I'm going to the hospital... to see a patient."

Across town from the modest Powell residence, at the big house on the Whitewater River, Helga scowled at the clock on the night table. It was 7:30 AM. She and Emily had been awake for more than four hours and most of that time had been devoted to the resurrection of Anna Sterling. They tried to force black coffee, and wrapped her limp, unresponsive body in cold, wet towels. They shouted her name over and over.

"Please let me hit her!" Helga begged, but a horrified Emily shook her head. They struggled to get Anna to her feet; if they could just get her walking, they could get her dressed, they hoped. Anna's height and bulk, dead weight, proved too much for them, for while she seemed to rally at times, mumbling incoherently and swinging at them defensively, she always fell back to the bed, snoring loudly.

"That's it!" Helga groaned. She moved her bulk toward the door, waving both flabby arms in the air. "You deal with Mrs. High Ass, I have baking to do."

"Don't you dare go off and leave me with this mess, Helga. Besides, who are you cooking for? No one is at home to eat." Emily slammed her dainty foot down hard, her tone now taking on a whining quality. "I've been up all night, too, doncha know?"

"The late Mrs. Sterling hired me to cook, not play nursemaid to a drunk. I most certainly do have folks to feed, my 'Missy girl' will starve sitting in the hospital, not to mention Miss Rachael who needs, and God knows, all the strength she can get. And when my poor Paul wakes up, he'll be screaming for my cookies!"

In spite of her mood, Emily had to smile. Could it be that the wonderful 'Missy girl' and 'poor Paul' were the same two ill-mannered little monsters that regularly provoked the swing of Helga's broom. Strange how a crisis suddenly changes everything. Emily had a yen for one of Helga's cookies, herself, and her tone softened.

"You go on, Helga. I have an idea."

"And what would that be? We've tried everything short of setting fire to the house."

"When Mrs. Steinburger called to tell us about the accident, she said she would be at home if we needed her. Well, we need her."

"Are you daft? You can't honestly expect that skinny, snooty society bitch to move that..." Helga gestured at Anna's bed. "Heavens, she might break a nail!"

"Then I'll call Millie Anderson."

"She hasn't got a phone."

"Then I'll go get her." Emily managed to squeeze past Helga and was through the door, moving rapidly down the carpeted corridor when Helga's voice caught up with her.

"You best have Billy drive you. Not a safe neighborhood."

"Why, Helga? Because 'Niggers' live there?" Emily had long been the target of ethnic hatred; she became militant at the first hint of bigotry.

Helga narrowed her eyes. "No, Miss Smarty Pants O'Shea! Because ignorant, whiskey-gussling, shanty lace curtain Irish live there!" 'So there!' her stare implied.

"The Irish don't cause no trouble," Emily tossed over her shoulder. "They're all afraid of the smelly, lard-assed Swedes!"

148

Helga laughed, her belly shaking as she turned for the backstairs, back to the serenity of her kitchen. She always enjoyed a good "go round" with Emily, but it was particularly therapeutic this morning, when so much was wrong with their world. Good for Emily... gave as good as she got.

By the time Emily returned to the house with Millie, Anna was slowly coming out of her stupor. Millie entered the bedroom with care, noting that Anna looked terrible. Dark circles ringed her eyes, her color was gray. Millie mistakenly assumed that the accident was the cause of Anna's alarming condition, for Emily had reported very little. A good whiff of Anna's breath, the pill bottles on the table told a different story. *Anna didn't know!*

"You had better get yourself together and moving, lady. There is much for you to do today."

Anna looked at her, stunned. "Wha..."

"There is no time to sugar-coat this for you, Miss Anna, big trouble in this house while you slept. Paul is in the hospital, near death. Rachael and Lillian are there with him now. Mac is in jail, and Jack is God knows where. I will help you make yourself presentable... hurry with your bath and get dressed." Millie spoke rapidly, matter-of-factly. She told Anna about the accident, filling her in on the most necessary details, omitting those that served no purpose at the moment. Anna asked no questions, simply stared at her old friend as though Millie's story was some sort of horrible cruel joke, and she was waiting for the punch line.

Chapter 25

It seemed to Rachael that she had spent a lifetime at Paul's bedside, waiting for him to die. She sat mesmerized, staring at what little she could see of his pale face that was surrounded by white gauze. She started at every twitch, every movement, however slight. The horrible days at the Vermont Military Academy flooded and flowed over her memory, and she wondered if the past eight years had actually happened, or had she simply dreamed it all.

The pearl rosary had not left her hand for the past seven hours, and she was surprised to discover that she had clutched it so fiercely that the crucifix had left its imprint on her small palm, like a stigmata.

Lillian dozed on the small sofa. Rachael smiled at the girl, grateful that she had arrived very early, carrying a small valise containing Rachael's things and a welcome basket of food still warm from Helga's kitchen. After they had exchanged news, most of it bad, Liz announced that she had made arrangements to stay there in the room with Rachael and Paul.

"What about school? Graduation?" Rachael protested.

"School is over in two weeks. My teacher said she would arrange for me to take the finals privately, as though I need to take them at all." The remark would sound smug uttered by anyone but Liz, who accepted her "A+" status rather matter-of-factly. "I don't care about grade-school graduation," she continued. "I need to stay here with you and Paul... please, Rachael!"

Rachael was secretly relieved. Liz was always good company, so grown-up sometimes that it was like talking to a forty-year-old. It would be helpful to have her here. Rachael's lip trembled when she thought about Paul's graduation, two weeks away. "One day at a time," she told herself.

They were silent most of the time while they awaited the arrival of Dr. Drake. They stared at the rigid young man in the bed as if they could somehow will him to awaken. When they exchanged comments, they did so in whispers. "So we don't wake him up," Liz joked, and Rachael smiled, once again grateful that she was here.

The door opened and the surgeon Drake appeared with Father McKay at his side. Rachael almost fainted at the sight of the priest, for it could only mean disastrous news that would require spiritual comfort, she reasoned. The doctor was quick to register the fear on Rachael's face. "No need to panic," he said. "I ran into the good Father as he was doing his rounds and he just came along to see you. May he stay?"

Rachael nodded, happy to see her confessor, her friend.

Tom McKay gently pressed Rachael's trembling hand, smiled and nodded at Liz, and pulled a straightback chair to the other side of the bed, where he held Paul's left hand in both of his.

"We have relieved the pressure caused by the blow to Paul's head," he began. "With proper care and time, his injuries will heal. He is young and strong. These things take a long time, and we can never predict the outcome with certainty, because the brain, when traumatized, can react in many ways. The effect can be delayed, sometimes for several years. I'm sorry I can't tell you more at this point, Mrs. Unger, but you understand, it is too soon."

"When will he wake up?" Rachael's small voice was a croak.

"The sooner, the better," Drake answered. "We cannot control that, of course, and a certain amount of his coma is due to all of the trauma, first the accident, then the surgery. Sleeping is the brain's healing mechanism, and when the cells have satisfied that need, he will, hopefully, come out of it."

"Hopefully?" Rachael cried. "You mean, he may not...?"

"There is no way we can know, for certain. As I told you, the sooner the better. After a few days, the longer he remains unconscious... well, let's just say we will all be relieved when he wakes up!"

Rachael's head dropped into her hands and she softly sobbed. Father McKay started to move around the bed, but Liz was there first, like a shot across the room. On her knees, she wrapped her arms around the woman, holding and rocking with her for several minutes. The men exchanged serious looks and stood by, helpless.

"I am glad that you have your daughter with you," Drake commented. No one bothered to correct him. "It may be a long siege. Sister Therese Marie has arranged a room for you," then he added, "for both of you, if you wish. We are also trying to reach Dr. Powell, who is Paul's physician, I understand. I will confer with him when he arrives."

Rachael raised her eyes and looked at the doctor for a long moment. "I'm sorry," she said weakly. "I just don't know what I am supposed to do."

"Just be here when he wakes up," Drake answered. "And pray."

Chapter 26

The praying began, and except for the basic necessities of life, sleeping, eating, and going to the bathroom, it continued almost non-stop for days. A du pri was placed on each side of Paul's bed, and they were seldom without an occupant. Father McKay made a beeline for the hospital as soon as he had uttered the "Missa est." Skipping breakfast, he packed the communion host and presented himself at Paul's bedside as the gray dawn gave in to the sunlight of spring. The black satchel that held the Holy Eucharist also contained the oils appropriate to the sacrament of Last Rites, awaiting the appropriate moment of their necessity.

After Rachael had received the host, Thomas McKay's beautiful tenor voice intoned one of the litanies, chanted in Latin and answered, also in Latin, by Rachael's lyrical soprano response. One or two at a time, the available staff filtered into the room, chanting as they entered, usually in English, some in Latin, some still in Spanish. They pulled rosaries out of uniform pockets and stayed for the recitation that followed. As some of them were required to leave, others took their places, and the small room was never without at least fifteen prayerful participants.

Lillian watched with fascination for the first few days, as one might take in a theatrical performance. She was particularly intrigued by the nuns who glided in and out of the room, administrating to Paul's physical needs while they prayed Prime, or Vespers. She marveled at how they never seemed to tire, never hinted that they might feel "out of sorts," never anything but patient, and kind, and loving.

Isaac arrived late every afternoon, carrying a large basket of food and another containing clean clothes that Emily had carefully ironed and folded, so as not to wrinkle. He was very much Liz's "special friend," and while he took pains to be very polite to Rachael, his reason for being there was obviously his young admirer. Since she could polish off a novel in a day or two, he worked very hard to keep up with the demand for books.

"You need to give the writers a rest," he teased.

"Here's a list," Liz instructed him. "Try the library first, then Father McKay at St. Rose's." The titles were strange to him: *Introduction To The Devout Life* by St. Francis DeSales, *Saint Catherine of Siena* by Johannes

152

Jorgensen, and *The Imitation of Christ* by Kempis. "I'll give you another list tomorrow," she said.

Isaac rolled his big eyes and scratched his head. "I can't wait until the librarian catches this poor black boy checking these out," he laughed.

On the third day, Rachael pulled an envelope from the bottom of the clothing basket. It was in Anna's hand, addressed to Liz. The girl took it without expression or comment, tucked herself into a corner to read, and reread the note.

> These are trying times for us all, I know. You have demonstrated such courage and concern for Rachael and Paul that I am moved to tell you how very proud I am. Please do not neglect to take reasonable care of yourself, since you are now a grown-up and seem to need no one to do it for you. Also, try to remember that I am your mother and in my own, strange way, I love you. Anna

Rachael watched Liz for some indication that the note had upset her, but she saw none. Liz smiled, in fact, and tucked the envelope away in her Bible, which was never out of her reach.

While they ate, Rachael tried to answer Liz's questions about the prayers, the sacraments, and all of the other hundred details that "cradle Catholics" just somehow know. Lillian sat cross-legged at Rachael's feet while the woman talked about her faith and her unfaltering love of God. There was a quest for knowledge, a hunger in Liz that soon became too much for Rachael, and she directed her young friend to Sister Therese Marie.

"It can't be forced," Sister told her. "True faith is a gift from the Holy Ghost, the third person in the Trinity. If you believe that you are called to a relationship with God, then you must ask the Holy Ghost to guide you. I know that you have had no formal spiritual training, dear, but certainly you must have heard some of it in school."

Liz thought about most of the girls her own age that attended one of the private, parochial schools in the city. A Catholic education was indeed the best that the friends of her parents could secure for their children, even those who were not Catholic. Mac had attended St. Rose's for awhile, she remembered, but she had been enrolled in public school. Why?

"I'm afraid I did not learn any of it in school," Liz told the nun, regretfully.

"I suppose I was very fortunate," Therese Marie continued, "even though

I lost my mother at a very young age, my father sent me to a wonderful boarding school, run by the Dominicans. That beautiful campus was my home forever; I took the veil immediately after I finished high school. It is also the Motherhouse of the Order."

"Why do they call it 'the Motherhouse'?"

"Because all of the sisters of the order can always come home, back to that special, wonderful place. That is where our Mother Superior lives."

"Could I go there, just to see it?"

"Someday, perhaps. I will be returning to Adrian in the fall. We shall have to speak with your parents about it."

Liz was so excited about all that she had learned in just a few days that she rarely slept. By the end of the first week of Paul's coma, she was saying the response to the "Ave" in perfect Latin. Soon she had learned litanies, novenas, and specific prayers to the saints. She prayed with a fervor, often so entranced that she lost all concept of time or place. She read the Bible for hours, and when Rachael insisted that she take a break, Liz would open one of the other books that she continued to demand from Isaac. Her questions never stopped: "How can there be three persons in one God? How could a loving God allow us to suffer? What must I do to earn heaven?"

"I am sure that you must miss your mother," Rachael said suddenly one evening.

"Not really. You are my mother now," Liz answered, and Rachael began to worry.

Father McKay was also concerned. "It is not uncommon," he told Rachael. "Young ladies of that age are very emotional and often turn that energy to religion. That is why those who believe that they are called to the religious life have a 'vocation;' both males and females have to be so carefully counseled. The Church needs valid vocations, Rachael. Much time and energy is invested in each candidate. The decision cannot be decided on a whim, and many young people get 'caught up' in the fever of the moment. It will pass when Lillian's life returns to normal."

"She is serious about being a Catholic, I believe," Rachael told him. "I don't want to discourage that if she is sincere. How can I know for sure?"

"You can't. But for now, let us concentrate on Paul and his recovery. The Holy Ghost will take care of Lillian."

Sister Therese Marie was also concerned about Liz's apparent conversion. On Wednesday of the second week, she noticed that the girl was looking thinner than usual, and exhibited other symptoms of fatigue. "She never sleeps," Rachael told her. "When she is not hovering over Paul's bed, she is reading the Bible or on her knees, praying."

Rachael didn't need more to worry about, Sister decided. The nun insisted that Lillian cease her vigil immediately and follow her to the private room where Liz and Rachael slept, when they slept. Sister drew a hot bath for Liz, helped her into a clean nightgown and tucked her in. "I will sit here with you until you fall asleep," she told Liz.

But the girl chattered on and on. What was it like at the Motherhouse? When could they go? How did Sister know she wanted to be a nun?

"I'll be right back," Therese Marie said as she bolted out the swinging door. It was moments like these, she thought, that missing out on motherhood didn't seem so bad after all. Getting this girl to sleep was a major undertaking.

"Just a little something to help her sleep," she asked the pharmacist on duty. He cocked his head at her and smiled.

"I know I should ask Dr. Powell, but it's a routine thing..."

"Is she a patient, Sister?"

"No, but... well, you'd have to hear the whole sad story, Bobby."

"Spare me," he replied dryly. "About ninety pounds, you say? This should do nicely."

She took the pill cup he extended to her and looked at the little blue pill. She was a nurse. She should know what this medication was, but its name eluded her at the moment. Bobby could be trusted, so she watched as Liz swallowed it with a glass of warm milk. Seven minutes later Sister Therese Marie stopped into Paul's room to assure an anxious Rachael that Liz was soundly asleep, and she then rushed away to check on another patient.

Chapter 27

Mac thought his bladder would burst if he didn't pee soon, but he would die before he would use the common toilet in the corner of the holding cell. The plumbing was so ancient, it had long ago ceased to function as a flushing depository, and had become instead a "piss bucket." Where the hell was his mother? Why would she do this to him, leave him here in the company of drunks and perverts and God knows what else? Jack was still furious with him, he understood, and the stinging pain on the right side of his face testified to that fact. But where was his mother?

"So what's it gonna be, pretty boy? Do you have any smokes, or not?"

Mac looked at the bleary-eyed drunk who sat on the bench across from him. Sure, he had smokes, wanted one badly in fact, but would not share with this filth, so he went without. This Great Depression was a pain in the ass. The poor were everywhere now, unlike the prosperous twenties when they were more or less confined to their own areas. He didn't belong in this place. He was not a drunk or a criminal. It had been a simple accident, and he hadn't meant to hurt anyone, lest of all Paul. Paul! God, when would someone please tell him about Paul?

Mac was painfully aware that he was a disappointment to his father. Everyone was. Except perhaps Lillian, who had somehow wormed her way into the old man's cold heart. Jack had even bought her an Arabian last year, a beautiful animal she named "Pegasus," and Mac had to admit that his baby sister looked very good astride the horse. But then hadn't he also presented Mac with a yellow convertible yesterday, an early graduation gift. Where was his car?

When would she come for him? This apprehension reminded him of the night he had arrived home from the academy, longing for the look of surprised delight in her eyes, only to discover that she was not at home. It hurt so much more than he dared to admit, so he had gone to his room without supper, locking the door behind him. Was that only four years ago? What happened to that boy, that little soldier who was so proud that he had taken a marksmanship trophy? What did he have to be proud of now? He wished he had stayed at the academy, made something of himself. Whose idea was it that he leave the school?

The cars that cruised down Market Street passed a black limousine driven by Isaac Thomas Anderson. The limo parked in front of the brick municipal building, next to the sign clearly marked "No Parking." Isaac walked around to the curbside and held the door for Anna, who told him, "I won't be long."

Two officers, about to exit, jumped back at the sight of her, and stood somewhat at attention with their backs pressed up against heavy oaken doors. She didn't bother to thank them, but breezed past as though she had anticipated the assistance. Two dozen pairs of eyes fixed on her as she stood in the center of the room, eyes that took in every inch of the tall, elegant woman in the white gloves and feathered hat. Conversation ceased, typewriters stopped mid-word, even the telephones dared not ring. Anna's scent, the expensive Paris cologne, permeated the stuffy air and she stood frozen in place, only her large gray eyes moving as they swept the room. Although it was warm, she felt the chill in the air, the curious looks of men who regarded her as just another uppity society mother come to rescue her rich, spoiled, wayward son.

Sergeant Harry O'Toole approached her slowly and with reluctance. "Bail is five hundred dollars," he announced curtly. She opened her purse, extended five brand new hundred-dollar bills and smiled at the look of disappointment on his face. He had hoped, she knew, that she would ask to write a check, which, of course, would be unacceptable.

"May I have a receipt, please?" she asked sweetly, while the look in her eyes reminded O'Toole of his grandmother's warning: "Watch out for the evil eye."

Receipt in hand, Anna pivoted swiftly on her heels, and let her long, stiff stride carry her out of the building. She gave no instructions, simply moved herself smoothly into the limousine and waited.

"Your mommy paid your bail," O'Toole sneered at Mac as he unlocked the cell. "That makes you free, for the time being, to resume your drinking and tom-catting until you go to trial, or kill someone else, whichever comes first!"

Mac looked at the Sergeant like he had been kicked in the groin. He ran from the room like a man pursued by a hungry tiger, so fast that he failed to stop, and collided with the side of the car. "I can't believe you left me in there!" he shouted at Anna. Backing off while the door opened, he continued his tirade. Why had no one come to tell him about Paul? What was wrong with this stupid family?

"Get in, sit down, and shut up!" Anna interrupted. She caught Isaac's eye in the rearview mirror, noting a slight smile. Anna leaned over the seat and handed Isaac a slip of paper on which was written an address. He nodded, adding a slight tip of his cap for effect and wordlessly moved the car into traffic.

Anna ignored Mac's inquiring look, busy with the notations she was making in her notebook. When Isaac failed to make the usual turnoff that followed the river toward home, proceeding instead downtown, toward the slum areas, Mac could hold his silence no longer. "Where are we going?"

"I'll let you know when we get there." She didn't look up when she spoke.

He had witnessed her cold, "Anna's in a mood" persona a few times, but never before had it been directed to him. He must really be in the doghouse, he imagined, for he honestly could not recall any previous display of disapproval. What did he have to lose?

"I have decided that it would be best if I stay away from the house for awhile," he boldly began. "Jack is furious, about the car I guess, and you won't even talk to me. Please tell me, Mother... please tell me Paul is alive!"

"Paul is alive. Just barely, but alive. He had surgery early this morning and is in a coma. As for your alternate residence, I agree. What exactly do you have planned?"

Surprised at her response, Mac pressed on. "I am old enough for a place of my own, an apartment, perhaps."

"Really? And how will you pay for it?"

Mac grinned nervously. "Well, I'll need some financial help, of course. Can you carry me awhile?"

Anna stopped writing, raised her eyes to look at him. She was someone he had never seen before. Her large gray eyes were void, cold. "I carried you for nine months, next to my heart. Everything I have done since has been for you, your comfort, and your security. As you say, it is time that you become a responsible young man. I have, therefore, arranged other accommodations for you, to that end."

"What are you talking about, Mother?"

"Your future, my son. Here's our stop."

Mac looked out the window at the dirty, shabby building that looked as if it may fall over on them. He started to protest, fairly certain that his mother had lost her mind, but she was already out of the car and on her way up the steps. She turned when she got to the door and silently motioned for Mac to follow her. Isaac instinctively knew that he must remain with the car, for that was where the greatest danger existed.

They climbed a winding, rickety staircase for several floors, and Mac marveled at Anna's stamina. She seemed to float from one level to another, without benefit of deep breath, while Mac found himself panting on the second landing. On the fourth floor, they entered a dormitory-type room that held about twenty cots, some of them occupied by sleeping men.

Mac tried to inquire about the purpose of this visit, but Anna ignored him. Her eyes scanned the room until she saw, evidently, the person she sought. "Follow me," she instructed her son, and they crossed the room precariously, stepping sideways at times through narrow spaces between cots. It was only April, not even hot yet, but the air in the room made Mac's stomach lurch in protest. His nose identified urine, body odor, stale whiskey, and something that suggested that it might be long dead. When would the nightmare of the past twenty-four hours be over? He had endured a car crash, a beating, incarceration, and now this. He looked to his mother, ready to register one final plea when she stopped suddenly and stared down at a dirty, unshaven old man.

"Hello, Father," she said softly and without emotion.

The creature on the cot opened red-rimmed eyes and stared at her. Mac stared at her. She was crazed, he decided, gone over the edge.

"Hello, Anna," the man answered flatly.

"This is MacGregor Sterling. Mac, say 'hello' to your grandfather."

Mac's eyes grew very large. His head turned from side to side as he looked, first at his mother, then to the old man, like a tennis fan, he thought. His mind was racing, trying to recall something, anything, that he had ever been told about his grandparents, or any relative for that matter. Nothing. Now he knew the reason. This was no joke, this was cruel reality.

"Why are you doing this?" Mac asked, his voice cracking, his eyes filling with salty tears.

She turned to look into his eyes, offering her full and undivided attention.

"Because this is what you came from, my son, and what you are cursed to become. Someday soon, I will tell you all of it, how this miserable man sold an innocent young girl into white slavery for... what was it, Malcomb? Thirty pieces of silver?"

Malcomb MacGregor grunted and uttered a quiet profanity under his breath. He gave her one more contemptuous look and rolled over on his side, turning his back to his unwelcome visitors. He offered one parting remark in the form of a long, loud expulsion of very offensive gas.

Anna took Mac's hand and quickly led him out of the room. He felt as

159

though he were three years old again, crying and moving his legs to keep up with his mother. He hadn't noticed that she was also crying.

"Glad I could be of some assistance," Malcomb whispered before he dropped off to sleep.

Chapter 28

Traffic was light at the early hour. While stopped at a red light, Adam glanced at the patrol car directly beside him and recognized the man in the rear seat as Jack Sterling. Jack's Buick, driven by a uniformed officer, followed the police car.

"Am I under arrest?" Jack asked the officer who appeared to be in charge, a Captain Jeremy Rager.

"Not at the moment. Unless, of course, you would care to take on a few more of my men. After we finish our questioning and the paperwork, we will escort you home safely, Mr. Sterling," Rager answered.

Jack was subdued, Adam noted, and appeared dazed. Why he needed to be "escorted for his own safety" was unclear, but Jack was exhausted and unable to argue. Lillian had tearfully begged her father to allow her to remain with Rachael and he agreed by offering no objection. An officer would drive her home later, it was decided.

Walter Bernstein's office took Jack's message, and Walter questioned the instruction to meet Jack at his home rather than at the station house. Jack quickly bathed and dressed. He was at the dining room table, stuffing poached eggs and Helga's wonderful biscuits into his mouth as if he might never eat again when Emily approached him.

"I packed a few things for you, as you requested," she said. "Mrs. Sterling left about thirty minutes ago. I think she went to..." Emily hesitated, reluctant to mouth "the jail," but Jack knew that she had gone to see Mac.

"I hope she didn't drive down there alone. Did Billy drive her?"

"Billy's still in his apartment, his day off. Isaac drove her. Oh, and Mr. Bernstein is here to see you."

Jack frowned and wiped egg yolk from his mouth. "Send him in."

"You look very troubled, Jack," Walter joked as he deposited his briefcase on the massive table.

"My driver, the one I pay an exorbitant salary, is enjoying his day off, while Millie Anderson's nappy-haired nephew is driving my wife around town in my car. What do you think?"

Walter shook his head, rolled his eyes, and answered, "I think that you have many more important things to worry about at the moment."

"Such as?"

"Such as your minor son driving drunk, for starters. Then there is the possibility of a massive lawsuit if, God forbid, the boy dies. How is he, by the way?"

"I have no idea. I am not included in the chain of information." Then, quieter, "I'm afraid I have behaved badly, Walter."

"So I hear. I have to admit I was surprised, Jack. You are not one to react with such raw emotion. I have done my homework, however, and I think we can minimize the damage. My contacts at the hospital tell me that Paul's coma is very likely the natural result of the surgery, and chances are this side of even that he will recover, or at the very least, regain consciousness. It goes without saying, of course, that you will be responsible for all medical expenses."

"Of course."

"The car is a total loss. Why on earth would you hand it over to Mac before you insured it?"

"I didn't 'hand it over.' Mac took the keys from the hall table. The ladies and I were still at the club."

"I see. Well, about the other thing, just be concerned and solicitous, and we'll deal with it one day at a time. Mac will require more work. He will no doubt be charged. It will cost you plenty to avoid punishment of any kind."

"What makes you think I have any interest in what happens to Mac? On the contrary, I believe that he is overdue. It is time for that young man to learn a few of life's difficult lessons."

"What about Harvard? The fall term is just months away."

Jack shrugged. He stood, dropped his napkin on the table and gestured for Walter to follow him. Emily stood waiting at the front door, holding Jack's favorite Panama hat.

"Your bag is in the car, sir."

"Thank you, Emily."

Walter raised an inquisitive eyebrow.

"I will be at the club, or the office, Walter. Call me when you have more information."

As the two men walked down the circular steps, Jack said, "It is doubtful that Paul will be ready for Harvard in the fall. As for Mac, he can go to Harvard when he can pay for it. Or he can go to hell. I have no preference."

****

Adam Powell ordered a blood sample STAT within seven minutes of entering Paul's room, for one good look at Paul's yellow hue alarmed the doctor into immediate action.

"When did Dr. Drake last see him?" Adam inquired of Rachael, who was relieved to see him.

"I couldn't say for sure," she answered. "I haven't seen Dr. Drake since early this morning, after the surgery."

He wanted to sit with Rachael while they awaited the lab results, but found that he was too nervous to maintain a conversation. He had worried her, he knew, and that fact made him more uncomfortable. "Try not to worry," was all he could muster as he patted her hand and left the room quickly, racing down five flights of stairs to the laboratory. There he hovered over the technicians, making a general nuisance of himself until they were forced to provide at least preliminary results.

"Liver numbers are out of whack," the tech said. "Better run it again."

The numbers were critically high, but just what the doctor expected and confirmed his fear. "Yes," he answered. "Run them again."

After the fifth confirmation, Adam grabbed the report and raced down the hospital corridor to the cafeteria, where he had reason to believe that he would find Dr. Bennett.

He ran so fast that he literally slid through the double doors, scanning the faces of the sea of white uniforms, finally settling his eyes on the serious countenance of Leonard Bennett. Thank God he had caught him before he left, Adam thought, as he made his way past tables of chattering doctors and nurses.

Leonard was paging through his *AMA Journal,* lunching on a Hershey bar with a black coffee chaser. He smiled briefly at Adam and gestured for him to sit. Adam passed a lab report across the table.

"What do you make of this, Leonard?"

Bennett looked at the name at the top of the page: "Paul Unger"

He stretched out long legs and sat back in his chair. His eyes ran down the page quickly and he handed the report back to Dr. Powell.

"Normal, considering. What are we looking for?"

"Liver functions. Look again."

Leonard uttered a long-suffering sigh and took the paper from Adam's hand. He was beginning to regret that he had pushed Adam's return to the position of primary caregiver in the Unger case, for his colleague had become obsessed with Paul's recovery. Leonard had reminded Adam several times that brain injuries often result in coma, and the length of unconsciousness is beyond control. It would be necessary to humor Adam, he supposed, as he glanced again at the lab report.

"Holy shit!" he exclaimed. "This can't be right!"

"I thought so too, so I asked the lab man to run it again. And again."

"This number is off the chart. Why isn't this kid dead?" Bennett looked at Powell with new appreciation. "What tipped you?"

"It was something I read in the police report. The Sterling boy admitted that he had too much to drink, but he kept insisting to the officers that Paul only drank one beer. I believe him... what would be the incentive to lie? He had no reason to, quite the contrary really, when you think about it. How could one beer do this to a liver?"

"Chemical imbalance. Alcoholic poisoning?"

"That's what I'm thinking. If he has liver damage, his coma could go on forever."

"Good work, Adam! What does Drake say?"

"Haven't talked to him yet... I wanted to confer with you first. I spoke with the chief pharmacist, and he tells me there are new drugs that can 'probably' resolve the problem. I need to be sure, proceed carefully. There is so much at stake."

"Your license, for one thing. Do you really plan to render treatment without Drake's approval, knowledge even?"

"He will never agree. As far as he's concerned, Paul's condition is due to acute head trauma, nothing else. Anything that can't be corrected by his scalpel is out of the question. Besides, as I told you, I don't know where he is."

"Did you tell me that, Adam? Shall we have him paged?"

"Leonard, please. Just answer one question... given what I have just told you, what would be your recommendation if you were making the decision?"

"Elementary, my dear Powell. First year med school stuff. 'Lavage or emesis by apomorphine, followed by solution of acetate of ammonia.' In other words, try to drown the kid, make him throw up, and slap him awake!"

"Precisely! Let's go."

Dr. Bennett stared, his mouth open to utter vehement protest. "You can't be serious! Do you actually believe that I am going to assist you in this madness?"

"It is the only answer, I'm betting my life on it. I don't need Drake's permission, just the mother's. I am, after all, the boy's attending physician. Are you up for a little heroics or not?"

"Whatever happened to 'first, do no harm'?"

"The harm may have already been done, Leonard. If Paul stays in that coma much longer, he will never come out of it."

Bennett shook his head slowly and rose from his chair. He picked up his coffee cup, tucked the magazine under his arm and smiled at Adam. "You know, I've really always wanted to be a vet," he chuckled. Let's do it!"

Chapter 29

Anna Sterling never left anything to chance. She was also never impulsive, seldom spontaneous, and rarely emotional. Once awakened from her stupor, she reverted to type… clear-thinking, rational, "in charge."

Mac was still dazed when the limousine approached the front gate of the Sterling mansion, so he missed the instruction that Isaac drive around the back of the house. When the car halted in the rear circular driveway, Anna turned to Mac and spoke to him for the first time since they had left the shelter.

"I have some errands to run, so I will be gone for a few hours. The boathouse has been cleaned and stocked with some provisions. Your things were moved there this morning. Helga will feed you in the kitchen. You will find a list of conditions and if you have any questions, we can discuss them . tomorrow morning."

While Mac continued to stare at his mother, she reached across him and opened the car door. After a moment of intense eye contact, he got out of the car and walked across the lush green lawn, to the boathouse.

"Take me to the hospital," she told Isaac.

Rachael was kneeling beside the bed, her tired knees very sore on the hard tile. She rested her head on the cool linen, close to Paul's left hand. She would will it to move, she decided. If she stared long and hard enough, it would move. Without a sound, neither footstep nor the opening of a door, Anna was suddenly standing inside the room, and Rachael sensed her presence immediately, when the sweet aroma of Channel teased at her nostrils. Rachel looked first at Liz, who dozed fitfully on the short sofa, then at the tall woman. She sighed, rose slowly, and walked around the bed to greet her employer.

"Anna, it was kind of you to come."

"I would have been here sooner," Anna greeted her, "but other matters demanded my attention. I see the flowers have arrived. I hope you like roses."

"Yes, thank you. They are beautiful."

The amenities over, silence prevailed. They stood a few feet apart, awkward and uncomfortable. *People say such silly things to each other*, Anna was thinking. *We waste valuable time trying to be nice, to say the "right" thing, and nothing comes out the way it should.*

"Please," Rachael said suddenly, "please sit down. I seem to have forgotten my manners."

Anna smiled and shook her head. "I won't intrude," she said. "I just wanted to be sure that all of you were all right. Is there anything that I can do?"

"No. We just wait and pray. We won't really know anything until Paul wakes up... if Paul wakes up." Rachael broke off with a short sob and turned away. Rachael had no desire to let Anna see her break down, for Anna was always so stoic, so in control. A show of strength, however contrived, must be demonstrated now. Quickly composed, she asked, "How is Mac?"

"I have taken him home. He is shaken, but uninjured. Do you and Lillian have everything that you need?"

"For the time being, yes. The sisters have been very kind. Thank you for allowing her to stay, Anna. She is a God-send."

"Tomorrow is her graduation," Anna replied. "I made her a dress. I know she doesn't think so now, but someday she may regret that she missed it."

"I will ask her again, but Lillian has her own mind."

"How well I know."

The silence returned. They were each aware that the other was busy in thought, and it seemed that they could read each other's thoughts. *What does she want from me? What am I supposed to say? Why won't she let me help? Is this how our thirteen years will end?*

Anna waited expectantly, anticipating that Rachael would share some confidence, a plan for the immediate future, something... anything.

Rachael waited in anticipation, hoping that Anna would reveal the real purpose of the visit, for Anna did nothing without purpose.

There seemed to be nothing left to say, except "Goodbye."

Anna made the first move. She removed her long white gloves from her purse and slowly put them on, smoothing each finger with intense concentration. "I will leave you to your prayers, Rachael. Please let me know when I can do something."

"Of course. Thank you, Anna."

Most women would hug, Anna suspected, but her fear of physical contact and her self-consciousness forbade the overture. Rachael looked as though she might cry again, and Anna could not deal with the oppressive aura of emotion surrounding them. She gave her housekeeper one more questioning look and turned to go.

"Anna?"

Rachael's soft voice stopped her. Anna waited, her gloved hand on the door handle, her eyes stinging. "Yes?"

"I know how difficult it was… your coming here. I want you to know that there is no blame. Whatever happens is the will of God."

Does your God tell you that I must be punished, Rachael? Does He tell you that if your son dies, I am to blame, and you may replace him with my daughter?

Anna made her trademark exit, without warning or parting remark. Isaac already had his orders, so there was no need of conversation when she re-entered the car. Isaac was comfortable with this lady, relieved that he wasn't called upon to make small talk, especially today when she seemed so very sad.

Anna was armed with a new purpose when she entered the law office of Dennis Jacobs, Esq. His secretary didn't bother to ask if Anna had an appointment, for Anna never made appointments. "My time is just as valuable as his," she was fond of saying. "Considering what he charges, he will see me at my convenience." Anna walked rapidly past the outer desk, offering a strained smile and a slight wave of her gloved hand as her right to admission.

Dennis was on the phone, uttering slightly obscene little love sounds to his mistress. He paled when he saw Anna enter his office, and muttered, "I'll call you later," and hung up without saying goodbye. Anna smiled knowingly, passed on the cryptic comment that ran across her mind, for she was in a business mood, and in a hurry.

There was no need for a casual exchange. Dennis had been her attorney for 16 years, her only confidant, really. While he knew only a few of her many secrets, he knew more than any other living being. She had first approached him when Mac was a toddler, requesting information about a possible divorce, and after Dennis had researched and carefully run the figures, the two decided that leaving Jack was not an option at that time.

"What is it this time, Mrs. Sterling?" he said dryly.

"I gather that this is not a good time," Anna snickered. "I will be brief, so that we may conclude our business quickly and then you can get back to your 'tootsie.' I need to give someone a large sum of money, a gift, but it must be done surreptitiously."

Anna lit a cigarette and waited for his reply. Dennis stared at his client, his mind desperately trying to define her last word. He hated it when she did this to him. Why couldn't she just speak English, like everybody else?

"So," he began, "you want to give money away, but you don't want… I guess you mean you don't want…"

"Exactly. I don't want the recipient to know where the money came from."

"I see." He made a mental note to buy a dictionary. "Why?"

"That is my concern. Can you do it?"

She was unusually abrupt, even for Anna. She would share little with him today, a fact that made him just a little angry, and to his surprise, a little hurt. *I really need to jazz up my life when I find myself living vicariously through a middle-aged woman!* he thought. "Let me make a few notes," he said, shaking his head slowly.

"It is to be in the form of a cashier's check, paid to the order of Rachael Unger," she told him, and without waiting for his question, spelled the last name.

"Address?"

"Have it delivered by messenger to her, and only her, in room 142 at St. Rita's Hospital. Today."

That directive might present a problem, he had planned an early day. He started to protest, noted the look on Anna's face, and decided it would be best not to mention the inconvenience, the complete disregard of his schedule.

"Amount?" He kept his head down, writing rapidly.

"Ten thousand, six hundred and forty-seven dollars and 28 cents." When the attorney's head jerked up in alarm, he found her passbook directly under his nose. "As you can verify by the bank balance, that is every cent I have." She then laid an envelope on his desk. "It's all there, every penny. I managed to get it out just before the bank closed. Please count it. You may bill me for your fee, of course, and any expenses."

Jacobs laid the pen down, and leaned so far back in his chair that he had to catch himself. He was stunned. "That is one hell of a lot of money, Anna! Are you absolutely sure that you want to do this? Why, in God's name, would you want to do this? It took years to build this nest egg, your security, you said. Why?"

"Don't make me say this again, Dennis. It is a very private matter. It also, I believe, comes under the heading of 'attorney-client privilege,' and is never to be revealed to anyone." There it was again, why did she persist in treating him like a child?

"How about the IRS? Can we at least claim it as a tax write-off?" He was being facetious, of course, an effort to lighten the tension with a little levity. One glare from Anna assured him that he had been unsuccessful.

"And just how do you suggest I explain this 'gift' to the very fortunate Mrs. Unger?"

"You will figure it out," Anna replied curtly. "That's what I pay you for."

Chapter 30

The surface of Jack's office desk was littered with the evidence of doom. The *Richmond Hearld's* front page shouted the "sins of the sons" in bold print. The article speculated widely, hinting that the boys were returning from a "wild party." A picture of Mac's beautiful new car caressing a large tree was included, reminding Jack that he had just spent $1200.00 on a pile of junk.

A letter lay beside the newspaper, from his corporate headquarters in Baltimore. His supervisors suggested that an audit would soon follow, due to reports of "certain irregularities in collection policy and procedure." He would need to revise some reports, he decided, and proceed carefully. Jack had an excellent mind for figures, an accountant's intellect, in fact, and knew well enough that the best accountants make the best thieves.

A bill from his attorney, premature and excessive in Jack's opinion, demanded his immediate attention. Rather than payment for "services rendered," the usual notation, this invoice was obviously a retainer for "services not yet rendered but sure-to-be expensive."

As further proof that he was "unwept, unhonored, and unsung," today was his birthday, his forty-eighth .His birthday was usually unnoticed and uncelebrated, and he might have forgotten it himself had it not been for the small card from Mrs. Nelson on his desk this morning. Not one mention of it last night, while he paid to wine and dine his beloved family. It was just one more "poor me" to add to his list.

Weighing most heavily on his mind, however, was his self-imposed distance from the rest of his family. Anna evidently neither needed nor desired his presence. His beloved Lillian had taken refuge with Rachael. Mac, he was certain, still carried on his face the sting of Jack's anger, and Rachael suffered most, while he was unable to offer anything other than money. His room at the club no longer held the old appeal, for it would seem now more like a lonely cell. Perhaps he would go home and get the dog.

"Mrs. Sterling is here," Mrs. Nelson informed him.

Jack's melancholy mood shifted to one of alarm and defense. He opened the top drawer of his desk, pulled out a bottle of Dewar's Scotch and took a long draw. "Have Mrs. Sterling come in," he said into the phone.

She looked rather fetching, considering the fact that she had "tied on the dog" last night. After one of Anna's prescription binges, she usually slept for fourteen hours and napped an additional ten. This time she had downed several Manhattans, joking that she only drank them because she "needed the fruit." It was a minor miracle that she was able to walk, Jack mused, and somehow she had managed to present herself well.

He rose when she entered the room, very unlike him, for Jack took no pride in behaving like a gentleman. Why had he done that, he wondered, and would the gesture give her an edge in what was certain to escalate into a major war?

Anna was in a state of nervous excitement, pacing the room while she tugged at her gloves, and finally settling on the sofa where she lit a cigarette and caught her breath.

He watched her without greeting or comment, best to determine her mood first, he reasoned. Finally she looked at her husband, really looked at him as if she were appraising an object at an auction.

"Are you all right, Jack? My God, what a perfectly awful day this has been!"

Correctly assuming that the question was rhetorical, he didn't bother to answer. He needed yet another clue, so he waited silently.

"I made a list this morning," she began again, "of everything that needed to be resolved today, in the order of importance. We have much to discuss, so much I don't know where to begin:"

Jack bristled a little, his self-pitying mood kicked in once more and he found his voice. "Perhaps we could begin by trying to determine why the welfare of your husband of eighteen years is so far down on your list of 'importance.'"

"Jack, please... just this once, could we cut through the bullshit and talk about some very serious matters?"

"I suppose so," he conceded. He hadn't intended his comment to be a joke, but Anna was right, they needed to get to the point. "Is there any news about Paul?"

"He is still unconscious, but that is to be expected, I suppose. The surgeon corrected whatever damage he suffered, let off the pressure... the fluid in his brain, and now we 'wait,' as Rachael says."

"You've seen Rachael?"

"I just came from the hospital. So you see, you are not so far down the list after all."

Jack grunted, as close to an apology as she was likely to get, and asked the next question. "Diz? Is she all right?"

"Our daughter 'Lillian' seems to be doing well." Anna frowned at Jack's use of his pet name for the girl. No matter what the issue, Anna never passed on the opportunity to correct his grammar, or any other misuse of the English language. "She seems quite content, although I can't be sure because she was asleep when I was there. But I am sure that she is happy to be with Rachael."

Jack's ears tingled at the edges. He thought he detected a definite tone... something he had never recognized before in Anna's speech. It sounded very much like... regret? Jealousy?

"Have you spoken to Walter? Does he speculate on liability?" she asked him.

Strange mood, this one. Anna seldom bothered to concern herself about financial matters that did not directly affect her bank account.

"Yes, and no."

"What does that mean?"

"It means, 'yes, I have spoken to Walter' and 'no, he does not speculate.' The car is a total loss. I have instructed Walter to handle all medical expenses, as my accountant, not as my attorney. We don't have any idea where this thing is going until Paul either comes to, or..."

"Or dies."

"Yes."

They were both silent while they each drifted into that possibility. Jack was surprised to see Anna's head drop into her hand, and even more surprised when he realized that she was softly crying. He opened the drawer once more, retrieved the scotch and two clean glasses. He poured her a full glass, crossed to the sofa and held it out to her. She looked so pathetic, childlike. He felt a strange stirring, an uncommon feeling of warmth. He liked her as she was now, unarmed and vulnerable.

"Didn't your mother ever teach you to carry a hanky?" he asked. He handed over a white linen square and smiled when she blew copiously.

"I was a motherless child, remember?" she retorted, looking fiercely into his blue eyes. Jack flushed, debated with himself. Should he return to his desk, or stay here with her? He sat down next to her, slipping an arm around her trembling shoulders, much like an inexperienced adolescent making his first move.

"Perhaps I could help if you would tell me what exactly has brought you to tears," he prompted. "Is it the loss of your mother, that son-of-a-bitch of a father, Paul's injury, Diz's attention to Rachael? What?"

"Has it occurred to you to even ask about Mac?" she sniffled. Her long nose was very red, her make-up badly smeared. No doubt about it, Anna was out of control for once.

Jack sighed and pulled his arm away, resting his head in hands, elbows on knees. This was tricky; he had better choose his words carefully. "Of course it has, Anna. I just needed to cool off, you know. So much happened last night, and I am not proud of most of it. Sooner or later we need to discuss Mac. I assume he is out of jail. How is he otherwise?"

"'Our son' is at home, in a matter of speaking."

"What does that mean?"

She took her time, blew her nose, wiped her eyes. Had he noted her "our son" remark? She suspected that he had, quickly relegating it to that mental file of "things we won't talk about."

She told him all of it, how she had gone to the police station and posted Mac's bail, how she had taken him to the flophouse to meet Malcomb. She talked about her anger at Mac's cavalier attitude, how he had suggested that he would move out of the house and declare himself independent, except, of course, for the funding.

"I have arranged for him to stay in the boathouse for the summer," she told Jack. "That way I can keep a close eye on him. I considered putting him up with Billy, but Billy has women up there from time to time, and Mac doesn't need to be exposed to that."

"What is he going to do all day in the boathouse?" Jack asked.

"He will be up every morning at 5:30, since Mr. Gonzales will pick him up at 6," Anna announced proudly. "Mac has a summer job, working with the gardener. I thought it was about time he got his hands dirty."

Jack was astonished. His approving smile soon became a grin, and he gave Anna a massive bear hug. "Well done!" he told her.

Anna was encouraged by Jack's admiration. "There's more," she continued. "No car, no booze, no girls. I have imposed a ten o'clock curfew, and will collect one-half of his earnings each week to apply to the car. He'll never get it paid for, I am certain, but at least he'll get the point."

Despite the encouraging news, Jack looked tired, beaten. "I haven't been a very good father to Mac," he said very quietly, speaking more to himself than to Anna. "I meant to be, wanted to be, but I suppose I simply didn't know how." He rose and walked to the dirty window of his rather shabby office, certainly not the accommodations to which he considered himself entitled.

His superiors in Baltimore did not appreciate his efforts. If not for the money that his business dealings made for him, there would be no point. He had pinned his hopes on his dream of a family, but there was little appreciation for him there either.

"Come home with me, Jack. We will have the rest of our lives to analyze our failures. For now, we are tired and hungry. I could use another drink."

Isaac drove the long black car back to the Sterling garage without benefit of Anna's company. She and Jack decided to go to the club for a quiet celebration.

"After all," she told her husband, "it is your birthday!"

Chapter 31

Lillian's feet were cold. She had the sensation of moving along a corridor, green tile burnished to a spectacular shine. She reasoned that the floor must be freezing, but while she could see her feet when she looked for them, they didn't seem to quite touch the surface.

Then there was this fog thing, a thick billowy mist, like the moors of Scotland. She supposed that she should be alarmed about the strangeness that surrounded her, but her mind was on a more important mission. She reached the door, pushed it open and entered Paul's room.

The light from the hallway spilled across the room. Before the door closed behind her, Liz looked up and down the hallway one last time for Sister Therese Marie. Not only was there no sign of the nun, the halls were void of any activity.

She expected that she would be in total darkness when the door closed, but the room held a glow that reminded her of the Christmas poem… "A luster of mid-day."

She had no need to cross the small room, for the hospital bed was empty and neatly remade with the proverbial "hospital corners." She had entered the wrong room, it seemed, and turned to go when she saw him standing quietly in the corner, watching her.

"Paul! Oh, dear God, Paul!"

He was fully dressed in the same clothes he had worn the night of the accident. They were clean, all traces of blood and vomit were gone, and the pants were neatly pressed and pleated. He looked wonderfully healthy, without bandages, his curly blond hair once again thick and shiny.

"Hello, Gretch," he whispered. He pressed his index finger against his lips and gestured to the sleeping Rachael on the sofa. Liz was confused. Why was Rachael sleeping? She should be awake… awake and dancing, and laughing, and crying.

"We must wake her, Paul! Rachael, wake up, Rachael!" Liz was shouting now, moving to shake Rachael by the shoulders, but Paul stepped between them and held Liz gently, confining her movement.

"Listen carefully, Gretch, we don't have much time. I have to go now; they are waiting for me. Please promise that you will look after my mother. She is so good, so kind. Don't let anyone hurt her ever again. I have loved you like my own dear little sister. Don't forget me, Gretch." His eyes were no longer blue, but black marbles, void of light or life. A tear appeared at one corner, pooled, and began to exit southward, down one ivory cheek.

Lillian felt a sudden, overwhelming sadness. This was a terrible dream, she knew, a nightmare that would linger in her memory all day tomorrow, and her pillow would be wet with her tears.

"What are you saying, Paul? Who is waiting for you?"

He turned her slowly and pointed to two male figures standing near the window. They were almost identical, tall, silent men whose faces were partially covered by the hoods of their brown, belted robes. She should be afraid, for she was certain they were not in the room when she entered. There was no fear, however, only the awe of their presence.

Liz patted Paul's arm as if to say, "I'll take care of this," and boldly approached the men. One turned away, as if in deference to the other, who stood very still and allowed her to face him. He reached up and slowly lowered the hood from his head, a silent signal that he would be open to her plea.

His face was magnificent! Perfect features, large round eyes the color of ebony, skin that had never seen any blemish or any slight imperfection. His jet-black hair was thick with curls that lay in rich clusters down his long swan-like neck. He was, beyond all doubt, the most beautiful creature that she had ever seen.

Liz's voice came out in a small whisper. "Where are you taking him?"

"I 'take' him nowhere, Gretch. We are simply here to journey with him." The voice that reached her ears was melodious, a symphony of beautiful tones."It is Paul's wish to go home."

"This is his home, he belongs here with the people who love him. Please, mister, please don't take Paul away." Hot stinging tears flowed easily now, rained effortlessly down her face until she could feel the wetness on her nightgown.

"My name is Michael," the voice said gently. "The choice belongs to Paul, only Paul. Your fears are needless, Gretch, for this is only a passage. Do you remember the moment of your birth?"

"No."

"Neither does Paul, and neither will he remember this passage, although both are his choice. You will understand when the time is right. For now, try to remember not to cling too tightly to the tiny speck that is this life, for there is so much more."

Suddenly, Michael was gone. All three were gone, and Liz whirled around the room, around and around, crying out Paul's name and frantically seeking some glimpse of him, as one might search for a tiny, precious stone.

She ran to the door, flung it open and stood on tiptoes, stretching to see as far down the empty corridor as possible. Nothing. She spun around just in time to catch sight of the three young men moving slowly through the double doors that exited the ward.

She ran. Breathless when she reached the spot where she had last seen them, Liz collapsed in a heap of white flannel, her bare feet tucked under her small body, as she sobbed and pounded her fists against a solid wall.

****

Rachael looked up from her prayer book and smiled when she saw Adam and Leonard come into the room. It had been many years since she had seen Dr. Bennett, but she remembered his concern during Lillian's delivery. Rachael also recalled that he had ceased to be the family physician soon after that event, but she had never asked any questions.

"So nice to see you again, Dr. What brings the two of you here at this hour?" she greeted them.

Bennett nodded and smiled. They had no time for courteous chitchat. He looked at Adam, who caught the silent message and cut Rachael off abruptly.

"Forgive me, Rachael, but we must speak with you regarding a very serious matter," Adam began. He tried not to react to the look of terror on her face and forged ahead. "We... that is, I have very good reason to believe that Paul's liver is in distress and if that major organ shuts down... well, I don't have any other way to say this. It will be fatal."

All color drained from her face and he feared she might faint. Leonard was at her side immediately, always prepared with his vial of ammonia. One good whiff brought her back, coughing. Between gasps she asked, "What happens now?"

"We believe that we can resolve the problem with a rather simple treatment, Rachael." The speaker this time was Leonard, for Adam looked like he could use some support. "Dr. Powell picked up on Paul's jaundiced condition very quickly and we are prepared to treat him. We need your permission."

"What does Dr. Drake say?" she asked the question they had been waiting for. They looked at each other for a moment. Adam was prepared for anything now that he believed so strongly in his mission.

"The truth is that I haven't consulted him."

"Why?"

"Because I can't take the chance that he will not approve, and may even try to prevent it."

"Why would he do that, if it will save Paul's life?"

"This explanation is an oversimplification, Rachael, but we doctors are very territorial. He may fear that it would compromise Paul's healing process. It was excellent surgery, no question. The problem is not the coma; the problem is what is happening to Paul's system that may prolong his coma, even worse. Do I have your support?"

She lowered her head on folded arms and silently prayed. Why was she forced to do this? Hadn't they suffered enough, she and her precious Paul? This "treatment" may kill him, she knew, although Dr. Powell had not actually told her so. How could she go on, living with such a tragic mistake in judgement? She lifted her head and looked at Paul, so quiet, so helpless. *Tell me what to do, Paul. Someone, please, tell me what to do.* She could say "no," keep her vigil and pray that the deepening yellow tint to his skin was something else, something unrelated. Or she could act bolder than she had ever imagined she could, take the chance, reach for the miracle. There were tears now when she looked at the doctors.

"Do it."

Leonard sprung around the bed and began to wheel IV poles into the room, while Adam stood and smiled at Rachael. It was somewhat of a personal victory, her faith in him, he concluded. "I am more sure of this than of anything I have ever done," he told her.

"I hope so."

Leonard stopped for a moment and looked around the room. "Where is the girl... Lillian?" he asked suddenly. "Will she be popping in?" He secretly hoped that the answer would be "yes," for he would like to see her again, after all these years.

"No," Rachael answered. "Sister Therese Marie put her to bed some time ago. It is after midnight, you know."

"Good," Adam said." This is not a covert procedure, by any means. I am sure that when the good Dr. Drake reads the chart, my ass will hang in the proverbial sling. I'll deal with that when I have to. Let's get to work."

By dawn, the small hospital room looked like a battle zone, with IV poles and wet towels strewn from wall to wall. Rachael and the doctors were exhausted from the labor of the repeated treatment, and collapsed in available chairs, or on the floor. Still, they had energy left to continually smile at each other and at their young patient, who was now sitting upright in his bed, demanding to be fed.

Chapter 32

1934

Prohibition was over… not that it made much difference to Jack and Anna Sterling, who, although they avoided the "speakeasy" scene, continued for the fourteen years between the 18th and the 21st Amendment to imbibe at will. For those less fortunate, however, the repeal of prohibition at 5:32 PM on December 5, 1933, signaled a welcome end to a very long dry spell.

This was the year to sing the blues. More Americans were unemployed than ever before, 13 million of them, in fact, and the mood was reflected in such tunes as "Stormy Weather" and "Boulevard of Broken Dreams." If "buddy" could "spare a dime," it might pay for one's movie theater ticket to see *Little Women*, starring Katherine Hepburn, or *King Kong*.

Franklin Delano Roosevelt occupied the White House and would remain there for almost four terms. The first Democrat elected in almost twenty years, his mandate, he believed, was to bring the county out of the dark poverty of the Great Depression and into the warm light of prosperity, which his predecessor, Mr. Hoover, had declared was "just around the corner."

It was a year of "comeuppance" for lawbreakers. "Pretty Boy" Floyd was shot by the G-men. Clyde Barrow and Bonnie Parker were gunned down on a lonely Louisiana road. John Dillinger went to a movie in Chicago with a woman in a red dress, and died on the street when he, too, was killed by agents of the government. "Baby Face" Nelson avenged the deaths of his buddies Dillinger and Floyd, only to be ultimately killed in like manner.

Adolf Hitler was named President of Germany, a title added to that of "Chancellor." Europe seemed not to notice that this one little man, son of an Austrian civil service worker, had more power than Stalin or Mussolini.

Soup lines were still long, and banks were still closed. Despite high unemployment, labor unions gained even more power, calling numerous strikes in their effort to force management to improve upon wages and working conditions.

Rachael accepted a generous severance in addition to the "anonymous" gift, enabling her to purchase a very nice home in Spring Grove, a few miles outside of the city limits. Paul's new room, freshly wallpapered and painted, was barely familiar to him, however, when he left for college at Ohio State. Still true to his word, Jack made a substantial contribution to Paul's tuition fund.

"I suppose I could take in borders," Rachael remarked to Millie. "The house has three bedrooms. It might be nice to be alone for awhile, though." Rachael had a few lingering doubts regarding the source of the cashier's check presented to her, but she dismissed them in the end and saw the windfall as a gift from God, intended to grant independence to her and her son. Dennis Jacobs had done his job very well, even went to the trouble to hire an out-of-work actor to pose as an agent of the Kentucky Mining Company, who handled the payment of the "accidental death claim of one John Unger and others" as part of a large settlement.

"You must understand very clearly," Dr. Powell admonished Rachael, "that Paul's system reacts severely to even trace amounts of alcohol." The medical term is 'Alcoholic Poisoning,' and it could kill him." Adam then addressed Paul directly, "Your drinking days are over, young man!"

Mac served out his summer "on parole," used most of the money he earned to pay off his fine, and considered himself fortunate that no charges were filed. He enrolled at Heidelburg University at Tiffin, Ohio, for the fall term, but he found that his interest was not in academics and left to join the Navy before the winter term had ended.

"Why would you do such a thing?" Jack ranted. "If you wanted to be in the military, we could have applied to the Navel Academy or West Point. How will you ever make Officer's School by enlisting as a nobody?"

"You keep telling me to grow up, Dad, make my own decisions. This is what I want to do. Besides, it may be time for you to realize that there really are some things in life that your money cannot buy!"

Lillian became so involved in her new found faith that she set her sights on converting Isaac away from his Baptist roots. She spent so much time with the young man, in fact, that Jack moved from mild nervous anxiety to downright panic. When she requested to be allowed to attend the Dominican boarding school in the fall, Jack reluctantly agreed, for he had evidently begun to share Anna's obsessive concern about the girl's virginity.

"It is the perfect solution," Anna insisted. "There will be no opportunity for dalliance surrounded by only female classmates and nuns."

Anna was very generous to Rachael regarding the furnishing of her new home, offering much-needed items and a few pieces of value that would lend "ambiance." Rachael's departure gave Anna the incentive to "take back her house" and she spent less time at the boutique. Jacob's "fee for services" practically wiped out what little she had left in her cash reserve, so she was once again totally dependent on Jack. She chose not to discuss the matter with Jack, although she suspected that he probably had come to the correct conclusions.

While the rest of America struggled with hunger and despair, the Sterling family fell into a relative calm. Roosevelt's "fireside chats," the weekly radio broadcast, became a private joke between Anna and Jack, who used the time to sit by the fire in her bedroom, sip brandy and improve upon a new closeness between them. Jack was invited to stay the night upon occasion, and for the present, a warm truce prevailed.

Part 3

Chapter 1

1937

The three girls huddled in a corner of the trunk room, that section of the basement level of Madden Hall that held the empty luggage belonging to the students. Martha and Betsy were trying to keep a cigarette lit, giggling as they took turns puffing. Lillian was the appointed "look out," and she frowned at her best friends between nervous glances at her watch.

"Hurry it up. We will be late for chapel, and Dennis Michael is on duty this morning. She is never in a forgiving mood."

"What are you worrying about?" Martha whispered back to Liz. "You are her pet."

"She doesn't have any pets." Lillian walked around the scattered trunks and headed for the staircase. "You two are on your own, I'm not going to be late for chapel again."

"We're coming," Betsy said, tossing a cigarette butt into the large, fiery incinerator. As they darted up the stairs, they pulled blue beanies from pockets and donned them. Through the "rec" room, with its squeaky wooden floorboards and into the marbled hallway that led to Holy Angels Chapel, they raced the chimes of the massive clock. The girls could see their classmates standing in line on the chapel steps, waiting for the latecomers. Sister Dennis Michael, OP, was centered at the chapel door, her arms folded under the white scapula of her habit. She was not smiling.

"How nice that you could join us, ladies," the sister said. "I trust we didn't inconvenience you."

The trio fell into line and stood very still, heads down, not daring enough to look her in the eye. Lillian stifled a giggle when she recalled reading that one should never challenge a dog by making direct eye contact. Sister Dennis Michael, or "Dennie Mike," as the students dubbed her, was about to comment further when the organ bellowed the opening prelude. It would keep, she decided, for she would not risk the embarrassment of entering the chapel late.

Once the choir of Novices began to chant the "Kyrie," Lillian lost all thought of impending discipline and fell into her spiritual trance. She felt as if her very soul was lifted from her slight body, straining toward heaven. This feeling would never leave her, she vowed. Her conversion to Catholicism had been the most memorable experience of her life, for she was blissfully content in her love affair with God.

Dennis Michael watched Lillian's face when the girl returned to her pew after communion. She had seen that look before, for her teaching tenure spanned over twenty-five years and hundreds of adolescent girls. It was rare, special. But something was different about this one, something the sister couldn't quite define. By the time Mass was over, the peaceful mood had engulfed both teacher and student, and their next conversation was congenial.

"Sister Catherine Ann has asked that you report to her office," Dennis Michael told her as they left the chapel. "I'll tell the kitchen to hold your breakfast."

Lillian looked worried. "Did she say why?"

"Did 'Sister' say 'why,'" the nun corrected. Sisters were never referred to as 'she,' it was considered disrespectful. "I think it best that Sister tell you." Dennis Michael turned quickly toward the stairway, her skirts whirling around long black stockings, floor length rosary clicking. By the time Betsy and Martha caught up, Lillian had closed the door to the office of the Senior Dorm Mother, Sister Catherine Ann.

"Come in, Liz." Catherine Ann smiled as she peered over the glasses perched precariously on her stubby nose. She was Liz's favorite faculty member, warm and sympathetic. Even the use of Lillian's nickname was an effort to put the girl at ease. "We have much to talk about."

Liz remained standing until invited to sit. "Have you received my note, Sister?" she asked.

"Yes. But first we need to secure the plans for next Sunday's crowning. You must be very excited."

The traditional May crowning of the Blessed Mother was the highlight of the sophomore year, and being chosen to carry and place the crown was a very high honor. The student must excel in academics, carry at least an "A" average, and display proficiency in music, sports, and most of all, attitude and decorum. It was a much-coveted appointment, decided only by unanimous decision of the governing board.

"I guess I am a bit nervous," Liz conceded. "I keep thinking that there are so many girls more worthy."

"Nonsense. You were chosen for very good reasons. We have watched you these past two years, and your development has been a source of pride."

186

"Thank you, Sister."

"Now, the plans. As you know, it is the closing event of the school year. After the crowning, there will be a small reception for students and guests. Besides your parents, who else will be attending?"

Liz was caught off-guard. Anna and Jack had been notified of the crowning, certainly, but they had given no indication that they would attend. Mac was unlikely to be there, for he was now enrolled in pilot's training. Rachael's letters hadn't mentioned whether she and Paul would come, for Paul's last letter had hinted at summer school. That was everyone, her entire "family," except for....

"Is there a young man? You can tell me about him, you know. I wasn't born a nun. I was sixteen once."

"He won't be here," Liz blurted. The look on her face was so pained that Sister quickly dropped the subject.

"I see. Well, we won't worry about the numbers. I'm sure the kitchen won't run out of cookies. Now, dear, about your note... your request to remain on campus for the summer... I'm sorry to report that I cannot grant it. You will have to be packed and prepared to go home with your parents."

"I don't understand, Sister," Liz protested. "You granted the request last summer."

"I did. I should not have. I realized later that allowing you to avoid your family had only deepened the distance. This is the last discussion of the matter. You will board the bus to the train station next Monday morning if your parents do not attend on Sunday."

Catherine Ann removed her glasses and pinched the bridge of her nose, bracing herself for whatever reaction might follow. There was only silence. She looked at Liz, whose chin now rested on her chest. "I know that you are disappointed, but you need to have some fun, dear. Go swimming, ride your beautiful horse and go dancing with a handsome boy. We will, God willing, all be here in the fall, waiting for you."

Lillian jerked her head up suddenly and announced, "I want to enter as a Postulant next fall."

Catherine Ann had seen it coming and she was prepared. "All the more reason to have this summer, Liz. Before you can give up the world, you need to see at least some of it. If it is truly meant to be, it will. But know this with certainty, the convent is not a place to hide, and the feelings that you may have for that young man will not disappear when you cross that threshold."

It was well after midnight when Betsy and Martha tiptoed across the room and slid into Liz's bed. It was a serious infraction, one that could get them expelled, but their friend was crying. St. Paul's was a small dormitory, only eight beds, and the resident dorm mother, Sister Luke, was not yet in her curtained alcove, for she usually worked very late at the laundry.

"Are you sad because you have to go home?" Betsy asked gently as she stroked Liz's long blond hair. "At least you and Martha can see each other, are in the same town. I will be stuck in Ann Arbor with no one to talk to."

"She's sad about Isaac," Martha ventured. "You really miss him, huh? Has he kissed you yet? Please, Lizzy, tell us all about his thick warm lips... did he squeeze your boobies?"

Betsy was stunned by Martha's bold approach, and gave a warning glare, which Martha missed in the darkness. She was about to reproach her soundly when they heard a giggle from the direction of the pillow.

"What boobies?"

The tension broken, they doubled over in peals of laughter until a roommate "shushed" them to silence. They hugged in a circle and the two barefoot girls returned to their beds just in time to say "goodnight, Sister" to the weary nun who moved past their beds.

Chapter 2

"So I said to Fred...' don't be silly, Fred, of course we'll be invited. Why wouldn't we be? Jack and Anna have been our friends for years and years.' Have you decided on a caterer yet?" Mary George was beginning to get on everyone's nerves, for she had chattered like a magpie since the foursome had seated themselves for a serious game of bridge.

"Sophie, dear, did you bid?" Doris interjected. Perhaps a change of subject would get Mary's mind off what would certainly be the social event of the year.

Sophie rolled her big brown eyes. "Yes, Doris dear. I bid three spades."

Anna smiled indulgently, grateful that she had been excused from answering Mary's constant questions. They were all invited, of course, their invitations would be in their morning delivery, but Anna enjoyed the game of letting them worry for awhile. It was good to be back in the weekly game, a pleasure she had forfeited when her expanding boutiques had taken so much of her time. Anna's life was very pleasant these days. Mac was advancing himself promisingly in the Navy, she had the house to herself, except for the usual staff, Jack was particularly caring and kind, and Lillian had blossomed into a lovely, charming young lady... a daughter to be proud of.

Mary would not be silenced. "I saw Lillian's picture in the paper," she gushed. "So pretty, that girl! I don't know much about Catholic boarding schools, but I understand that 'crowning of the May ' is quite an honor. We should introduce her to our David."

"It is the crowning of the Blessed Virgin Mary," Anna corrected. "I doubt that Lillian will devote any time to dating this summer. She has a very full agenda, with music lessons, her equestrian training and all." Anna caught the deflated look on Mary's face and considered adding, "David will, of course, see her at the ball." but she didn't want to encourage Mary's matchmaking.

"One would think that you have no interest in Lillian's introduction to eligible young men," Mary persisted. "Isn't that what a 'coming out' is supposed to be about? Sophie, you rat, you just trumped my ace."

Sophie grinned and lit a cigarette. "If you paid as much attention to bridge as you do to social climbing, Mary, you'd have noticed that I won the bid!"

Mary blushed. Anna felt a little uncomfortable with Sophie's remark and turned her full attention to the bridge game. Jack had refused to attend the crowning ceremony, mumbling about "heathen witchcraft stuff," and Anna chose not to argue the point, for Lillian seemed unconcerned with their absence.

Lillian couldn't have cared less actually, and was secretly relieved. Her mood changed quickly, however, when Martha's mother waved an engraved invitation under Liz's nose and spilled the beans about Anna's greatest adventure. "You must be so thrilled, Lillian," Mrs. Singer chirped, "a debutante ball! The lady then proceeded to fill in some of the more auspicious details, using such terms as "huge lawn party," "catered," "thousands of dollars." Lillian stared, dumbfounded, while Martha jumped and squealed and starting chattering to her mother about the dress she would buy for the occasion.

"I'm so excited, I may pee my pants!" Martha went on. "You will be positively the envy of everyone... my best friend!"

Lillian felt her face grow warmer, her pulse quicken. She mumbled something unheard by the Singers and raced through Madden Hall in search of Catherine Ann.

"Liz, whatever is wrong?" the sister said when Liz gripped the sleeve of her habit.

"Did you know about this... this party?" Lillian demanded. Under normal circumstances, Catherine Ann would have been compelled to correct the student's manners, but Liz's pallor and obvious agitation worried the nun.

"Your mother told me about it a few weeks ago," Sister said. "I gather she has been planning it for some time, but it was supposed to be a homecoming surprise. I suppose the cat is out of the bag now, someone has told you about it."

Liz began to cry a little. Tears were a new experience, for she seldom indulged in emotionalism. "I won't do it!" she almost shouted. "I won't allow her to parade me in front of the whole town like a piece of meat on the block. Why can't she just leave me alone?"

They were standing in the solarium, bright spring sunlight spilled across the polished tiles where parents and students sipped tea and nibbled cookies. Most of the faculty was there. People began to stop speaking, looked in the direction of the excited young girl who was standing with the nun.

"Liz, lower your voice please, you are creating a scene. Come over here with me." Catherine Ann led Liz to a quiet corner behind a staircase. "What is so terrible? Your mother wants to introduce you to society, that's all. What

190

is so wrong about that?"

"Why can't you see?" Liz whined. "She doesn't care about me, what I want. This is just another excuse to take credit for what she wants me to be, not who I really am! It's uppercrust phony, a sham! Let's spend a lot of money and put on a big show and maybe, just maybe, we can marry her off to someone who deserves to be our son-in-law! Well, she can go to hell... I won't do it!"

"Lillian Gretchen Sterling, amend your tone! You have the rest of your life to follow your own agenda; this is one day that you can give to your mother. Remember the fourth commandment... 'Honor thy Father and thy Mother.'"

Lillian stopped crying and glared at her favorite nun. She felt a pang where she supposed her heart was, but she would not let Catherine Ann know how hurtful her reply had been. Liz stiffened, holding the Sister's gaze. "I prefer the first, Sister: 'I am the Lord thy God.'"

The nun took a deep breath and closed her eyes. She wanted to wrap her arms around the girl, comfort her. When her eyes opened, the belligerent look had only hardened.

"You, dear child, are willful and without compassion. You will, of course, do as you please, but you must know this if you intend to enter the order. There are three basic rules: poverty, chastity, and obedience. That last one will be the one that trips you every time." Catherine Ann watched Lillian walk away. "Dear Lord," she whispered, "that didn't go well at all."

Lillian stepped off the train the next afternoon to be met by Billy. She requested that he drive her directly to Jack's office. Her father was delighted to see her, looking so grownup, radiant really. She returned his rare embrace with cool acceptance and as was her tendency, came right to the point.

"If you are really happy to see me, perhaps you will grant me a homecoming wish?"

"Of course, dear. Anything."

"Persuade my mother to call off this... this party thing. 'Debutante ball,' whatever she calls it. Please, Papa, I beg you. Don't make me do this!"

Jack gave her a shocked look. "You mother has spent months in the planning," he said. "She wanted you to be surprised, thrilled. It would break her heart, not to mention the humiliation of recalling hundreds of engraved invitations, the expense.... what on earth is wrong with you, Diz?"

"I'll die, just die if she makes me play up to her society friends and their stupid sons. I have never asked you for anything that is more important to me.

Please, Papa."

"And I, Lillian, have never denied you. Tell you what, ask me to do something considerably easier, like stopping a speeding locomotive! I'll make it up to you, I promise. A few hours, that is all, and it will be over forever."

She had challenged her father and lost. He used the name "Lillian" when he spoke to her, the name she hated. She was no longer his "princess," she concluded. The one person in her life that she could always depend upon had defected in her absence, and Anna now occupied Diz's place in his heart. It was a painful betrayal to the trusting daughter.

She left the room without another word, leaving Jack wondering how he would survive the ongoing war between mother and daughter.

Considering her age and her level of life experience, Lillian Sterling had a remarkably uncanny ability to analyze, resolve, and rectify. These useful traits were passed to her at birth, a gift from her gene pool, for both parents were masters at the art. Unburdened by emotionalism, the Sterlings were like cats who always landed on their feet, for each of them could grasp and regain control when they felt it slipping away, quickly calculate how their own interest would best be served, and make it happen. Two factors were known to complicate this capacity, however. The first was pride, which confused the issue and often resulted in rash judgement. The second was a tenaciously stubborn will which allowed for absolutely no change of mind, no second-guesses, no recant. Once the evaluation had been completed, the plan formulated, nothing in heaven or on earth would change it.

Lillian needed time to think. She asked Billy to drive to the park, where she found her favorite bench next to the pond. What were her options? She could run away, she supposed... and go where? She could attempt to reason with Anna. No. Those two words didn't fit in the same sentence. She could try again with Papa. No. That door had closed.

She could ruin the whole affair, create a nasty scene, heap humiliation on the heads of her beloved parents, and bask in the glow of satisfaction. Too mean, too much planning involved... what would it gain her? The key, Lillian reasoned, was to determine the best possible outcome and work backward.

Billy watched her from the car, leaning on the rear fender while he smoked. When Liz approached him, she was smiling. "Let's go home," she told him.

Chapter 3

Paul considered making up some excuse to cut this telephone conversation short, but on the other end, Mac went on somewhat nervously. They had spoken only a few times since the accident four years ago. Strange, Paul thought, they were once so close, like brothers, really. "People float in and out of our lives," one of his professors had said. "Like a stage play, enter, exit stage left. That very person who plays such a vital role in your life today may be beyond your recall five years from now. Unless, of course, they are related to you, and then they are forever in your memory."

"I don't think there is any option," Mac was telling Paul, who stood first on one leg, then the other. The frat house was buzzing tonight, young men up and down the hall where the telephone was almost never without a user. "It is a command performance, you know, show up, look good, play the dutiful son and brother."

"Why do I have to go?" Paul retorted. "I am neither."

"Baloney. You can't get off the hook that easy, buddy. Besides, the Navy owns me now, so I may not get the leave I requested. You'll need to represent the masculine end of the family."

It was true. The Sterlings had once seemed like a family to Paul. Somehow, that was no longer the case, not because of the accident... just because. Perhaps it was the new life he enjoyed now, the distance. He was happy at Ohio State, happier than ever before, and while he missed his mother, he had nothing else to go back for.

"What about Lillian? Doesn't she matter to you anymore, Paul?" Mac's question hit him with a bolt, causing him to jump out of his reverie. It was spooky, like Mac had read his thoughts, or had he actually expressed them? Sometimes Paul was confused. And there were dizzy spells, short-term blackouts.

"Of course she does! How could you ask me that? I love her like a sister."

"Well, there you have it! This night is all about her, you know. Her big debut into Anna's social heaven. Sis will be very hurt if you are not there."

"I'll think about it."

"Good. Hey, call me once in awhile, will 'ya? We need to keep in touch."

"Yeah. Bye, Mac."

As he hung up the phone, he felt the light pressure of a body against his back. He smiled and turned slowly to look into the emerald green eyes of Caroline Bradley.

"If you're trying to avoid me, it won't work," she whispered. "I always know where to find you."

His heart pounded rapidly, just as it did every time he even so much as thought about her, which was more often than he cared to admit. He tensed, tried to think of something witty and clever to say that would make her laugh, but as usual he stumbled over his words like the head-over-heels-in-love schoolboy that he was.

"Wow," she said seriously. "Something is really wrong. You look like you just got hit with a brick."

Paul had the entire scene planned, had gone over it a dozen times. The diamond ring was in the top drawer of his dresser, upstairs. He had made dinner reservations for Friday evening at the finest restaurant in Columbus. On Saturday morning they would pack up the Ford·Roadster that his mother had presented to him and they would drive to Spring Grove to share the glorious news with Rachael. It would be perfect, just as Caroline was perfect, in every way.

"We can't talk here," Paul whispered. Frat house rules forbid the presence of female visitors without chaperones, and the continual flow of "brothers" who passed them in the corridor with knowing smiles was making Paul nervous.

"Wait for me on our bench in front of the library," he instructed her, and kissed her quickly. She nodded, stepped away from him and waved merrily as she strolled down the front steps. He raced to the second floor, taking the steps two and three at a time, grabbed the black velvet ring box from the drawer and raced back down to the same door. He sniffed the air, confident that it was her sweet Chantilly scent that still lingered.

"I am so excited about summer school," Caroline exclaimed when he found her at their "special place." She threw herself into his arms, wrapping her long legs around him in a lock. "We can be together for the entire summer, just imagine! The sun, the surf, the warm, wonderful summer!"

"Surf?" Paul chuckled. "Not much surf in Columbus, honey."

She frowned. Then she brightened and pulled him by the hand to the bench. "Paul," she said very sweetly, "I want us to transfer to Southern Cal."

The look on his face made her frown again. "Oh, please, Paul. Let's do it! It's one of the best schools in the country. We can finish our degree programs early, get wonderful jobs and settle out there. If it is your mother you're thinking about... well, she can come with us, later. I need you to help me, Paul. I can't do this alone."

He hadn't seen it coming. He had never entertained the possibility that they would finish their education anywhere but here at OSU, or that they might reside anywhere but Spring Grove. Why hadn't he?

"I am committed to this program," Paul told Caroline. "I can't just pick up and move three thousand miles away and start over. It's out of the question."

"I thought you were committed to me," Caroline said. "But I understand now that your commitment has limits. I don't want to stay here, Paul. I hate the winters. Most of my friends are there, and I would love it if you would come with me. But I'm going, in any case."

"Then there is nothing more that I can say. Your mind is made up, and you seem to think you can make decisions for me while you're at it. I have family obligations, my mother..."

"Your mother. You won't even discuss it with her, will you?'

"No."

They continued to see each other for the rest of the week, but when Paul left on Friday, Caroline didn't come by the dorm to say "goodbye." He packed the ring box away, along with his stamp collection and *Short Wave Radio* magazines. His last exam was over, his belongings packed in the car, there was nothing more for him here, he decided, as he drove around her sorority house ten, maybe twelve times. He watched the window that was her bedroom's, cruising slowly, hoping to see her standing there, looking for him. As he stepped on the gas toward the front gate, a frat brother waved him down.

"There's a phone call for you at the dorm," he told Paul.

"Who is it?" he asked, his heart beating wildly.

The housemate shrugged, and ran off across the green to the commissary.

Paul left the motor running and took the stone steps in two bounds. The phone at the end of the hall dangled by its cord and he grabbed it, expecting to hear her say, "I changed my mind, darling. I can't live without you, even in California."

"Paul, are you there?" the voice said. It was his mother.

"Yes," he said flatly. "Yes, I'm here."

"I hope I didn't take you away from anything, dear. I just haven't heard from you for awhile and I wondered about your plans for the weekend."

"I... I don't... I don't have any plans, I guess."

"Honey, are you all right?"

"Yeah. Look, Mom, I don't mean to cut you short, but the car is running and I'm all packed. I'll see you tomorrow sometime."

"Oh, that is wonderful, Paul. I'll have your favorite dinner ready. Hurry home!"

"Yeah."

"Paul, tell me, what is wrong?"

"We'll talk when I get home, Mom. Everything is fine, really. Don't worry."

"All right, dear. If you say so. Oh, I almost forgot the reason I called. Mr. Porter called from the men's store downtown. He said to tell you that he was holding a tux for you, but he needs your measurements right away. I know what they were, but I needed to check. Still the same?"

"What? What do I need a tux for?"

"Lillian's coming out party, dear. Did you forget? It's black tie."

Chapter 4

"It was like *Alice in Wonderland*, Martha," Liz was saying. She slurped through her soda straw. "You know, tea with the Mad Hatter."

"Did she tell you about the party?"

"Not one single word. I pretended not to notice that the whole house was in an uproar; there were six gardeners mowing grass and pruning trees. Party stuff was piled all over the place and Helga was cooking up a storm. We sat there eating cucumber sandwiches and sipping tea. I tell you, it was so strange, like I was a visitor in my own home."

What Liz didn't tell her friend was that she felt like a visitor who was not particularly welcome, but necessarily tolerated. Nevertheless, her homecoming reunion with her mother had not disappointed her, for it had been just as she expected.

Anna made an effort to play the doting parent, but her feigned interest in Liz's academic achievements and music awards was all too obvious. They simply had very little to talk about, this mother and daughter, for they avoided intimacy at all cost.

"Have you told her yet that you intend to enter the Dominicans?" Martha asked.

"Heavens no! It would be war all summer. I will wait until about three days before I leave. Papa will sign, I know he will. Maybe I can persuade him to break the news after I've left."

"Do you want to see my dress? It's a gas!"

Liz had been so preoccupied with trying to avoid discussion of the ball that she had given no thought to the details. A dress! Of course she would need a dress. Her mind wandered while she tried to picture what she might wear.

"Liz?"

"What?"

"I asked you if you wanted to see my dress. We can go over to my house and I'll show it to you. Mother said I could have any color except white, because white was for the debutante. That's you, I guess."

The girls left the soda shop and took the cross-town bus to the Singer house. "I hate riding the bus," Martha complained. "I begged my dad for a car, and I almost had him talked into it, but he changed his mind. He said I could have one if I stayed home and went to high school here, but it was a waste of money just to drive it for the summer."

She gave her friend a sideways glance, testing Liz's reactions. "I was pretty tempted to drop out of boarding school."

"How could you even consider it?" Liz exclaimed. "We are a team, the three of us. Betsy would die if you didn't go back."

"It's not the same for me, you know," Martha explained. "I am only there for the education. We are Jews. I don't get the same spiritual high that you and Betsy seem to."

"You could convert," Liz suggested. "I did."

Martha frowned. "It's not that simple. I don't want to be anything but what I am. Furthermore... I'm sorry, Liz, but I sure as hell don't want to spend my life hidden away in a convent, wasting my ovaries."

"Is that what you think I am doing?"

"If you really want to know what I think... here it is. I think you are hiding from your mother. And I think you are in love with Isaac, but you know that you can never have him, so you are throwing yourself into some sort of ... I don't know, self-persecution, maybe. It seems just all too tragic."

They lapsed into silence. Martha tried to think of something to say that might lighten the moment, for she had said too much. She envied her friend, the girl who had everything. Everything except joy.

Liz was thinking about Isaac. Was it true? She had to admit that he was in her thoughts more intensely since her return to Richmond She found herself looking for some glimpse of him everywhere. She hummed his favorite tunes, read his favorite books, tossed and turned for hours every night as he dominated her dreams. She was so confused about her feelings. It was as if she were a twin, one, devoutly religious who aspired to the pursuit of heaven, the other a very flesh and blood young woman who yearned to realize the mysteries of passion. Was Martha correct in her analysis? Did she retreat to the Motherhouse in order to forget him?

Lillian read the *Rules of the Order*.

RULES OF THE ORDER OF ST. DOMINIC

"The prospective postulant must conduct herself at all times, both publicly and privately, with the utmost decorum. Virtue is not something to be exercised in one location and discarded in another, but an intregal part of the total spirit. Remember that you, as a possible member of the order of Saint Dominic, must do or say nothing that might, in any manner, bring shame upon yourself, your family, or the order. This rule is particularly true as regards the sixth commandment."

The guidebook went on to explain the importance of daily mass, monthly confession, and the preference the "perspective postulant" should give to good companions. Liz tossed the book off her bed and sighed. She was bored. Her internal balance was off because her routine had been abandoned. Her academy days had been filled with prayer, study, and the treasured time with her friends. She missed everything about the Adrian campus, even the teeth-grinding clang of the awakening bell at 5:40 AM, followed by the eyeball-blinding glare of the overhead light. The students sat upright in their beds, eyes wide open and staring at the nun with the bell, standing in the doorway. Sister pressed an index finger to her lips, said, "Glory be to God," followed up by, "20 minutes."

Complete silence was imposed until after breakfast, and there was little time to chat then, since the girls went directly to class. Lunch was taken in silence. At three o'clock the students were free to partake in some outdoor activity, visit with classmates, or request a conference with one of the sisters or Father Gaynor. Dinner was at 5:30, followed by two hours of study hall and one hour in the music room.

Liz missed the simple routine, the buttered noodles that tasted like rubber bands, the soggy oatmeal. She missed the serenity of the chapel, the sound of the vespers bell, the sweet soap and water smell of the sisters.

I was right, she thought. Less than a week at home, she had no one left to talk to. Rachael lived twelve miles away, and while she was certain she could quickly learn to handle the automobile, Jake was reluctant to allow it. Martha was leaving next week for summer camp. She had ridden Pegasus for hours every day, resulting in an injury the vet called a "shin splint."

Lillian had never felt lonelier in her entire life.

Chapter 5

Jack rarely announced his homecoming. If no one noticed his car winding up the long driveway from the gothic iron gates, he could be in the large house for hours before anyone was aware of his presence. It was a game with him, to find out how much he could overhear from the kitchen, or who he could catch in the act of doing what. Helga had dealt with his "little habit" since he had been old enough to walk, but he could still scare the hell out her, sneaking up behind her and grabbing a slice of her meal preparation.

A call from his accountant had given Jack a raging headache. "Have you seen these bills, Jack? Flowers, linens, candles... you name it, Anna's ordered it. This party will cost you a fortune."

"Pay them," Jack answered, and he hung up. He took two aspirin and drove home. He let himself into the den, napped for about forty minutes and then poured a large scotch. He stood at the large beveled window and watched Lillian as she and Pegasus approached the stables at a canter. Jack smiled to himself and was about to turn away when he caught sight of Isaac as he came out the barn door and stood ready to receive the reins. Jack turned then to open the desk drawer that held his high powered binoculars. He managed to focus just in time to see Lillian slid down from the saddle, into the arms of Isaac Anderson. Closer inspection confirmed for Jack that their bodies were pressed tightly together for more than a few seconds. Jack watched as Isaac nuzzled the side of Lillian's neck before they walked hand in hand, into the barn.

He put the field glasses away and picked up the telephone.

Anna was accustomed to finding Jack napping in the den or floating in the pool. This afternoon she was in the pantry off the kitchen, reaching for something so high that even her considerable height needed the assistance of the stepstool. Like Jack, she often showed up in unlikely places, but for Anna it was no game. She pulled drawers open to check for the dreaded roaches. She examined the shine of the silver, inventoried the food supply, and was known to strip any bed that did not meet her very high standard.

When she found the basket she had been seeking, she descended the small ladder and began to search for the silver napkin rings that had belonged to her grandmother. She had decided to pass them on to Mac, as they were the only heirlooms from her side of the family. She had been a little hard on him, that day she had taken him to meet Malcomb. She would take them to the jeweler, she thought, have them cleaned and polished. She examined the engraving: "M." It was fitting and proper.

She sat on the stool and thought about Mac's homecoming, a few days away. Perhaps the excitement of the party, the family together again, would heal old wounds. She hoped so, for she dearly missed her son.

"I tell you, Helga, I couldn't believe my eyes!" Anna heard a voice from the nearby kitchen. It was Emily, sharing some tidbit that aroused Anna's natural curiosity.

"There they were, in broad daylight, carrying on like a couple of love struck puppies. I tell you, I saw it all! They were as close as I am to you, and I could hear every word."

"And what were you doing, Miss O'Shea, sneaking around in the garden on your hands and knees?" Helga chuckled.

"I was looking for Buddy. He sometimes chases rabbits or mice. If he slips through the fence, he might get out on the road and get hit."

"We're half a mile from the road, Emily."

"Do you want to hear this story or do you want to argue with me, Helga?"

"Go on, go on. You're just bursting your buttons to tell me, so get on with it. I have a mess of cooking to do, in case you didn't notice. Damn party!"

"Well, suddenly there they were. She walked up from the stables and he followed her. He had Miss Lillian pressed up against the brick wall under the eaves. He was whispering in her ear and... that part I couldn't hear, but she was telling him that yes, she loved him. 'But it can never be,' she was saying. 'Why, because I'm a black man?' he says to her and she said that his race was only part of it. She is promised to someone else, she tells him, and can never be with Isaac 'that way.'"

"Who?" Helga demanded to know. She gave full attention now, laid down her ladle and faced Emily, hands on hips. Anna strained to hear.

"Christ!" Emily exclaimed.

"What's the matter?"

"Nothing. Christ."

"There you go again. Are you daft, girlie? What are you cussin' about?"

"You're the one who's daft, Helga. I am trying to tell you that Miss Lillian says she wants to be the bride of Christ. She told Isaac that she wants to be a nun."

"Well, don't that beat all!" Helga whispered, plopping her bulk into a nearby chair. "You better hand me that brandy, girl."

Anna would have preferred to join the ladies with the brandy, considering that she was stuck in the pantry until Emily went about her duties and she heard the bathroom door shut, signaling that Helga was on a "necessity trip."

Maybe I should spend more time in the pantry, Anna thought as she made her way through the house. This was news, indeed, and not news that she wanted to share with Jack, at least not until after the festivities.

It was barely dawn the next morning as Isaac left his mother's small house and walked three blocks to the bus stop. "Be here before six," Emily had instructed him. "There is much to be done." A car pulled up behind him and a man's voice said, "Are you Isaac Anderson?" Isaac's basic instinct signaled a slight alarm when he turned to face not one, but two well dressed white men. They were not from the neighborhood, and it was not likely that they were seeking directions.

"Yes."

"Well, Isaac, this is your lucky day. We are here to escort you to work, so you won't be catching the bus today. Get in." One of the men held open the rear door while the other stepped closer to Isaac, his hand in his jacket pocket.

"I don't have any money," Isaac told them.

"That's all right, boy. You won't need any."

Isaac quickly surveyed the terrain and tried to force his panicked mind into a reasonable conclusion. He could outrun them, probably, for he was very fast and knew the area well. The street was vacant at this hour, so no one would likely witness a scuffle or hear his cries for help. Did the man have a gun, or was he bluffing? Isaac decided not to take the chance.

One of them got into the back seat with Isaac as the other drove the car away with moderate speed. Experience had taught Isaac that asking questions of white men was usually a waste of time, for they would tell him what they wanted him to know. Although he gave the appearance of calm acceptance, he was very afraid.

"Here's the deal, Isaac," the man beside him said. "We will drive you to your new employer, who will pay you a very fair salary as long as you do as you are told. The rule is that you are not, under any circumstances, to cross over the bridge to the other side of town. You will not see Lillian Sterling again; you will not contact her in any way. Understood? Your new job is driving new cars to Florida, so you will be on the road for long periods of time. Any questions?"

"If I don't... do as I am told?" Isaac asked.

The man seated next to him looked out the car window at the passing houses. He was silent for so long that Isaac considered repeating the question, but he waited until the man was ready to answer.

"I grew up in a place very much like this," the man said. "Once in awhile, not often, but once in awhile, a little girl would get lost, or come up missing, or something. Sad, I used to think, how bad things sometimes happen to little girls. How old is your little sister, Isaac?"

Isaac turned away to look out the other window. He had his answer.

Chapter 6

"What is this?" Anna was looking at the small package in her lap. "My birthday isn't until September."

"Why don't you open it and find out?" Jack grinned. "Since when do I need a reason to honor my wife? Consider it your trophy for a job well done."

They were in her bedroom, the place that had become their sanctuary. No fire blazed, for it was balmy, early June and well after midnight. They drank their brandy, still dressed in their party finery. Monday's newspaper would feature the gala event, complete with photographs of a tuxedo-clad Jack and the elegant Anna. The real surprise would be a shot of Lillian, lovely beyond belief in her eggshell chiffon, dancing with the son of Richmond's mayor.

"It really was wonderful, wasn't it? An unqualified success?" Anna asked her husband. It seemed that the more she gained his approval, the more it became necessary to her.

"I would call it a triumph!" Jack answered. "Now, open it."

It looked like something that could wait, for the small package was clumsily wrapped in brown paper and tied with string. "Oh, Jack... how can I ever thank you enough... a bar of Fels Naptha soap!"

"Things are not always what they seem, my dear Anna," he teased. He was enjoying the moment, for he didn't want the evening to end. He only wished that his mother could have been there to witness how the most important residents of the small city had reveled in his hospitality. Richmond had never seen anything like it, the massive white tents, the caviar and champagne, the lobster, the wonderful orchestra whose strains of Glenn Miller and Tommy Dorsey still lingered in the warm air. And, of course, "his girls," his beautiful "September girls," as he called them... for that is what the press would call them, captioned under a photograph of a beaming Jack flanked by Anna and Lillian.

She opened the end flap and pulled out a wad of white tissue paper. This wasn't soap. The paper fell away under the weight of a diamond and ruby bracelet, so exquisite and so expensive that some might call it "ostentatious."

Jack had given her many lovely things, costly things: the new Cadillac, a fur coat, her silver service, the list was endless. She had never taken any of it for granted. Growing up severely poor, each gift was very appreciated, and even a little unreal. Somehow it was as if the car, and the coat, all of it, didn't belong to her. Not really. They were props. But this... this was hers. It came from his heart, she knew. She would treasure it forever.

She was so moved, so overwhelmed, that she chose silence. A brief hug was all Anna could manage before she turned away.

Jack's proud smile faded. "Don't you like it?" he asked. His tone reminded Anna of Mac at the age of ten.

"More than you can ever know," she told him. "More than I could ever express to you. You are so good to me, Jack. I'm not sure that I deserve your kindness."

This was a strange mood, brought on perhaps by a dip into nostalgia, the victory of the party, the brandy. Their embrace was brief and without passion, but it was warm and it conveyed all the love that they each had within them to give.

Jack awoke in the very early hours of the morning with a vague feeling of uneasiness. He was sitting upright on Anna's chaise lounge, his short legs covered with an afghan. In the moonlight that streamed through the window, he could see the form of his wife in her bed, and he sat for a moment, listening to the soft sound of her snoring. He never slept well in this room, and they had spent very few nights in the same bed. He rose slowly, quietly, so that he would not disturb her, requiring an explanation. He glanced at the window, hesitated, and groped his way to the door, back to his own room.

Had he spent time at the window, Jack may have observed his daughter asleep on the front lawn, under a large oak tree. She was dreaming the she was Cinderella, just home from the ball. It had been a magnificent evening, for she had filled one dance card after another, laughing and twirling with handsome princes. One in particular made her heart stir lightly, like the flutter of butterfly wings, for he was the beautiful Paul. He carried a solitary rose when he approached her on the dance floor, and everyone moved away when he took her in his arms. Liz moved like a vision in the yards and yards of vanilla chiffon, her glossy brown hair pulled up in a diamond clip. Around her long neck was the solid gold chain that held a golden key, a mysterious gift from her Papa.

"Keep it with you forever," Papa had said when he secured the clasp. "Someday, when the time is right, you will understand how to use it."

She danced and danced. All of the other girls watched with envy as the would-be dance partners pushed and shoved at each other to get to her. Suddenly Paul was gone, and she was dancing with someone else, a dark stranger, and the only man wearing a white jacket. But he was not really a stranger, she knew him well, even though she could not clearly see his face. He carried her in his strong arms to the terrace and he kissed her. His lips were so warm, so soft. She felt as if she might melt under the spell he held over her, and her heart kept telling her to "give in," "surrender."

It was a magical night, one that she would remember, or try to remember, for the rest of her life.

Chapter 7

When Lillian opened her eyes, she saw the large man standing over her. She jumped, giving a little gasp. She struggled to sit up, but the grass was slippery with dew and her head pounded harshly. She was disoriented, confused.

"Easy now." The voice was Billy's, and Liz relaxed a little. "Let me help you, Miss Lillian. What on earth are you doing out here?"

She didn't answer for a moment, but held her hand out to him. He slowly lifted her to her feet and she leaned against him, shivering. Billy wrapped his denim jacket around her shoulders and held her tightly against his chest.

"I don't know. I guess I fell asleep."

Billy's keen eye surveyed the area. An empty champagne bottle lay a few feet away. Next to the bottle was a white cummerbund, crumpled and wet. His watch said five seventeen. The sky was still gray, the air close and noisy with the sounds of birds who demanded the advent of dawn.

"Let's get you back to the house," he said gently. "Can you walk?"

"I think so."

He began to lead her slowly, but her legs buckled, so he deftly reached under her and picked her up. She laid her head against his broad shoulder while he effortlessly carried her across the large lawn that was littered with the remnants of last night's reverie.

It gave him time to plan ahead. The front door would be locked. He had in his pocket a key to the back door, so he carried Liz around the house to the kitchen entrance. He put her down, balancing her body against his while he fumbled for the key. Once in the kitchen, he hesitated. If he carried her to her room, he would very likely make enough noise to be heard, for Jack was a light sleeper as well as an early riser. If he took her through the downstairs rooms to one of the couches, he might encounter one of the maids. What the hell was he going to do with her? He couldn't stand here all day!

She weighed barely more than one hundred pounds, but he felt her weight. If he sat her in one of the kitchen chairs and went to find help, would she fall or wander off?

Billy had run out of options. He carried Liz down the hallway toward the servant's quarters, where he kicked at Helga's bedroom door until it opened just a crack.

"What the...?" Helga's eyes opened wide at the sight of them, all thoughts of sleep suddenly just a memory.

"Hush, woman!" Billy hissed. "Open the Goddamn door!"

The door swung wide and he pushed past the near naked Helga, who gasped and grabbed at a robe in an unsuccessful attempt to cover herself. Billy laid Lillian down on the already-made bed and looked around for a cover.

He turned to face the stunned Helga, still clutching the robe to her naked, ample body. It didn't cover much, Billy observed. He chuckled. "Great God Almighty! You sleep in the raw!"

Helga snapped like she had been awakened with a spray of ice water. She whirled around to face the door, exposing a large pink backside that vaguely reminded Billy of two pigs nestled tightly together in a barn stall. He continued to stare as Helga fumbled with the robe, its edges reluctantly joining at the belt.

"Just never you mind how I sleep, Mister!" she retorted. "What the hell are you doing in my room, and what is wrong with that child?" Helga's face was scarlet, hot, and twisted in anger and embarrassment.

"You'll need to get this wet dress off of her, quickly," Billy instructed, ignoring her outburst. "I think she'll be all right, if she doesn't catch her death. Too much party, I'm guessing. I found her asleep under the big oak." Best not to tell Helga too much, but then he didn't know too much.

They stood in silence, looking at each other. Someone had to move, sooner or later, so Billy took a step toward the doorway. Helga jumped over a few feet to let him pass. "What am I supposed to do with her?" she asked.

"Do I have to tell you everything?" Billy sighed. "Get her undressed, keep her warm, and get her to her own bed as soon as you can. Emily can help you, I have work to do."

He opened the door slightly, looked up and down the corridor. "Oh, and by the way, the fewer people who know about this, the better."

"Why?"

"I'm not sure yet," he answered, "just a hunch."

By this time Helga was reluctant to see him leave. He knew something that he was not telling her and it would drive her mad. She forced a gentler tone in an effort to draw him into continued conversation.

"So... don't you?"

"Don't I what?"

"'Sleep in the raw'?"

Billy laughed now, a welcome belly laugh that was really more one of relief that he was almost out of there than a tribute to Helga's wit. "Not unless I have company. Are you hiding a man in here, Helga?"

She flushed deeply and batted at him, her fleshy arms flaying in the air. He winked at her and chuckled all the way down the long hall, shaking his head.

Retracing his steps, Billy retrieved the empty bottle and the piece of clothing still under the tree. As he turned to return to his apartment for a much-needed cup of coffee, his eye caught a glimmer in the wet grass. Sun on the dew, he thought at first, but closer examination produced a gold cufflink. Billy picked it up and noted the initials.

"Must have been some party!" he said to the birds as he pocketed the shinny disk and walked toward the carriage house.

Chapter 8

The summer of 1937 was a boon to the newspaper industry, but nothing affected the country more than the searing heat wave that caused the death of 109 Americans. Temperatures hovered well over the 100-degree mark for weeks at a time, stretching tempers to the breaking point. Domestic violence was on the rise, reported the *New York Times,* as the dry, hot weather doggedly jockeyed for attention, bumping such auspicious headlines as the wedding of the Duke and Duchess of Windsor and the mysterious disappearance of Amelia Earhart.

The article that Jack read one August morning was very disturbing. Four of the "Scotsboro Nine" had been released from prison, after a six-year wait for a new trial. The accused rapists, poor southern blacks, had the US Supreme Court to thank for their spared lives.

"Why does this bother you so?" Anna asked her husband as they sipped their coffee on the west porch. It was still early, and relatively cool. "Hitler has just constructed another concentration camp… why don't you get excited about that?"

"We have no control over Hitler, he'll do what he has to do," Jack retorted. "America is my back yard, and when niggers can rape white girls and get away with it, everyone should get excited. Don't the people of Alabama have guns? Where is the local justice?"

Anna fell silent. It was futile to debate with Jack, for he would never consider that the accused might be innocent. She thought about Isaac… what had become of him, she wondered. She had been more fearful of the answer, she admitted, than of the anger Jack would display at the question.

Now that Jack had broached the subject, Anna ventured, "Lillian keeps asking about Isaac." It was a lie, but it would serve the purpose.

Jack lowered his paper and glared at her. "Isaac," he said slowly, "is no longer with us. Lillian will have to get used to that fact. I keep reminding you that those people are not dependable." The paper went up again, and discussion closed.

Anna felt a chill shimmer up her spine, and she shuddered a little. Isaac had simply disappeared two months ago, just days before the party. Jack had something to do with it, she was certain.

"I need to speak with the carpenter," she said to the newspaper. "About the addition to the sewing room. I am running out of space." After the devastating blow to her business empire in 1929, Anna had focused her dressmaking talents on the one remaining boutique. At Jack's suggestion, she had sold it to Millie Anderson two years ago, and set up her equipment in one of the downstairs sunrooms, where she flourished as Lima's exclusive designer. Jack was far more supportive this time, for Anna was at home "where she belonged," and he could keep an eye on her.

Jack was relieved at the change of subject, and quickly forced himself toward a more civil attitude. "Yes," he said, folding the paper. "I will leave it up to you to instruct the workmen about the details. Whatever you want. Spare no expense."

Well, there you have it, Anna thought. That was her husband's method of dealing with any unpleasantry... to close his mind and open his checkbook.

"Speaking of expense, the accountant called yesterday," she told him.

"Are we broke?" he chuckled.

"Very funny. He said something about an invoice for a very large, very ornate trunk. He thought that the price was excessive and he wanted to verify it with you before he mailed the check. Are you planning a murder?"

"I beg your pardon?"

"Well, according to Walter, the thing is huge," she said. "'Big enough for a body.'"

He studied her face, searching for some indication that she was more than mildly curious. He found none. "It's for Diz," he said casually. "A going-back-to-school gift. She has so much stuff..."

The reference sent her off in a different direction. "I can't believe that the summer is almost over. It went by so quickly, so much time taken up with the party. But it was wonderful, wasn't it? We gave her a night to remember... the whole town is still talking about it."

"It was a triumph!" Jack smiled. "You outdid yourself. I don't deserve any credit, all I did was authorize the checks."

"All that spoiled it was Mac's absence," Anna said wistfully. "We haven't seen him in so long."

Jack wanted to move her away from discussion of Mac. She became strangely dark when she spoke of him, retreating into a chasm of depression.

"Paul was certainly looking hale and hearty," Jack offered. "I had very little time to speak with him, but I gather that all is well with his degree program."

"He seemed preoccupied to me," Anna said. "I didn't see much of him either, only when I inquired about Rachael's ankle. Shame she couldn't come at the last minute."

"If she has a mole problem, she needs to hire a yard man. Perhaps you could send Mr. Gonzales."

Anna flushed a little. It was a directive, she knew, not a suggestion. Jack had been obvious in his disappointment when Paul told them that his mother had sprained her ankle and had stayed home. Anna sipped at her coffee and listened to the quiet singing of the whippoorwill. They needed the rain that the bird solicited to cool the oppressive heat.

Jack kept the paper in front of his face and pretended to read. He had covered himself on the Isaac business, he was certain. Anna was just fishing, and he didn't believe for a moment that Diz had shared any concern about the boy with her mother. He didn't give a rat's ass, he decided, what Anna knew or thought she knew. When it came to protecting his own, Jack would take any measure necessary… no regrets, no apologies.

He knew that she was more than just curious about the trunk. He slowly reached into his watch pocket and pulled out the timepiece. Attached to the gold bob was a small gold skeleton key, identical to the one that he had given to Lillian. He smiled. The trunk was indeed a masterpiece, oak based, metal slats, and trimmed in brass. It was four feet in length, three feet deep, not counting the high domed lid. The engraved initials on the front drop lock read: "LGS." In addition to its impressive size and handcrafted beauty, the trunk had one other unique feature: it contained a false bottom, which extended over the entire base and measured eight inches in depth. The brass corner pieces were hinged to expose a hidden lock, which could be opened only by the key in his hand or the one that nestled between Lillian's breasts.

****

"What, again?" Helga asked.

Emily sat the breakfast tray on the butcher block in the center of the kitchen and nodded. "I tried everything this time, short of sitting on her and shoving in oatmeal. I sat with her, offered to eat with her… nothing. I don't know how long this can go on. That girl hasn't eaten in weeks."

"She never comes to the table. Why haven't they noticed that?"

"Because they are not paying attention, that's why," Emily snapped. "Like they don't notice that she sits in that room all day, lighting candles, and praying her rosary. She doesn't sleep, walks around the house all hours of the night. It's damn spooky. There is something else."

"What?"

"She is sick all the time. Throws up. I'm sure I catch the whiff of vomit when I clean her bathroom."

"What can she be throwing up? She doesn't eat! I don't care if they fire me," Helga announced. "I'm going to call Dr. Powell."

"He just saw her, at the first of the week. She had a physical for school. He must have noticed that she looks terrible."

"Not if she piled on Anna's makeup."

"She's taking pills," Emily added.

"What kind of pills?"

Emily shrugged. "Miss Lillian showed them to me, just before the party. She said they helped to calm her down. I think they were her mother's, you know… prescriptions. I'm sure they must be all right if Dr. Powell prescribed them."

Chapter 9

"Routine this time," the nurse said. "So routine, in fact, that Mama Bear didn't even come with her. Lillian goes back to school in two weeks, so she needs a physical."

Adam Powell breathed a sigh of relief and told Nurse Manning to take Lillian to exam room number two and help her undress. So Anna, or "Mama Bear," as Manning so appropriately called her, was not in attendance. It was a sign of better days.

"Well, young lady," he greeted Liz. "Are you anxious to get back to school?"

Liz smiled broadly. "Very."

She looked a little peaked, he thought. But her cheeks showed traces of color. She was thin, as usual. No doubt the nuns would see that she got the right balance of proper diet and exercise.

"First we'll need to draw some blood, then I'll complete the form. Any problems?"

"Not really."

"'Not really'? What does that mean?"

"I have had some stomach problems. I think Helga feeds me too much, and some of it is too rich for my system. We eat very simply at the Motherhouse."

Adam's antenna went up. "I guess I didn't realize that St. Joseph's was a Motherhouse. Do you plan to enter the order?"

"Yes. But I haven't told anyone yet."

"I see. Well, then it will be our little secret."

After the blood had been drawn, Dr. Powell listened to Liz's heartbeat, took her pulse and blood pressure. "Your vital signs are a little elevated, Liz. Have you been sleeping well?"

She hesitated, cautious. If she said "no," he would press for a reason. If she said "yes," it would be a lie. Should she tell him the truth... that she slept twelve to fifteen hours a day because she took Anna's sleeping pills on a regular basis? Better not.

"I read a lot at night," she answered evasively. "Steinbeck has written a new novel... *Of Mice and Men*. Have you read it?"

"I'm afraid I don't have much time to read anything other than the medical stuff," he answered. He sensed her evasion. "Any muscle soreness? Cramping? Anything we should check out?"

"I'm as healthy as a horse," Liz told him. "You don't have to... you know, do that other thing, do you?"

Powell knew that his young patient was referring to the regular pelvic exam imposed by her mother. He thought for a moment, decided to skip it. The prospect was obviously unpleasant to Liz and things were going so well.

"I don't think so. Any problems in that area?"

Liz flushed. "No."

"Well, then I suppose we are finished. Good luck in your school year, Liz. Perhaps we'll meet again before it is over."

The rest of the week passed without incident. He saw the usual patients, gave baby shots, stuck tongue depressors into gaping mouths, dispensed pills and advice. Friday was a heavy day at the hospital, and the office was crowded when he finally got there two hours late. Two old men with heat stroke, one severe sunburn, inflamed tonsils, a sprained ankle, three expectant mothers, and six other miscellaneous ailments. The paperwork piled up on the doctor's desk, necessitating an early Saturday morning catch-up session. Soon he was joined by Maggie Manning, who also had some work to do.

"I didn't know you came in on weekends," he said.

"How else could I keep up with you?" she chuckled. "I am really not the world's most organized woman, you know."

"I know," he teased. "Make some coffee."

He began to shuffle through the pile. His hand fell upon a lab report designated "Rush." The name at the top read: "Lillian Sterling." Why had he asked the lab to rush it? He had seen her at the beginning of the week, simple school exam. He tried to recall what it was that raised "rush" suspicion.

Maggie brought in a cup of steaming hot coffee and sat it down on his desk.

"Are you familiar with the phrase 'self-fulfilling prophesy'?" he asked her.

"I think so. It means that if you harp on something that you fear long enough, it will happen."

"That about sums it up," he told her as he tossed the lab report back on the desk. "Lillian Sterling is pregnant!"

They stared at each other for a long moment. Maggie walked away, shaking her head. Adam put his head down on the desk and tried to will himself somewhere else, an island in the South Pacific, the moon, anywhere but here, now.

He had to admit that he was more than curious about the father of Lillian's baby. But he could come to no conclusion, for she never mentioned a love interest, and he doubted that Anna would permit her to date. Adam's head came up suddenly. Had she been raped? There was no way to know for sure unless Lillian herself confided the details, for he had done no exam in the pelvic area. Shit. He could smell trouble, feel his feet being drawn closer to the fire. He reached for the phone.

"Damnit, Adam. I am not your mentor," Leonard Bennett snarled. "Where did you go to medical school anyway?"

"Harvard."

"Oh. Good school Harvard."

"Chew on me some other time, Leonard... real trouble this time."

"Meet me at 'the place.'"

"The Place" was a small, intimate bar directly across from St. Rita's hospital. It was a favorite of the large staff, and provided a quiet corner where the two doctors could confer without attracting attention.

"More medical decisions made here than in the conference room," Leonard chuckled as he slid into the booth across from Adam Powell. "Wow, you look like shit!"

Adam confirmed that he felt as bad as he looked. "Lillian Sterling is pregnant."

"What? How?"

"The usual way, I suppose. There hasn't been a virgin birth in almost two thousand years."

"Does Anna know?"

"No one knows, except me and Maggie, and now you."

"And the lab people?"

"Yeah."

"How are you going to handle this?"

"Why do you think I called this little meeting?"

"Oh, no! Don't even think... don't look at me! I told you before, I don't deal well with those people."

"Help me, Leonard. I need a plan."

"Well, right off the top I'd advise that you bypass Anna. That leaves Jack. Boy, talk about a rock and a hard place!"

"It has to be one or the other, if not both. The law says so, I looked it up.

She is a minor."

"Lillian doesn't know?"

"Evidently not."

"Whose is it?"

"How the hell do I know? Anyway, it doesn't matter. That's not my problem."

"Right. Be prepared for Anna, sooner or later. She will demand an abortion."

"That's not my problem either. I don't do abortions. I need to rehearse it in my mind, pick a setting that won't result in my death, and get out quick."

"Why don't you send him a certified letter? Slip a note under his door?"

"Why are you being so flip? This is not funny!"

Leonard wiped the grin off his face and looked at his colleague with sympathy. "You are correct, it is not funny. Sorry. I guess I am just so damn relieved that it is not happening to me. I went around with that guy about sixteen years ago, and I can still feel his spit on my face. You are the messenger, Adam, not the responsible party. Just tell him how it is. That is all you can do."

Adam looked at his watch. It was 5:10 PM on Saturday, August 21st, 1937. Lillian Sterling expected to return to her beloved academy in ten days, but circumstances beyond her control had altered her plans, for she was now eleven weeks pregnant. If Adam drove over there now, he could perhaps salvage at least part of the weekend.

Chapter 10

When Dr. Powell arrived uninvited and unannounced at the Sterling's front door, he was not enthusiastically received.

"The Sterlings are dressing for dinner," the newly hired Sharon informed him. "Perhaps this could wait until tomorrow."

"It is a matter of some importance," Powell retorted, mildly miffed at being put off so curtly when he had spent considerable time gathering his courage for the mission. "I must speak with Mr. Sterling at once." Sharon nodded with resignation and led the doctor into a small foyer where he sat on the edge of an elaborately upholstered bench. From the area of the living room, he heard the sound of a small cocktail party... muted laughter, ice clinking.

"Dr. Powell, is someone ill?" Anna greeted him from the doorway.

One look at her explained why he was now faced with Anna rather than Jack, in spite of his best-laid plans. In what other marriage, Adam pondered, was the lady of the house dressed and ready to go before her spouse? She was elegant, as usual, in a gown of gray satin that matched the color of her eyes and accented the slight graying at her temples.

"I... I apologize for the intrusion, Mrs. Sterling. I have some news regarding Lillian that can't wait, I'm afraid." He was trapped. She would block any effort on his part to speak to Jack, and if he didn't get it out now, he might never be able to satisfy his professional duty. He was sweating, and she was watching him squirm with mild amusement. Wordlessly, she waited.

"Lillian is pregnant!" he blurted.

Her eyes grew into large spheres, pupils black and dilated, but if she was shaken by his pronouncement, she hid it. "Have you been drinking, Doctor? Or is this some pathetic attempt at humor?"

"The tests are positive," he went on. "She is displaying the symptoms. I'm sorry, Anna. It's true."

"What test? What symptoms? It is impossible. My daughter is a virgin, Dr. Powell. Now if you will excuse me, we have guests. I trust you are able to see yourself out." She disappeared as suddenly as she had appeared, leaving Adam feeling foolish. Well, he had done his duty, and there was nothing more that he could do.

"What was that all about?" Jack asked his wife when he came down the staircase just in time to see Adam Powell leaving by the front door. Jack was fumbling with his French cuffs, and Anna smiled as she approached him to lend assistance.

"Nothing important. Some business about the hospital auxiliary." She straightened his black tie, smoothed his labels. "Our guests are waiting." She smiled at him.

"The trunk," the long-awaited new addition to Lillian's luggage, arrived on Monday amid much fanfare. It required two deliverymen and three staff members to move it from the pickup truck into the front foyer, where it was decided that it must remain. "If we try to lug this thing upstairs, we'll never get it down once it is loaded," Billy said.

Guided by the list forwarded to Anna from the Dominican Mistress of Postulants, the remainder of the week found every available female in the house washing, ironing, sewing name tags, and packing the grand trunk with items of black clothing. The skirts were black muslin, ankle length and made to the specifications of the order. Blouses matched the skirts, long sleeved and high-collared, and even the buttons were black.

Black leather shoes, oxfords with two-inch square heels and, of course, black laces, had to be specially ordered, for they were hardly in fashion. Long black cotton stockings completed the ensemble. The only items in the trunk that were not black were the long white flannel nightgowns and the cotton bras and panties. One wool shawl was permitted, color... black. There would be no need for a winter coat, in spite of the Michigan cold. Lillian would not leave the confines of the Motherhouse for one full year, except to travel from building to building by way of heated tunnel.

"Why do they call this a "trousseau?" Helga wanted to know.

"I suppose because she is to be the 'bride of Christ,'" Emily answered. "After she completes her first year of prayer and study, she will officially accept the full veil and white habit, at the 'wedding ceremony.'"

"Will she wear a white wedding dress?"

"Yes, in the beginning of the ceremony. Her hair will be cut at the altar, and then she will go out to dress in the habit."

"It will surely be something to see. I think I'd like to be there."

"So would I. I hear it is quite beautiful."

While the entire household buzzed around her, seeing to her needs, Lillian remained sequestered in her room, praying for hours in front of burning vigil candles. She refused almost all food, somehow subsisting on juices, toast and

Jell-O. Once or twice a week, Emily managed to get some hot soup down her, but the nausea continued and it came up again.

The staff informed Anna that Lillian was not well. Since the doctor's visit, Anna had been in total denial, and continued to avoid her daughter's bedroom. The stronger the signs, the more she persisted in ignoring them.

It was all a terrible mistake. It couldn't happen to her daughter... or to Anna. She willed it to go away. Once Lillian was safe behind the walls of the Motherhouse, all would be resolved. Somehow they would get through this long, long week. There were no going-away parties, no departure dinners.

"Paul called today," Anna said to Lillian. "He will be home until fall, since he decided not to attend the summer session. He is worried about you. He would like to see you before you leave."

"I don't want to see anyone," Lillian insisted.

Lillian refused all telephone calls, even Martha's. She relented only once, to speak with her brother.

"Oh, Mac! I miss you so much. When are you coming home?"

"Not for awhile, Sis. I have been assigned to the Pacific Fleet, for training. It is so exciting, taking off and landing these new planes off the carriers. I hope to be able to remain there permanently."

"You sound very happy, Mac."

"Happier than I have ever been in my entire life. There's a girl, Sis."

"Just one?" she teased. "You must be losing your edge."

"I grew up. Thinking about the future, a family. Listen, Sis, don't mention this to the folks. Somehow the less they know about me, the better off I am... know what I mean?"

"Do I ever! Mum's the word, I won't tell."

"How are they, anyway?"

"The same. Papa wheels and deals, Mother plots and schemes."

They shared a laugh. It was so good to hear his voice; she would not spoil the mood with her own fears. "I leave for school in a few days; promise you will write," she said.

"Every week, I promise. Hey, I sent you a package. It should arrive before you leave. It's a tapestry bag I found in New Jersey. Bought it the day the Hindenberg went down."

"I'll watch for the mail. Thank you in advance, big brother."

"You are most welcome. Take care of yourself, Sis. I love you."

"Mac?"

"Yeah?"

"I love you too. Be careful. Don't drown or anything awful. I couldn't bear it."

"You should know by now, I am indestructible."

"Do you know where you'll likely be stationed?"

"Pearl Harbor. Bye, Sis."

On the morning of Lillian's departure, Anna pleaded a migraine and sent a message to Jack that he would have to drive to Adrian without her. He protested.

"We have forms to fill out, to sign. This is a major thing, this consent to enter the convent. It will be a whole year before we can see her again. Take a pill and get dressed. You are going."

Anna didn't argue, for she had taken three pills and was soon unconscious. Utterly frustrated, Jack hurried Lillian and one small valise into the Cadillac at the last possible moment, for the trunk had been shipped by rail. His mood was peevish during the three-hour drive across the state line, and he found little comfort in his daughter, who suffered from "car sickness."

They were greeted on the front steps by two nuns who inquired of Lillian, "What do you ask?"

"To be admitted to the Order of St. Dominic," she answered softly, and was allowed one awkward, quiet moment with her father before they took her away.

Jack spent the next few hours with Sister David Paul, Mistress of Postulants. She gently led him through the admission procedure, answered his questions and concerns, accepted his generous check, the "dowry," and gave him the official tour.

"I am not a practicing Catholic," Jack admitted. "My parents were, and I was raised as a Catholic, but there were some problems..."

"I understand, Mr. Sterling," David Paul said. "The important thing right now is that you are a father, and I know how difficult this must be for you."

"Yes."

He left suddenly, for he felt very vulnerable. A flood of memories washed over him, some bittersweet. The gray day had given way to drizzle by the time he backed his car out of the parking space and left the front gates. Before he had driven a mile, he pulled over to light a cigarette, and he sat for a long while on the brim of the road, smoking. More intense than the overwhelming sadness that enveloped him was the powerful dread that he could not dispel. Something was wrong, very wrong. The longer he sat there, the more he thought about it, the stronger and more ominous the feeling grew.

He aimed the chrome hood ornament toward Richmond. Perhaps the thought that he would not see his daughter for one full year had settled too deeply.

Chapter 11

Less than twenty-four hours after her arrival on the campus, Liz was sent to the infirmary.

"She is probably dehydrated," the nursing nun reported to Sister David Paul. "It may be even more serious. I have contacted Dr. Agnew and he is on his way.

"Has she been fasting, Sister?"

"Apparently. There is another problem. In processing Lillian's paperwork, we find no admission physical from her attending physician, Dr. Powell."

"Strange. I will contact Dr. Powell at once. Thank you, Sister. You may go."

David Paul was becoming increasingly alarmed. While it was true that the campus was abuzz with the arrival of students and prospective candidates for admission to the Order, it was unlikely that something so important as a physical was misplaced or overlooked. It was vital to the security of the Motherhouse that candidates be carefully screened, both physically and mentally.

"He is with a patient, Sister," Maggie Manning said. "But I will make sure that he calls you back as soon as possible."

When Sister telephoned the Sterling house, Helga offered to take a message. "I need to speak with Mr. Sterling, please give me a number where I can reach him," Sister replied.

The Sterlings were on their way to Florida, the nun was told, on an impromptu vacation. "They left this morning, but as soon as they call in, I will give them the message."

David Paul left her desk and hurried to the infirmary. "Patch the call over there when Dr. Powell calls," she informed the switchboard.

The elderly, kind Dr. Agnew moved slowly due to advanced arthritis, but he was already coming out of the ward when David Paul caught up with him, breathless from the dash up the stairs. It had not taken his experienced eyes very long to determine exactly the cause of Miss Sterling's "illness." "Let's go somewhere where we can speak quietly," he told the nun. "You will need to sit down."

One hour later, Emily signed for a telegram marked "urgent."

"Something is wrong," she told Helga. "I am going to call Rachael."

Rachael called George Steinburger, who arranged for Jack's Cadillac to be intercepted as it traveled south. Jack and Anna had just crossed the Ohio state line and stopped for lunch when a uniformed officer approached their table.

"Are you Jack and Anna Sterling?" he inquired.

"Yes, officer. Is there a problem?" Jack asked. There was suddenly a knot in the pit of his stomach.

"The message is that there is an 'emergency at home,'" the officer said. "You are to call..." he consulted his notes, "George Steinburger, at this number."

Jack used the pay phone outside the diner as Anna watched him through the window. He appeared agitated as he spoke to George. After only a minute or two, he returned to the table.

"The telegram said that Lillian is on the afternoon train, headed for Richmond. She is escorted by two sisters. 'Medical considerations,' the wire said. Why do I have the feeling that I don't know everything I should know?" Jack asked his wife,

Anna did not answer him. She would need the long drive back to Richmond to come up with an answer. The Cadillac exceeded the speed limit, accompanied to the Ohio state line by two police motorcycles. A cruiser and two members of the Ohio state police met the car there. Jack was rapidly moving toward utter panic. After he had driven another twenty miles, he pulled over to request that one of the officers drive the Cadillac. "I refuse to sit in the back seat of any automobile I have paid for," he told Anna. "You can ride in the cruiser."

The next twenty-four hours warped into a blur in Jack's mind. George Steinburger was on the front steps when the Sterlings pulled up. A city taxi was parked directly in front of the cruiser. Anna nodded to George and waited while Jack attempted to pay the cab driver.

"I haven't finished the fare," the driver told him. "The sister asked me to wait, said they would be leaving very soon."

"Where is the trunk?" Jack asked.

"What trunk? I didn't load any trunk."

The trunk that holds $100,000 dollars in cash, bonds, and stock certificates, you fool! Where the hell is my goddamn trunk? Jack stood there, staring at the empty cab. He couldn't speak, couldn't move.

225

"Jack?" Anna prompted. "Are we going inside?"

Of course! The trunk wouldn't fit in the cab. It is being shipped. He handed the driver a $10 bill and went into the house, followed by Anna and George.

"I asked them if they wanted tea," Emily explained. "But they said they would not be staying. They are in the library."

The sisters rose to their feet when the trio entered the room. Liz remained seated between them on the sofa. Anna looked very worried, while Jack's face was flushed and angry. *Evidently the trip was not important enough to send out the "first string,"* Jack thought. The younger one was obviously an aide to the old geezer with her.

"How dare you?" he addressed the women draped in black cloaks. "What is the meaning of this... you bring my daughter back to me like discarded trash! Wasn't my check big enough?"

The sisters stood silently. Their faces betrayed no emotion, no offence.

"Mr. Sterling, we haven't met," the old one answered gently. She crossed the room and extended her hand. "I am Mother Mary Cabella, Mother Superior of the Order of St. Dominic. This is Sister Therese Ellen."

If Jack and Anna didn't have the good sense to be duly impressed, George certainly did. His eyebrows shot up and he watched his friends for reaction. *Even this old Jew knows that it takes a minor miracle to get the Mother Superior away from her charges. Wow, big guns here!*

"You must be Lillian's mother." Mary Cabella offered her hand to Anna.. "I am sorry that we haven't met. Now that we have seen Lillian safely home, we won't impose upon you any longer. Our cab is waiting to take us to a local convent for the night." She handed Jack a white envelope with his name neatly inscribed on the front. "I believe you will find what you are looking for in here." Mother Superior turned to Liz, who had now risen to her feet. "Goodbye, dear. God bless and keep you."

George had seated himself in an inconspicuous chair in the corner, amused as he watched the little drama play out. Anna and Jack stood as if in shock, neglecting even to introduce the other gentleman in the room.

"That's it?" Jack demanded. "No explanation? If she is so ill, what is wrong with her? Diz? Are you sick?"

"This is difficult for all of us, most assuredly for you and your wife," Mother said. "When Lillian explains, it will all become quite clear. But it is a private, family matter, and we are intruders. Please accept my apologies, but we must leave now. Here is the number where you may reach me if you have any other concerns or questions."

They were suddenly gone. Before the cab had reached the gate, Anna asked her husband, "What now? Do you want George to stay?"

"You and George may do whatever pleases you," Jack replied dryly. "My daughter and I have much to discuss, so we will be in my office. Have Helga bring a tray for Diz. She has a hungry look." With that said, he took Lillian by the hand and they left the room.

After he had locked the door, he turned to look at her. She looked terrible, so pale and so thin. She huddled in the leather chair, her long legs drawn up in a pseudo-fetal position, staring at nothing and chewing on a bleeding fingernail. He wanted to comfort her, to return to the feelings they had held for each other on that day when they fished and laughed. But there was no time for that now.

"You listen to me very carefully, young lady," he began, "for I have had quite enough bullshit for one day. You and I are locked in this room and we will remain here until I am satisfied with your answers. I am very tired, and I would imagine that you would be more comfortable in your room, so let's get to it. Neither one of us will leave here for any reason until it is settled, or one of us is dead."

It was 4:35 PM.

Three hours later, Paul tapped lightly on the door. Jack admitted the young man, blocking Rachael's entrance. "I wish to speak with Paul alone, Rachael. Please forgive my rudeness, but I must insist."

One hour and ten minutes later, the door opened. Rachael was still sitting alone in the corridor, waiting for her son.

"You may come in, Rachael," Jack announced. "Paul has something to tell you, and I will leave you two alone for now. Anna and I will come in when you are ready."

Jack took Lillian's hand and helped her up from the chair. "You look very tired," he said gently. "Go on upstairs and I will be up later."

Jack found Anna in bed, with a hot towel on her forehead.

"Get dressed and come downstairs," he ordered briskly. "Rachael is here and the two of you have a wedding to plan."

Chapter 12

It was understandable that Anna would avoid the weekly bridge game. It would give the girls a chance to get it out of their systems, she thought. They could whisper and speculate, titter about the "shame" and "humiliation," and delude themselves that it could never happen to their daughters, just as she had done.

"It smacks a bit of 'incest,' doesn't it?" Mary George asked her friends.

Doris Steinburger snapped, "Mary, you just shut your filthy mouth or I'll do it for you!"

"Well, I'm sorry, but..."

Doris turned away from Mary and addressed Marge. It would serve no purpose to attempt to change the subject... the best she could do was to steer it in a different direction. "I hear the banns have been published at St. Rose's. Such a beautiful church for a wedding."

At the Sterling home, negotiations were underway. Rachael, Jack and Anna pretended to enjoy lunch on the veranda. Rachael called upon every ounce of restraint that remained within her, Anna chain smoked and made copious notes and Jack silently drank scotch.

Anna suggested that Judge Steinburger marry them at the courthouse. "It was good enough for us," she insisted. "That way it can just be quietly done and we can print an announcement later."

Rachael reminded the Sterlings that Paul and Liz were devout Catholics, subject to the publishing of banns for two consecutive weeks and marriage by a priest.

Jack had no preference. He simply wanted to get the whole affair over with.

Paul confided to his mother that he had taken a job at a local petroleum plant, working the midnight to morning shift because that was all that was available to him. "What about school?" she wanted to know. "It is your senior year." If it was a matter of living arrangements, the two of them could stay with her, she said. Rachael could look after Liz and the baby while Paul completed his education.

As the couple was considering Rachael's offer, Anna got wind of it and overreacted with vehement protest. "They should stay here," she reasoned.

"We have far more room and help. This is my daughter and my grandchild… why are my wishes so callously disregarded?"

What about a reception? Honeymoon? Bridal shower? What would Lillian wear? More importantly, what would Anna wear? What were they going to tell their friends? How would Anna ever live this down? How much money should Jack give them? Perhaps Jack should build them a house.

The battle raged on for three days. Rachael and Paul stayed in Spring Grove, where they sat up all night, every night, discussing the reasons for this "situation," and possible solutions to the many questions that plagued them. Paul did most of the talking, for he needed to unburden himself. "I honestly don't remember much of it," he told his mother. "We were dancing and then the party was over. We took a walk, to say 'goodbye.' The waiters were loading up and someone gave us a bottle, I think. Nothing is too clear after that."

She didn't waste precious time in scolding him. What was done, was done. She would be forever grateful that he had not lied to her, nor had he tried to make excuses. "I don't understand," she said. "How you could just leave her there under the tree?" He looked at her blankly. Tree? "That is where Billy found her the next morning," Rachael prompted him. "He also found this." She held the cufflink out to him in the palm of her hand.

"I don't know what to tell you, Mother," he said. "I wish I could tell you all of it. I'm trying, but it is just not there."

Liz refused to discuss details with her mother, and after the marathon session with her father in his office, there was nothing more to talk to him about. No one asked her what she wanted to do. Decisions were made and plans were implemented all around her, as if she were invisible. With Mac gone, she had no one in which to confide, for she had lost her friend Paul, she realized. He was now part of the "them," the tight little circle that surrounded her and regulated her life.

Jack believed that Anna was resentful because she had been left out of the "confession" scenes, and because she was denied the opportunity to convert the family "problem" into another social triumph.

"Save yourself the embarrassment," Jack told his wife. "The girls are having a field day with this… be assured that we and ours are the talk of the town."

"I was cheated out of a proper wedding, and now Lillian… do you have any idea how I longed to create a beautiful wedding dress? Fate had granted me that opportunity when she decided to enter the convent. Now… nothing!"

"Stop whining!" Jack snapped. "In case you haven't noticed, Lillian and Paul are the people this is happening to. It is our duty to make it as painless as possible."

"You are suddenly a candidate for 'Father of the Year,'" Anna retorted. "She tells you what she wouldn't dream of telling me, and you are so understanding and patient. Sometimes life with you is like dealing with a split personality."

Jack decided to cease the war of words, retaining the trump card that he would use against her when it became necessary. He had not yet chastised her for her failure to inform him of the purpose of Dr. Powell's visit.

What no one had considered was the possibility that the "children" would take control of their lives. Before the end of the week, Paul and Liz had agreed upon the details… they visited Father McKay, who would publish the first bann in two days. Their wedding date was set for September 18th, eleven days after Liz's seventeenth birthday. They paired their savings, Paul's substantial bank account and Lillian's "stash" of twenties still under her bed, and went shopping. Paul even took his bride-to-be for a soda and he teased her good-naturedly. "Drink up," he told her, "then I'll order another. We need to fatten you up."

She laughed for the first time in weeks. "I have a feeling that will happen, regardless of what I eat."

"I don't know much about babies," Paul admitted. "But I suppose we'll catch on. This is all very strange, isn't it, Gretch?"

"Like it isn't real," she agreed. "Scary. Neither of us wanted to be married, at least not to each other. There is someone else, isn't there?"

"Not any more."

"Ohmygosh, Paul! I forgot all about witnesses. We need someone to stand up with us."

"I have it covered."

"You do? Who?"

"It's a surprise. Beginning now, you'll need to learn to trust me."

They ordered their own wedding cake, arranged for music and flowers, and asked Father McKay to hear their respective confessions. Then they drove to Spring Grove and rented a small garage apartment from Paul's neighbor, Mr. Gleason, three houses down the street from Rachael. "Wait until Anna hears about this!" Liz giggled.

By the day of the wedding, Liz was feeling and looking better than she had in a long time. She presented a very pretty picture in her powder blue silk two-piece suit, patent leather pumps and simple white Spanish veil. Paul was resplendent in navy blue, calm and in control.

At 9AM Paul and Liz sat in Father McKay's office, drinking coffee and listening very carefully to the priest as he consoled them. "Do not be dismayed," he told them, "because your choices seemed to have been made for you. Something brought you together, and that union has created God's new life. You are His instruments. Trust that He has a purpose far greater than any you may have planned." They signed the appropriate papers, joined hands and accepted the priestly blessing.

"Now, before we go into the church," Father said," we must meet with your attendants. Are they here?"

"I'll check outside," Paul said as he rose to leave. "They should be here by now."

"Who?" Liz asked, and she smiled at him.

"You'll see."

Betsy came in first. The girls hugged each other and cried. They held hands and danced around in circles, squealing with such abandon that Paul and Father McKay pressed hands to their ears, laughing.

"I'd better fetch my best man," Paul announced.

"Mac! Oh my God, Mac! You're here. You're really here!" She flung herself into his arms. He picked her up and swung her around the room while she laughed and cried.

"Wouldn't have missed this for the world," Mac grinned. "Let's go get you two married."

Mac extended his arm to Betsy and they walked into the church to the strains of "Here Comes the Bride" as if they were presenting royalty.

"It took some doing," Paul explained as he slipped his arm around Liz's small waist and pulled her to him. "We had to apply for a special dispensation for Mac to serve as Best Man, because he is not a Catholic. Father McKay did all the paperwork. Do you like your surprise?"

She smiled at him, a long loving smile. She nodded and kissed him gently on the cheek. "You have given me so much already. All I have to give you is this child, and my promise that no matter what ever happens to us, I will always be your friend."

"That's enough for me. Now, let's go make your mother cry!"

Chapter 13

It seemed for the moment that "all was well that ended well." The wedding dinner provided a rare atmosphere of "family" and forgiveness, for Anna had worked her usual magic… an elegantly tasteful affair on very short notice. As the wine flowed, the mood became very mellow indeed for the Sterling family and a few carefully selected guests.

There was no time for a honeymoon, Paul decreed. His new job began on Monday, and he and Liz still had a few things to transport up the long twenty-two steps of their garage apartment. "You don't have to do this, you know," Jack told Paul as he pulled him aside. "You would be far more comfortable here." Paul politely declined, wishing that he had the courage to tell his father-in-law about the pact that he had made with his bride.

"No handouts, no interference," were Paul's terms. "We will make it on our own, or we won't make it." In return he agreed that he would be very patient with Lillian's lack of homemaking skills and her admitted reluctance to engage in "marital relations." "We will have to make some adjustments," Paul said. "And we should be very clear and honest about what we expect from each other."

Regardless of their resolutions, the union was doomed almost from the very beginning. At Rachael's urging and with Lillian's blessing, Paul enrolled in night school to complete the courses that would ultimately gain him his four-year diploma. His job at the refinery began at midnight and the shift ended at 8 AM. It was dirty, boring work, checking gauges and machinery all night, with little else to challenge his mind. He dragged himself home in the morning, needing sleep but resentful of the need. It was a beautiful autumn, alive with foliage and clean crisp air. He was hungry and horny. He found his bride in their double bed and discovered that when he slipped in beside her, he was no longer tired.

"I am so tired all of the time," Lillian told Dr. Powell. "I go to bed when Paul leaves for his night class, and most of the time I don't hear him come home. Then he goes to work at midnight. I can easily sleep until noon. We barely see each other."

"It should resolve when you are well into your second trimester," Adam replied. "Keep taking the vitamins I gave you. If you can really sleep that much, your system must be requiring it."

While Lillian slept, Paul's greasy, smelly coveralls piled up on the bathroom floor. Food was purchased but was rarely cooked. Every available pot and frying pan was crusted with evidence of some attempt to prepare a meal, yet Paul nursed more than one constant hunger.

"I can't sleep in this bed," Liz announced one morning. "The sheets are filthy. At home my bed was changed twice a week."

"Get out of bed once in awhile and wash the sheets," Paul responded. "Take them över to Mom's. You can use her washer."

By the time Liz wrestled a pile of laundry down the twenty-two steps and over to Rachael's house, she was exhausted. Once there, she broke down in tears while she related to her mother-in-law her failure as a wife. "He wants the sex thing," Liz confided. "He becomes very angry... the other day he told me to see a priest! What does that mean?"

"I imagine Paul is referring to the Church's admonition. It compels a wife to fulfill her duty to her husband. Perhaps Paul doesn't understand how difficult this pregnancy is for you. Do you want me to speak with him, dear?"

"No. It will only make him more angry."

"Let me help. I can come twice a week and pick up the wash. When you have days that you feel up to it, you can come over here and I will teach you how to prepare Paul's favorite dishes. It will be all right, Liz."

By Thanksgiving Paul was merely "stopping by" the small apartment to bathe, change clothes and check on his young wife, who was either asleep or at some level of nausea. It began slowly in the beginning, dropping in for Rachael's pancakes after work. He would then stretch out on the couch for a short "nap," eventually giving up all pretence and retiring to his old bedroom. He ate a hearty early supper and left for class. He would return for cake and coffee before he left for the refinery, gratefully accepting the lunch that his mother packed for him.

When Paul wasn't at Rachael's house, Lillian was. "I know he is very disappointed in me," she told Rachael. "I felt so guilty that I forced myself to be awake the other morning so that we could make love. I threw up all over him."

Rachael winced. There is nothing worse than standing by while your children suffer, unable to help. Should she insist that they learn to depend on each other, turn her back on both of them, for the sake of the marriage? She patted Liz's hand. "Let's make some cookies," she offered.

Eleanor, Rachael's next door neighbor, began to visit on a regular basis, usually soon after Liz arrived. She chatted merrily while she sipped her tea, watching Liz move around the kitchen. Rachael was embarrassed by the obvious stares at Liz's midriff, but she was at a loss about how to tactfully discourage Eleanor, who was obviously confused.

"She doesn't look pregnant to me," Eleanor told her sister the next day. "If your information is correct, she should be in her fifth month. I tell you... nothing. That girl's belly is flatter than mine."

"It is unusual, I'll admit," Dr. Powell told Rachael when she accompanied Liz for a checkup. "But it does happen. Her pelvic region is very broad, and she carries the fetus horizontally. She'll pop out one of these days, you'll see."

"I wonder," Paul confided in Rachael, "if it could be something else. Maybe there is no baby." His face darkened at the thought. Had he been duped? Was all this misery for nothing?

Rachael finally recognized the obvious. Paul and Liz were "playing house," living out a lie. They were not devoted to each other; there was no passion between them. In desperation, she telephoned Anna.

"I tried twice," Anna said coldly. "I trudged up those miserable steps to spend some time with my daughter, and she hardly invited me to sit. I took groceries, cash, and some things for the baby. Paul returned the groceries and the money by messenger the next day. I don't go where I am not welcome."

"You must understand that Paul is a proud man, Anna. Perhaps he doesn't behave appropriately, but he is proud."

"Read you Bible, Rachael. 'Pride goeth before a fall.' They want to be independent, do things their way. This mess is of their making, so let them work through it."

Paul was the adult, the head of the house. Rachael would reason with him, impress upon him that he must be more patient, more understanding, and more attentive. She broached the subject when he arrived for breakfast.

"Did you know that Jack has a gun?" Paul interrupted her.

Rachael was stunned. If that were true, and Rachael doubted that it was true, what on earth did it have to do with her concerns about their life together?

"I saw it when he opened his desk drawer the night that I was summoned to his house. I remember that I stared at it and thought about what I would do if he aimed it at me."

"Paul, for the love of God, what are you trying to tell me?"

"Nothing, I guess. It just struck me as strange. Why would Jack need a gun?"

"I don't know and I don't care," Rachael snapped. "It is his concern. My concern is the status of your marriage. You are about to become a father, Paul. Job and school cannot take up all of your time."

"What about her time, Mom? She does nothing except sleep. We live in a tiny three-room dump. If I don't pick up after her, yesterday's clothes are still on the floor. I am trying to earn a living, finish my education. What more do the two of you expect from me?"

"I am not your enemy, Paul. I love you more than life. But the two of you are acting like adolescent siblings rather than married adults. I am exhausted from running interference. You can't blame Liz for the way she was raised... always a maid to pick up her clothes, always a cook to prepare her meals. This would be a considerable adjustment without the pregnancy. Try to be patient."

A few weeks before Christmas, Lillian took a bad fall down the steps leading to their apartment. Paul carried her down the street to Rachael's house and Dr. Powell was called.

"She will have to be watched very carefully," he told them after a long examination. "At six months she is extremely prone to go into premature labor. She must have complete bed rest. I recommend hospitalization or a home nurse."

Lillian adamantly refused to go to the hospital, promising to follow the Doctor's orders. "Please, no nurse," she pleaded. "I will stay in bed."

"Let me take care of her," Rachael said. "I will make sure that she takes her medication and does everything that she is supposed to do. This is my grandchild... let me help."

"She can't climb stairs," Powell ordered. It was agreed that a hospital bed would be ordered for the living room, where Rachael could watch Liz's every movement.

Liz flourished under Rachael's loving care. Within a few days the color in her sunken cheeks was rosier than ever before. Daily appointments with the bathroom scale confirmed a steady and healthy weight gain. "Look, Rachael... boobies!" Liz exclaimed one morning, and she unashamedly opened her pajamas to demonstrate. Rachael was so astonished that they both collapsed in uncontrolled giggles.

"Don't think you are just going to lie there and waste time," Rachael teased. "Paul, please go up to the attic and bring down the quilting frames." The bed was adjusted to a sitting position and the ten-foot frames were placed over the bed. Rachael sat for hours, coaching Liz on every stitch. Within two weeks, Liz was laboring intensely, creating beautiful patterns until her fingers bled.

"She says that she has never been happier," Rachael reported to Paul as they drank their coffee in the kitchen. "I think she was just lonely."

"I think I know the feeling," Paul said dryly. He was withdrawn since Liz had become a permanent fixture in his mother's house. It was as if he somehow resented the intrusion.

A few days before Christmas, Rachael asked Liz if she could stay alone for a few hours. "Paul and I have some shopping to do. I can pick up some things for you, if you give me a list."

"I'll be fine," Liz answered cheerfully. "You two go make a day of it."

"Remember, up to the bathroom or to make some tea. No push ups!"

The doorbell awakened her. The clock on the mantel told her that it was 3 PM, and she had slept since noon, after a morning of concentrated sewing. Liz pulled on her robe and went to the door. It was Mr. Spoon, the mailman. "Certified letter for Paul," he announced." Sorry to disturb you, Miss Lillian, but it must have a signature."

"It's all right, Mr. Spoon. Time I was up anyway." She took the envelope from his hands. The small cursive script was lovely. On impulse, she sniffed at the white rectangle with embossed roses. Chantilly. Very nice. She took the pen from the mailman and scribbled "Mrs. Unger."

She didn't remember saying "thank you" to Mr. Spoon, so involved was she in staring at the letter. She carried it to the mantel and propped it against the picture of Paul's father that smiled back at her. The heat from the fireplace warmed her legs, a welcome feeling for she was suddenly very cold. She sat down in the nearest chair, staring at the envelope. It was for Paul, his personal correspondence. She had no right. But she was his wife, wasn't she? His friends were her friends. They should have no secrets. It seemed a very short time, but the clock chimed the half-hour. If it was to be done, better get on with it. They would be home soon.

My darling Paul,

I have begun this letter so many times, but lost courage. I was so foolish to walk away from the one man in the entire world that I will ever love. I don't deserve your forgiveness, my love, and you would be justified in turning me away. I made a terrible mistake, Paul. Please find it in your heart to forgive me. I will live anywhere, go anywhere, and be anything that you want me to be, if we can only be together.

I have returned to Ohio, and am staying with my aunt and uncle in Toledo. You will find the address on this envelope. I will wait for your answer. Please make it soon, Paul, for I am on pins and needles until I know how you feel.

All my love, forever.

It was signed "Caroline." A phone number was printed below the signature, next to a drawing of stick people holding hands. Liz stared at the drawing; it was so childish, so juvenile, that she wondered how Paul could have loved this girl. She should feel something, she supposed, but only numbness enveloped her, that strange feeling of detachment that one might experience when death strikes... that sensation of sleepwalking.

Before she could think about the advisability, the consequences, the right or wrong of it... before she had given the letter and its implications another moment's thought, she decided that she was indeed almost asleep, and she tossed the envelope into the fire.

Chapter 14

On the spring morning that her daughter was born, Lillian felt better than she had in a long time. She had gained a healthy 20 pounds. Her skin was clear, her eyes glistened. She had abandoned her bed rest in mid-January, and now filled her days with caring for her apartment. She rose at 5 AM and accompanied Rachael to Mass. She threw herself into cooking with such a vengeance that Paul complained of indigestion and weight gain.

"Paul told me last night that your apple pie is better than mine," Rachael said. "I think I shall have to change my recipe." While Rachael pretended to be peeved, she was very proud of Liz's efforts, and Liz grinned at the compliment.

"Why couldn't he tell me that?' she asked.

Rachael smiled. "Well, dear, we all know how men are. Have you thought about a name for the baby?"

"Yes! If it's a girl, she will be baptized 'Margaret Mary.'"

"For your friend, Betsy. It has a pleasing ring to it."

"You aren't disappointed are you... about the name?"

"Of course not. There will be more babies."

"I hope so."

Paul was at work when the pains started, a full week early. Rachael had gone to bed and Liz placed a clock on the quilt so she could time the intervals. When the pangs grew alarming, she called for Rachael, who drove her to the hospital.

Liz was alert and excited when Dr. Powell examined her. "Better tell Paul to hurry," he told Rachael. "It may all be over soon. She is progressing nicely. Routine delivery."

By the time Paul rushed breathlessly up the staircase, Rachael had expected to have wonderful news. But it had been over an hour since she had last spoken with the doctor.

Something had gone wrong.

"The baby turned suddenly," he told them finally. "Breach. Liz is all baby, it seems. Very large... almost nine pounds, I'd guess. This is not going to be easy. Liz is a first-time delivery, very young and somewhat underdeveloped."

"Paul, you should call Jack and Anna," Rachael prompted. Paul frowned, then nodded. He went off to look for a public phone. Four hours later, the four of them took turns pacing the waiting room, changing and exchanging chairs.

When Adam Powell came into the room, all eight eyes were upon him."A girl!" he announced. "A big pink girl. Lillian is asleep in recovery. She has lost a lot of blood."

"Margaret Mary," Rachael whispered to Paul.

"Who?" Anna demanded.

"Margaret Mary, the baby's name is Margaret Mary."

Anna made a face."Dreadful..." she started to protest, caught Jack's warning look and clamped her mouth tightly shut.

Jack shook Paul's hand and presented him with a cigar. "I think I'm supposed to give the cigar to you," Paul mumbled. "I am totally unprepared, I'm sorry." He looked like he might go into shock at any moment, overwhelmed by the shear reality of fatherhood. Jack sincerely wanted to help, do something for the boy.

"Well, I imagine that your little apartment is getting rather crowded. Have you found a two bedroom yet?" Jack's question fell on seemingly deaf ears, for Paul was still staring straight ahead.

Rachael nudged her son. "Paul, dear. Jack is talking to you."

"What? Oh, yes! I mean 'no'... that is, she is very small, Jack. Won't take up much room."

Jack laughed heartily, sure that Paul was joking. One look at the ladies changed his mind. "It's not the size of the baby, Paul. It's all the stuff they need... crib, bassinet, buggy, diapers, bottles, tons of things."

Paul looked even more confused. "Oh, those things. Well, we haven't... I mean, we'll have to buy some diapers."

The look that passed between Rachael and Anna predicted a battle of words would ignite at the first recrimination. Suitable preparations had not been made. Rachael had been so involved in Lillian's care and comfort, Paul's immediate needs, and keeping the peace between them that she had not pressured them to shop for the baby's arrival, still a week away.

"We have the basics," Rachael said apologetically. "We thought there would be more time... I'm sorry."

Adam felt the tension in the room. "Lillian will be required to stay for at least two weeks," he offered.

Anna was unusually calm. "But my granddaughter is doing well?" she asked him. "She can be released... when?"

"In a few days, if all goes well," Adam answered cautiously. Something was going on here, something he could not define.

While Jack remained silent, Anna continued to be pleasant. "Don't worry about it, Paul," she told him. "Everything will work out."

When they drove back to Spring Grove that evening, tired and emotionally drained, Rachael had a feeling of impending doom. The beautiful little girl had arrived, whole and healthy. Lillian would recover in good time, with only her newly diagnosed anemia to worry about. Paul would graduate this year, and even the continued high unemployment rate would not hold him back, considering his college education. They had no really serious money problems. There was much to thank God for, yet so much seemed to go missing.

They visited the small apartment and Rachael looked for once with a critical eye. This would never do for the small family. There was no place for a crib and all of the other things that the baby would need. "You will need to make some plans," Rachael told her son. "You have a family now."

Within forty-eight hours of delivery, Lillian's temperature was an alarming 104 degrees. Adam Powell consulted with a specialist by phone, confirming his fear that she had retained a portion of the placenta. "We can certainly treat this condition," he told Paul and Rachael, "but it will require careful watching and a longer stay."

Liz floated on a feverish cloud, in and out of total comprehension. She dreamed that she had somehow lost her baby, and that she wandered around in a gray mist, crying and calling for "Margaret Mary." Paul sat with her as long as he could, praying and begging her to wake up and be well.

When he could no longer bear to watch her suffer, he left the hospital on a mission of his own. The next morning he advised his mother that he had purchased a house close by, and had requested double shift-work in order to make the payments.

"Let me help, Paul. The money in the bank is more than enough, and it is rightfully yours… because of your father's accident. Please let me do this for you!"

But he could not, he said. True to their mutual pledge to accept no financial aide from Jack and Anna, he would not take from Rachael either.

When Lillian forced herself to open her eyes, Anna was smiling down at her.

"Lillian dear, I know that you want your daughter baptized as soon as possible. I have made arrangements for Father McKay to do it this very afternoon, if that is all right with you."

"Yes... soon. Yes," Liz mumbled, barely grasping the thought.

Anna made a beeline for the nursery, where she ran into a little opposition from the charge nurse. "It is highly unusual, Mrs. Sterling. You realize, of course, that once the infant has left the hospital, she cannot be readmitted. Under most circumstances, the baby is discharged with the mother."

"But these are not usual circumstances, are they?" Anna asked, arching an eyebrow. "Has Dr. Powell signed the release?"

"Yes, but..."

"Then we will be taking her to the church now. Please get her ready."

Father McKay also thought that procedure had been compromised when Jack and Anna announced that they would stand as the child's godparents. Jack produced a yellowed copy of his own Baptismal Certificate, in a new envelope that also contained a check for $200, made out to the "Parish of St. Rose." The priest shook off the feeling of uneasiness long enough to inquire, "What is the name of this child of God?"

"Nellie Lee," Anna answered proudly.

Hardly a saint's name, but then nothing else was as it should be.

"Nellie Lee, I baptize you in the name of the Father, the Son, and the Holy Ghost," he intoned as he poured holy water over blond curls and made the sign of the cross on her small forehead. "Go with God."

She went with Jack and Anna, "home" to the Sterling estate where a newly furnished pink and ivory nursery awaited her arrival.

Chapter 15

"Gretch, please, don't go on so. You're supposed to be resting. Calm down, honey, please."

He looked rather pathetic, the new bridegroom, very new father, standing beside his young wife's hospital bed, both hands clutched around a bouquet of fresh flowers.

"You don't understand! You don't know her, Paul... what she is capable of. She has my baby and I want you to go there right now and get her back!"

Paul sat down on the bed and spoke very softly to his wife. His tone was soothing, his gestures loving. He stroked her hair while he talked her down from a hysterical high. He explained that the baby's stay at Jack and Anna's was only temporary, only until he and Rachael could complete the move into their new home. He talked about the house, how they would shop together for furnishings and linens, how much fun it would be. Everything Paul said made perfect sense and Liz soon began to wonder if she had overreacted. "After all, Gretch, they can't keep our baby. It's against the law, I think."

"They are feeding her with bottles, Paul. I wanted to breast feed."

"You are weakened from the delivery, anemia, and now this infection, Gretch. How could you possibly give milk?"

"Are you sure we can afford the house?" she asked.

"Yes. I am sure. Now will you please stop fretting and just get well so you can come home and we can begin our lives all over again? We are a family now; we have a daughter. Let's try to act like grownups."

"I know you don't love me, Paul. Why do you go to so much trouble?"

It was not an accusation, just a simple statement of fact, and the question was one of wonder and curiosity. He looked into her intensely blue eyes, Jack's eyes. He could never lie to her, for she saw all the way to his soul.

"Oh, but I do love you, Gretch. I always have. You are my very best friend."

Liz was released three weeks later, happy to discover that late April had brought with it the promise of spring while she was confined. Paul drove her to the new house, even carried her over the threshold. A smiling Rachael met them there, moved to tears as she watched the couple explore every room. A two-bedroom bungalow with white picket fence, it was everything they needed, complete with a garage and workshop for Paul and a sewing room for Liz.

"Oh, Paul, it is just perfect!" Liz cried, and he smiled with satisfaction. Soon he would begin the sixteen-hour workdays that were required to pay the mortgage, but for now he could focus on the pride of a man who had provided well.

The sound of a beeping horn announced the arrival of Anna and Jack, bringing the fat and happy Nellie Lee to her parents. Liz was so happy that she allowed her mother to kiss her, and she hugged her papa like she would never let go. Just as Paul had predicted, everything worked out very well.

Before the end of the week, however, it was evident that the new parents had their hands very full. Nellie developed colic, fussed day and night as she pulled her little legs up to her chin in protest. Paul came home late in the afternoon, demanding food and sleep. Liz couldn't seem to establish a routine that could put a hot meal on the table while she carried the baby around all day in aching arms. She began to note each and every time she was forced to call upon Rachael, fearful that her mother-in-law would tire of running to her rescue.

Every casual comment ("I worry about Paul," Rachael remarked one day. "He is looking so tired.") sent Lillian into frenzy of anxiety and guilt. *He is tired because of me*, thought Liz. Every day began with new resolve and ended with exhaustion and despair.

She almost missed her six-week check up. Miss Manning called several times to remind her, but Liz was too busy with motherhood. After two weeks of Liz's nausea and vomiting, Rachael insisted that they hire a sitter, and she drove Liz to Dr. Powell's office.

"Have your monthly periods resumed?" he asked Liz. "Are they normal?"

"What? I don't remember having a period." she answered.

Frowning, he quickly examined her. "I don't believe it!" he exclaimed. "What?"

"You are pregnant. Honestly, young lady, you should give your body time to recover from one baby before you incubate another one."

"We only did it once," Liz protested. She looked as if she might cry.

"Well, once is all it takes." Dr. Powell smiled. He tried to sound casual, but he was concerned. Babies, wonderful as they are, have a way of creating chaos in experienced households. Both Paul and Lillian had serious health problems, and considerably more ground to cover on the road to maturity. He wanted to give her some pamphlets about birth control, but he thought better of it, considering her dedication to the precepts of the Church. "Rhythm" was the only salvation for Lillian, but she would need to allow her body to establish that pattern first.

This time it was up to Liz to make the announcement. She was very quiet on the ride home, fielding Rachael's questions while she pondered how she would tell Paul, who should be the first to know. It would have to be tonight, before she lost courage. He didn't hear her over Nellie's screams, so she had to shout at him.

"I said that I saw the doctor today. I'm pregnant!"

He glared at her as if she had slapped him. Then he quickly walked to the bedroom, waving his arms in a gesture of desperation, and slammed the door.

Even Rachael, sweet wonderful Rachael, who was her only ally, seemed less than pleased. It was for Liz the final judgement, and she slowly retreated into her private hell, suffering alone in the fires of self-recrimination and confusion. She didn't understand what she had done that was so wrong. She had tried to be a good Catholic wife, to fulfill her "marital obligation" to her husband. Was this now her punishment, a life without rest, drowning in dirty diapers and crying babies? What had she done that was so terrible? She longed for the luxury of crying herself to sleep, but there would be no sleep tonight, nor for many nights to come.

"You are dangerously dehydrated," Dr. Powell told her one-month later. "According to my scale you have lost eight pounds."

"I can't keep anything down," Liz answered. Her blue eyes were dull and lifeless, large sunken orbs in bony sockets. Her skin was gray, especially under her eyes; her clothes hung like sacks. "Even the vitamins and the pills you gave me for anemia come right back up."

He decided to hospitalize her immediately. "Where is the baby?" he inquired.

"She is with my mother. Rachael had to go to Fort Wayne to visit her sister, so Papa brought me into the city."

Adam asked Jack to come into the exam room. "This young lady is very sick," he told him. He pulled Jack aside and whispered, "I want to admit her to the hospital this afternoon. You and Anna can work out the particulars with Rachael when she returns, but under no circumstances is Lillian to continue to deal with this pregnancy on her own, or we may lose both of them."

When Paul arrived home from his long shift, he found Jack busily packing up the baby's things. "When Lillian is released from the hospital, I will take her home with me," he told his son-in-law. Paul dropped his thin lanky body into the nearest chair and ran his fingers through his hair. He was so tired, so defeated. He had fought until there was no fight left. The mortage, the bills, a crying baby that refused to let them sleep, a frail, sickly wife who couldn't cope, not to mention the stirrings within him that cried out for love and understanding. He looked up at Jack and nodded slowly. Jack had won, now he had all of them.

"You had better get some rest yourself," Jack said gently. "You look like shit."

Chapter 16

November 26, 1938

Dear Betsy,

As promised, I have visited with Liz during the Thanksgiving break. I am sad to report to you that all is not well with our dear friend, for she is already on the slide to deep depression and falling further every day. The rumor was correct; she is again pregnant, due to deliver in January. This pregnancy is especially hard on her delicate constitution, what with the anemia, nausea (I thought that was supposed to stop after three months!) and her separation from her husband Paul.

She does not confide easily, even to me. She mentioned you quite often, and I think there is a deep sadness that she is apart from her closest friends and the academy that she loves so much. It is difficult to talk privately with her, even in her own bedroom, because "Mama Bear" (Anna) buzzes in and out with all sorts of excuses. "Now, don't tire her out," she told me. I really didn't feel very welcome. Your namesake-to-be, baby Margaret Mary is not "Margaret Mary" at all, but "Nellie Lee," much to Liz's disappointment. But that is another story, for another time. Anyway, the child is a cherub, blond curls hanging in ringlets, and the most beautiful little face that you can imagine. She is a good, happy baby... as long as she is with her grandmother. She really has no use for anyone else, although she will tolerate being held for a minute or two.

There is more, dear Betsy... so much more. I really need to come back to school and somehow break the iron wall that separates us so we can talk. Perhaps you could ask Sister David Paul for special permission. I know that postulants are cloistered, but I sincerely believe that Liz's sanity, perhaps her very life, may depend upon whatever support we may be able to give.

God bless, I will see you after the holidays, even if only to pass you in the hall.

Love,
Martha

As Martha's letter to Betsy suggested, there was indeed more to the "confinement" of Lillian Sterling Unger. She was literally a prisoner in her father's house, although she was not aware of it at the time. Paul and Rachael were received cordially, encouraged to stay as long as they liked, even invited to stay for dinner, but Lillian seldom left her room. Nellie Lee would smile and coo at her father, granting him permission to hold her until she spied Anna walking by the doorway, and then she held out her little arms in a plaintiff plea... "Nana, Nana, Nana," she would chant, and then her lower lip would pucker and tremble. Once the crying started, it wouldn't stop until Nellie Lee was once again in her maternal grandmother's arms.

"The visit seemed to go well last night," Jack remarked to Anna at the breakfast table. She nodded in agreement, only half-hearing, for she was totally engrossed in talking to the baby as she shoveled oatmeal into the laughing mouth. It gave Jack great pleasure to watch them, for he had never seen Anna so content.

"You are certainly going to miss that child," he said casually. Whenever he broached the subject, Anna would react with anger or complete denial. Her response this morning was a new twist.

"Perhaps I won't have to give her up," she said sweetly.

Jack's eyebrows shot up. "And just how do you propose to pull that off?"

"I'm not sure yet. But the fact that our daughter's marriage isn't working out is not totally lost on you, I presume.'There's many a slip between cup and lip.'"

"There you go, talking in parables again. I never quite understand what you are trying to say. As for Paul and Lillian, forget it. That is a Catholic marriage, sealed in cement. Rachael would never allow a divorce."

"Rachael may not have anything to say about it."

"What the hell does that mean? What do you know that you haven't told me?"

Anna smiled at her husband. "Caroline Bradley," she said.

"Who?"

"A very dear friend of mine happens to be a sorority sister to Marion

Bradley, whose daughter Caroline was once 'almost' engaged to Paul Unger, and carries, I am told, a gigantic torch for her lost love." She continued to smile in satisfaction as she again turned her attention to Nellie's breakfast.

"Promise me that this story isn't something you heard on 'Ma Perkins,'" Jack tittered.

"On the contrary, I have it on very good authority."

"From who?"

" 'Whom.'"

He gave her that "I have had enough" look and she put the spoon down and faced him. "Mary George's sister was a classmate of the girl's mother. Mary told me all about it, at bridge."

"Mary George is a duplicitous old bitch, and I wouldn't believe her if she told me that Roosevelt was the President." Jack picked up his newspaper and opened it to the stock market page with a loud snap.

She smiled again. She would let him think about it for awhile, roll it around in his mind until curiosity got the better of him. Then he would ask her what she had in mind, and he would help her. For the moment, she needed to plant the ground work, sow the seeds of doubt in Jack's mind that Lillian's life could pick up where she left it when she last slept in her own home

"It was very nice to see Martha," Anna continued, attempting small talk. The truth was that she hadn't been at all pleased to see the girl huddled with Lillian and whispering "girlie" secrets. But Anna had played it out, always the gracious hostess.

"Oh, speaking of Martha, that reminds me! I had almost forgotten! The Mistress of Postulants called yesterday, Sister-What's-Her-Name. She wanted to know what we wanted done with Lillian's trunk. It is still in the basement at Madden Hall. I suppose they may as well just keep it; there is nothing in it that is of any use to Lillian, and it will cost a fortune to ship it back."

Behind his newspaper, Jack paled. His heart beat widely as he realized that the precious trunk was indeed still in Adrian. How could he have overlooked it? He struggled to regain composure; he had to think quickly. He almost wished he could leave it there, for it would certainly be safe from prying eyes. But anything could happen, the old building may burn, or the nuns might force it open and God forbid, discover his treasure.

He tried to keep his voice level as he questioned her. "What did you instruct her to do with it?"

"Nothing. I told her I would get back to her about it. It is, after all, your pride and joy. I never understood all that fuss and brass. Lillian didn't really need another trunk, and they are certainly welcome to the contents. What do you want me to tell the Sister?"

"Don't tell her anything. Don't give it another thought, dear. I will take care of it."

Jack put the paper down. It was time to change the subject.

"I had a long chat with Dr. Powell. He thinks that Diz is about ten weeks from delivery, and so far, so good. She has gained seventeen pounds, he said, and her anemia is under control."

"How can he know that?"

"Blood tests. The 'red count' is up. Her vital signs are normal. She could go home if she had someone with her."

"Nonsense. She is better off here. You just told me how much better she is than she was when the hospital released her."

"Well, she is certainly sleeping better, I have to admit. I used to bump into her at all hours, prowling around the house like she was lost. Now she is sound asleep when I look in after dinner, and Emily tells me she is hardly ever awake before noon."

Anna had cause to smile again. When would the people in this house admit that "mother knows best?" Several weeks ago, Anna had prepared a concoction that she labeled her "toddy." She added a shot of scotch to a cup of boiling water and flavored it with sugar and cinnamon. Lillian protested at first, but after a few sleep-filled nights, she accepted the hot drink without comment. More than once, when Lillian became anxious, Anna had added a few grams of sleeping powder from her endless supply of pharmaceuticals.

Although, the nausea continued; Anna and Helga struggled to pour food into Lillian. They insisted that she allow them to weigh her every day, cheering loudly at every pound gained.

"It's like living with a parasite," Lillian complained to her mother.

"It is a parasite," Anna agreed. "And it really never stops eating away at you." Anna wanted to seize the opportunity to suggest a sterilization procedure at best, some type of birth control at least. It would be a waste of breath now, Anna decided. Perhaps she would be more likely to succeed after this baby was born.

Jane Rachael Unger was born on a cold winter night in mid-January, 1939, ten months after her older sister. She was an instrument baby, requiring the use of forceps that forced her reluctant entry into the world. She was a lightweight compared to Nellie Lee, only six pounds, two ounces and the world welcomed the bruised, bleeding and jaundiced infant by confining her to incubator. Her mother was so exhausted that she couldn't sit up to hold her for more than a week.

Her father took one look and remarked, "Aren't we ever going to have a boy?"

Chapter 17

1939

Europe was seriously at war. Every day the headlines grew more alarming, as Hitler cut a wide swath through the continent, intent on his mission to rule the world. The release of Chaplin's *Great Dictator* was ill timed. Intended, as a humorous spoof, its character "Adolf Hynkel" was no longer funny by the time the film premiered in October of 1940. President Roosevelt, elected to his third term, kept Americans both alarmed and informed through his "fireside chats," announcing a proposed 1.8 billion dollars for defense, resulting in an additional tax increase of $460 million.

All of the news from Washington these days was bad news. While American ambassadors attempted to talk peace, five thousand new pilots were being trained, and naval troops were dispatched to Greenland and Iceland, as well as Alaska.

"Mac has been assigned to the USS Reuben James, on convoy west of Iceland," Jack told Anna.

"Did you get a letter?"

"No, Paul did. It seems our little soldiers have reunited with a common interest, the defeat of Nazi Germany."

"Are we at war?"

"Not yet. Washington is saying that it is a 'precautionary measure.' It is significant, however, that the Queen Elizabeth had to race across the ocean to safe harbor in New York. The ship isn't even finished yet."

"I spoke with Millie this morning," Anna commented. "Issac enlisted yesterday."

Jack smiled. "Good for him. Europe is the perfect place for Issac."

On the home front, Paul and Lillian's lives together could be said to have at least stabilized. Following a collapse at the refinery, Paul was ordered to have a complete physical, resulting in a cutback of his working hours. He was reassigned to the day shift, a blessed relief that enabled him to get at least six or seven hours of sleep per night. With Jack's assistance, Paul was able to renegotiate his mortgage to a lesser payment, backed by a second mortgage co-signed by Rachael.

There remained, therefore, only two major problems. The first was Jane, whose temperament required almost constant attention. She was a bright toddler, quick to learn, precocious almost, and she could at times behave like any other little girl. But she was subject to sudden changes in her behavioral patterns, and simple temper tantrums could turn quite ugly. She was prone to fits of violence, head banging, and destruction. She would scream uncontrollably for hours, without apparent reason. The plain little child was far more than Liz or Rachael could control… only Paul could quite her, and then not always.

Anna and Jack contributed to the quest of peace by "taking Nellie for the weekend," every weekend, beginning on Thursday morning and ending on Sunday evening. Paul's only objection was that she would miss Sunday Mass, so Anna dressed her to the teeth and trotted to the Cathedral of St. Paul every Sunday morning. As for Nellie, she tolerated her parents because her reward for doing so was her precious time with "Nana" and "Pawpa."

The second obstacle to the couple's wedded bliss, although Lillian was unaware of it, was the reappearance of Caroline Bradley. It was strange how she just suddenly "popped up" after almost four years.

It was a hot August Saturday. Paul was sweating while he pushed the mower across his front lawn, grateful that the girls were not there to "help" him, for they had gone to the movies with Rachael and Gretch to see *Dumbo*. He caught the approach of the car as it pulled up very slowly at the curb. It was a beauty, a Packard Clipper, price tag… $907.00 plus tax. Paul was more interested in the car than the driver, since he had coveted the automobile since Detroit had released it.

He was not curious enough to cease his labor, until a familiar voice said, "Hello, Paul." His back to her, he froze in place while his heart skipped a beat or two. He turned slowly, fully expecting to see those incredible green eyes.

"Caroline! Is it really you? What on earth brings you here?"

She looked wonderful. Her young beauty had only been enhanced, for she was even lovelier than he remembered. Smartly dressed in a cool linen sundress, white pumps and matching straw hat, she smiled at him.

"I could say that I was just in the neighborhood," she chuckled, "but I was never any good at fibbing. I drove down here last night, just to see you."

"Why?" As soon as the question had passed his lips, he recognized that it sounded rude. It was too late to take it back.

"Good question. I am not really sure. Impulse, perhaps. Or the desperate need just to see you again, to be sure that you weren't a dream. And I need an answer."

Paul glanced uneasily around the neighborhood. Cars passed. Walkers passed, waved and nodded. He felt somehow that he had been attacked on his home turf. Caroline noticed. "Is there someplace we could talk... privately?" she asked. He held her gaze, her eyes were sad, pleading.

"My family..." he hesitated.

"Are at the movies," she finished his thought. She looked at her watch. "It won't be over for another hour. By the time they stop for ice cream and drive home, it will be two hours."

He nodded and dropped the handle of the mower. He led her to the front door, held it for her, catching a whiff of her familiar scent. She pressed lightly between Paul and the doorframe, pausing long enough to smile up at him. He had an immediate erection.

"Damn!" he mumbled.

Caroline smiled again as she followed him through the house to the kitchen. She made no polite comments; she was not interested in his dwelling, his wife or children. She had no time to waste.

She didn't wait to be invited to sit down, pulling out a chair that broke the strained silence of the house with a loud scrape.

He was beginning to get angry. How could she just invade his life this way, causing him to suffer nervous anxiety? "What do you want?" he asked her.

"You first, Paul. What do you want?"

"At the moment, I want to finish mowing my lawn so I can listen to the Yankees game. DiMaggio is on a homerun streak."

"Hooray for him. I want to know how you could so coldly ignore my letter, after I agonized over it for weeks, poured my heart out to you? We meant something to each other once; how could you do that?"

"What letter? What are you talking about?"

"The letter I sent you four years ago, the one that begged you to forgive me, give me another chance."

"I didn't get any letter. Maybe it was lost in the mail."

She sighed and opened her purse. A US Mail return receipt was at the end of her long arm, extending across the table to him. He looked at it. It was signed "Mrs. Unger."

"I can't believe, after everything you have told me about Rachael, that she would deliberately withhold this letter from you!"

It was all too clear to him now, for the signature was not Rachael's. What could he say? Should he apologize? Try to explain? What was the point?

"Look, you walked out on me... left me standing in that frat house, brokenhearted and holding an engagement ring. How was I supposed to know that you would change your mind? You couldn't even come to say 'goodbye' the day I left. I'm sorry that we somehow disconnected, but you obviously got on with your life, and I got on with mine. End of story, nice to see you again. Goodbye."

"What has happened to you? Why are you so cruel, so cynical?"

"Is there any purpose in dredging it all up? What's done is done. I am married, Caroline, married. I have children."

"Two little girls, I know. Are you happy?"

"Whether I am or am not, it's none of your damn business. You know too much about me already; you make me feel violated. Stop it. Go away."

"I love you, Paul. It's that simple. I have always loved you and I will go on loving you until the day I die. There was something very special between us, a 'grand passion' that happens to a handful of people once in a lifetime."

She got up from the table and they stared at each other for what seemed like hours. He wanted her. He wanted to hold her, bury his face in her sweet-smelling, long red hair. He wanted to make love to her, here, now. He held his breath, standing rigid and without expression, until he heard the front screen door close.

After a few moments, he moved toward the table where she had left a small piece of notepaper. It was her address and phone number. He folded the note and put it in his shirt pocket, dropped into a kitchen chair and cried.

Chapter 18

1941

By October of 1941, America's involvement in the World War was a foregone conclusion.

"It's just a matter of time," Paul said to Liz."Germany sank the Hood; Britain sank the Bismarck. The world is out of control."

"You're scaring me." Liz shivered.

He shrugged. "It won't go away if we bury our heads in the sand and pretend it's not there. We'll have to fight."

"Don't you mean 'they'll have to fight'?" she countered. "You can't possibly consider…"

"I can and I will, Gretch. Make no mistake about it, if my country goes to war, I go with her."

"First Mac, then Isaac, now you. Isaac's last letter hinted that this war was going to get a lot worse before it got better. Would you like to read it?"

"No, he didn't write it for me, it was for you. It was private. I wouldn't think of reading mail that was addressed to you." He held her gaze for a long moment. He had made his point; he could see it on her face.

"I will say a novena," she answered. "For peace."

Peace eluded them. On October 30th, the USS Rueben James was sunk off the coast of Iceland. Mac was among the 44-surviving sailors rescued, and although he suffered from hypothermia caused by long hours in the icy water, he was otherwise uninjured and would recover.

> October 14,1941
> Dear Mac,
>   So good to hear from you (finally) and also good to hear that you have fully recovered from your little dip in the North Atlantic. I know it has been a lousy year for you, pal, and for what it's worth, it scared the hell out of all of us, especially your mother. Anna has actually mellowed out some since your ship was sunk; I think she "saw the face of God."

So now you just lay on the beach at Pearl Harbor and take life easy! Some guys have all the luck. How is the training coming along? Are you a certified fighter pilot yet? Every month I resolve to sign up, and then Gretch starts to cry, I think about her and the kids. I almost wish the draft lottery would nail me so I can come over there and save your ugly ass, and your sister won't be able to blame me.

As for your "let's get serious" question, no, I haven't resolved it yet. I am 25 years old, Mac, just like you. I haven't done anything of any value with my life. I have moved very close to death twice, but I have not yet lived. I work in a dead-end job, just to pay the bills. Gretch doesn't need me, really. All she needs is someone to take care of her, and I can't compete with your father on that level. My oldest daughter prefers the company of her grandparents; my second daughter prefers no one

So, how's your love life? It hardly seems fair that you're getting more action than this old married man!

Take care, pal
Paul

November 5, 1941
Dear Paul,
Greetings from Pearl Harbor, the lovely pacific paradise! Yes, the weather is great here, except when it rains. Sure beats freezing my ass off on some tub in the North Atlantic. Sometimes I think I will never be warm again. I still have the nightmares, so real, so vivid. I was almost asleep when the torpedo hit us. I remember that the ship pitched and I rolled out of the bunk to the hard, cold floor. Then the icy water started rushing in, so cold that I couldn't get to my feet, couldn't catch my breath. I relive it every night, Paul, just like it actually happened.

Yes, I am cleared to fly now. Graduated with honors, in fact. (Tell my father, will 'ya?) Dozens of new "fly boys" are arriving here every day. Something big is about to happen, I think, but I can't say anymore or it will be blacked out and you won't be able to read it.

256

As for you and Sis, I guess it is time to be honest, if you want my opinion. I could never really see the two of you together, you with your normal (?) sex drive and Sis hung up on chastity, and all that. Catholic girls are the coldest, I am told, because they grow up saying "no, no" and then someone puts a wedding ring on their finger and expects them to say "yes, yes!" Combine that fact with having Anna as a role model. I overheard Jack tell George Steinburger once that he had never seen her naked. Not that he missed much, I guess, but if I had to live my life like that, without passion, I would have preferred to go down with the other 76 of my mates in the North Atlantic. So there, I said it. You have to come to your own conclusions, my brother.

Don't do anything rash, like signing up right away. Sooner or later we will all have to fight, Paul. Put it off as long as you can.

No leave for me this Christmas; we are "on alert," like the rest of the country.

Happy New Year,

Mac

PS Almost forgot... I ran into someone from Ohio here on the base. She is a Wave, hometown is Toledo and she said she went to OSU with you. Her name is Caroline—can't remember her last name but she sure is a looker. How did you miss out on this one?"

Paul put Mac's letter back in the envelope and carefully slid it under his dress socks. He had read it at least once, often twice a day since it was delivered, almost three weeks ago. Yesterday he had walked to the church determined to go to confession, to rid himself of the guilt of his desires, but once there he had merely lit a candle and returned home. He could not remember a feeling that compared with the one that now lay heavy upon his heart. He wanted out, wanted it so badly that he could think of nothing else. He dreamed of Caroline every night, made love to her, listened to her soft words, experienced such happiness that he was afraid his heart would burst. Before dawn, just before he awakened, an oppressive cloud of sorrow flowed over him, and there were tears in the corners of his eyes when he awoke.

"Paul, are you ready?" Gretch called up the staircase. "Your mother is here and we have twenty minutes to get to Mass."

He slammed the drawer shut and frowned. He hated it when his routine changed, and he seemed always to be at the mercy of Gretch's whims. She and Rachael usually attended the early Sunday Mass, leaving him and little Jane to sleep in. Sometimes the toddler would join him in bed, snuggle down close to him and sing softly some little song she had learned at church. Sometimes she remained soundly asleep in her own bed, and sometimes she screamed the entire time, causing him to pull his pillow over his head and mumble curses. When the women returned, he could walk to the 10 Mass all by himself, providing him the blessed time he treasured these days… time to day dream, time to think.

"Why can't we ever all go together, as a family?" Gretch would ask every Sunday during dinner.

"Because Nellie Lee is at your mother's house, and Jane Rachael cannot behave in church, that's why," he answered every Sunday at dinner, and Rachael would look at the two of them with doe eyes that said "I worry about the two of you."

But this morning was different. His wife had insisted that they must try it again, so Paul was being obedient, trying to keep the peace. He had been moving toward "the decision" all week. Today he would tell her. He would try to make her understand that it was not her fault, but all his. He braced himself for the look that would assault him from the eyes of his mother. He wondered if he really had the courage to do this.

Rachael greeted him with a soft kiss when he came downstairs. Her expression said "patience, Paul, patience." He heard the screams from the kitchen, where Gretch was trying to clean some unknown substance from the front of Jane's pinafore with a dampened dishtowel while the child screamed and kicked, and pulled handfuls of brown hair from her head.

Gretch looked pathetic when she looked at her husband. It was not necessary that he comment, for she already knew what he was thinking. "You two go ahead," Paul said kindly as he removed the towel from Gretch's hand. "I'll do the best I can and maybe we'll join you, maybe not. There's no point in everyone being late."

Gretch began to protest, but Rachael shook her head. "Paul's right, honey. We'd better hurry."

Paul gave her arm a gentle squeeze. "It's ok, Gretch. You tried."

"But you'll miss Mass!"

"God will forgive me. Now get going, or we'll all miss Mass."

She gave him a grateful smile and nodded. At least he hadn't said, "I told you so."

They took the car, to save ten minutes. It was a silent ride until Liz said, "Paul is different."

"Different how?" Rachael asked her. She sensed it too, so the question was really a plea for clarification.

"He doesn't want me at all anymore. The last time we made love was five weeks ago. Before that it had been six months. He doesn't have any interest."

Rachael blushed. She didn't want to have this discussion. As they entered the church's parking lot, Liz pulled a hanky from her purse and dabbed at her eyes.

Rachael's heart ached for her. "Are you all right?"

As though she hadn't heard the question, she continued, speaking so low that Rachael strained to hear. "I think he will leave me."

"That's impossible! Paul would never do that, Liz. Whatever is wrong between the two of you will work out if you want it to. Concentrate on that, pray, and work at it."

Liz bit her lip and nodded. Rachael was so dear, so trusting, but Liz wanted to grab her and shake her hard and scream, *"Shut up and listen, you fool! My marriage is over and all you can do is prattle on in platitudes!"*

Still at home, Jane was quiet now, watching her father while she sucked on her thumb. He was sitting at the desk in the bedroom, writing a letter of resignation to his supervisor at the refinery. He sealed the envelope and placed it beside the other two in the desk drawer, one addressed "Gretch" and the other, "Mom."

He turned to the bed where his daughter sat, her little legs crossed, smiling at him. He smiled back, finished packing his suitcase and slid it under the bed.

"Daddy has to go away for awhile, Punkin," he said. "I hope it won't be long, but however long it is, I promise, I will come back for you." It broke his heart to leave her, for in spite of her problems, perhaps even because of her problems, she was his favorite. She put her chubby little arms around his neck. "Bye, bye, Daddy," she said, and she patted his shoulder. "Don't be sad, Daddy. Punkin loves you."

At ten minutes after 1, the small family sat down together for Sunday dinner for the very last time. At the exact moment that they bowed their heads for the blessing, nearly 4000 miles away some 360 Japanese warplanes were closing in on the Hawaiian Island military base at Pearl Harbor. It was December 7, 1941.

Chapter 19

1943

One hour into the interview, they still had much to talk about... two men in serious discussion of the mental health of Lillian Gretchen Sterling Unger. The man behind the desk was Dr. Robert Maxa, Chief of Psychiatrics at Wedgeworth Convalescent Center. Jack Sterling sat across from him, intently interested in everything that was being said.

"Given her history, and the circumstances of her life during the past six years, she has made remarkable progress. Please don't assume that she is somehow fragile, or unable to cope with everyday life. One difficult pregnancy and delivery, and the resultant post-partum depression would have in itself be quite enough to bring on a complete breakdown. Lillian has suffered far more than that," Maxa was saying.

"Prognosis?" Jack asked.

"I would like to say 'excellent,'" Maxa continued. "Unfortunately, we have done all that we can do for her here at the Center. The real test will be the reunion with her family, her level of self-esteem and her perception of acceptance and support. The next few weeks are critical. Now, tell me about the home environment, what preparations have been made."

"The children are with us... Anna and me. Our house is quite large, easily able to accommodate everyone. We have hired a nanny. Should we consider a nurse for Lillian?"

"Not quite yet. It might suggest to her that she is still very ill, and we want her to feel competent. It may become necessary, but let's hope not. What about the ex-husband? We are aware that he has had no contact since the divorce, since her admission here, but will he be an active part of her life once she is home?"

"At last report, Paul was on a battleship, somewhere in the South Pacific. Mac may know for sure, but this damn war has split us badly. I'm not even sure that Paul knows that he has a son, or that he even cares."

"How old is the boy?"

"Just a year, last month."

"And the husband left... when?"

"The day after Pearl Harbor was attacked."

"So Lillian herself was not aware of her pregnancy until after he was gone?"

"Correct."

"Is the baby's Paul's?"

Jack bristled. Immediately angry, he had to compose himself, struggle to understand that the question was not a judgement or an accusation, but simply a clinical inquiry. He had learned much the past nineteen months, more than he wanted to know.

He took a deep breath. "Yes."

Maxa smiled. "Good job, Jack. That was a little test. You are learning how to react appropriately, and that will be vital to Lillian's recovery. What about her relationship with her mother? Are you able to deal with both of them at once?"

"I don't have much choice, do I?" Jack almost chuckled. "I had my hands full with Anna after Pearl Harbor. Mac was there, you know, and after the Rueben James incident, she just couldn't deal with the fact that Mac was in mortal danger. It has certainly changed her, but to what extent, and how it will apply to Lillian, I can't say."

"What about you, Jack? You are the major caregiver; it's all on your shoulders. What deep-seated resentments are you hiding?"

"Am I being analyzed, Doctor?"

"Not at all. Much has been dumped on you. It is only natural that you assign blame."

"You're goddamn right I 'assign blame.' I treated that boy like my own son, and he deserted my daughter, leaving her with two small girls and pregnant. He didn't even have the balls to say a proper 'goodbye.' It was like the day the nuns brought her back, one more rejection."

"According to Lillian, it was not a happy marriage. Were you aware of that?"

"So what? Who says you're supposed to be happy? You grow up, get married, you die. If you want happiness, you find something you want and you buy it."

The doctor made a mental note for the chart. "Family patriarch is cynical, neurotic."

He wondered what Anna was like.

"About the 'desertion,' don't you see any justification? Many young patriots enlisted after Pearl Harbor."

261

"It wasn't Pearl Harbor… he would have done it sooner or later, so spare me the 'I love my country' bullshit. She is mine. My daughter, my blood. He took her from me, but he didn't want her. When he finished with her, he threw her away, and she ended up here. Am I supposed to thank him for that?"

"He gave you three beautiful grandchildren."

"No, 'she' gave me three beautiful grandchildren. Each one almost killed her."

"Lillian said she never wanted to be married. Did you know that?"

"All she had to do was say so. It was her mother who insisted that we had to make everything 'look right.' It didn't fool anyone. I would never have forced her into marriage."

"What do you want for her now?"

"Peace. I want her home where she belongs, with me. I can take care of her. She doesn't need anyone else."

Maxa reluctantly put his misgivings aside and released Lillian to the care of her father.

"There is no other option," he told Adam Powell on the telephone. "I agree with you that there are some serious problems with the family, but she won't make any further progress here, and sooner or later she will need to 'mainstream.' We can only hope that in familiar surroundings, she will somehow recover."

Actually, she did quite well. Little by little, Lillian created a healthier self-image. She applied for admission at the City College, where she was politely reminded that she had no high-school diploma. So determined was she to advance her education that she broke her own rule and asked Jack to intercede with the school administrator. After some "persuasion," Lillian was permitted to challenge the entrance exams, which she aced, and audit one or two classes. She excelled in the schoolwork, applied her energies. One of her instructors volunteered to assist her in completing the high-school graduate program. Her spirits lifted. Her complexion cleared, her eyes began to sparkle, just a little, and she was seen around town with one or two eligible young men, having lunch. Very soon, however, the propositions began to filter in, subtle at first. Most of the interested gentlemen were the husbands of friends, hers or Anna's. Still at ease with Rachael, Lillian confided in her. It was no easier being a widow, Rachael told her.

Liz almost never went out at night, and it pleased her father that she honored his curfew when she did. She made elaborate efforts to avoid confrontation with her mother. Lillian's self-perception had been shattered.

Her marriage had failed. Her relationships with her children were precarious. Somehow, she reasoned, she must maintain a civil existence with Anna, because as Jack told her, "a happy Anna is a silent Anna." So when Anna suggested that she see this young man or that young man, Lillian accepted invitations to dances and parties that bored her. Most of the time the date ended badly, a groping session in the car, but Lillian kept the unpleasant details to herself.

Paul wrote often to his mother, passing along cordial messages to Lillian and loving comments to the girls. He never mentioned Liz's pregnancy; although, Liz knew, he must have certainly been aware of it. Rachael moved quickly to pay the balance due on Paul's mortgage, in desperate hope that Liz and the children would remain there.

"Too many memories," Liz told her. The third pregnancy, like the two preceding, soon developed into serious complications, and by her fifth month, Liz was confined to bed. "Guess I'll never get the hang of this," she joked. But it was different this time. Anna did what she could to see to her daughter's comfort, but there were no medications or "tonics" administered other than those prescribed by Dr. Powell, who visited twice a week. In late August of 1942, a healthy boy was presented to Liz, and her maternal juices flowed in abundance when she held him, her one and only joy. She held him for hours, beginning to understand the pain that had permeated the hearts of both Anna and Rachael, who grieved for their sons constantly.

"I don't really blame Paul," she wrote to Betsy. "The terrible truth is that I would have run away too, if I had had somewhere to go. We should have never been married, but still I hold a place for him in my heart." A few weeks later, when the reality of what she referred to as "failures" joined forces with severe post-partum depression, Liz suffered a total mental breakdown. She was admitted to Wedgeworth.

As Christmas of 1943 approached, Liz steadily gained new strength and she was relieved to come home. While Anna kept herself locked in her room, preparing for the expected announcement, any day, that Mac was dead, Liz assumed the duties of running the house and caring for the children. In many ways, it was a relatively happy period, for she had begun to discover that she was indeed a strong woman, capable of taking care of herself and her own, if only her parents would allow her.

Chapter 20

1944

The waiter placed two Manhattans on the table and smiled. "From the gentleman at the bar," he said.

Liz and Martha looked at each other and giggled. Good manners prevented them from staring at the handsome dark-haired stranger, but Liz did manage a small salute. He grinned and waved back. "Your mother would be fainting about now," Martha laughed. "I wonder which one of us he's working up an itch for."

"You, no doubt, in your new chic outfit," Liz replied.

"Look who's talking! You are looking mighty good these days, missy. By the way, did you keep your married name?"

"Of course. The children are confused enough."

"Here he comes, right on cue," Martha whispered. "What's it going to be? Shall we be cool and aloof like the cultured young ladies that we are... or shall we both drag him under the table and pleasure him?"

Liz pretended offense. "Honestly, Martha! Get your hormones under control."

"Good afternoon, ladies," he greeted them. He smiled at Martha. "I like the second idea better," he said.

Martha blushed and stammered something completely unheard by the other two, who were now laughing with genuine glee. "Please join us," Liz said. She had never laughed so hard, and it felt very good."How did you possibly hear that?"

"I read lips," he laughed. He slid in beside Liz, took her hand and introduced himself. "I am Mitchell Southerland... will you marry me?"

Martha gasped, Liz grinned. "Later," Liz answered. "First I must finish my drink."

After hurried introductions, the trio chatted and laughed for the next two hours. Suddenly Martha looked at her watch and exclaimed, "Wow, gotta go. I was supposed to meet Chet thirty minutes ago." She blew Liz a kiss and hurried off.

Liz felt a little self-conscious now that they were alone. She had been dodging advances for so long that it was becoming instinctual, and she didn't want to offend this very charming man who had provided her the best afternoon of her life.

"I'm afraid I must leave also," she said. "There are people waiting for me."

He smiled knowingly. "I understand," he said, and instead of the expected protest, he moved out of the booth and offered his hand. "May I see you again?"

She took in the full presence of him now. He was taller than she, a pleasant surprise, for most men weren't. Tall enough to dance with, tall enough to allow her to wear the fashionable new heels. His black wavy hair was thick and shiny, and if she had consumed one more Manhattan she may have given in to the urge to run her manicured nails through it, wrapping it around her slender fingers.

"I would very much like to say 'yes,' Mr. Southerland," she said gently. "But we have not been properly introduced, you see. Thank you for the drinks, and the charming conversation."

He stepped back to allow her to pass. He clicked his heels together and bowed, and she noted that his shoes were buffed to a perfect shine. He certainly was dapper, this one.

When Liz arrived at the house, a harried Sharon greeted her. "Call Miss Martha at once," she ordered. "She has called four times in the last hour."

"So?" Martha prodded.

"'So' what?"

"Don't be coy. Did you go out with him?"

"Not exactly. We did make love though, twice behind the bar and once in the taxi. I really need a nap."

"Go to hell. I never expected that anyone would make me forget my Chet, but that was one gorgeous man. Are you going to see him again?"

"I think not. A man like that usually has at least one wife, two mistresses, and a bevy of girlfriends. I'd grow old standing in line."

"I suppose so. Are we still on for shopping on Friday?"

"I'll have to bring Mama Bear. She wants to buy new shoes for your wedding."

Anna insisted on wearing her new heels, "to break them in," and she teetered precariously as they strolled the downtown streets.

"Mother, please be careful," Liz warned. "You are going to break your neck in those things."

"My feet are killing me," Anna announced after a few blocks. "There's the Congress Club ahead. Let's stop for a drink."

As they approached the Club, Liz spied Mitchell Southerland seated on the same bar stool that he had occupied a few days ago. She panicked, certain that an introduction to Anna would only invoke endless questions. She whirled around to concoct some quick reason why she needed to go immediately home. "Nellie has a piano lesson," she started to say. But Anna had stopped short in back of her, lost her balance, and was now sprawled out on the sidewalk, clutching her ankle. Her silk stockings were torn at the knee, which was bleeding profusely.

Shit! What was she going to do now? A two hundred-pound woman was down for the count; pedestrians were stepping around her, gawking. Suddenly the door opened and he was there.

"Get some ice," he told Liz, "from the bar." By the time she returned, he had hailed a taxi, and he and the driver were lifting the swooning Anna into the back seat. Liz climbed in beside her, and Mitchell got in front with the driver. Liz gave the driver the address and they were off, barely seven minutes after the fall.

In spite of her obvious discomfort, Anna was alert to the fact that the handsome young man and her daughter were not together for the first time. She closed her eyes and groaned. Her foot was swelling rapidly, throbbing.

"Are you in much pain?" Mitch asked from the front seat.

"Considerable."

"Mother, perhaps we should go directly to the hospital."

"This may help," Mitch said, and he passed a silver flask across the seats to Anna.

She looked surprised, then shrugged and took a deep swig. She took one more before she handed it back.

"Thank you."

"My pleasure."

Well, aren't you two just the cozy ones! Liz thought. Mitch winked at her.

When the taxi arrived at the entrance to the Sterling home, Liz ran ahead to open the door for Mitch, who was carrying Anna up the steps without even puffing.

"You are very strong," Anna told him, wrapping her arms around his neck, reluctant to be put down. He smelled very nice, a faint masculine musky scent, not Old Spice. "Tell me, how do you know Lillian?"

He grinned at her, their faces very close. "I met her at the Congress Club.

I proposed immediately, of course, but she turned me down."

"She is a silly fool," Anna answered. She was feeling no pain now; warm and fuzzy was how she felt. "Ask her again. If she still says 'no,' I'll marry you."

"We have a deal," he laughed.

He placed her gently on the leather couch in the den, and busied himself with propping pillows while Liz went to phone Dr. Powell. At Anna's invitation, Mitch fixed them each a strong drink. When Jack appeared, he was more impressed with the fact that Mitch had paid for the waiting taxi than the rescue itself. He offered to reimburse him, but Mitch declined.

"At least stay for dinner, please," Anna interjected.

"Some other time, thank you. I must go."

Liz walked him to the cab. "My father would bequeath to you at least one-half his kingdom about now," she chuckled. "I expected that you might ask to see me again."

He cupped her face and kissed her, slowly, gently. His lips were very warm and soft. She was disappointed that the kiss was short, for she found herself enjoying it very much. He got into the front seat.

"I don't need his permission," Mitch said. "You are a grown woman, all I need is yours."

She stood watching the departing taxi until she could no longer see any sign of it. She was smiling when she reentered the front foyer, for although she was not yet aware of it, she was, for the first time in her life, completely, desperately in love.

Six weeks later, Jack sat in a back booth of Kelly's Tavern. His eyes were gray tonight, behind the glasses. He seemed very engrossed in reading the material that had just been handed to him by the man on the other side of the booth.

"It is all there, Mr. Sterling, and quite complete if I say so myself." Randall "Snoop" Crosscut was a private detective, recently hired by Jack Sterling to investigate one Mitchell Southerland. "The report is yours to keep." Crosscut wanted to collect his fee and get out of here. He had a hot date that would cool down considerably every minute that he was late. "Snoop" was not Jack's "usual" informant, but John Randolph was not available, so Jack was reduced to using the yellow pages. He wasn't too sure about this guy.

"I am paying for your time, Mr. Crosscut," Jack retorted. "So you will remain. I may have questions."

"But what more could you possibly want to know?" Crosscut protested. "I have followed the man for weeks, talked to everyone who could possibly know anything about him, checked out the official birth records, everything. If you don't want him in your family, send him over to my house," he chuckled. "I would say that he is excellent son-in-law material."

Jack looked at Randall over his glasses, causing the man to wish he hadn't spoken at all. "You are perhaps not as particular who beds your daughters," Jack snarled. "As for me, I can't afford any more mistakes. I want to know when and where this guy pisses, what he had for breakfast, what movie he saw last week. Everything."

He picked up the manuscript and reviewed what he had already read. Southerland was the only son and grandson of a prominent old family. Homestead was established in 1860. Great-grandfather was president of Hardin County Bank, raised horses for Union Army.

Origins were Scot-Presbyterian. Assets were not in the Rockefeller league, but there was lots of old money. Mitchell's father was the family's "black sheep," liked his booze too much. He had married beneath him, or so the family thought. Mother was a bit of "good time girl." Southerland, known as "Sparky" to his many friends, was the darling of his sober grandfather and aunts, the heir apparent. He was college educated, drove a new car, and traveled easily in all social circles. No wife, no ex-wife, no children."

"Is he queer?" Jack asked Crosscut.

"Only if the Pope is a Jew," Crosscut chuckled. "I would call him 'discreet.' The ladies love him."

"Indeed," Jack mumbled, remembering the way Anna fawned over him. "It says here that he works for the Tappan Company. What does he do?"

"He's a time-study methods engineer. Very bright, uses a slide rule."

Jack snickered. "You are very easily impressed. Does it pay anything?"

"He certainly isn't a gold-digger, if that's what worries you," Randell offered.

"My worries are none of your concern. Why hasn't he been drafted?"

"He failed the physical. Scarlet fever as a child left him with some slight heart trouble."

"Must be more than 'slight,'" Jack came back. "In this war, if you are able to walk and breathe, you can fight."

"He flunked. What more can I say?"

"Politics?"

"Die-hard Republican."

"Arrest record?"

"Clean."

Jack removed his glasses and pushed an envelope across the table. It contained $1000 in cash. "You are anxious to leave, Mr. Crosscut, so here is your fee, plus a little extra .I will contact you if I have any more questions."

Driving home, it occurred to Jack that Mitchell Southerland was probably too good to be true.

Chapter 21

1944

Mac Sterling was unable to attend his sister's wedding, due to the fact that he was at the controls of a B-29 Fortress bomber, lead plane in the attack on Japan. The bride's ex-husband was also not in attendence, as he was a reluctant guest of the Japanese, a prisoner of war. President Roosevelt prepared to run for his fourth term, with Harry Truman as his Vice-President. The Republicans chose Thomas E. Dewey, an admitted long shot, to oppose the President.

As for the courtship of Lillian, Mitchell had done everything right. He was solidly "in" on the day after Anna's fall, when he sent Anna a dozen red roses, accompanied by a card that read, "Don't forget, we have a deal." Anna took great delight in concealing the message from both her husband and her daughter. It drove Liz crazy until she had hunted him down at his hotel, for by now she was so smitten that the mere glimpse of him would quicken her heartbeat. "He plays me like a maestro plays a violin," she wrote to Betsy, who was now Sister Mary Marcella, OP. "I simply never dreamed it could be like this."

By the time Martha and Chester Reubens had returned from their honeymoon, Liz was riding very high on the euphoric cloud of true passion. "He is an absolute master of the art," she told Martha, and launched into such descriptive detail about female orgasm that Martha was positively green with envy and didn't call for a week.

With Anna firmly in his corner, Mitch set about winning over the suspicious Jack. As with everything that he did, he was so subtle that no one noticed the effort. Mitch studied Lillian's "Papa," soon knowing just what to say and how to phrase it. Mitch introduced Jack to the game of golf, gaining for him a complimentary membership in the country club. They went out drinking together, Mitch pacing himself carefully in order to drive Jack home safely. They attended ball games, went fly fishing, and shared bawdy stories with the guys down at Kelly's Tavern. Mitch always picked up the tab.

Since Mitch was a frequent guest at the dinner table, Liz and Anna took great pains to insure that the children were dressed in their best clothes and on their best behavior. At six, Nellie was a beauty, reserved and cool, always polite. She had no particular interest in the pairing of her mother with this man, for it would not alter her life in the least. Jane, age 5, missed her father desperately. She was so openly hostile to Mitch, as she was to everyone else, that she was sometimes ordered to take her dinner in the kitchen. Scottie, the two-year-old, was an unqualified joy. Mitch romped and roughhoused with him, and never tired of his incessant chattering and demands for attention.

Lillian grew more beautiful every day. She spent hours getting ready for Mitch, was almost never seen without a smile, and she hummed "Always" until Jack threatened to break the record if she didn't stop. She worked now in her father's office, as a junior file clerk, earning a respectable $17.50 a week. Combined with the monthly check forwarded from Rachael (who claimed it came from Paul), Liz was feeling relatively independent regarding the support of herself and her children.

Some mornings when she awakened, still basking in the afterglow of last night's lovemaking, she wondered how she would ever exist without him. When would he propose? She wanted to die if he didn't want her the way she wanted him. Other times, she almost wished he wouldn't ask her to marry him. It was so perfect. Marriage might ruin what they had together. She reminded herself that many of her sufferings had been of her own making, the results of bad choices or no choices at all. If she had learned nothing else, she knew for certain that she must take control of her own life, take responsibility for her own happiness.

When she was really being honest with herself, she had to admit that Mitch's reluctance to tell her about his family bothered her a great deal. "They are different," he said once, "not like yours."

"That's a plus!" she quipped.

She knew that the family farm was in Hardin County, an hour's drive away. Soon, she assumed, he would take her there to meet his parents. But every time she brought it up, he changed the subject.

Everywhere they went, dozens of people knew him on sight. At first she resented the woman who brazenly threw their arms around him, locking his lips on theirs. But eventually she discovered that it meant little more to him than the men who sought out his company. He had friends everywhere. He was seldom permitted to pay for the drinks he ordered for "his lady" and himself, and he was always the center of attention, entertaining his admirers for hours with funny stories and Irish songs. Liz began to realize that she could be charming and witty simply by association, and she too came to be admired, by virtue of winning his heart.

He drank a little too much, but then, who didn't? He didn't share her faith, but neither did he oppose it. He didn't try to control her, never asked her to account for her time away from him, never hinted at jealousy or possessiveness. He encouraged her independence, supported her decisions, and was always on her side of any dispute.

Liz grew so confident in the warmth of Mitch's love that she began to consider a move away from the Sterling house, perhaps even out of the city itself. She could support the children, maybe even afford a part-time nanny to help with them, and they could be a real family. More than anything else, she wanted to make up for the time she had taken away from them, the months in the "hospital," the long convalescence.

He just showed up one afternoon, greeted the maid Sharon with his usual slap on the rear when she answered the door, and sprinted upstairs, where he found "his woman" soaking in bubbles. He kissed her lightly on the forehead, carefully avoiding the cold cream smeared all over her face. "How soon can you be ready?" he asked her. "I want to get married."

It turned into another hurry-up affair, but this time she wasn't pregnant. Anna propelled herself into high gear, and within three days all the arrangements had been completed for a tasteful but elegant wedding in the Sterling living room.

"Can't we, just once, do this the right way?" Jack moaned.

"Mitch is so romantic; he wants a small intimate wedding," Anna responded.

"'Mitch is so-o-o romantic,'" Jack mimicked. "You would throw yourself into a tub of sheep dip if Mitch suggested it."

Anna smiled and patted the top of his hairless head. She walked away humming. He couldn't even provoke her anymore, he thought.He was surrounded by crazy women, and loving every moment of it.

Liz naively believed that Mitch's failure to provide Anna with a guest list was an oversight, so she simply mailed the invitations to "general delivery," Kenton, Indiana. That done, she forgot about it until Preston and Ella Southerland called from the Carlton Hotel the night before the wedding. Mitch was less than delighted, but he covered as well as he could. Jack offered to cover the bill, but Mitch insisted that he would handle it.

"I don't think he intended to invite them," Jack told Anna later.

"Strange," she said. "I wonder why."

When the Southerlands presented themselves at the Sterling home, Anna was surprised to see that they were both dressed in black. Preston's pants were shiny at the rear, and Ella was draped in black lace, heavily made up and more than a little drunk. During the course of the evening, she made a pass at every male she encountered, including the father of the bride. Preston was well on his way to drunken oblivion, and Sharon was recruited to follow him around with an ashtray after he had burned two holes in the oriental rugs.

Judge Steinburger did the honors this time, since Lillian's divorce prohibited a Catholic wedding. Liz looked lovely in yellow organdy; Mitch wore an elegant pinstripe. The children were in attendance, the girls play-acting the parts of "little miss perfects," while Scottie delighted everyone when he made a head-down run for Mitch's arms, refusing to be put down during the exchange of vows. Mitch kissed Lillian full on the lips, unashamed and passionate. Then he hugged Scottie and exclaimed, "Hey, buddy, we're married!"

Part 4

Chapter 1

1945

Lillian held the card out to her handsome husband. "It's from Mother and Papa," she said. "An all-expenses paid honeymoon to the destination of our choice. So, where do you want to go, dear?"

"I suppose that Europe is out of the question," he laughed.

"It might be a little too exciting, considering. I have an idea. Why don't we pass on the long, long trip for now and just take a few days?"

He laughed and pulled her to him. "I don't care where I am, as long as you are with me," he said gently. "Just promise that you won't leave me sitting on a park bench somewhere when you get tired of me."

"Fat chance." She stood between his legs as he sat on the bed. Winding her long fingers into his black curls, she pulled his face to her breast. When he lay back, taking her with him, all travel discussion ceased.

They spent the next three days almost exclusively in their hotel room, granting occasional concession to sustenance. When they checked out, Mitch agreed that they could stop making love long enough to at least finish an entire sentence, so they drove out of the city for about an hour, stopped the car near a winding creek and spread a blanket on the grass.

Three hours later it was decided that they didn't really have to decide anything, at least not right away. They would rent a house in the Richmond area, settle in with the children, and take one day at a time while more permanent options unfolded. Mitch wanted to explore a new opportunity in Tennessee, he told Lillian, but it was not pressing. She wanted to keep her job at the Savings and Loan, even if only part-time.

"See how good we are together?" Mitch chuckled. "Can we make love now? Everything is settled."

"Nothing is 'settled,' silly," she laughed, and she threw herself into his waiting arms.

Jack was less than pleased with their plans. "Nonsense," he blurted out. "Renting is a bad waste of good money." He opened the top drawer of his desk and produced a deed, which he proudly presented to Mitch. "It has four bedrooms, three baths, a full basement, and a two-car garage; it sits on a five-acre lot just three miles down the river," he explained to the startled pair. "It even has a large barn, for Diz's horse." Mitch rose, put both hands in his pockets and walked across the room to study the antics of a large squirrel from the French doors.

Lillian's head began to buzz. It was happening again, the panic, the anxiety. Papa still had the document in his hand, waiting for a standing ovation, copious gratitude, anything.

Tension hung heavy in the air, and the silence seemed unbreakable. Mitch returned to the desk, lightly placing both hands on Lillian's shoulders. He could feel her tremble. This would go down in their personal history as their first crisis, he knew, and his reaction was critical.

"Thank you, Jack. We are delighted to accept your offer, but please retain the deed."

Jack's eyes narrowed. "Why?"

"Because you are a man who understands that I am a man who needs to provide. For the moment, I have no means to do so, considering that the provision includes three small children, but I will do it, and soon. Meanwhile, I thank you for your assistance."

Lillian held her breath .No one had ever said "no" to Jack, who continued to stare at Mitch, his mind clicking. Suddenly his face erupted in a rare grin, exposing short, stubby teeth. "Good man!" he exclaimed. "Well said, well said indeed." They shook hands. "If you find yourself ready to be a property owner, let me know," Jack said, pumping Mitch's arm.

"You saved my ass, Darling," Liz told him later. "I owe you."

"And what an ass." He smiled. "Let's make a pact. I don't want to waste our precious time debating or discussing what went on with your father. I learned a long time ago to chose my battles, give in on the things that don't really matter, or don't matter as much as other things. Just know this, my love, I am my own man."

"And what a man!" she whispered. "I know exactly what that cost you, and I have never been more proud of anyone in my entire life."

During the next few weeks, Mitch and Lillian were overwhelmed with moving, decorating, coordinating, Scottie's chicken pox, Jane's tantrums, and Nellie's arrogance. Anna was there every time they had time to notice, offering a second and third suggestion before they had time to consider the first.

"Those drapes are all wrong, Lillian."

"Mitch, I have a list of repairs for you."

"You can't be serious, don't think for a moment that you can put those two girls in the same room."

Lillian began to display a few of the old symptoms, but she balked at any suggestion that she see Dr. Powell, or that she might resume the mood-altering medications. "I have had enough of that stuff to last me a lifetime," she told Martha. "No more."

As the holidays of 1944 dawned on the horizon, the only element that prevented an unqualified disaster was the hope that the Southerlands and their little family could somehow manage to have an intimate Christmas together, their first. Optimism set in when Jack and Anna announced that they would spend the rest of the winter in Florida. It was short-lived when Mitch's parents arrived for a surprise two-week visit.

Nellie flatly refused to allow her sister to share her room in order to accommodate the guests, demanding instead to accompany "Nana and Pawpa" to Florida. "She will make us all miserable if we force her to stay here," Lillian pleaded to Mitch.

"If we give in to a seven-year-old tyrant, we are beaten," he countered. But he finally agreed, feeling that the cause of the problem was his family this time. Lillian amazed him with her hostess skills, preparing excellent meals while Ella propped her ample bottom on a kitchen stool, chattering endlessly and dropping cigarette ashes everywhere. Preston stayed quietly drunk and out of the way for the most part. Mitch took charge of Scottie, who was delighted to follow him everywhere. The moody Jane surprised them all when she suddenly and inexplicably bonded with Preston. "They are two of a kind," Mitch kidded. "Silent and moody. The only difference is that she doesn't drink bourbon."

"At least not yet," Lillian laughed.

Somehow they managed to get through it, without too much damage to the carpets, without too many tears. Ella used her rare sober moments to give Lillian detailed accounts of Mitch's former love life, vent her truculent hatred of anyone or anything Catholic, and make the not-too-subtle suggestion that she and Preston would require a monthly supplement to their limited income, now that Mitch was "making good money."

When the couple finally reunited, mentally and physically exhausted in their cozy bedroom, they drank and laughed about the day's trials and near misses, then made love long into the night.

"I told you that my family was different," he offered as clarification.

"I think we are about evenly matched." She smiled.

Nothing, it seemed, threatened to cast even the slightest shadow on their bliss. When Mitch announced that he would take Lillian's beloved Pegasus for a "good run," she was only concerned for her husband's safety. "He is a spirited Arabian," she told him. "Very sensitive. He has never been ridden by anyone except me."

"I grew up on a horse farm," he reminded her. "Trust me, I know how to handle him."

The beautiful stallion had to be destroyed when Mitch pushed him beyond endurance. Lillian thought her heart would break, but she never asked for an explanation, and none was offered to her. Mitch was far more upset about the airplane that disappeared over the Atlantic Ocean, carrying bandleader Glenn Miller to his death.

They looked to the New Year with hope and promise. 1945 would bring the liberation of Auschwitz, the complete defeat of Nazi Germany, and peace at long last. In February, Americans celebrated the raising of Old Glory at Iwo Jima. April announced the death of FDR and the suicide of Hitler.

"I pray every night that the boys will come home alive and well," Lillian told Mitch. "There is so much death; it is difficult to believe that we will be spared."

"Talk about life," Mitch answered. "New life. When is our baby due?'

"How could you possibly know?" she sputtered. "I was keeping it as a surprise! No morning sickness, and I don't even show."

"I know everything about you, don't you realize that by now?"

The August bombing of Hiroshima and Nagasaki brought the Empire of Japan to its knees, and the document of unconditional surrender was signed on September 2nd. Five days later, on her own 25th birthday, Lillian gave birth to a curly-headed baby girl. "It was a piece of cake," Lillian told the grinning father. "If every baby could be this easy, I'd have one every year."

"It is my birthday too, you know," Anna said. "I imagine that you will want to name her after me."

"Not this time, Anna," Mitch interjected. "Her name is Kathleen."

Chapter 2

1946

While life appeared to be placid and content, rumbles of disaster began to move silently beneath the surface of Mitch and Lillian's happy home, much like the infestation of termites. It began with Mitch's trip to Tennessee, where he met with old political friends in the Estes Kefauver camp.

"We are waiting for you," they told him. "Estes will run for the State Senate if we can recruit enough help." It was the perfect solution, Mitch reasoned. The weather was warmer, the pace more conducive to his ideal existence, for it was "Dixie," the land of the easy-going, where even the ambitious found time for an afternoon nap. He began to form concrete plans for housing, took time to look into the school situation, and rehearsed his plea to Lillian.

Jack received a call from Randolph, his old friend and occasional private investigator. "I hear by the grapevine that you hired my competition to do a job for you, Jack," he began. "Sorry that I was out of town. Was it something that couldn't wait?"

"You might say that. I needed to check out my prospective son-in-law. Snoop did all right, I guess. Competent, but not as thorough as I had hoped."

"I bumped into Snoop at Kelly's the other night. He introduced me to Mitch. They were mighty friendly. Did you know that they knew each other?"

"No."

"It may mean nothing, Jack, but I thought it was a bit strange. Figured I'd better check it out with you."

"I appreciate that, John. What do you recommend?"

"Give me a few days, let me ask some questions, see what I can find out. I'll get back to you."

Randolph's report was similar, for the most part, to the one delivered by Crosscut. It was the discrepancies that sent the paranoid Jack into frenzy. Southerland had been called up for the draft because the father of his discarded ex-girlfriend was on the local draft board. Local gossip revealed the assumption that Mitch had married a woman with three children in order to avoid military service.

"'He married a rich girl,'" quoted Randolph. "Speaking of money, he doesn't handle it well. He borrows much, repays some, talks his way out of the rest."

Mitch's basic credentials were legit, college degree, good job. He had a string of questionable discharges behind him, and there were rumors of a drinking problem and a proclivity for "telling off the boss."

"It seems your fair-haired boy has quite a temper," John told Jack. "He has a reputation as a 'hot-headed Irishman,' been known to swing a punch or two. He sure is a hit with the ladies, however."

"Tell me more about that."

"He developed very early, evidently. Typical big farm boy, rolling in the hay. Could charm the pants off an eighty-year-old virgin, I'm told. No proof of bastard children, but there are plenty of 'maybes.' Sheriff was called once or twice when he got a little rough with a persistent ex-lover. He has no arrest record because the local law are his drinking buddies."

Jack did not look pleased. The more he heard, the less he liked. "What else?"

"Well, the family has lots of old money, that part is true. Grandfather and great-grandfather were pillars of the community, and owned most of the county. His father's sisters are OSU graduates and very proper. Southerland's uncles were very respected; one died in France during WWI, and the other is the family patriarch. But his old man is a drunk who gambled away his inheritance and spent six months in the pokey for vehicular homicide. He is reported to be 'Peck's bad boy,' and Mitchall is very defensive of his father, very devoted. There is bad blood with the mother, however, for some unknown reason. All of this is just usual family stuff, not worth much concern."

"But there is something else, right?"

"Right. If he were related to me, I would worry about his friends."

"Pardon?"

"He moves in some mighty diverse circles, and he is not always discreet. He's been seen drinking with 'family.'"

"Like in 'Mafia'?"

"The same. More interesting, however, is his current interest. He is planning to move to Tennessee to work on the Kefauver campaign."

"The 'moving' part concerns me, but what is the deal with this—what's his name?"

"Kefauer is a democrat. The Southerlands have been registered

Republicans since God created the world. Southerland is usually reluctant to aggravate his wealthy aunt... she is his 'cash cow,' and she is very anti-Democrat. Kefauer has his eye on a US Senate seat, as he comes up the rank, maybe even the White House. He is devoted to fighting crime."

"I don't follow. What has that to do with me?"

"Nothing at all, unless you have something to hide, which, of course, you don't. I'm just laying it out for you. Don't you think his association with Kefauver is a bit at odds with his other 'friends'?"

"Maybe. I'll have to think about it. Honestly, John, all I gather from your report is that he can't hold his booze, pinches a few asses, and is ambitious. He may not be the cream of the upper class, but he's no yokel. My main objection to all of this is that I paid Crosscut to do a job, paid him very well. He sold me out, evidently. "

Privately, Jack had more concerns, but he was not about to confide in Randolph.

"It's a stretch, but he might be a 'plant,'" advised George Steinburger. "Be very careful, Jack, what you tell him about your business. If he knows anything at all, he knows too much already."

Anna's notable interference in the new family moved into high gear. Her visits became more frequent, and her suggestions took on a condescending tone.

"Can you believe it?" Lillian complained to Mitch. "She took my pork chops back to the butcher... said they weren't lean enough. He won't wait on me now. It is so humiliating!"

"Nellie doesn't want to attend the school you have chosen for her," Anna told Lillian. "I would like to enroll her in private boarding school, perhaps the Academy."

"But we want her home, with us."

"Perhaps with Nellie away at school, you could spend more time with Jane. She is the one who requires careful watching."

"Meaning what?"

More infuriating than Anna's comments were her lapses into stone silence when she was challenged. She gave her daughter one of her "you know what I mean" looks and walked away. Lillian was unnerved. She was beginning to come undone, a little at a time, around the edges. Mitch reacted to Anna's constant "helpful" hints with an aggravated groan whenever he encountered her car in the driveway upon his arrival. He maintained his composure with

Anna, however, feigning delight to see her, turning his displeasure on Lillian after Anna left.

"What do you expect me to do about it?" she challenged him.

"I expect you to control your own house," he snapped. "It is time to stop being a weak papa's girl and stand up to her. Your children are farmed out all over the place. Nellie Lee spends every weekend with Jack and Anna; Scottie goes to Rachael's every other weekend. If you can find someone to take Jane, you can give up 'mothering' altogether! On second thought, good luck."

"I guess I had forgotten that they are only 'my' children," she countered. "I thought they were 'ours.'"

"It is difficult to establish a family atmosphere when we are rarely a family," he said.

The debate continued, escalated into a serious quarrel, and he slapped her that evening for the very first time. It was not to be the last.

He spent the night on the couch, and left her a note the next morning that he needed to give them both a little "breathing space." He was going to Tennessee, he said, to check on his job prospect, and he hoped to have a wonderful surprise for her when he returned. She was a wreck until his car pulled into their garage, afraid that he had deserted her, blaming herself for yet another failed marriage.

Their reunion was sweetly passionate. Thus the pattern became established. They quarreled; sometimes the quarrels became shouting matches. When the shouting began, Mitch usually inflicted some physical harm, depending upon how much he had had to drink. She cried, recriminated herself, reinforcing her low self-image. She concluded that she had deserved what she had gotten, that it was always her fault. He was always repentant in the morning, when he often cried and begged her to forgive him. She always did. She made excuses when asked about the bruises, careful not to use the same one twice in succession, and she even convinced a few people that she was just "accident-prone." Jack had doubts, but he would wait until he had more information. Besides, Diz would not stand for much of it, he was sure, and he would see to it that the children were not alone with Mitch.

Lillian was home alone when the telephone rang. Scottie had gone to the circus with Rachael, and the girls were shopping with Anna.

"Mrs. Southerland?"

"Yes?"

"This is Henry Meeder at National Bank. Sorry to bother you, but we need to clarify the amount requested on the recent note. Five thousand dollars is a considerable sum, and we prefer not to issue the loan in cash, as requested. Would a cashier's check be all right?"

Lillian initially thought that the caller had made a mistake, confused her with someone else, a clerical error. "I'm sorry, Mr. Meeder, I didn't catch that. Would you repeat it, please?"

He patiently went over the details again; she had supposedly applied for a $5000 loan, "signed" a personal note, and requested payment in cash. Mitch! There was no other possible explanation. She was shaking, struggling to control her voice. "Let me get back to you, Mr. Meeder," she said. "Things are a little hectic here."

Chapter 3

"Five thousand dollars, Mitch! Did you think I wouldn't notice? How dare you sign my name to a note?" Lillian was angry, so angry that she was hardly aware of his silence. He would let her vent this time, get it all out. Then he would answer only in soft, reasonable words that would ultimately win.

Mitch had concluded weeks ago that his only option was to get out of town, even before his conversation with Morelli. "You can believe it or not, Sparky, but I tell you here and now that I have experience in these matters. Your ass is on the block."

Mitch had laughed. "You have been watching too many gangster movies, Morelli. There is no 'hit man;' no one is going to kill me. I'm a family man, legit and clean. I make my money honestly; I have no deep dark secrets."

"Your father-in-law thinks different," Morelli warned. "He has two PI's on your tail now, asking a lot of questions. I'm not your priest, so you don't have to confess to me. Maybe you have something on the side; maybe you beat the little woman. He is sniffing for something, so you'd better look over your shoulder."

It was that comment that made Mitch conclude that a "leave of absence" might be in order. But he needed cash, lots of cash. Then he could go to Tennessee, take Lillian and the children with him. Once he was established with the Kefauver people, he would convince her to stay. They would be away from Jack and Anna, away from the bookies that hounded him, away from the return of the war hero Paul, who might try to take back what was once his.

"It was going to be a surprise," he told his wife. He kept his tone low and contrite.

"Well, it worked. I'm very surprised."

The new things for the house, the household bills had taken most of his earnings. He should have discussed it with her, asked her to slow down on the spending, but she was so happy with the new nursery and being able to provide piano lessons, dancing lessons and practically everything that she thought would make the children content. His pride stopped him from telling her about his money concerns, for he didn't want her to know how little they really had... no savings, no buffer for an emergency.

He was on his knee in front of her now, pleading his case. "A family vacation is just what we need," he was saying. "We won't tell anyone where we are going. We'll cash the check from the bank, pack up the car and just go. The kids will love it."

"What about school? Your job?"

"School is over soon; we'll just take them out a little early. I have some time off coming. Please, darling. We need some time as a family."

In the end, she agreed. It was a romantic notion, considerate. Just the type of thing that Mitch would do, so why had she been so upset? She liked the idea of stealing away without having to account to her mother.

"I'll pack the car on Friday and we can leave early Saturday morning, while the kids are still sleepy," she suggested. "That way they will be quiet for awhile. Where are we going?"

"It's a surprise," he said.

Lillian decided not to tell the children, for fear that they would tell Anna. She spent the rest of the week making careful preparations and by Friday everything was ready. She was excited, ready to go.

The disaster began with pureed peas. Mitch was late coming home, and when he made his way to the dining room, Lillian could see that he was very drunk. Nellie and Scottie had gone to bed, but Jane remained at the large table, spewing spit and salty tears into a bowl of peas. Lillian sat across the table, with Kathleen on her lap.

"The doctor says she must eat her vegetables," Lillian explained to her husband. "She has a vitamin deficiency. She refuses."

When he bent down to kiss her, Lillian pulled away, for his breath reeked of alcohol. One look into his bloodshot eyes made her regret her gesture. He walked around the table and stood behind the child's chair.

"Eat your peas," he growled. The six-year-old looked first to her mother, then turned her head and locked her defiant brown eyes on Mitch.

"I hate peas!" she shouted. "And I hate you. I don't have to do anything you say, my grandmother told me so." Lillian caught her breath as Mitch's arm swung up, but he did not strike the little girl. He grabbed the tablecloth instead, yanking it violently from the table and sent china, silver, and scraps of food flying across the room. Jane let out an ear-piercing scream and scurried out of the room, headed for the second story.

Lillian jumped up, balancing the crying baby. "Mitch! What in the name of God...?"

He came at her, his face twisted in rage. She backed away quickly, clutching the baby, until she felt her back against the far wall. She was terrified, trapped. She looked around, desperately searching for something, anything that would serve as a defense. Over his broad shoulders she saw the children standing in the archway, Jane with her thumb in her mouth and Scottie in hysterical tears as he struggled against Nellie, who was holding him back. "You leave my mommy alone!" Scottie blubbered.

Mitch turned away from Lillian and snarled, "Go to your rooms! Now!"

They ran for the stairs, but Nellie returned long enough to announce. "I called Pawpa. He is on his way."

Mitch glared at Nellie Lee, who was by that time halfway upstairs. He could hear the sounds of doors slamming and locking. He went into the living room, smashing a vase of fresh flowers on the way. His arm swept the mantle, sending glass from the picture frames and clock flying in all directions. Lillian stayed against the wall, afraid to move.

Jack heard the commotion as he and Anna got out of the Cadillac. "We should have called the police," Anna told him. Her voice trembled.

"No police," he answered. "I'll handle this." He patted the pocket of his jacket, reassuring himself that he had remembered to bring his revolver.

When she heard the front door open, Lillian dashed through the kitchen and up the back stairs. She did not want her mother to see her like this. She would get the children calmed down, powder her nose and come down when Mitch had composed himself. She had no idea how she would explain the breakage.

"Good evening, Jack," Mitch said from the sofa. He had a drink in one hand, a cigarette in the other. "If you came for dinner, I'm afraid you missed it." Anna looked around in horror, then hurried upstairs.

"Drink?" Mitch asked his father-in-law.

"What is going on here, Mitch?"

"Little family discussion. Peas. None of your business, actually."

"You are drunk."

"Really? How can you tell?"

"Let's keep this reasonable. I am taking Lillian and the children home with me. You can talk to her when you sober up."

"No one is going anywhere, Jack. This is my house."

"I beg to differ, Mitch. It is my house."

"Ah, yes. So it is. My apologies, I stand corrected. But Lillian is still my wife, so you will not 'take' her anywhere."

"Hello, Papa." Lillian stood behind her father, her eyes slightly red, her face pale. She was calm.

"Are you all right, Diz?"

She almost lost her composure when he called her "Diz," and she suddenly wanted to hide in his arms and cry. "I'm fine, Papa. We are all fine. I appreciate that you are concerned, but Nellie should not have bothered you. I think it would be best if you and Mother would just go home."

Mitch smiled at her, lifted his glass. "My sentiments, exactly," he slurred.

"Shut up!" Jack barked. "Diz, honey," he turned to her, "this place is a mess. Don't ask me to walk away and leave you here with him. He is dangerous."

"He will sleep it off; we'll clean up in the morning. Everything will be all right. Please, Papa, I am a grown up woman now. Don't treat me like a child."

Before he could answer, Anna descended the stairs with all three children in tow. She carried a small suitcase in one hand, led Scottie by the other. Nellie and Jane were holding hands, much to Lillian's surprise. "Tell your mother," Anna said to Nellie.

"We want to go with Nana and Pawpa," Nellie said. "We don't want to stay here... with him." She inclined her head toward Mitch. "If you try to stop us, we will run away."

It was the only defense Liz knew, conditional and limited acquiescence. What she could not directly control, she would pretend to allow, buying her at least a small role in the decision. So here it was the ultimate showdown, the ultimate choice. Her husband and her baby, or her children. If she left with Papa now, she would lose Mitch forever. If she could effect a compromise, she might somehow save them all.

"You may go with your grandparents tonight," she told the three little faces turned to her. "Mitch and I will come and get you in the morning, for a big surprise." She looked at Anna, held her eyes with steel determination. "Just for tonight," Lillian repeated. "Have them ready by 10 o'clock." Anna ignored the comment, and hurried the children to the car. Lillian wished they had at least kissed her "goodbye."

She turned to Jack. "Will you go now?"

"Are you sure?"

"Very sure."

He looked at Mitch. "If you even consider laying a hand on her, I will kill you."

Mitch laughed."Threats, Jack? Should I worry? You can't even stand up to Anna, you pansy! Do you really think you can take me on? Or will you hire one of your goons to do it?"

"I don't know what the hell you are talking about," Jack snarled. "But I am warning you…"

"That's enough!" Lillian shouted. She ran up the stairs, to her crying baby.

Jack thought about the gun in his pocket. It would be so easy, he could plead self-defense. But the children were outside in the car. If he tried to force Diz to leave, things might get worse. He would leave, for now, and he would be back when he had a court order.

Chapter 4

Mitch was snoring heavily. He snorted, waking himself just enough to wonder about the time. He glanced at the mantle, but the clock wasn't there. "We've been robbed," he mumbled, and closed his eyes again. It was dark outside, probably around midnight. He coughed, coughed again, and suddenly he was racked by a fit of coughing. "Damn," he mumbled. Maybe he should cut back on the cigarettes. It was then that he noticed that the couch was on fire.

He jumped, grabbed the afghan that covered the back of the sofa and began beating at the flames. It only made the problem worse, so he ran to the staircase and shouted for Lillian. When he looked back, the entire couch was aflame, spilling smoke across the hardwood floor, smoke that curled around his feet.

"Lillian! Get up, Lillian. The house is on fire!" He dashed up the stairs, first to the nursery where he swooped up the sleeping baby. He threw a blanket over her head and rushed to the master bedroom. His wife was awake but disoriented. "Get out, quick!" he commanded. As was he, she was still dressed. Her head throbbed as she strained to understand what was happening.

"The baby!" she cried out to him.

"Right here," he said. "I'll help you down the back stairs. Get her to the car."

"The children... where...?"

They stood for an awkward moment, finally reaching the same conclusion at the same time. The children weren't here. They ran. "Mitch! The money!" All they had left in the world was in her purse, the result of yesterday's visit to the bank.

"Forget the money," he shouted at her. "Take the baby and run!"

"You take her," Lillian shouted back. "I know where it is. I'll be right behind you."

There was no time for further debate. He ran down the stairs and out into the night air, clutching Kathleen tightly to his chest. "Daddy has you, honey," he kept saying to her. He fumbled for the car keys, shaking. He finally secured the child in the car and ran back around the house to the back door, where he expected to meet his wife, coming out. She was not there!

"Lillian," he screamed. His heart was beating wildly, painfully. His chest felt as if it might explode. He put his head down and dashed into the kitchen. The smoke was very black and thick now, but he could not determine the location of the flames. It was extremely hot, more than 120 degrees, he imagined. When he tried to call for her, the smoke choked him, so he ran silently from room to room, looking for her.

He almost tripped over her as she lay on the floor of the back hall. She was breathing, but almost unconscious, her purse clutched in her left hand. He picked her up, and almost dropped her due to the stabbing pain in the area of his heart. *Dear God*, he prayed. *Help me.* His wife would die in his arms if he couldn't carry her. Perhaps he would die also. His child was alone in the car, which might explode at any moment if he didn't pull it away from the burning house.

She stirred, opened her eyes. "Put me down, Mitch, I think I can walk. Lean on me, I'll help you."

They hobbled to the car, Mitch bent over and clutching at his shirt. "Get in back with the baby," Lillian told him. "I'll drive."

She pulled the car over when they reached the highway, and turned to look in the back seat. "Are you all right?" she asked him.

"I think so. I just need to sit a minute, take in some fresh air." He looked awful. His face was a pattern of singed flesh, overlaying a surface of gray. His hands shook as he held the baby on his lap. Kathleen chirped merrily between pulls on her thumb.

"I suppose I should try to wake up the neighbors," she said, "and call for a fire truck. I don't want to leave you alone."

"No point," he coughed. "It's gone."

She looked back. The entire house was engulfed in flames, billowing giant clouds of black smoke into the sky. She reached over and started the ignition.

"Where..." he coughed again.

"To the hospital."

It was seven AM. when the fire chief pounded on the Sterling door. Sharon asked him to wait while she went to find Jack.

"I'm afraid it is a total loss, Mr. Sterling."

"What about my daughter?"

"The police have their own report, but I am free to assure you that no remains were found. As far as we can ascertain, either no one was home, or they got out safely."

"Was it the wiring?"

"We can't say for sure until we finish our investigation, but I would guess not. I'd say it was more likely a dropped cigarette. The fire started on the living room couch."

Anna came up to stand beside Jack. "Are they…?"

"No, Ma'am. No fatalities. Bad fire, though. They were very lucky."

"Thank God," Anna murmured. "But where are they? I mean, if … they weren't in the fire. Where did they go?"

"I don't know, Ma'am," the chief said. "I'm sure you'll be hearing from them soon. There is much to be grateful for."

"Yeah," Jack retorted. "We should be grateful as hell… that son of a bitch burned my house down!"

Mitch caught Lillian's arm as they got out of the car at the emergency entrance.

"Don't tell them any more than you have to," he whispered, his voice now almost gone. "Jack can't know where to find us."

"I can handle this," she assured him, and she gently touched his hot hand. A piece of burned flesh came away with her hand. "I need help!" she cried out.

The physician on duty wanted to admit Mitch immediately, but Mitch kept shaking his head with such adamant refusal that the doctor gave in and treated his burns. A nurse took the baby aside, where she was thoroughly examined and declared to be in good condition.

"How did this happen?" the doctor asked Lillian. Mitch gave her a warning look.

"We were burning leaves and the fire got away from us," she replied without hesitation. The doctor kept his head down, eyes on the application of salve to Mitch's hand. He lifted his eyes only slightly to catch the look that passed between the couple.

"I see."

Lillian refused treatment, not wanting to be further delayed. "We are on own way to a funeral," she told the doctor. "We must be on our way. Thank you for your kind assistance." He started to protest, although he was unsure how far he was prepared to proceed when she handed him a twenty-dollar bill. "Will this cover it?" she asked.

They left the hospital parking lot tired, hungry, and in need of a bath. Lillian wanted to go to Martha's house, rest and make plans. Mitch kept insisting that they needed to move on, quickly, and the fewer people who knew about it, the better. When she pushed the issue, he began to cough violently, so she gave in. They drove south for a few hours, until the baby's hungry fussing forced them to pull over to a circle of roadside cabins near the Ohio state line. Some provisions had already been secured in the trunk, so Lillian left Mitch and the baby in the small unit with crackers and water from the adjacent bathroom while she drove down the road to a general store.

They stayed long enough to get some much-needed rest, taking turns with the baby. Driving south again, they stayed overnight in Kentucky, stopping for whatever provisions they needed along the way. When they reached Lewisburg, Tennessee, and checked into a hotel, Lillian told Mitch she would call her father to check on the children. It was time to stop stalling, Mitch decided, and tell her the truth.

"I have no job to go back to," he said. "I was fired the night of the fire. I guess I stayed too long at Kelly's, drowning my sorrows."

"Why didn't you just tell me?"

"It was difficult to work it into the conversation, what with the fire and all."

She had to laugh, despite her worry. "What will happen to us now?" she asked him.

This time he laughed. "So dramatic! We won't starve, honey; it's only a job. I was looking for one when I applied for that one. We have a chance for a good life here. Please, can't we give it a chance?"

"But... what about the children?"

"We'll send for them as soon as we are settled. First, I must meet with the contact people. Then we'll look for a place to live. Everything will work out, you'll see."

Mitch made his phone calls, and within an hour the small hotel room was overrun with cigar smoking men, who sat around drinking bourbon and plotting "strategy." She sat in a rocker in the corner and rocked Kathleen, pleased to see her husband happy again, but still...

She didn't understand Mitch's fear of Jack and she suspected that there was something more that Mitch was not telling her. But she had taken her stand, for better or for worse.

Dear Martha,
Mitch and the baby are asleep, but I find myself lying here wide-awake, thinking. I need to make a connection,

touch someone at home. Mitch doesn't want me to call, because he and Papa had a terrible argument... I'm not sure I know what it is all about, but Mitch seems convinced that Papa is out to destroy him somehow.

We are all well. Mitch's burns are healing and I am not quite so tired these days. We will be leaving this hotel soon, for we have rented a little house on the outskirts of town. Mitch is quite happy with his new job, and I will play homemaker for awhile, until we can send for the children. I miss them so much; sometimes I just lie here and cry until I can sleep.

I will write again when we have a permanent address. For now, just know that we are still alive. I haven't deserted my children, Martha, please don't let anyone tell you that. I simply must prepare a proper home for them, and that will take some time.

Love, Lillian

Chapter 5

"What is he like?" Paul asked his mother, "Gretch's husband, I mean. Is he a good man? How is he with the children?"

Rachael smiled. "I can only answer one question at a time, dear. He is very polite and kind. He sometimes brings Scottie for the weekend, and he stays for coffee and chats. He even offered to put a bulb in the porch light; you know I can't abide getting up on a ladder. Scottie likes him." Rachael was telling the truth, as always, but she played down Scottie's fondness for Mitch. More than anything in the world, she wanted Paul and his son to become close.

"What about the girls?"

Rachael laughed. "Well, Nellie ignores him, of course, but then Nellie ignores everyone, except Anna. Jane is her usual passive little self, but I don't know of any real problems."

"No 'real' problems? What kind of problems, then?" Paul seemed very intense.

Rachael wanted to change the subject. Any additional information she might have about the remarriage of her former daughter-in-law was the result of gossip, which Rachael was loath to repeat. She had traveled all the way to California to meet the hospital ship that brought her son home. She had sat with him, again beside his bed, while he recovered from his war wounds. It was too painful to talk about his life with Liz and the girls, the life he had thrown away when he enlisted in the Navy.

"Did I tell you that Scottie and I went to the circus?" she asked him.

"Only about four times."

"I'm a proud grandma, I guess. But he is so incredible, Paul. So smart. He looks just like you, at his age."

He wheeled away from her, across the solarium to the glass wall that looked down on perfectly groomed grounds. Nurses in white strolled beneath him, pushing veterans up and down the walkways. Paul lit a cigarette, inhaled deeply and watched the laughing nurses. He forgot for a moment that Rachael was still there until he heard her voice.

"Why can't we talk about him, Paul? You ask endless questions about Liz and the girls, but when I mention Scottie, you drift away. Why?"

She saw his chin drop to his chest. Her heart ached for him, and for herself. Conversation was strained between them now; Paul was different. Perhaps she was different. She was quicker to speak her piece, she had to admit. In her letters to Paul she had expressed her disappointment regarding his behavior, his "quickie" divorce, and the fact that he was no longer welcome to receive the sacraments. Harsh as it may have seemed to her son, Rachael believed that he had broken a covenant with God, as well as with his wife.

"I have made so many mistakes, Mom," Paul said quietly. "Sometimes I wonder if there is any use to go on. I wanted a son. Each time Gretch told me that she was going to have another baby, I prayed for a son. But I walked out, used the war as an excuse to get away from so much unhappiness. I didn't know about the boy. Then the demons in my brain said 'maybe he isn't your son.' By the time I realized how very much I wanted to be Scottie's father, Gretch's husband, a father to my girls... well, by then it was too late."

Rachael dropped to her knees in front of him, looked into his eyes. What could she say to him that would ease his pain? All of it was true, everything he had said was true, and she would not deny it. While Rachael struggled to find the words that would help him heal, Paul cried. She thought her heart would break for him, and she laid her head on his trembling legs and cried with him.

"Paul is suffering far more from the trauma of war than from his injuries," the doctor told her later. "His physical condition will gradually improve; he will, in fact, probably recover completely. His mind is horrified, because of the things he has seen, the things he has been forced to do. It will take some time, perhaps a long time. He needs to be surrounded by the people who love him and those he loves."

"When can he come home?" Rachael asked.

"Actually, very soon. I would say that within two weeks, he could be released to home care. It would be best if you could stay long enough to travel with Paul, take him home. Is there something or someone waiting for you back east that would prevent that?"

"I miss my grandson." Rachael smiled. "But he is being cared for. I will stay with Paul, and take him home. He is my life, all I have."

In 1945, America opened her arms to her patriot sons, and she treasured every one that returned to her. Some were bona fide heroes, whose acts of courage had been testified to. Some wore the Medal of Honor, the Purple Heart, and the Bronze Star. Hometown newspapers ran exclusive interviews and community bands met their trains. Most were simply soldiers, or sailors, who were assigned a job and tried to complete it without losing their lives in the process. They too had their moments of raw courage; the only difference was that no one in particular noticed. The common bond was that they all, heroes and non-heroes, slept in the same cold mud, dodged the same bullets, witnessed the same atrocities. Too many came back to Mother America cold and dead; some didn't come back at all. Still others came back alive and well, most came back somewhat alive and not so well.

Paul Unger was one of the latter. He walked down the ramp of the plane, carrying his own duffel bag. He smiled and waved at a few friends and neighbors who just happened to be there, and he told his mother that it was very good to be home, back in his old room. He sat on his bed after dinner, a dinner he hardly touched, and rolled his football around in his hands while he played "Sentimental Journey" over and over on the phonograph. Then he took two of the sleeping pills given to him in the hospital and slept for the next 18 hours.

After ten days, Rachael was worried. She felt isolated, like she and Paul were alone in a life raft, floating on an ocean of despair, going nowhere. After four years of living alone, responsible only for herself, Rachael realized that it was much like having an infant. She could not leave him alone for long periods of time, because his moods moved from silently morose to screaming nightmares in the middle of the day. Gratefully, the local grocery delivered, and the food rations were a thing of the past. She could still attend daily mass, and the rest of the time she and Paul were like Siamese twins, joined at the hip.

Reluctantly, she telephoned Anna. "I tried Lillian's number, but the operator said it was disconnected." Anna didn't comment, so Rachael continued. "Paul needs to see the children. I was hoping we could work something out that won't be too traumatic since he is still recovering..."

"Well, it will be difficult, since the girls are in boarding school. They won't be home until Christmas. As for Scottie, I suppose I could bring him. I don't think Jack will come." Anna was not being unkind, Rachael understood, just simply stating the fact. Jack was still upset with Paul about the divorce. But why had Nellie and Jane been sent away to school? Why was Scottie with Anna and Jack?

"You may as well know it all," Anna sighed. "You'll hear about it sooner or later. Right after you left for California, Lillian and Mitch came up missing. We haven't been able to locate them yet, although we have had a private detective on it for almost a month. There was a fire, a bad one. The house is a pile of rubble." Anna's voice cracked, and she silently waited for Rachael's questions.

"What happened? Are they all right? What about the baby?"

"We really aren't sure how the fire started, but the examiner said 'probably a cigarette.' Since we don't know where they are, we can't be sure that any of them are all right."

"Oh, Anna. I am so sorry! Why didn't you call me? I have been back for over a week."

"There was nothing you could do, nothing to tell you really." Then, after a pregnant pause... "Have you heard from her, Rachael?"

"Of course not! I would have told you, Anna."

"Yes... yes, I think you would have."

They had reached a truce. Somehow they had managed to commiserate as only anxious mothers can, and they hadn't even realized that they walked the same road.

"I imagine the children are devastated, poor dears," Rachael offered.

"Only Scottie really. He is a bit of a 'Mama's boy.'"

If Anna had kept on talking, if the comment had been sandwiched between some other thoughts, it may not have the impact on Rachael, who responded instinctively and quickly. "Like his father?"

"Let's not quarrel, Rachael. Too much has happened." That concession was, Rachael knew, Anna's unique version of a half-hearted apology. "Scottie has been very unruly since the fire. He may not be very responsive to Paul right now. Well, you know what I mean."

"Paul is a stranger to the child, I know." Anna was right... a rejection from Scottie might make things much worse. Paul was already a bundle of nerves, chain-smoking, sleep walking. And then there were the nightmares.

"Call me again. I will do what I can with the boy. You have your hands full with Paul, I'm sure."

"What about Mac?" Rachael asked. "When will he be home?"

"Mac isn't coming home. He sent a telegram to say that he was reassigned to the Pentagon and will be living in Arlington."

Then Anna added, "He and his bride, that is."

Chapter 6

Rachael had been dreaming. When she opened her eyes, she couldn't focus on the dream, couldn't remember what the dream was about, but she was glad to be awake. A sound, coming from downstairs... what was that? Knocking. Someone was knocking.

Two uniformed policemen stood on her front porch, their silver insignias gleaming in the porch light that she had left on for Paul. Rachael could see them clearly through the lace door curtain, but she held back. The clock on the mantel struck the half-hour, 2:30 AM.

Don't open the door. This is not good news. Something has happened. Don't open the door. Too late, they have seen you! Run!

"Are you Rachael Unger?" the officer asked her when she opened the door.

"Yes. What is it? What's wrong?"

"May we come inside, ma'am?"

She began to back away, finding that she couldn't stop. Slowly, deliberately, she continued to walk backward, away from the uniforms, away from the horror of whatever it was that the policemen wanted her to know. "Please stop!" one of them said. He looked into her eyes and then he looked away. "Please, Mrs. Unger, please come over here and sit down." He held out a hand to her, and she saw his wedding ring. Funny that she would notice that, she thought, but somehow her senses were acute, taking in every detail of this scene that she was playing. She stopped moving, shook her head. She would not sit down. If she sat down, he would tell her... tell her... what?

The three stood now in the center of the dining room, for they had advanced on her. "Are you alone?" the other one asked her very softly. She looked from him to the second uniform. She would concentrate on the uniform, she decided. She stared at the badge and nodded.

"Is there someone we can call, someone who can be with you?"

She shook her head.

One of them was looking around the room, trying to compose himself for this grim duty. Damn, he hated this part of the job. No matter how many times, he never got used to it. His eyes fell on the crucifix and he nudged his partner. They both stared for a few seconds, looked at each other, and the older man nodded.

"May I use your phone?"

It was one of the advantages of living in a small town, Officer Brady thought. An Irish Catholic, his mother cleaned the rectory of the local parish, had an "in" with the priest. When he spied the crucifix, he knew that Rachael was probably a member of the parish, and he called Father Kreigel.

"I know it's late, Padre," Brady apologized, "but this nice lady has no one with her and we have bad news. Please come as soon as possible... we need help here." Kreigel could hardly hear the cop's whisper, but he heard enough to know he needed to get there, and fast.

Rachael and Brady's partner had progressed to the living room, where she had seated herself on the sofa. Brady checked his watch. It would be at least 15 minutes before the priest would arrive. The men looked at each other. It was so quiet that the sound of the minute hand of the clock made them jump. Rachael was close to shock, Brady decided, and she might go over the edge if something didn't happen soon.

"Mrs. Unger," Brady said quietly, "will you do me the honor of praying with me?" He pulled a black rosary out of his pocket and began to intone, without waiting for her answer... "Hail Mary, full of grace..."

"You forgot the first part," Rachael blurted out.

"I'm sorry. Could you say it? I always forget."

She closed her eyes. "I believe in God, the Father Almighty, creator of Heaven and Earth..."

By the time they had begun the "Glory be," Rachael was entranced in her prayers. She continued to pray, unaware of the presence of the men in the room, She was still praying aloud, staring straight ahead when the priest arrived, and he shook his head when the policeman reached to touch her shoulder. "No," Father Kreigel said, "let her finish."

Immediately after the last "Amen," Rachael said, "Tell me. Tell me now."

Brady cleared his throat. "There was an accident, earlier... Paul Unger hit a train, just outside of Richmond's city limits. I'm sorry. He is dead."

The priest closed his eyes and made the sign of the cross. Rachael stared at nothing.

"You shouldn't be alone tonight, Ma'am," the older cop said. "Are you sure you don't have the name of someone we can call?"

"What did you mean, 'he hit a train'?" she asked clearly. "Don't you mean that a train hit him?"

They looked at each other again. "No, Ma'am. My report says that his car ran into the side of a moving train," Brady answered. "He was... that is, he had been drinking, Ma'am."

Rachael closed her eyes. They sat in silence. Finally, Brady added, "We don't have all of the details. For instance, we don't know where he had been. We assume he was driving back to Spring Grove."

Her eyes flew open. "Scottie! What about Scottie? Is he all right?"

"Who is Scottie? There was no one with him, Mrs. Unger. He was alone in the car. Do you know where he went; what he was doing in the city?"

Rachael's mind began to replay the past week. Paul had been even more depressed after her conversation with Anna, as if he somehow knew that there was trouble. She wondered how long she could stall his constant questions with vague answers. No, she didn't know how the children were. No, she hadn't spoken with Lillian or Mitch. No, she didn't think it was a good idea for Paul to just drop in on them. He was smoking about three packs of cigarettes a day, while he paced the floor and talked aloud to himself. When she realized that even a mother's love was not enough, she called Dr. Powell and made an appointment to consult with him and a specialist, James Bracken, who treated "shell shock."

After an interview with Paul, Dr. Bracken asked to see Rachael alone. "There is no doubt that Paul has a serious case of "shell shock," Bracken told her. "Please forgive me if I seem insensitive, but there is a lot of that going around these days, Mrs. Unger, and it is very difficult for me to explain it. It will also be difficult for you to understand, for anyone to understand who has not experienced it first hand."

"Is it treatable?" Rachael inquired.

"There are several new medications, and we will find the right one for Paul. Meanwhile, allow me to tell you as gently as I can... stop trying to run interference for him. Let him be a man. He is, after all, almost thirty years old. He has been through a terrible war, and he perceives that he has lost everything, his wife and children. Give him more space, let him work his way through it."

When Rachael looked at Adam Powell, his expression was passive. He gave no indication of agreement, but neither did he seem to disagree. Had she been too protective? Had she turned him into a whimpering "Mama's boy"?

Then, just last evening, (had it only been a few hours ago?) Rachael walked home from the church, where she had dusted, vacuumed, and laid the freshly ironed linens on the marble altar. The car was absent from the driveway, and on the kitchen table she found a letter. It was from Mac.

Rachael's eyes scanned the script, falling upon one paragraph.

> The folks are, of course, quite concerned about Sis and her family since the fire, for there seems to be no trace of them yet. Jack has hired a detective, who will hopefully find them soon. Try not to worry about the kids, Paul. They are safe with the folks.

Rachael laid the letter down and picked up the note beside it.

> Mom,
> I know that you believe that I have gone off the edge, but I am resolved at last. I have a purpose finally, a chance to be what I should have been long ago, a father. I have gone to get my children. Please don't interfere, I need to do this alone. And don't worry. Love, Paul

Rachael sat quietly now, between Officer Brady and Father Kreigel. Paul had gone to the Sterling house, but he was alone when he left. If it were the last thing that she ever did, she would learn what had occurred during the last hours of Paul's life.

"I'm afraid I have no information for you, officer," she said. "I want to see Paul. Where is he?"

"At the city morgue. We will drive you, if you wish."

"Yes, thank you. I will get dressed."

****

Technically, there was little need for Rachael to identify the body, since Paul had sufficient paperwork on his person, and he still wore his "dog tags." It was only natural that she held out the hope that there had been some terrible mistake, and that the rigid form on the gurney had merely been assumed to be Paul.

"He is not a pretty sight," the attendant warned her. "Are you sure you want to see?"

"Yes."

The attendant frowned, gave the officers a meaningful look and pulled back the sheet that covered Paul's face. Rachael felt her knees move, and the officers, one on each side, supported her. Why hadn't they at least cleaned him up?

She was presented with a paper bag that held his clothing, his watch and wallet. At the very bottom of the sack her hand felt the hardness of a bottle. She took it out. Jack's Scotch. Empty. She signed for the items and walked away from the desk, toward the elevator that would take her to the street level. Officer Brady caught up with her brisk stride. "We will take you home now," he announced.

"Thank you, Officer, but I have other people to see, arrangements to make. I will take a cab."

"But it is still very early, not yet 5 o'clock," he reminded her.

"I know, but there is someplace I must go. Please, I will be all right."

But the officer insisted. She knew that he would not relent until he had delivered her, so she asked that he drop her at St. Rose's Rectory, where she was greeted by the kind Father Kreigel. He prepared strong coffee, added a generous shot of bourbon, and just let her make herself comfortable on his overstuffed couch, where she kicked off her shoes and pulled her shaking legs up to her chin, under a warm woolen blanket. He sat near her, sipping coffee and listening to her talk about Paul… what a beautiful baby he was, what a delightful child. When she finally gave in to her tears, he patted her hand and prayed.

"I must go now, to prepare for the early Mass," he told her. "I will get someone to sit with you."

Rachael looked at her watch. It was almost seven-thirty on Sunday morning. "No." She smiled. "Please call a taxi. I need to go to talk to someone. I will be back later, to make funeral arrangements."

"Do you feel up to staying for Mass?" he asked her.

"No. I can't." She couldn't go to Mass because in the deepest recesses of her heart, she harbored hatred and rage. Her soul was racked with sin, reaching for the sweet coolness of revenge. The empty space that was once her heart was not a fit habitat for the Lamb of God.

Chapter 7

Jack rarely slept beyond sunrise. He liked to spend the quiet, pre-dawn hour in his study, writing in his journal. On this particular Sunday morning, however, he was listening to a voice on the telephone... the voice of John Randolph.

"Lewisburg, Tennessee. He is working for Tappan again, so he is either a star performer or someone pulled some strings. She works part-time at a shoe factory. I have listed all of the details, addresses, and contacts in the report. I will send it over to you today, by messenger."

"No! Don't send it here. Wait until Monday and send it to my office. I guess that is all I needed to know. Good work, John."

"Don't worry, Jack. You won't have to be grateful after you get my bill. Goodbye."

Jack hung up the phone and then dialed Billy's apartment extension. A sleepy Billy answered, "Yeah?"

"Twenty minutes," Jack said, and hung up. The two men would meet for coffee in the kitchen to review the status on each of Jack's automobiles. It was their Sunday morning ritual.

Meanwhile, Jack needed to pace, to think. He wasn't sure how to proceed, now that he knew where she was. He could hardly drag her home without Mitch, and Jack was not anxious to push his son-in-law into confrontation. For the time being, he would wait. She knew how to reach him, and when she needed help, as she most assuredly would, he would come to her rescue. Meanwhile, he held the trump card, the children. As long as he had the children, Diz would ultimately have no choice but to return to her "papa."

He picked up the note from Henry Meeder and tossed it into the wastebasket without re-reading it. Meeder could think again if he thought he would recover his money from Jack; let the stupid bastard hang for it. Maybe next time Meeder would ask for a proper co-signer. Jack crossed the room and opened the door, intent on a cup of fresh coffee from the kitchen.

He let out a little gasp when he came face to face with Rachael.

She had a strange look about her, not quite Rachael. Her usually perfect blond hair was uncombed and rumpled, like she had just gotten out of bed. She wore no makeup, her dress was crookedly buttoned, and her stockings were in ruins. She wore only one white glove, on the hand that gripped the neck of an empty bottle. The most striking aspect of her total look, however, was the sinister way in which she looked at him.

"Rachael! What on earth...?"

She walked into the room as if she were in a trance. He moved aside to let her pass, watched her walk to his desk and deposit the bottle on its polished surface. "I believe that this belongs to you," she said. "I have come to return it to you, and to ask a few questions."

He was suddenly and inexplicably frightened. This was not Rachael, the Rachael he knew. This woman had the persona of madness. "I have an appointment," he protested.

"I won't keep you long, Jack. I want you to tell me about Paul's visit last night."

He blanched. So, Paul had told her about it. How much had he told her?

He shrugged. "There isn't much to tell. He wanted to take Scottie, but it was very late and the boy was asleep. We talked awhile, and I persuaded him to wait until this afternoon. I told Paul I would bring the boy to Spring Grove."

"But you had no intentions of doing that, did you?"

"Look, Rachael, Paul is not well. That must be painfully obvious to you. I don't think that having Scottie with him is a good idea."

"What gives you the right to make that decision? He is Paul's son, not yours. You have a history of forgetting whose children are whose, Jack. What else did you say to him?"

He was angry now. How dare she interrogate him in his own home? "If you need a complete account of the conversation, ask Paul," he growled.

"I would like to, but you see... Paul is dead."

Jack's face registered total shock. "That's impossible!" he stuttered. "When? How?"

Rachael picked the bottle up by the neck and flung it at him. Jack moved quickly out of the way, and the missile crashed against the wall behind him, very close behind him.

"Have you gone crazy, woman? You could have killed me!"

"Yes, Jack, I have gone crazy. My son is dead, so nothing else matters anymore. You are responsible, you and your Scotch, you and your constant control over the lives of innocent people. I would like nothing better than to send you to hell, where you belong."

She was standing behind the desk now, her back to the window. Her eyes caught the open drawer, the one that held his precious journal and the gun.

306

With one swift movement, the gun was in her hand, pointed at Jack Sterling.

"Don't... Rachael, be careful with that thing! I swear, I had nothing to do with... whatever happened to Paul. He was alive when he left here. Please, Rachael, don't do this... put the gun down and we'll talk."

"You have nothing to say to me, Jack, nothing that would be true, anyway. Nothing that will take away the terrible pain. I have lost everything. I no longer want to live, and the idea of taking you with me is the only consolation I have. You gave him the liquor, didn't you? Patted him on the head and gave him something to drink and sent him away to run his car into a train!"

Jack winced. Good God, could it be true? Paul dead? His mind moved quickly over the details of the visit. Paul had been very distraught, they had had a drink together, but Jack didn't remember anything about a bottle.

"One drink! One lousy drink, Rachael. That's all. I don't know where the bottle came from."

"'One drink' is all he needed. You knew that, Jack. You knew that Paul was allergic to alcohol, since the coma, since that last time one of the Sterlings tried to kill him." She brought the gun up now, level and aimed at his chest. She supported her right wrist with her left hand. "I know how to use it, Jack. Don't worry. I won't miss and leave you crippled. See?" She pulled the hammer back.

Jack closed his eyes and tried to think. If he rushed her, she would most assuredly fire. If he did nothing, she might fire. Had he known about the alcohol thing? Had someone told him? He couldn't remember, but did it matter? Even if he knew, did he deserve to die? He waited for the shot, the impact. He waited for the searing hot pain that would rip through his body and send it sprawling against the wall behind him. He opened his eyes when he heard Billy's voice.

"Put it down, Rachael. You want to... you know it and I know it. Put it down and come over her to me, Lady Rachael. Let me help you."

Billy stood between them, directly in front of Jack and within four feet of the barrel of the gun. Jack felt woozy; he would need to sit down, and fast. He felt stupid and cowardly, but he willed himself to stay conscious.

Rachael looked at Billy for a long moment; the gun now cocked to fire and pointed at his midline. She did not lay the gun down, as he requested, but simply opened her hand and let it drop to the floor. The resulting discharge made all three of them jump, as the bullet ripped across the floor, shattered a china umbrella stand, and lodged in the far wall.

Rachael sank to her knees, cupping her face in her hands. "Oh, Billy!

Paul... Paul..."

He was instantly there, his large brown arms wrapped around her, enveloping her. "I know, Lady, I know," he cooed. "I heard it on the news this morning." He rocked her back and forth until her sobbing quieted to a low pathetic whimper.

Jack dropped into the nearest chair, pulling a handkerchief from his pocket. He took deep breaths while he wiped copious sweat. "It's not my fault. I didn't know," he kept saying, but no one was listening.

Rachael accepted Billy's hand. She rose slowly, wiping her wet cheeks with the back of her arm, and quickly returned to composure. She had unfinished business in this house.

"I will take him now," she said quietly to Jack. "Scottie."

He looked at her, into her eyes. There would be no argument, for she would hear none. Jack nodded slowly.

Several hundred miles away, Lillian prayed in the small church that had become her Mecca. She had decided to confer with the local priest regarding an annulment. Next to the separation from her children, her greatest heartache was the separation from her church. She had researched the information, and she felt confident that she would be a likely candidate for the official dissolution of her marriage to Paul. She had, after all, tried to be a good wife. He had left her, divorced her. If she could attain her goal, she and Mitch could be remarried in the church, bringing God's blessing on their union. Somehow, she would convince her husband that it needed to happen, and they would return to Indiana and reunite their little family. She wanted it more than anything she had ever wanted in her life.

While she waited for Father Bush after Mass, Lillian tried to imagine what they were doing just now. The lazy Nellie Lee would still be asleep, her golden curls covering the pillow. Jane would be awake and giving Anna a hard time about something. Scottie was, no doubt, tearing through the house, playing the cowboy and terrorizing the old, long-suffering Buddy. She smiled. Soon, very soon.

Before Lillian and Father Bush had concluded their discussion, Scottie was on his way to Spring Grove with Rachael. She tried to listen to his prattle, but her mind was reeling. Somehow, with God's help, she would get through the next few days. She would bury her beloved son and begin her life anew, with Scottie. This was God's consolation prize.

Chapter 8

The children of Paul John Unger were an impressive show of family unity and proper decorum as they sat on folding chairs under the green tent. Their spines stiff, their gloved hands folded neatly on their knees, they silently awaited the commencement of their father's funeral service. It was bone-chilling cold in the gray November rain.

Their grandmothers flanked the trio, one on each side. Anna was on one end next to Nellie Lee, age seven, and Rachael was on the other end next to three-year-old Scottie. Six-year-old Jane was in the middle, and no one held her hand. The occasion would become memorable to them many years later as the last time they were all together, but had a photograph been taken at the moment, it may have revealed something more... who belonged with whom. Jack Sterling was not in attendance because Rachael had asked him to stay away.

"Such a pity!" Martha's mother whispered to her daughter in the row behind the children. "No mother, now no father. Orphans, poor motherless children."

"Mother, hush! No one knows that for sure... that she is dead, I mean."

"Well then, where is she? Certainly not here to comfort her children."

"Keep your voice down, they will hear you!"

The children heard, but they asked no questions, made no comments. If the women heard, they ignored the exchange. The five of them stared at the gray casket covered with the American flag and a spray of red roses. Only when Master Sargent Isaac Anderson presented the flag to Rachael did the floodgate open, spilling waves of memories and emotions over them. Anna regarded the flag with terror. How close had she come, she wondered, to being a recipient of this dubious prize? Mac crowded her thoughts, for in a very different fashion, she too had lost a son.

Nellie was relieved that they were seated at last, for the day's events had been very unpleasant. She hated the attention of strangers, the way the men fawned over her and reached out to touch her, the way the women clucked their tongues and pitied her. She smiled weakly at first, made some attempt to politely accept their expressions for "her loss," but she soon abandoned the effort. What "loss?" her child's mind wondered.

She was the oldest, had known Paul the longest. She should feel something, and she wished that it were so as she tried to envision her tall, handsome father. That was all he really was to her, an illusion that smiled from a recruitment poster or the photograph that comes inside a new wallet.

"I want to go home," she said to Anna, not bothering to whisper, for she had determined that the more that heard, the better her chances.

"Soon, dear," Anna said quietly, patting the small hand. "It will be over soon."

Nellie sighed and thought about her mother, the missing Lillian, more like an older sister actually. Nellie missed her. Why had she left after the promise of a surprise? Was that it? *Surprise! We are running out on you!* What had happened to her, the pretty lady who was her playmate?

Nellie tried to listen to the priest. He wanted her to throw dirt on her father's casket, an abhorrent idea to a sensitive child. *What is it that Papa always says?* Oh yes, now she remembered.

"This is bullshit," she said to Anna.

Jane perked up when she overheard her sister's profanity, and she looked about for someone to whom she could relate the transgression. She was disappointed to discover that neither Rachael nor Anna seemed interested, for only Scottie reacted, bringing his hand to his mouth to cover his giggles. She scowled at her little brother. He didn't understand that Daddy was "dead," and she knew that "dead" meant gone away forever, not just until after the "war" was over. Who would tickle her now? Who would carry her to bed on his shoulders and read to her? Who would comfort her when everyone else was angry about something she had done? "Daddy," she whispered, "Daddy, you said you would come back for me." The tears began suddenly, blubbery breathtaking sobs that shook her and she wanted to "die" too, go with him wherever he was going. She waited in vain for the arm that might wrap around her small shoulders, but she was in the middle and there was no one to hold her.

Scottie ceased his laughter and followed his sisters to the big hole. He watched and then imitated their movements, dropping a handful of soil into the gaping crevice. It was a likely game, something that he could manage, so he grabbed several more handfuls before Rachael gently pulled him away. The loud boom from the honor guard sent Scottie scurrying up on Rachael's lap, to the safety of her arms. When it was all over, when he finally slid down to walk to the waiting limousine, he saluted Master Sargent Isaac Anderson, who returned the salute with a friendly wink.

Rachael turned to Anna as they started for the cars. "Please relate to Jack that I appreciate his acquiescence to my request." she said. "He will understand the message. I know you are anxious to return home, so we will talk some other time." Without another word, Rachael assisted Scottie into the limousine and left Anna standing there with the girls, wondering just what in the hell Rachael was talking about. One thing was quite clear, however. Anna had been summarily and unceremoniously dismissed.

Jack took advantage of the family's absence to confer with his attorney.

"What took so damn long?" Jack wanted to know.

Walter frowned. "You are not my only client, Jack, and it has only been three days. The information you requested is not readily available. I had to spend some money."

"So bill me."

"Count on it. Nothing very unusual about Paul's estate. His house is free and clear, he had considerable savings, and the government insurance is still effective since he died within 90 days of discharge. By the way, did you know he planned to re-enlist?"

"No."

"That entitled him to more than the usual insurance. Add that to his other assets, plus the policy he carried on himself, private insurance that pays double for accidental death, he had a tidy sum to bestow upon his children. If it is invested well, they should be set for life."

"They won't need it. I can take care of them."

"Well, that may be true, but there is another consideration. All that money is going to go someplace. By law it will be at the discretion of the children's legal guardian, so I guess whoever has the kids will get the dough."

"What's your point?"

"My point is that you should never, never lie to your attorney, Jack. It is foolish and dangerous, not to mention unnecessary. You know where Lillian is, have known for some time. Have you considered that she might pop in at any minute and take the children away with her?"

Jack narrowed his eyes and glared at Walter. He didn't like being caught in a web of deceit, but the fact that he had somehow slipped up angered him more.

"You are not my priest," Jack snarled. "Don't you ever dare to lecture me. She left those children with me, and this is where they will stay until I decide otherwise."

"It's your party," Walter answered flippantly. "Just don't say I didn't warn you. Lillian is the surviving parent; she held custody before Paul's death. No problem, then, if she has a yearning to play "Mommy" again. Better read your own report, Jack... the one from the private dick you hired. If Mitch gets his hands on that money... well, I don't even want to think about it."

Jack sunk deeply into concerned thought. Walter was right; there was no way around it. Ideally, Diz will leave Mitch and come home where she belonged. But every day that passed made that dream more and more unlikely. He would have bet anything, in fact, that she would have been back by now. He remembered the note at the bank, still unpaid. He thought about the house that was destroyed, Mitch's temper, Mitch's proclivity to use other people's money, piss it away.

"What are my options?" Jack asked the attorney, his voice cracking.

"Only one. File for permanent guardianship. Given your contacts, it should be quite easy. Of course, you will have to proclaim in court that Lillian is..."

"Is what?"

This was the hard part, Walter realized. Lillian was Jack's life, his pride and joy, his princess. In order to protect the interest of his grandchildren, Jack would need to convince the court that they would somehow be endangered if they resided with their mother and her husband. Touchy stuff.

"At the least, incompetent. At the worst, unfit. It could get very nasty, Jack. Are you sure you can do this?"

Jack was silent for so long that Walter began to feel very uncomfortable. He didn't want to repeat any of it, but he needed an answer. Jack had turned his chair to the window, his back to the attorney, and sat staring into the rain. Finally Walter cleared his throat, placed the last of the documents in his briefcase, picked up his hat, and moved toward the door. As he reached for the doorknob, he heard Jack's voice, low, strained, barely more than a whisper. "Do it, Walter. Do it now."

Chapter 9

1946

Spring came early to Tennessee that year, arriving with a flourish that thumbed its nose at the snow-capped mountains. Lillian hummed as she took down the wash and folded each piece carefully before she deposited it into the wicker basket. An occasional warm breeze brought with it the sweet aroma of freshly washed clothing, spring flowers, and the muted laughter of children playing. She stood on tiptoes and peered over the line of sheets, checking once again on Kathleen, who was playing in the yard, although she had done the same only three towels ago. She would take no chances with this one. She would never again allow her babies out of her sight.

"Babies," she said aloud, touching her abdomen in a greeting to the child she now carried there. "I sure hope you have all the boy stuff," she told the little lump. "Daddy says the world is running out of Southerlands." She managed to carry both toddler and basket into the house, where she put the baby down for a nap and fixed herself a glass of cool tea. She would prepare a special dinner, and when they sat on the front porch with their coffee, she would ask him again about the children.

"Maybe we will do the frog legs thing again," she said to the cat, and she smiled when she recalled how Mitch had urged her to add more salt to the skillet. Soon the damn things were hopping and jumping all over the kitchen, sending the two of them into peals of laughter. She never dreamed that life could be this good, this much fun. There was only one cloud on the horizon, and she prayed that it would soon blow away.

They had discussed it again last week, when she said to him, " It's been more than a year since the fire. Can't I at least call Martha and find out how they are?" Mitch had run out of even lame excuses. His function on the Kefaufer committee prohibited him from confiding in his wife, for his was on a special undercover assignment, and Jack must surely know the extent of his involvement by this time. He had been able, in the beginning, to convince Lillian that some harm might fall upon them if their location were discovered, but now she pressed for details that he could not give. The truth was that he dreaded the reentrance of any member of the Sterling family into their quiet, happy lives.

"Tell you what," he told her. "Give me a few days to check it out."

He had run out of time, run out of stalling methods. He hated to see her so unhappy when he caught the faraway look in her eyes, saw the tiny tears at the corners. Against his better judgement, he made the necessary inquiries.

"There is big news from the homefront," Mitch's informant was saying now. "What do you want to know first?"

It was late afternoon and they were seated at the bar. Mitch wondered how long this recital was going to take. He hadn't heard one single word, yet he had an ominous sense of foreboding.

Driving home, Mitch tried to sort out all of the information he had received. What must he absolutely tell her immediately; what could wait; what could he skip altogether? Paul's death was certainly at the top of the list. That fact alone would send her into a frenzy, so how was he going to tell her about the pending court order that would deny her the children? Could he convince her to fight Jack, take him on in court? Or would she close down, devastated by her father's betrayal?

It was dark when he pulled into the driveway. He didn't want to go in, so he sat for a few moments, smoking, thinking. Their life together was about to change forever.

He went in through the kitchen door, but there was no sign of Liz. No dinner simmered on the stove, no radio played the mountain music she loved. What he heard were the incessant screams of his daughter. He ran to the nursery to find Kathleen standing in the crib, crying fiercely. Her mother lay on the floor in a pool of bright red blood.

The next few hours would later prove difficult to recall, for he moved as if in a dream He remembered using the phone to call for an ambulance. When it arrived, the neighbors gathered, and someone tried to take the baby from his arms, protesting that she would be better left with them. Mitch shook his head and clung to the little girl as if she were a lifeline. Kathleen was quiet while he held her, in spite of a soaking diaper that was dripping all over him. When the emergency room doors slammed shut in his face, a kind nurse offered to change the baby, give her some milk and crackers.

"Don't worry, sir. I'll bring her right back," the nurse said.

Kathleen fell asleep in his lap, so he sat rigid, barely breathing for the following three hours. He should call someone, for he desperately needed help, but there was no one to call. They were private people, kept to themselves. Mitch's associates at the Kefauver campaign office knew very little about his personal life or his past, and he wanted to keep it that way. As the hours dragged by, he grew more frightened. If Lillian died, it would be his fault, because he had brought her to this place, away from home and family. She had lost her children because of him, would he also become the reason for the loss of her life? His aching arms felt as if they were broken, his head pounded, his bladder screamed, and he badly needed a drink. A nurse brought some very official forms for Mitch to sign... permission for surgery, she said.

The man who approached him three hours later looked weary and worried. His surgical whites were splattered with blood, and he sat down next to Mitch. "I am Dr. Lucus, Mr. Southerland," he said softly. He reached over to touch the moist spiral curls of the sleeping child. "Will you let one of the nurses take her while we talk?"

"My wife is dead," Mitch tried to say, but his voice cracked. Two nurses were immediately at his chair, gently prying Kathleen away from him. His head dropped into his hands.

"No," Lucus quickly replied. "Your wife will recover. She has hemorrhaged, lost a lot of blood. The baby... well, the little fellow never had a chance, you see. It was a tubular pregnancy. We were forced to do a complete hysterectomy, so I'm afraid there won't be any more babies. I'm sorry."

"I want to see her."

"Of course. But she is in recovery right now, and she will sleep soundly for the rest of the night. Is there someone you can call... to take the baby?"

"No. No one."

"Then let us put her to bed. There's an old lumpy couch in my office where you can get some rest. I'll let you know when she is awake."

Mitch went to the men's room, splashed cold water on his face, and tried to digest all that had happened in the past few hours. He needed to think clearly, make plans. "I know someone I can call in Indiana," he finally told Lucus.

"Come with me, you can use the phone in my office."

It was almost midnight when the telephone rang. Chester Reubens had just deposited the cat on the front stoop and bolted the door. "Hello?"

"Chet, Mitch Southerland. I know it's late, but..."

"Mitch! Where the hell are you? What's wrong?"

Chester listened very intently to Mitch's hurried recital of events, scribbled down the address, asked a few questions. "We'll be there as soon as possible, Mitch. Or at least Martha will, I'm not sure I can get away."

"Don't let her come alone, Chet. These roads down here aren't the best...
and please, don't tell anyone else."

"Try not to worry. Help is on the way."

It took them two days to make the trip, Martha, Millie Anderson, and
Billy. Billy did most of the driving, a relief to both women, as well as to
Chester, who demanded that they take someone dependable with them.
Millie joked to Martha, "Maybe you better paint your face, lady. A white
woman with two 'darkies' is mighty suspicious in these parts."

"Don't be silly," Martha laughed. But soon after crossing the Kentucky
state line, the trio was observed with interest by the occasional passing
motorist. They were stopped twice by law officers, state and local, who
checked all licenses before waving them on. It was not unexpected, but it did
slow them down.

Meanwhile, Mitch kept his vigil beside Lillian's bed, usually holding
Kathleen. After she had reacted so intensely to the loss of the baby, he
couldn't bear to tell her more. "There will be no more boys born to your
family," she cried. "No one to carry on the Southerland name."

"When you think about it," Mitch laughed, "isn't it just fitting that I
should be the last?" He talked non-stop about their future. He sang to her for
hours, his beautiful tenor voice repeating "Always" over and over. His
performance became so popular that the staff gathered to hear, and soon he
was doing requests. He put on a large bathrobe, donned a borrowed wig and
did an outrageous skit that had the entire hospital doubled over with laughter.
By the time the Indiana reserves arrived, Mitch was exhausted.

After hugs and handshakes, Mitch told them about the baby, the surgery.

"How much does she know?" Millie asked.

"Just the events of the last three days," Mitch replied. "She can't cope
with the rest of it, not yet."

Martha took charge. She would take the first "watch" with Lillian while
Millie and Billy took Mitch home for some rest, food and fresh clothes. Millie
would stay there with Kathleen and Billy would drive back to relieve Martha.

"Is there a local hotel?" Martha wanted to know.

Mitch smiled weakly. "You are south of the Mason-Dixon now. Better if
you stay at the house."

After a full week had passed, Mitch began to worry about Billy's job. "I
don't really give a shit," Billy assured him. "Let Jack fire me. I'm tired of
being his nigger, anyway."

As Lillian regained her strength, she pressed Martha and Millie harder for news of home. They had stalled and evaded as long as they possibly could, and Lillian was growing suspicious. The group held a meeting, and it was decided that it would be best to break the rest of the bad news while she was still hospitalized, in case there were any complications. "I'll do it, Mitch," Martha offered. "You have had so much put on you already."

"Thank you, Martha, but I can't let you do that. I will tell her."

He stopped at the best jewelry store in town and bought his wife a special present, a beautiful silver bracelet engraved with the words that would tell her what was in his heart, "Grow old along with me... the best is yet to be."

Chapter 10

It was still very chilly in Richmond. Jack stood on the veranda, taking occasional sips from his steaming coffee cup, watching the gray sky that threatened snow. He shivered and turned to enter the kitchen through the French doors when he caught sight of Anna, and almost changed his mind. It would be no warmer in there, he concluded, given the intensity of last night's discussion.

"I can't believe that you would do such a thing!" she had screamed at him. "When will you stop making decisions for members of this family without consulting anyone? How dare you!"

"There was no time for a consensus, Anna. I had to move quickly, before the insurance checks were issued and the property sold. Surely you can understand that."

"What I understand is that you have saddled me with three children, Jack. I am almost fifty years old. I'm tired. I want to retire to Florida, plant a garden. You had no right to do this to me. Considering the fact that neither of our children is currently speaking to us, one might reasonably conclude that we weren't very good at parenting the first time around! Now you want to do it all over again."

"Are you willing to ship Nellie Lee off to Tennessee to be with her mother and that man she married? Would that make you happy, dear?"

Anna stared at him. "Tennessee? You have known all along, haven't you? You knew where she was, that she was alive... what else?"

Jack silently cursed himself. God, he must be getting old, too. He was apparently slipping, giving out bits and pieces of information intended to remain exclusive to him. "What does it matter where she is and how long I have known? She won't be back as long as she is bedded by her wonderful Mitchell."

"He is her husband, Jack. She loves him. Why can't you just accept that?"

"Perhaps because I have never had the experience of being loved as a husband."

"You are jealous!" Anna cried. "That's it, isn't it? You tolerated Paul because you knew that there was no passion, but you can't abide the thought of Mitch and your precious 'Diz.' Do you even begin to recognize how sick it all is?"

His hand itched to slap her. He put his fist into the wall instead, leaving an ugly imprint."That is quite enough!" he shouted." Enough."

Anna had struck a nerve, and although she hadn't really believed her own accusation, it was painfully close to truth. She looked at her husband of thirty years, sadly shaking her head. "I don't know who you are," she said softly.

"Don't you? Well, I know who you are... Queen Anna! I am only your pawn, here to do your bidding... 'Jack will fix it'... 'Jack will make it go away'... whatever I have become, whatever I have done, I have done for you."

She dropped to the nearest chair, rubbing her forehead. The worst headache of her life was moving across her brow, hot and blinding.

"Her children think she is dead," she whispered. "Lost in the fire. What are we going to do now?"

"Well, who in the hell told them that? I didn't. And we'll tell them nothing else. All remains the same. Scottie is with his grandmother. The girls are away at school. Everything is under control."

"Not for long. Jane's tuition check was returned by certified mail yesterday, along with a cryptic note from Becky... Sister Mary Marcella, I mean. They have requested that she not return to the Academy after the Easter break. It seems she has become even more of a behavioral problem since Paul's death."

"So, that's that. We'll deal with it."

"You can deal with it, now that you are her legal guardian. I want you to tell me where my daughter is."

He turned his back on her and walked out of the room. His final words were, "When I'm damn good and ready."

Jack waited outside the double doors until Anna left the kitchen. Helga and Emily were seated at the long table, having their morning tea. "Will someone please tell me," Jack began tersely, "where I might find Billy?"

The two women exchanged meaningful looks. Jack followed their eyes with his own, as they continued to look slyly at each other while blowing into hot liquid. "He isn't here," Emily offered finally.

Jack was in no mood to play games. "I have figured that out for myself. Now, where the hell is he?"

Helga spoke up, giving Emily a firm kick under the table. "He was called away... family emergency."

Jack was shouting, "Where?"

Emily interjected, "Georgia, I think. Somewhere down south. His sister is dying, so who knows how long he'll be gone." Jack looked at the women suspiciously, but since he had no information to the contrary, he was forced to accept their explanation. He had formulated a plan that required Billy to do some driving, but it would have to wait.

At the office, Mrs. Nelson was relieved to see Jack at last. "Your attorney has called every ten minutes for an hour. Do you want me to get him on the phone?"

"Why didn't he call me at home?"

"He said it was very personal. He didn't want the conversation overheard."

Maybe the urgency had to do with the purchase of the Florida property, some little problem with the paperwork. "I'll call him," he told her.

"Walter, what's wrong?"

"Big trouble, Jack. We have underestimated Lillian. She has filed suit against you in Superior Court, for the return of the children. Do you want me to read it to you?"

"No. Not necessary. Where do we stand?"

"Well, for openers, we will have to prove that there was positively, absolutely no way we could have known her whereabouts at the time of the court order. That's problem number one. Add to that the fact that she may be able to prove "special circumstances" on the order, because your friend and business associate, George Steinburger, issued it. I was afraid that this might happen."

Damn lawyers, always second-guessing, always saying "I told you so" after the fact.

"You must be getting soft in your old age, Walter. I never knew you to run from a good fight."

"This isn't a good fight, Jack. This is nasty, dirty stuff. I've done it, and I don't want to do it again. Do you have any conception of what will be required? We would have to tear Lillian apart, hint at terrible things. All this to keep money away from Mitch. Let them have it, for Christ's sake! You didn't need it before, you don't need it now."

"You didn't feel this way when we filed."

"Two factors, Jack. First of all, you swore to me that you didn't know where she was, so there was no way we could advise her of this action. That was a lie. You knew. Second, like you, I assumed that they would simply roll over for it. We were wrong, they will fight."

"So let them fight... we'll win."

" It's the 'we' part that is eating at me. Not this time, Jack. I have no stomach for it. Get yourself another hatchet man." Walter hung up.

"Cowardly bastard," Jack mumbled, slamming down the receiver. No one could talk to him in that tone, no one. There were other attorneys, hundreds of them. No one was going to stop him now.

When the messenger brought the "Notice of Hearing" to Jack's office the next morning, he had already retained the best attorney in the state, a specialist in family law. As was his habit, he told his attorney only what he thought necessary.

"I don't like to lose, Mr. Sterling," Ralph Jennings told him. "I need your assurance that you won't get cold feet when we get rolling on this."

"Don't worry about me," Jack retorted. "Just do your job."

On the morning of the hearing, Jack managed to avoid the group from Tennessee. He refused to even glance in the direction of the petitioner's table, staring straight ahead or whispering to Jennings. The Southerland's attorney had a "good old boy" demeanor and more than a trace of "hillbilly twang" to his melodious voice. Jackson Potter was overweight; his suit was brown and ill fitting. He wore a bolo tie, had a toothpick sticking out of his mouth and looked every ounce of his 300 pounds like a genuine yokel.

"This isn't even going to be a fun sport," Jennings remarked to his client. "Like shooting fish in a barrel. For two cents, I'd leave the official reply to the petition on the bench and go to lunch."

Jack reached into his pocket and handed his attorney two pennies.

Even the Judge, His Honorable J. Clyde Snyder, was amused by the motley look of the petitioner's attorney. He would cut out of here very early and get in a round of golf.

When the gavel went down, Potter rose to his feet, an obviously painful effort, due to the resident corns on each small toe. He grinned at everyone, paused purposely in order to allow them to have their fun, and then he spoke.

Seven minutes later, every occupant of the small room sat stonily silent. Never had they heard a more eloquent presentation. Potter's command of the language of law, his unequaled power of reason, his appeal for compassion, his legal references were flawless. He described the blameless mother of the children as a victim of circumstances, hovering near death in a Tennessee hospital while her children were stolen from her. When he took his seat, the court recorder had to squelch the urge to applaud.

Jennings was so unnerved, so very unprepared, so shaken, that his reply fell short of the mark. He had decided that the case would be so easily won that he was "out gunned," skating lightly on the fringes of the issues with platitudes on his feet.

In a recovery effort, Jennings hinted that the Southerlands were "unfit," but he had no proof; no one that would say so. He contended that they were "deadbeats" who left Richmond owing money, but a "paid in full" receipt was presented to the contrary. Every corner he turned, every rock he unturned was met with logical, reasonable dispute. He sat down, regretting that he had subjected himself to such humiliation.

"That's the ball game," he whispered to Jack.

"The hell it is, you shyster," Jack snarled. "Get up off your lazy ass and request that the court interview the children."

"What for? From what you have told me, the little girl is hostile and unpredictable. The little boy is too young. Besides, he likes the stepfather. We won't accomplish anything, and we'll look stupid."

"We already look stupid, thanks to you. Do it!"

The request was made, and as Jennings had predicted and Jack had expected, Scottie and Jane were eliminated as potential witnesses. As luck would have it, however, Nellie Lee was readily available, outside in the corridor. Emily escorted her, because Anna had refused to be any part of it.

While Lillian and Mitch looked at each other in stunned silence, Nellie Lee walked through the swinging gate and accompanied Porter and Jennings into the Judge's private chamber. Jack left the courtroom, so confident was he that it was suddenly unnecessary to remain for the finding. Lillian stared at him as he passed, but he would not look at her.

Porter returned forty minutes later. "It's over, folks," he told them gravely. He looked at Lillian. "I'm sorry, Ma'am, but that is one tough little girl. Never seen anything like her." He cleared his throat, embarrassed. "She has testified to some very serious accusations against both of you, but primarily Mitch. Snyder bought it, hook, line and sinker. I'm sorry."

They were confused, incredulous. "What kind of accusations?" Liz demanded.

"Physical abuse, mostly." Then he paused. "And worse."

Mitchell's face went pale. "It's a lie," he said. "All of it."

Lillian reached out to touch his sleeve. She loved him more than life. She believed him, but it had been said and could never be completely taken back.

The next morning, Jack ordered Emily to pack a small valise for Jane and to put it into the truck of the Cadillac. At the breakfast table, he smiled at her.

"Put a pretty ribbon in your hair," he said. "We are going for a drive."

She was silent in the car, giving her grandfather shy glances between counting telephone poles along the highway. They had never been alone together; he had never invited her to go anywhere with him. One of the voices in her child's mind told her that this was a good thing; the other warned her of vague sorrow.

He drove to Spring Grove and parked in Rachael's driveway. When Scottie came running around the house to greet them, Jack said, "Go play with your brother. I need to speak with your grandmother." The conversation was short, and his decision was not open to discussion. When the children went into the house an hour later, Jack was gone, and they didn't see him again for many, many years.

Chapter 11

1975

"Hello, Sis."

To the casual observer, it might have appeared that the man and woman who stood face to face in the Washington-Baltimore Airport were bitter ex-lovers, competitive business associates, or even strangers. They shook hands politely and remained frozen in place, indeed in time, as they each regarded the other in cool inspection. A second look, however, would reveal the unmistakable similarities in stature, facial feature, and expression. Only their eyes set them totally apart, for hers were a deeply penetrating icy blue, while his were as black as ebony marbles.

"I was surprised and delighted when I got your wire," Mac continued. "I wasn't sure you would come."

"I had to," she said flippantly. "I have never been summoned before. My curiosity got the better of me."

"I was wondering," Mac replied, "if we could just sit and talk for awhile, before we drive to the apartment. We have some catching up to do."

Liz nodded. "It's your party."

"Coffee shop or bar?"

"Bar."

He relieved her of the carry-on. "Is there more luggage?"

"No. I travel light. Easier to get away."

He ignored the comment and led her through the terminal to a cozy saloon where they ordered drinks, lit cigarettes, and settled in. "You look wonderful," he offered.

She smiled to acknowledge the compliment. It was true. In her mid-fifties, Lillian was a very attractive woman, even stunning. She was tall and sleek, but had lost the gaunt thinness of her youth. Her skin was flawless and perfectly made-up, her eyes very bright. The slight graying at her temples accented high cheekbones and lent the illusion of graceful maturity.

Liz found it difficult to believe that her brother was almost sixty years old. He was still very tall and incredibly handsome. His blond hair was a little thin, but there was no sign that he would completely lose it.

"You are looking pretty well yourself," she told him.

"Well, we got that out of the way," he laughed, and they both relaxed a little. "It has been a long time, Sis."

"Twenty-nine years, but what is that when you compare it with eternity? We have probably set a record, however, as sibling rivalry goes."

"There was never really any contest. You were perfect and I was the bane of their existence.

"Is that what you want to talk about, after all these years... how I got more allowance than you?"

Lillian sighed. "I don't want to talk about anything in particular. You sent me a telegram, remember? 'Important family matters,' you said. Well, here I am. What's up?"

Mac took a deep draw on his beer. "I flew out to Arizona about a month ago, to close up the house. Mother and Dad are no longer able to be alone, so I brought them back to Arlington with me. Dad's in the hospital... he is dying, Sis. Mother is at the apartment with us, but she is not well either. I had hoped that we could make some long-term decisions."

Liz's face remained passive. "Sounds to me like you have everything under control, big brother. What is it that you think you need from me?"

Mac reddened. "A little concern for your parents would be appropriate," he retorted. "We may not be the Waltons, but we are a family, for better or for worse."

His remark stung. Perhaps she had been too flip, too defensive, but what did he expect, after all, after everything that had happened?

"I apologize," she answered softly. "But what I remember most is the 'worse.'"

He had hurt her, he knew, and he regretted it. "I was sorry to hear about Mitch," he offered.

"Mac, please. I don't want to talk about Mitch, or Paul, or the children, or even about Anna and Jack, although I suppose we do need to discuss that subject. I cannot, will not, pretend to feel something that I don't feel."

"He is an old man, Lillian. Almost ninety. Can't you find it in your heart to forgive him?"

"When I am long cold and dead, perhaps. Until then, never."

"He is asking for you."

"He can go to hell."

Mac sighed. Better get off this particular road, for now. "There are financial issues," he went on. "Mother has been diagnosed with Alzheimers.

Her care alone could become quite costly, assuming that Jack doesn't live much longer."

She leaned back in her chair and regarded him with a gaze that registered just one level below contempt. Smirking, she said, "It took awhile to get to it, but I understand now. You called me 700 miles to hit me up for money? How dare you! Spend your friggin' inheritance." She reached behind her to slip into her jacket, and began to gather up her belongings, preparing to leave.

Mac bristled. "Hold on," he almost shouted. They both looked around the room. They were alone. He lowered his voice. "First of all, even if I did, which I did not, why would that be so offensive? They are no more my responsibility, my parents, than yours, Sister dear."

Actually, they are less. She wanted to hurt him. Should she tell him now, tell him that he was not the son of Jack Sterling? Why had he not figured it out by now? How long had she known? She struggled to remember. Would it really matter to him now, after all this time?

She stopped a few feet from the table, resumed her seat and finished her drink in one swallow. "Then why?"

"There may be no money left after it is all over. I wanted you to know that. Also, Jean and I think it would be better if Mother went to a nursing home. That will be costly, about $5000 a month actually, as long as the money holds out. Then she would need to apply for Medicaid."

"What you and Jean decide about Anna does not concern me. I certainly have no intentions of playing nurse to her, so don't even think about it. I do want to know, however... what the hell happened to all the money?"

Mac shrugged. "There will be some coming in from the sale of the properties, if I can get Jack to sign. Other than that, wiped out. The bank says there are no stocks, no bonds, very little cash, under $10,000."

"Impossible! Jack made good money, invested very wisely. He inherited a bundle from Grandmother Sterling. I don't believe you, Mac. Someone has it." Her right hand instinctively touched the gold key that was hidden under her silk blouse. She was unaware of the gesture, a sub-conscious reassurance that it was still there.

He held out both hands, palms up. Liz was confused. She had practically called him a liar and a thief to his face and his reaction had been mild irritation. Either he was very cool and controlled, or he was telling the truth. "I'm open to suggestions," he said.

"Nellie?"

"That would be my guess. But even if we could prove it, which is unlikely, what recourse do we have then? If it was a gift, I mean."

"I don't know," she said vaguely. She was thinking about Nellie, trying to remember when she had last spoken to her eldest daughter. Ten years? Twenty? "Where is she now?" she asked him.

Mac laughed a genuine chuckle. "You're asking me? She's your kid... how the hell would I know where she is? This dysfunctional family doesn't exactly stay in touch."

He looked at his watch. "If you want to go the hospital, we'd better leave now, it's a thirty-minute drive. The old boy isn't awake much, and they'll be giving him something very soon, to make him sleep through the night."

They rode in silence for about ten minutes, Mac straining to reach his exit in a blinding downpour. Liz relaxed a little, lulled by the "s*wish, swish*" of the wiper blades.

A hundred images played out on the screen in her mind. Mac and Paul chasing her around the infamous oak tree. Sitting on the roof with Paul, eating Helga's cookies, all the more delicious because they were stolen. Paul smiling at her. Mac smiling at her, so handsome in his uniform. She was shocked when she realized that she had spoken aloud when she said to herself, "I miss them. I miss them all." If he had heard, he didn't let her know it.

At the door of Jack's private room, Mac reached out to her. She let him take her in his arms, grateful for the gesture. "Do you want me to come in with you?" he asked huskily. "Your call."

She laid her hand gently on the side of his face. "Thank you, but no. This is something I must do alone. I guess I never thought about how very painful it would be."

"I know. I thought I had paid my dues that day on the deck of the Indianapolis, when we came into Pearl Harbor... swarming with Jap warplanes. I didn't think that anything could be worse than that."

"At least your war is over," Liz cried against his chest.

"Yours could be over, if you want it to be; I'll be in the cafeteria."

Liz watched her brother walk away. She hadn't even asked him about what he was feeling, how he was. So many lost years. Mac laughed when she called after him, "You still owe me for the bike!"

"You must be the daughter," the nurse said. "He has been asking for you."

Yes, she was "the" daughter. The only daughter. The only anything, as a matter of fact. Why didn't he honor his only child? Why couldn't he treasure her?

"Is he awake?" Liz asked the nurse.

"Not at the moment, but he goes in and out. If you want to sit with him awhile, I have some paperwork to do at the nurses' station." She showed Liz where the call-bell was and left.

She walked to the bed with trepidation. Liz hadn't seen her father in almost thirty years. Common sense told her that he had certainly changed, but nothing could have prepared her for the sight of him as he was now. Her first impression was that he was so small, so shriveled, like a tiny, ugly gnome. He lay on his side, in a fetal position, his toothless mouth gaping open. She closed her eyes and tried to conjure up a memory of Papa that would seem familiar... Papa laughing, Papa smoking, Papa playing with the babies. When her mind finally caught a fleeting vision, it instantly dissolved in a cloudy puff and she saw again the thing on the bed. He was so pathetic, so impotent. How could she have ever feared this man? For that matter, what had she loved in him?

Chapter 12

Liz was suddenly fearful, the victim of a full-blown panic attack. She had to get out of the room before Jack opened his eyes. She rushed out into the corridor, breathlessly asked directions to the cafeteria, where she raced to Mac's table and demanded that they leave at once.

Once back in the car, she began to breathe easier again. She lit a cigarette with shaking hands, deeply inhaling several times.

"Are you all right?" her brother inquired.

"I think so. I'm sorry, Mac. I just couldn't take it. Could we just sit here a minute?"

"Sure. Then what? Tell me where you want me to take you... to the apartment, to the airport, a hotel?"

She felt like such a whimpering coward. She was a grown woman, educated, sensible. Certainly she could cope with two senile old people long enough to purge them from her mind once and for all. "Let's go see Mother," she finally answered.

Mac's wife, Jean, was gracious enough in her own clumsy way, for as far as she was concerned, Lillian was just another member of Mac's crazy family. Lillian took her time, settled into the guest bedroom, washed her face and slipped into cozy, comforting silk pajamas. When she could think of nothing else to detain her, she walked down the hall to the room that Jean had identified as Anna's.

"Come in," Anna's voice answered in response to the knock.

Lillian tried to remember how long it had been. Anna had attended Mitch's funeral, she recalled, breezing into the small country funeral home that was filled to standing room only capacity with unwashed old boys in coveralls and frumpy women in cotton dresses. Anna's mink coat and mink-trimmed hat, the haughty attitude, and the condescending looks had embarrassed Liz, and now she remembered that had been 1960, fifteen years ago.

"You are looking well, Mother." It was true. The years had been very kind to Anna, who seemed only a few years older, and maybe even a little prettier, a little softer.

"Who in the hell are you?" Anna sneered.

Lillian almost laughed. Jean had warned her that Anna was "sometimes confused," but she hardly expected this reaction. "I am your daughter, Lillian. Don't you remember me?" *If she said that she didn't,* Liz thought, *I could leave without any guilt. I will have done my daughterly duty.*

But the old woman moved closer, narrowed her gray eyes and studied Liz carefully. Liz held her breath. God, why did she agree to come here? After all the pain, all the years, she had almost succeeded in pushing it into the far recesses of her mind. Now it was all there again, screaming at her.

"Oh, yes... Lillian. I suppose you have come for the Haviland. Well, girlie, you'd better get it fast before that fat old cow breaks every last piece."

"I didn't come all this way for your china, Mother. I came to see you."

"Why?"

"Because it has been a long time. Because we may have something to say to each other before..."

"Before I'm dead?"

Anna sank down to the edge of a chaise lounge and began to pick at lint from the woolen blanket. "Sometimes I wonder if I am already dead," she said quietly. "The worst part is that no one cares, not even me."

Liz sat down on the window seat, a few feet away. She tried to decide what to say next, but somehow the silence suited her.

"Have you been to see your Papa?"

"We stopped at the hospital. He was sleeping."

"He sleeps too much, if you ask me. I suppose you finally hate him almost as much as you have always hated me. Have you come to tell us that, Lillian?"

Liz was reminded then of something she had once read about inhibition. It had something to do with a chemical in the brain, a substance that the very young had not yet developed and the very old had depleted. "Children and old people will tell the truth without hesitation," the writer had explained, "because they have no 'editing factor.'" At this point in their strange, cold relationship, why shouldn't she behave the same?

"Yes."

"Well, you've said it, so you can go now. Take that ugly thing with you."

Liz followed Anna's gaze to the large trunk that spanned the end of Anna's four-poster bed. She had forgotten about the trunk, the one that would hold all of her mementos, her papa had told her... and treasures "beyond belief." Liz thought about the fire, the irreplaceable items that were gone forever.

"Are the pictures of my children in there?" Lillian wondered aloud.

"How the hell would I know what's in there?" Anna barked. "It was to be your private property, your father said. I haven't looked in there since I packed it for the convent. Except for..."

"Except for what?"

"Your father's journal is in there. He gave it to me with instructions not to open it. 'Put it in the trunk,' he said. 'For Diz.'"

"Did it ever strike you as strange that this family claims such respect for 'personal property,' but rudely intrudes in every other aspect of its members lives?"

Anna just stared. Liz would get more satisfaction talking to the trunk, she realized. How ironic, how unfair, that having finally reached the pinnacle of her development, having matured and mellowed to the point where she now was, able to confront the two people who she held responsible for all of the misery in her life, they were deaf to her. Liz sighed. Better to lay it down, go home.

"I'll have Mac ship the trunk, get it out of your way. Goodbye, Mother."

When Liz reached for the doorknob, she felt a hand on her shoulder, fingertips, really, a light touch. "Don't go yet. You just got here."

She turned to protest, but was startled at the sight of the frail Anna. Liz took in the look of her for the first time. Her mother had shrunken, was now below eye-level. She was very old; her still gray eyes pleading for... something. Liz tried again to remember why she had come. Wasn't this it, her moment of truth?

"All right. Just a little while."

"Rachael is dead. Did you know that?"

"Yes, I know." Indeed she did. When she received Martha's phone call, Liz had boarded a plane. She took care of everything, the arrangements, and the expenses. Liz and the funeral director joined only the young priest at graveside, until Jane appeared.

"I am surprised to see you," Liz had said.

"Why should you be? She was the closest thing I had to a mother."

"Finally we have something in common. She was very special to me, also."

"We have nothing in common. I have children that I am devoted to. I also have a cat that is more 'Mother' than you could ever hope to be."

It was a painful memory. Jane could always stir the rancor in her, Liz recalled. Why? Brought abruptly back to the present, she heard Anna's voice again.

"Tell me about your life, your work. Tell me about the children."

"You missed the best one. The 'pick of the litter.'"

"Kathleen."

"Yes. The one I raised. Pretty damn good job, if I say so myself."

"Are you happy? What kind of work do you do?"

"Well, I work in a library, in Cleveland."

"You always loved books. What exactly do you do there?"

"I am a librarian, Mother. I run the place. As for the children, I wouldn't know. I haven't seen them since... I can't remember."

"Why?"

"'Why'? Did you ask 'why'? You must know the answer to that. After you and Papa took them from me, you told them that I was a slut. Then you told them that I was dead. Nellie discarded me because she had you, Anna. Scottie became Rachael's. Jane simply hates all of us. I don't receive many cards on Mother's Day. How about you?"

Anna sighed and returned to the chaise. "Some of us were not cut out for motherhood. I was one of those. I failed miserably."

"No kidding. Perhaps you should have considered that fact before you conceived. You could have saved us all a lot of suffering."

"Like you did?"

Liz flushed. "Touché. I'll plead guilty to that one; I hadn't planned on Nellie. But I might have had a chance if you hadn't grabbed her from my arms and took over."

"You were seventeen! Little more than a child yourself, and pregnant with Jane. I was only trying to help you."

"Bullshit! You wanted her because I had been such a disappointment to you, because you and Jack thrive on control and manipulation. Did she turn out to your satisfaction?"

"She's had a tragic life. Jane still behaves very strangely, I'm told. And Scottie... well, no one even knows where he is."

"There you have it, Mother. Congratulation, three for three."

"I don't know what I could have done differently. I tried to stop him... your father. You ran off, I couldn't find you. Jack was afraid Mitch would get his hands on the children's money and..."

"It was always about money, wasn't it? And politics. Jack turned on Mitch when he worked for Senator Kefaufer. Why? What did Mitch have on him? And did you ever in your entire life care about anything except money and your social image? Why did you marry him?"

"Well, it is a bit of a long story. How much time do you have?"

Liz eyed the old woman carefully. Alzheimer's or no, this conversation was the longest and most honest of their entire relationship. Anna no longer had anything to hide, no reason to twist the truth, no personal agenda. It would also, very likely, be their last.

"Go on," Liz said. She kicked off her shoes, lit a cigarette and propped herself on Anna's bed. "I have all night."

Anna produced an ashtray from the dresser drawer. Handing it to Liz, she said, "Could I have one? I have to beg to get a smoke around here. Usually I bribe Mac's boys. Sometimes they bring me some of that other stuff... what's it called... marigold?

Liz laughed. "You mean, 'marijuana'? Great God, Mother! How much of that stuff do you smoke?"

"As much as I can get," Anna giggled between puffs. "Where should I start? Oh, yes... it was 1915, and there was this knock at the door...."

Anna talked for hours, telling her daughter long-held secrets. There were gaps, lost years, lost thoughts, confusion, wrong names, and wrong dates. But the overall message was clear, and Lillian listened with intense interest.

"I always thought of you as made of iron," Liz admitted to Anna. "Why couldn't you ever stand up to him.... defy him? How could you have let him do all of those terrible things to your own children?"

"I tried," Anna whimpered. "I undermined him every way I could, but I kept it secret. He never knew... like when I forged his name to a check and paid that note at the bank so that the court would not hold it against you. I did what I could but I was no match for Jack. No one was."

There were occasional interruptions, like Mac's knock."Is everything all right?" he asked, appearing very worried. "Can I get you anything, Sis?"

"No, thanks. I'm fine..."

"Yes!" Anna interceded. "We'll have a pitcher of Manhattans. And how about some cheese and crackers?"

Mac looked at his mother strangely, then at his sister. His thick eyebrows rose questioningly, and then he jiggled them up and down in a silly gesture.

Liz laughed. "Well, I guess you have your orders, Major."

He bowed deeply and backed out of the room. "Watch her," he mouthed to Liz. "She's a lush."

"Does Mac know?" Liz asked Anna when the door closed.

"Know what?"

"About his father. You know, the ecstasy on the sofa thing."

"I suspect that he may have figured it out by now. If not, what's to be gained? He thinks I'm crazy... wouldn't believe me. Did I say 'ecstasy'?"

"You implied it."

"Well, I guess it must have been, considering what I had in store for me. I read once that there is a 'grand passion' in every woman's life. Mine missed the train. I was so naïve that I actually used to believe that there was no conception without orgasm. If that were so, you would not be here."

Liz flushed. "I'm not sure we should talk about 'orgasms.'"

"Why? Are they a secret? How many have you had?"

Liz was having a difficult time convincing herself that this was real. But it felt good somehow, like schoolgirls sharing the most intimate details of their dates. She forgot for awhile that she was talking to her mother, her enemy.

The drinks arrived, along with a tray of crackers and cheese, sliced ham, and pickles.

"Goodnight," they said to Mac in unison. He almost seemed regretful that he had not been invited to stay.

"Goodnight, ladies," he saluted them.

"Well? Are you going to tell me? How many?"

"Oh, that," Liz said. "Lots and lots."

"With Paul?"

"No. Never Paul. But with Mitch it was..."

"Don't tell me! I can imagine. He was such a handsome man, so virile, so charming."

Liz frowned. "He was until Nellie told her little story to the judge. Was that your idea?"

"Did you credit it to me? No, dear. I am guilty of much, but I had nothing to do with that. Lies, all lies. Everyone who knew Mitch knew that."

"It destroyed him. It destroyed us," Liz struggled to say, huge tears welling in her eyes, tears that seemed too heavy to fall. "It was never the same after that. All he cared about was staying drunk. He didn't laugh any more. He didn't..."

Anna rose quickly and came over to sit beside her on the bed.

"I am so very sorry," Anna said, and she held out her arms. Exhausted, more than a little drunk, Lillian did the most natural thing in the world. She fell into her mother's arms and cried.